Born in Omaha, Nebraska, Jozy Gusman grew up in Council Bluffs, Iowa. Around the age of seven, his parents divorced and he went to live in Nebraska. While still going to school in Iowa in 2016, his mother tragically passed away. He graduated high school in 2007.

Jozy Gusman

ARROGANCE

AUSTIN MACAULEY PUBLISHERS™

LONDON • CAMBRIDGE • NEW YORK • SHARJAH

Ordering Information
Quantity sales: Special discounts are available on quantity purchases by corporations, associations, and others. For details, contact the publisher at the address below.

Publisher's Cataloging-in-Publication data
Gusman, Jozy
Arrogance

ISBN 9781643788470 (Paperback)
ISBN 9781643788487 (Hardback)
ISBN 9781645365372 (ePub e-book)

Library of Congress Control Number: 2020924344

www.austinmacauley.com/us

First Published (2021)
Austin Macauley Publishers LLC
40 Wall Street, 33rd Floor, Suite 3302
New York, NY 10005
USA

mail-usa@austinmacauley.com
+1(646)5125767

Part 1: Japanese Frostbite

"Nothing burns like the cold." – George R.R. Martin

Chapter 1

Valentine's Day

The sound of pots and pans being washed echoed through the long, whitewashed hallway and slipped their way into a cracked door where the sunlight had already won the race. The origin of the sunlight was a window, whose curtains were not drawn, that was directly opposite the door. The light illuminated the dust that fell on a bookshelf to the left of the door, where such titles as *Ghost in the Machine*, a modern military tactics book, and an original copy of *The Killing Joke* were humbly present. To the right of the door was a computer with a holographic monitor and illuminated keyboard; a poster from *Serial Experiments Lain* hung above it. Farther to the left, there was a television hanging from the wall, where the 'play' menu for Mamoru Oshii's *Ghost in the Shell*, quietly danced with artistic life. Finally, there was a bed nestled below the window where a man, dressed in a black T-shirt, Crye combat pants, and boots, slept. His face was unshaven and the sides of his head were shaved, while the top was left short.

There was a sudden knock at the door, which was then followed by a voice, "Lovecraft. Hey, Lovecraft! Dude, get the fuck up already; you'll want to see the news."

Lovecraft's eyes slowly opened to glare at the man in the doorway.

"Aaron, do you have any idea what fucking time it is?"

Aaron lent inside the room and looked at the clock on the computer.

"It is nine o'clock, on February 14th, 2052."

"And when did we get in last night?"

"Five A.M. on the dot."

"Do you not see a problem here?"

Aaron laughed as Lovecraft sat up, cursing under his breath, when he realized that he had fallen asleep without shutting the T.V. off.

"I do, but as you could probably guess, I don't give a shit."

He shifted his gaze over to Lovecraft's attire.

"Nice to see that you didn't bother to change after we got back."

"Yeah, and why do you care?"

"Because you smell like shit."

Aaron grabbed his nose for added effect.

"Gunpowder and shit are two completely different things, I can assure you," Lovecraft retorted.

"Oh I know, come on, I wasn't lying about the news. Besides, breakfast is ready."

With that, Aaron disappeared back down the hallway, leaving Lovecraft to wipe his gray eyes and look out the window. He immediately lost interest when a giant eye, which was then followed by a nose, lips, and chin, moved in front of it. He got up and turned off the T.V. whilst muttering, "Damn holograms."

Shutting the door behind him, Lovecraft walked down the bland hallway, until he came into the dining area of his and Aaron's compound. It was colored in gray and at one point, it had been a small cafeteria. This was evident by the large window that was cut into a wall, it separated the dining room and kitchen. He could smell the scent of bacon, eggs, and smoked sausage, as he watched Aaron cleaning the skillet and other utensils he'd used to make the meal. Lovecraft noticed a white plate carrying the same food that his nose had just identified and grabbed it. He looked back up to where Aaron was and thought how ironic it was that they were not brothers.

Had Aaron not had brown hair and blue eyes, he could have easily been mistaken as Lovecraft's twin. They had the same muscular build that allowed them both to weigh right around two-hundred pounds, and he was only taller than Lovecraft by about an inch, bringing his overall height to that of 6' 3". The most shocking difference between the two of them though, was that Aaron wore a gold ring on his left ring-finger. Lovecraft gave it a quick glance before turning around and taking a seat at the white table in front of him, eyes drifting up to the T.V. hanging on the wall, only to be brought back down when he saw nothing but advertisements.

"How's Millie and the kids?" he asked, whilst cutting his egg with his fork.

"Fine, Martha apparently keeps asking when I'll be able to come back. I can't believe she'll be out of kindergarten in four months."

Martha was Aaron's youngest, and was more or less at the bottom of the food chain when it came to his three daughters. Well, that's at least how it was supposed to work. Lovecraft knew that Millie, Aaron's wife, had a special place in her heart for Martha. Maybe the reason for it had to deal with the fact that Martha would be Millie's last kid, or maybe it was something else, he didn't know. What he did know, however, was that if somebody bet him a thousand dollars that she hadn't coddled Martha a bit too much, then he would at least match the bet just to prove a point.

8

"She'll be six by the time she gets out; if my aging memory is still worth something."

"You're only 30; older people would cuss you out for such a complaint. She'll turn six the last week of school."

It was after he said this that the T.V. switched back over to the news and greeted the two men with the image of a young blonde who could have passed more for a prostitute than a news anchor.

"You know, I always wondered why people watched this shitty news station. Now, I know why. Big tits and a nice ass can turn anyone into a fucking genius."

Aaron laughed at Lovecraft's comment.

"Kara told me some time ago, that there were some nasty rumors spreading about her. Apparently, she has a history of claiming sexual assault without any reasonable evidence, but the court always rules in her favor because of equal rights and all that bullshit."

Lovecraft snorted at this.

"She's a whore, that when flipped over, is a total bitch. Man, and I thought all women were innocent." He placed the fork on his empty plate, "What else did Kara say?"

Aaron shrugged his shoulders, "She's more of a slut than a whore. She, allegedly, has receipts from almost every sex store in Chicago, and is also part owner of a strip club that runs prostitution out the back. She also gets first dibs on the new recruits, but that's just Kara's assumption."

Lovecraft bounced his head back and forth. Kara was as much a criminal as any other. She had been charged with grand theft auto, weapons trafficking, possession of stolen items, assault with a deadly weapon, illegal possession of a firearm, joy riding, and had been fined for overdue library books. She was a fence who had a passion for selling guns. Luckily, there were more pros than cons to keeping someone like her around. The first was that Aaron and Lovecraft got a fifty-percent discount on weapons and ammunition, the second was they could sell any illegal materials they found to her; it wasn't exactly legal in any way, shape, or form, but when it came to police work, nowadays, it didn't really matter. If you got private Contractors called against you, then you were basically guilty.

Lovecraft and Aaron had met her by way of bureaucratic incompetence. Some idiot had called in saying that she was armed and dangerous; a job usually reserved for the S.W.A.T. team, not the Contractors who were typically called in for active terrorist situations and general assistance on raids. Unfortunately, for Kara, a police liaison issued the wrong call and sent the two men into a house that, for all tense and purposes, looked like a meager family home than the 'Heavily Fortified' fortress that belonged to an international arms dealer. Lovecraft had to laugh a bit, as he thought of the look of terror on Kara's face. He'd never seen somebody twitch before, and in her underwear no less. Rather suddenly, Lovecraft was torn away from his mirthful memories by Aaron, instructing him to look toward the T.V.

The news anchor came back on and began speaking

"At seven A.M. this morning, the Japanese Prime Minister, Akira Kusanagi, and his wife, Ai Kusanagi, were ambushed on West Roosevelt road between Mount Carmel Cemetery and Queen of Heaven Cemetery."

Lovecraft grimaced as she pronounced 'Ai' as 'A-I' instead of 'I.'

"Ai Kusanagi, was eight months pregnant, and is believed to be shot through the stomach, before bleeding out next to her husband, who died from a gunshot wound to the head."

Lovecraft's brow furrowed as she continued on, like she was reading the text off a piece of cardboard. She made a better machine than Arnold Schwarzenegger.

"She has no respect, stupid bitch," he muttered, whilst grabbing the remote.

The screen faded to see through and Lovecraft rubbed his forehead, as Aaron asked, "What should we do?"

Lovecraft paused for a moment, as he collected his thoughts. He had been informed of the Prime Minister's arrival on Sunday evening, three days ago. He was asked to be a part of the security detail, but declined for fear that something worse might happen, like a terrorist attack or something of the like. Plus, he reasoned that if something bad did happen to Prime Minister Kusanagi, then he would be in a better position to counterattack his assailants, if he were left mobile and not tied down. This seemed to be a mistake, but there was no reason for him to be there in the first place. The Prime Minister's convoy was protected by Academi mercenaries, not the Contractors that Lovecraft would have put much faith in, but they could at least handle tactics well – even though they were usually in just for the money. He had a history with Academi, even killed some of them before, so the fact that the car ride would have been tense was just another reason for him not to be there. The problem though, was that they all had seemingly been killed without firing a single shot in return; it was either the most perfect ambush against paramilitary that had ever been orchestrated, or there was something else going on.

"Get your gear and the town car ready. We're going to the crime scene once I'm ready," Lovecraft instructed.

"Roger that."

Lovecraft watched as Aaron walked back down the white hallway. He looked away and back to the holographic T.V.; this was the underwhelming future.

The town car's electric engine waned down the streets of downtown Chicago. Holographic colossuses danced atop of metallic skyscrapers that reached so high that they appeared to have been built by God himself. This was the new age of advertisements. Big, flashy, holographic people and objects that were plastered with brand names, while propaganda for 274-L (The Contractor Act) floated next to the American flag; typical bureaucratic nonsense that tried to get people to trust the Operators that were blowing holes in their houses, much less their friends and family.

Lovecraft wiped his right, index finger over his upper lip before slipping it into his other Oakley SI Pilot glove; his MK. 18 Mod 0 assault rifle hanging lazily over his black duffle coat. Aaron sat next to him in the driver's seat in full kit. His gear was blacked out and included a level-three ballistic helmet, Crye J.P.C., and Crye Combat pants. His gun was a tan, full length MK. 16; more commonly known as a SCAR 16, that sat beside him on the console. His face was covered by a black balaclava that was emblazoned with the lower half of a skull.

"Police emergency in progress. All drivers must keep right or face prosecution. THIS IS YOUR FINAL WARNING."

Aaron looked toward the screens on the sides of the road that kept repeating, 'Keep Right.'

"Override the A.I.," Lovecraft ordered.

Aaron left one hand on the steering wheel while he fished a silvered card from his admin pouch. He slipped it inside of a small slot in the dash and waited for it to register.

"Override accepted. Thank you, Operator."

Aaron smirked as he turned right down another road bathed in holographics. People lined the streets, and watched as they held their chins to their breast; the cold chill of February was hell bent on snuffing out the warmth of Valentine's Day. Well, it was warm for some.

Lovecraft watched them with semi-interest as they passed by. Among them, he saw the faintest glances of people who were beaten; their bruises unable to be covered since the looks on their faces betrayed them. There were also people who tried to cling on to some form of their cushy lives, such as the women who wore their heels and mink coats. They were too busy on their phones to notice that he was looking at them. His full attention was garnered when he saw another Contractor standing on a street corner, with a machine gun in his hands. He was dressed in all black and wore thick goggles over his eyes that hid his whole face from view, thanks to his balaclava. It was from these three aspects that he saw the world and made him doubt whether or not things would actually change, if there was a future or not. Luckily, Aaron saved him from this impossible question.

"So why do you watch it?"

"Watch what?"

"Don't be stupid, the movie. You've watched it every night since we found it at that old ass store; it's been over a month."

Lovecraft could detect an edge of concern in Aaron's voice.

"I like it. It's like I'm looking into a future that we will either never have or could have."

"So you get hope from it?"

"I guess; nobody ever said that realistic dreams couldn't come true."

The two of them fell silent as they drove; the only noise made was from the outside world that was just trying to operate. Lovecraft could feel his pulse thudding in anticipation of what he would find at the crime scene; thirty bodies strewn about the road while the police kept people away? No, it was something worse: the F.B.I.

It was just as Lovecraft had thought. Underneath the gray, winter sky, sat a line of S.U.V.s with black body bags strewn around them that were rather haphazardly being loaded into ambulances. Parked next to the other black S.U.V.s was another one, only with blacked-out windows that featured four people: three men, one woman, decked out in armor that had 'F.B.I.' plastered all across them.

"Great, the Feds are here. I can't wait to hear the 'Federal Jurisdiction' bullshit they'll try and feed you," Aaron muttered, as he pulled up to the police line.

"You're not going to hear it, because you're going to wait in the car in case shit hits the fan."

Aaron looked at Lovecraft with question in his eyes.

"What do you mean?"

"Nothing, it's just a hunch. Now, are you going to unlock the door or do you want to talk about my feelings more?"

Aaron snorted and rolled his eyes before doing as Lovecraft asked. He watched as the door shut and shook his head, *You and your 'hunches,' L.* He looked out the driver's side-window and scanned the horizon of the nearby cemetery. His eyes were trained to notice small details, but one did not need trained eyes to notice that the cemetery was eerily calm for having a crime scene so close to it.

Like it or not, the living did visit the cemetery and on this particular day, loved ones typically visited their deceased spouses, so why was this cemetery deserted? Aaron grabbed the fore end of his battle rifle and unlocked his door, before jamming the barrel into the left-hand corner next to the steering wheel. He slapped the magazine to make sure it was seated in before switching the safety to single shot. Aaron rested his hand on the pistol grip and watched the horizon; now all he could do was wait and hope that nothing happened.

Meanwhile, Lovecraft ducked under the holographic police line and walked toward the center of the scene, his presence not going unnoticed by the F.B.I. The sound of heels filled his ears and his eyes were suddenly filled with a sea of red hair, as he looked toward the sound.

The agent herself was incredibly attractive with long hair that flowed just passed her shoulders. Her skin was a pale white that reminded Lovecraft of salt, and her eyes were assisted by amethyst colored contacts. It was too bad that her protective gear covered the majority of her body, otherwise he may have actually gotten to see whether or not her curves were worth the trouble. However, Lovecraft was not so naive. He knew that no F.B.I. agent's assets were worth the pounding headache the next morning; that's what liquor was for.

It was during his observations that she introduced herself, "Karen Alvarez, Chicago F.B.I. Might I inquire as to why you're here? This is a federal crime scene."

"Yes, it is a federal crime scene. One that happened in my jurisdiction and thus, have as much right to conduct an investigation. My name's Lovecraft and I'm a Contractor for the Chicago P.D."

"Be that as it may, you have to be aware that federal investigators outrank private Contractors when it comes to matters of national security."

This was how it always went. The F.B.I. would bring up national security and then Lovecraft would have to remind them of what the law actually stated. This was getting really old.

"Sure, but I will remind you that state's rights come before government rights when dealing with Contractors. Thus, if you were unwilling to share your crime scene, then you would be breaking a state law, as well as a federal law."

Lovecraft watched in amusement as his words caused the agent to bite her lip. He caught her like a fish and now, all he had to do was wait. Yet, her response would never come, as blood, as red as her hair, suddenly shot out of the side of her neck. Lovecraft's eyes widened as his ears heard the trademark crack of a high-powered rifle off to his left.

Instinctively, he dropped down and it was lucky that he did, since he felt the heat of another bullet whizz right over the top of his head. His back landed on the asphalt just a little bit after Alvarez landed, face down, next to him. Her men shouted her rank; she was apparently a sergeant, and called out, "Sniper." Lovecraft jumped into a crouched stance and squeezed off three 5.56 caliber rounds toward the cemetery; the location of the shot. His holographic sight gave him little to no magnification, so he could not see exactly what he was shooting at, but since the F.B.I. were shooting in that direction as well, he figured they could see. Unfortunately, it was the blind leading the blind, since the next shot dropped another of the F.B.I. agents.

"Fuck," Lovecraft swore, as he saw Aaron's door open.

He gripped the magwell of his battle rifle and sent three rounds of the heavier 7.62 cartridge. They impacted one of the larger headstones and made the fragile granite explode into a spectacular dust cloud. However, Aaron could see through his own holographic optic that there was still movement at the base of the headstone, which meant that he had, more or less, missed. He ducked behind his car door in time for another heavy caliber bullet to burrow itself into the bulletproof glass. Aaron then popped up again to shower the position with five more shots before slowly moving over to Lovecraft, who had his rifle poking around the trunk of a nearby car.

It was while he was watching that he heard somebody gasping and choking. He looked toward the noise and noticed that Alvarez was somehow still alive.

"You gotta be fucking shitting me. Aaron! Cross faster, I've got wounded behind me!"

"Roger that!" Aaron yelled back, as another round whizzed underneath his right arm and into the asphalt. The F.B.I. started shooting again, as Aaron completed his movement and Lovecraft went back to fetch Alvarez.

Lovecraft flipped her over as another shot flew right over his head and ricocheted off a car in front of him. To his amazement, there was hardly any blood coming from the wound on Alvarez's neck; she was extremely lucky. Lovecraft grabbed her by the shoulders of her tactical vest and dragged her along the ground, as Aaron dropped the magazine out of his rifle.

"I saw sparks when I hit this bastard," he declared.

Lovecraft pushed himself up against the car and motioned toward the medics to come check on Alvarez.

"Means it's a goddamn robot. Switch to A.P."

Aaron nodded and grabbed a tan magazine that featured black electrical tape. Meanwhile, Lovecraft saw a medic trying to move toward him. He hurriedly told him to wait before he started shooting at the sniper's direction. The medic took the cue and ran as fast as his crouched form could carry him;

the F.B.I. and Lovecraft's guns doing wonders to suppress the sniper. He set his medical briefcase down just as Lovecraft ran out of ammo. The young Contractor flung the magazine free of the assault rifle and took another one from his pocket.

"Aaron, last mag. Shoot this fucking asshole."

Aaron obliged by sending three armor-piercing rounds, ones that had a steel core in the center of their bullets, down range that impacted and sheared metal off their robotic attacker. It was after this that everything went silent and the only sounds that could be heard were from the barely conscious F.B.I. agent lying between Aaron and Lovecraft.

The latter kept his head behind the car as he watched the former keep their barrel pointed toward the headstone. A rush of cold ran down Lovecraft's neck and when his glove came back wet, he looked up to the gray clouds. The medic slowly did the same before covering the bandage he had attached to Alvarez's neck with his hand. All too suddenly, afterward, did a cold rain shower all of them; the water running rivers off of Aaron's helmet and a downspout dripping off the barrel of his SCAR. As suddenly as the rains came, he pulled his rifle free and took cover just like Lovecraft; his gloved fingers flexing over the angled grip. Lovecraft looked at him as if reading each other's minds, and like lightning. both shot up and started moving toward the sniper's position; the remaining F.B.I. agents following close behind.

Four barrels, three, the same caliber, one of one higher, appeared over the hill and spread out, as they looked at a sparking machine that resembled the human form. Its lower half was covered in a weird, shimmering distortion that vaguely looked like the dark clouds.

"Camouflage Unit!" Lovecraft announced.

"If I would have brought my fucking night vision, I would have seen it before it pulled the trigger," Aaron cursed.

He kicked the robot's sniper rifle, a Russian SV-98 chambered in 7.62 x 54R, away and down the hill.

"Nice to see the Russian Mafia is still getting this shit in the country. You fucking Feds suck at your jobs."

"Aaron, enough. We can argue politics and whose fault this is later."

Lovecraft bent down and rolled the machine over, which made him grunt, since it weighed almost three-hundred pounds. It was from there that they saw that Aaron had hit it in its main C.P.U., effectively disabling it. However, it was not the shot placement that had caught Lovecraft's attention, it was what was written in white paint on the front of the machine's chest. He read it aloud, "Interfere with the Master, and be exterminated."

Chapter 2
A Typical Day in Chicago

The sun was such a simple object to most people, but to Lovecraft, it was something else entirely. For him, it was a tool that belonged to the art of self-reflection; a necessary skill for one who often shot first and asked questions later. The giant, glowing orb was like some ancient god rising out of the abyss that was Lake Michigan, and it represented a beacon that told anyone that there was hope; there was a future. If they would put the work into it, then the future was never lost in the first place.

This was where Lovecraft looked every morning he didn't work at night, which was somewhat of rarity, but he made it a tradition when he could. He climbed his way up the stairs and to the roof of his compound, and took a position near the edge, which was where he now stood.

The winter had been strange this year. At first, it seemed normal; blustery winds and snow, but after January, the temperatures would fluctuate between thirty degrees and seventy degrees, with the latter being the one in higher favor. This was the reason why he dressed in a black T-shirt which was tucked into his combat pants, and tan, synthetic boots. He had gotten up early enough, a product of his training and childhood, to clothe himself in his combat gear which was comprised of a tan, Crye J.P.C., and drop leg holster. A rare Yugoslavian nine-millimeter was held with the holster's plastic confines and his assault rifle hung loosely from his back. Lovecraft had left his helmet back in his room, since he had yet to take the night vision off of it; he didn't want to get the expensive equipment damaged by banging it on a door frame or something stupid like that.

He rubbed his gloved thumb over the glass of his watch and read that it was a quarter past nine A.M. Lovecraft grabbed the pistol grip of his rifle with his dominant hand and turned to walk back down the stairs; they had a meeting with the chief of police in 20 minutes. He grimaced as he grabbed the handle of the steel door, *I hope he doesn't just go on about how he's going to lick his wounds.*

Unfortunately, that's exactly what the chief did, while Aaron and Lovecraft silently wished they could tape his mouth shut.

"Do you have any idea what you've done?!" Chief Barons yelled at them.

There was only a certain number of times one could roll their eyes before they got a headache; Lovecraft had reached that point 20 minutes ago.

"Investigated a crime scene within our jurisdiction and saved an F.B.I. sergeant from certain death after being engaged by a robotic sniper. It's in the report Lovecraft sent to you…if you took your head out of your ass to read it, that is."

"Why, you! If you were under my command, I'd have you fired!"

Lovecraft shook his head.

"But he's not. Thus, all you can do is toot your own horn. Now, I didn't get delayed a day to watch some fat bureaucrats tell me how to do my job. So, Barons, what are you going to do? Let the F.B.I. take it and get their heads blown off, or are you going to let me, a professional, take over and get results?"

Barons rubbed his face with his hands. This is how it worked for most police chiefs: they managed the police department, while the Contractors were essentially bounty hunters that did the jobs the police were ill-equipped to deal with. This often proved to be a double-edged sword, since the Contractors could say no at any point and time. Luckily, God seemed to be on his side, since Lovecraft and Aaron showed up a little over two years ago and actually liked doing the police jobs.

"Fine, do it your way. Just be aware that I will not be able to call the F.B.I. and convince them to stop their investigation."

"That's fine. We're creative and have an ace that even the F.B.I. don't have."

Barons' brow twitched uncomfortable at the admission.

"Right, the arms dealer. It's probably best we not speak of her while there are eyes all around us."

Aaron and Lovecraft looked around with suspicious expressions.

"I suggest you work this diligently, until then, there are more pressing matters."

Barons leaned back in his chair and folded his hands across his belly.

"I'm sure you are aware of the 'Chaos Killer.' Well, there's been a breakthrough."

"The cop killer's finally been found. Well, that took how many months? Three?" Aaron asked, in half-sarcasm.

"Yes, she covers her tracks very well."

"She?" Lovecraft asked.

Barons nodded his head.

"It's not official yet, but a Metropolitan C.C.T.V. camera found an unknown woman, around 5' 6" with black hair, jogging through an alleyway in the Flood Zone. We traced her facial features and found that she is a Miss Argentina Lagos, who is known to be living with her junkie boyfriend, William Carson. Apparently, she has quite the Heroin addiction."

"Aren't you just jumping to conclusions by just assuming that she is your murderer?" Lovecraft knew this was suspicious. The Flood Zone was a section of Chicago that had been flooded by a massive storm in 2047. The waters had yet to recede and this left several washed-out and rundown neighborhoods that still had several feet of water in them. The problem, however, were the taller buildings that had multiple floors and the areas that had already drained. It was a mess of illegal activity that reminded one of Hurricane Katrina. The biggest problem though, were the gangs that spawned from the rampant drug trade in the area. No people meant no police, and when there were no police, the Contractors stepped in. It was a literal militarized zone in northern Chicago, and was a glimmering bastion of the Contractor's sole order: Keep the peace.

"Maybe, but this is our best lead. Are you ready for your official orders?"

Aaron and Lovecraft nodded and waited patiently.

"Gentlemen, you are to make contact with the boyfriend and, by any means necessary, collect information about Argentina, or take her into custody."

Aaron raised his hand, "Should we meet resistance, what are the rules?"

"Taking her alive is preferred, but not necessary. Any other questions?"

Aaron looked to Lovecraft who shook his head and stood up from his chair. Aaron followed suit and exited the room right after his boss.

"Lovecraft," Barons called after them.

Sighing under his breath, Lovecraft stuck his head back in.

"I overlooked it this time, but we will discuss your team size. Five people are required to keep your Contracting License and eight is the standard. Keep that in mind." Lovecraft rolled his eyes once again and nodded. He disappeared around the door frame and Barons pulled a cigar from his top-desk drawer.

Lovecraft pinched the bridge of his nose as he caught up to Aaron; the police station smelling of bleach and ammonia. The noise of ringing phones echoed around them, as they walked past the main call center and then, as suddenly as it appeared, it disappeared, as they went down the hall and found themselves at a set of burgundy stairs that lead to the front door.

"Problem?" Aaron asked. Lovecraft knew he would ask and had already dismissed what Barons had said, even though it discouraged him.

"It's nothing. Just more regulations and requirements."

"He threatened you over the size of our team again, didn't he?"

"I'm starting to think you're psychic."

"No, just good intuition. Besides, when it comes to people like Barons, you don't need a Ph.D. to see that he's a pushover. I'm sure, that if you compared him and a puppet, you'd find that the only difference is one is covered in flesh."

Lovecraft wholeheartedly agreed with what Aaron said. There had not been one time during the two years Aaron and he had worked here, that Barons had made any 'big' decision. It was always, "Let me ask the state," "Let me ask the Feds," "Just don't put me in the spotlight." The man was a soggy piece of paper that only stood up because he was braced by sticks that were sent in by the Federal Government: The Contractors.

"True, but what can I do?" Lovecraft was the first to take the step down the stairs, "He holds the pen that signs our paychecks."

Aaron pursed his lips as he watched his friend walk.

"We could always find another employer. Although, I hate to admit it, Barons has given us a lot a freedom when it comes to our jobs."

"That's why we can't just go find another employer. There's no guarantee that it will be any better."

Lovecraft and Aaron had a certain way with conversations that told the other it had ended. They had planted and developed this kind of communication in high school; back before the Contractors were legal and Lovecraft had to do his work in the dark. It was times like these that he would suddenly be filled with a sense of nostalgia and wished that he could be home; back in Omaha. It was from this nostalgia that he formed a new conversation, as they walked down the multitude of crimson stairs.

"On the bright side, he didn't tell us we were being sent to Juarez, like Pammy."

Aaron stopped walking and looked at him incredulously.

"I haven't heard you call Pamela, 'Pammy,' since we were in high school."

Lovecraft immediately noticed his blunder when Aaron pointed it out.

"Right. It slips out sometimes due to force of habit. Usually when I'm thinking about her or one of our other classmates."

Aaron guessed that old habits die hard, but kept a grain of salt in the back of his mind. It was very unlike Lovecraft to 'accidentally' call Pamela, 'Pammy.' After all, Pamela was the only schoolmate to become a Contractor, besides Lovecraft and himself.

Pamela had been a quiet girl when she was in her freshman and sophomore year; some even said that she couldn't talk. However, it appeared that she blossomed in her later teens and became a developed and, rather boisterous, woman. She became so boisterous in fact, that she started dying her hair all sorts of insane colors, although purple was her favorite. Pamela had become attached to Lovecraft and Aaron when everyone learned about what they did;

it was like she had always wanted to help people and becoming a Contractor was the way she could do it. Thus, it was a bitter-sweet moment when she completed her training under the two men and went off to join her own team of Contractors; she still made sure to check in whenever she could.

"I wonder how she's doing. Hasn't called in a few days," Aaron said, absentmindedly.

"I doubt they have the communications we have here. I'm sure she's fine."

They reached the bottom of the stairs and were greeted by white tile that proved to be the source of the smell. At the beginning step sat a ladder that featured a tall, scrawny man, with his head stuck up inside the ceiling. He wore a unique visor that appeared to highlight the outdated wires, yet he was still looking for something.

Aaron and Lovecraft casually stepped past him and found themselves in a small waiting room with the front door to their right and a kiosk that was manned by a robotic police officer on the left. Directly across from them sat a row of chairs, along yet another whitewashed wall; there were around five chairs lined up. Five rows of five chairs lined the middle of the room and these faced toward the kiosk, leaving the five chairs along the wall rather lonely. Lovecraft had experience with the far set of chairs though, and knew their isolation was not by accident. This was the place where the victims sat who had nowhere else to go. Lovecraft had quite a history with this particular set of chairs, since he had more than once had to question a victim. Thus, it was no surprise that he gave the row a quick scan.

The first person was a black woman who really needed to be taught how to put on makeup; her face, a discombobulated mix of anger and frustration. The second was a woman with blonde hair and nails that looked like they could be worth a diamond ring; typical damsel in distress who probably got her purse stolen. Next to her was a man, to Lovecraft's surprise, who looked like he was either having a panic attack or it had been some time since he had a hit of cocaine. The seat next to him was empty, which surprised the Contractor even further. However, his surprise soon turned to confusion as he laid eyes on a woman whose nose, lip, and right eyebrow were covered in blood. Her prune colored hair, a very interesting and weird color choice, was mated and stained with the blood on her brow. It hung past her walnut eyes.

Lovecraft took a step forward and saw that her left eye was, in fact, swollen and purple, much like the rest of the bruises that patterned her pale skin like polka dots. She noticed Lovecraft with a start and began trying to wipe the blood off her face, jeans, and white button up; hurting herself in the process of trying to look somewhat presentable. The taller man found this small woman, she appeared to only be about 5' 2", peculiar. No, not for the fact that she was beat to hell, but there was something inside of her, something invisible that seemed so obvious that it made Lovecraft's intuition scream. She looked at him with a shy half-glance and proceeded to twitch her hands and move her head uncomfortably. It was this movement that allowed Lovecraft to see what his thoughts had picked up on; the woman had strange, vertical scars just above her earlobes.

He immediately turned away after learning this and sought out anybody who could help her, or at the very least, give her a bandage. Looking around, he found no one besides Aaron, who also turned to look around, after finally seeing what had captured his leader's interest. The robot at the kiosk would be of no help, it was only built to organize and take complaints, and anybody who could help had vanished, as if they weren't even there to begin with. Lovecraft's shoulders slumped in frustration as a black med kit was pushed into his view. He turned to Aaron with a questioning glance.

"Don't worry. I still have my primary on my belt. You'll be able to plug any holes if you need to."

Lovecraft nodded and took the nylon pouch in his gloved hand and walked over to the woman who was looking at them with eyes so wide, one would have thought she was a child. He opened the bag and immediately started wrapping her head and, after that was done, he used a disinfecting wipe on the small cuts that did not merit wasting a bandage on. Lovecraft wore a scowl on his face as he realized he couldn't do anything about her broken nose and the bruises that dotted her nubile body. The woman, on the other hand, could not believe what was happening. This was not the first time that she had been here, and this was most definitely not the worst it had ever been, but for the first time in the course of three years, someone had actually noticed her and wanted to help.

Unfortunately, before she could formulate any form of thanks, she heard the pouch zipping up and the tall man stood up and handed it back to his partner, *They must be Contractors.* Lovecraft nodded to her and started walking toward the door. Her mind started spasming and it led her to simply raise her hand to wave at them as they left; an innocent smile on her face.

Outside, they were greeted with a surprisingly warm sun. The water that coated the sidewalk was from a small downpour that had happened after Lovecraft and Aaron had already entered the building.

"Strange, I thought it was supposed to rain again," Aaron said, putting his hand parallel with his brow. Lovecraft, on the other hand, couldn't help but focus on the situation they had just experienced.

"I can't believe they just left her there," Lovecraft shook his head.

"It's just the way it works nowadays. Nobody helps each other anymore, and I can guarantee you that she was checked out and since she could stand, she was left to her own devices. It's sick, but what we did gave her hope; I could see it on her face." Lovecraft grabbed his sunglasses off his plate carrier and slipped them on his face.

"If only that kind of hope were so easy to give." He pulled his cellphone out of his pocket and found a contact that was just represented with a 'K.' It was an old flip phone that was untraceable; perfect for dealing with those you'd rather not tell other people about.

The line clicked and a woman with a thick, French accent said, "Hello, Mister Lovecraft, what can I do for you?"

"Hello, Kara," he began walking with Aaron toward the car, "I need a moment of your time. Are you busy robbing somebody blind?"

"As charming as ever I see. No, I've got enough time for you to stop by, and for your information, my 'specialties' keep the consumer alive."

"Yeah, yeah, you test each one on somebody who deserved it. I've heard it a thousand times. We're 15 minutes away, I'll see you then?"

"I look forward to it, just don't go announcing yourselves. Vinny got shot the last time and I had a hell of a time finding a new merc- guard." Lovecraft smirked as she said this and hung up, just as Aaron turned the car on.

"We're going to Kara's first and then the compound."

"Why?"

"Because I don't like just doing something in the Flood Zone on a hunch. That's how things like Black Hawk Down and Benghazi happen. Frankly, I'd like to know if I'm going to get pulled on by a bunch of gangbangers and Narco terrorists, before I just walk through the front door and get shot in the dick."

"Point taken," Aaron said, as he pulled away from the curb.

The drive was as uneventful as ever, and it only started to get interesting as they stopped in front of a metal, two-story building that featured a pink, neon sign reading, 'Lugers & Leggings.' It was a rather feminine name for a gun store, but it did match Kara's personality to a tee. The shop was located just north of Lincoln Park, and its trademarked symbol was of a scantily clad female holding a WWII-era pistol, naturally, against her leggings. Surprisingly enough, Kara did more business with men than women, but one could tell that the few women did appreciate the female-oriented venue.

Lovecraft undid his seatbelt and opened his door, "Let's go see what Kara's up to. I wonder if she dyed her hair again."

"Knowing how much hair she has, without a doubt, she did," Aaron said, clicking his weapon's safety on. Lovecraft did the same just before opening the door and listening to the jingle. Both men stepped through the door and saw a woman with long, green hair that was braided down to her knees. She was leaned over the counter, intently listening to a woman who looked rather uncomfortable being there; she looked scared.

Along the far wall, which was painted in a deep red, stood two men; one black and the other of Hispanic descent: his name, Sam, his brother, Vinny, used to be where the black man now stood. Kara, for her part, was dressed in an elegant burgundy dress that was cut deep down the middle and had a slit, all the way up to her right hip, in the skirt. 'Selling Death and Destruction with Sophistication' was her motto.

Lovecraft took a moment to look around and besides a few of the pieces on the wall being sold, the place hadn't changed since he was last here a few months ago. Red tapestries hung around the windows, plush red chairs were sat in key locations, a crystal chandelier hung from the ceiling, and blue L.E.D. lights illuminated the wall and shelves where the guns were on display. Even the carpet was kept at a kind of satin white that made one almost wipe their feet on reflex; if only people knew that this place was actually themed after a strip club in France…minus the guns, of course.

"I'll be with you in a second, gentlemen," Kara assured, after she reached a lull in the conversation.

"We're in no rush," Aaron responded. Kara nodded and continued listening to this woman that was still, extremely nervous. He took a seat in one of the chairs, while Lovecraft went over to Sam; Lovecraft was taller than him by about five inches.

"How are you doing, Sam?" The man scratched his shaven scalp before answering him.

"I'm doing better, Lovecraft. Thank you for getting me out alive… Even if you couldn't get Vinny out."

"Sam, I tried to save his life, but—" Sam stopped him before he could continue; he didn't want to hear about it again.

"I get it. There was nothing you could do and I know I didn't act in the most positive way after the incident, but I'm past that now." Lovecraft searched his expression and found that there was no deception in his eyes, so he let the subject fall with a nod. He turned back to watch Kara, just as their conversation picked up again.

"Okay, well, if you're needing something for home protection, I have many options. Is there any particular flavor you were looking at?" Kara asked, running her hand over the glass counter. The woman, who was still fidgeting slightly, calmed herself and pointed toward a piece located in the upper right-hand corner.

"Ah yes, of course. A revolver is an excellent choice when it comes to protecting the family. Do you have the necessary paperwork?" She reached into her purse and presented her pistol license to Kara's trained eyes.

The Frenchwoman smirked, "Perfect, it's cash only, so I assume you brought enough?" She nodded and started reaching for her wallet. While she did this, Kara, reached beneath the counter and placed a box of .357 Magnum cartridges on the counter, leaving the woman to shoot her a questioning glance.

"First-time customers, Contractors, Law Enforcement, Active Duty Military, and Veterans get the first ten rounds on us." She nodded over to a sign that read, 'The American Rule.' The woman looked over and smiled her first solid smile that anyone had seen, before reading the rest of the sign. She read a particular part that stated, 'Contractor's weapons are for Contractors. Don't like it? Tough shit.' Beneath this was a white emblem of an AK-47 that appeared to glow on the black background.

"What's a Contractor's weapon?" she asked, feeling adventurous. Kara looked at her for a moment, before she motioned behind the woman with her head. She turned around and found herself looking at Lovecraft, who stood there with his arms folded.

"Automatic assault rifles typically, but it can also be things like belt-fed machine guns, grenades," he pointed to the two on his belt and the one on his plate carrier, "rocket launchers – although highly frowned upon – and other forms of military equipment, like fifty-caliber machine guns." After hearing this, the woman looked like her hair was about to catch on fire, and simply nodded, as Kara told the black man, his name was Jamie, to fetch the box that the revolver belonged to. Aaron looked at Lovecraft and cocked an eyebrow, which earned him a shrug from his team leader.

After this small exchange, they would wait for the woman to fill out her paperwork before leaving, not ten minutes after Lovecraft and Aaron had first pulled up.

"What's her deal?" Lovecraft asked, as Kara now stood alone at the counter.

"Single mother, house gets broken into… You know, the usual stuff," Kara paused for a moment to nod toward Sammy, who went to the windows and swiped his hand over them to turn them almost as black as night, "So what brings you guys over? You usually call a day in advance, so I assume it's not because you miss me."

"Charming as ever," Aaron muttered with a playful smirk.

"Oh, believe me, honey, you have no idea how charming I can be. You'll never find out though; not without that ring under your glove coming off."

Aaron formed a fist with his left hand, "The ring stays on." Kara gave a satisfied smirk; it was strange for her, now that Aaron and she had once been shooting at each other.

She was brought back by Lovecraft clearing his throat, "Argentina Lagos," he pulled out his actual phone this time and pushed a holographic picture toward Kara, "Have you ever heard of her?"

Kara looked at Lovecraft and then the picture before shaking her head, "She's never come in my shop, why?" Lovecraft toyed with telling her the truth or lying to her, but she was a friend and had come to help them out of various situations before.

"She's believed to be the Chaos Killer."

"The one who uses the MAC-11?"

"That's the one, and as you have told me before, your shop is the only place to get rare weapons like that." Lovecraft glanced down to his holster where his birthday present from Kara sat; a Yugoslavian CZ99.

The MAC-11 was a cold-war-era machine gun that spawned off somebody thinking that a fully automatic pistol was a good idea. It was an unruly hunk of steel that showed its age, but when gunning down police officers who weren't paying attention, it did its job well enough.

"You're correct. I'm about the only person in the city who has the right contacts to get one of those, but the last one I sold was to a man named William Carson," Kara explained.

Lovecraft's eyes lit up as she said the name, "You did? He's one of our leads to finding her. Thank you, Kara, you've been a big help as always." Kara looked in confusion as Lovecraft moved faster than she had ever seen; even Aaron seemed to move like a crazed animal.

"L.C., wait!" Kara yelled after them. Spinning on his heel, Lovecraft almost kicked the door in front of him.

"The one I sold him was a semi-automatic, civilian version, which means he had to get an automatic conversion kit. Those are illegal for anyone without a class-three gun license." Lovecraft stood there and thought for a moment.

"That means he had help getting one. Any idea where he could have gotten one?"

Kara shrugged, "Take your pick. The Vipers out of Juarez, the Russians, hell, even the pussies who run the Familia out of California could get one...if they're not too busy getting off on graffitiing some abandoned building." Lovecraft nodded in agreement and turned back to the door.

"Thanks for your help as always, Menagerie." This earned him an eye roll from Kara, as well as the appropriate use of her middle finger.

"Fuck you too," Kara paused, as she ran her hands through her floral crown of hair, "Listen, you guys better come back. The only thing keeping this city from continuing its descent into Lake Michigan is you guys." Lovecraft and Aaron smirked at her sudden behavior.

Kara did not have many people she truly cared about, and most of them were back in her home country of France. Those that were in the United States could barely fill up a handful of fingers, and a majority of those were just people she relied on to help her with Lugers & Leggings. Thus, it would certainly not be too farfetched to say that Aaron and Lovecraft were her only friends, as well as the only semblance of family she had. This was the reason why they knew Kara's real name, 'Menagerie Alexandre.' A name much too long. She came to be known as 'Kara' simply because her grandfather was in the Russian Navy and commanded a Kara-class vessel; his daughter married Kara's father and then she was born. The name was quite a hit in the illegal arms trade.

"Don't worry, we always come back," Lovecraft said, opening the door, "Later, Kara." He walked through the door and Aaron said his goodbyes with a wave of his hand before following him. Kara put her arm on the counter and used it to hold her head up; a lopsided frown on her face, "You always say that."

After this, the two Contractors got back in their car and went back to their compound where Lovecraft was able to grab his helmet, as well as other equipment that would be necessary in the Flood Zone. Before they knew it, they were back in the car and driving north to a heavily fortified checkpoint situated on West Cermak Road, the Ruins of Chinatown.

The checkpoint itself was massive. Two guard towers were on each side of the street, four in total, and the same number of military Humvees were parked near their bases. They surrounded an old, tradition gate that stated Chinatown's name; only some of the symbols and letters had fallen due to age. The two men immediately noticed the increased security around the checkpoint and knew that it meant one thing.

"Contractors…well, if this mission was going to be a pain in the ass, I'd say this is a good omen to confirm that's the case," Aaron said, slowing down. Lovecraft knew that this could go one of two ways. The first, was they could get through without a problem because they had good relations with whoever's team this was. The second, was they would stop and then the other team would stonewall them, if not just to waste time. Unfortunately, there was no rule that said Contractors had to get along with other Contractors, and Lovecraft's team was on everybody's shit list, excluding a few notable teams who were mature enough to look past the fact that they were highest paid in the city.

As they grew closer, his eyes graced over the balaclava-wearing soldiers who grasped the Humvee's fifty calibers; he couldn't see their patches or their I.D.s. They stopped in front of a black man with broad shoulders, fat lips, and his hair cut into a Mohawk that was also bleached. Lovecraft immediately recognized the patches on his arms and thanked God; they would be getting a break today.

"Ah, Lovecraft!" the man said upon the window being rolled down, "You are a sight for sore eyes."

"It's good to see you, David, what's the deal here? The Israelis volunteer for guard duty?" David was the leader of a group of Contractors based out of Israel; they were called the T.W. or The Wall.

"They wish," he said, laughing, "The police got called to something else, so we're here to pick up the slack."

"We?" David nodded and pointed toward the end of the road; an old factory was off in the distance. Lovecraft focused his attention on the building and noticed the faint glimmer of light reflecting off the lens of a scope.

Lovecraft smirked and knew just who the sniper, and whoever was with her, was, "Nice to see that Maleene has been reduced to guard duty."

David laughed, "You should have heard her when she found out. 'What the fuck is he thinking?!' or, 'I'm a goddamn sniper! Where does he get off having me watch this stupid fucking road in the middle of this stupid fucking city?! Jesus fucking Christ, it's like I'm back in that shithole Afghanistan,'" David paused for a second, "My personal favorite was, 'When I get back, I'm going to shove a stick up that asshole's asshole!' I literally couldn't breathe for a good 20 seconds."

Both Aaron and Lovecraft laughed before the latter said, "Sounds like fun. Are we clear to pass?"

"I need one thing first. What's your call sign and channel?"

"Ruler. Channel 063." David nodded and withdrew a notepad from his plate carrier and wrote everything down, before bookmarking the channel in his radio.

"Welcome to the Flood Zone, Ruler."

Chapter 3
Call Sign: RULER

Old, water-damaged buildings appeared to fly by, as Aaron drove down the deserted Chinatown streets. The sky above had suddenly become overcast; they had only just left the checkpoint. All around them, the street, the buildings, the back alleys, even some exposed rooms, were covered in paper trash and downed banners which were a remnant from a festival that never happened.

Lovecraft had slipped his helmet onto his head, a level-three ballistic helmet, with its panoramic night-vision pushed up, and twisted his neck in order to get used to its weight. It was colored in dark earth.

"You think Maleene was really that angry to get guard duty? I mean, it is in her job description," Aaron asked, turning a corner.

"Who knows? Maybe she's on her period or something, but it's not something I'm interested in finding out. Did you know she served in Afghanistan?" Lovecraft shook his head.

"No, she may have mentioned it, but it would have been lost in the seas of conversation. Especially when you have the other Eclipses like Mark, Eugene, or Adam." Eclipse was the Contracting Team that Maleene ran out of Springfield; they were known for night operations.

"True enough." They rounded another corner only for Aaron to slam on the breaks, as a lake of water stood in their way. Both of them sat there for a second, as if they were seeing water for the first time; Lovecraft was the first to get out of the car.

"Well, shit," he said, pulling a piece of paper from his pocket.

"Was this on the map?" Aaron asked, as Lovecraft fumbled with said map.

"No, an old water-main probably burst and flooded the street." Aaron looked back to the water and grabbed a piece of broken asphalt next to his foot. He threw it toward the water and grimaced, as he heard a heavy splash and didn't hear it afterward.

"No way we're making through that. It's gotta be at least three feet deep, unless you wanna try breathing through your scalp?" Lovecraft chided, moving his hand up to his headset.

"Ruler 01 to Sandstone 01, message, over."

"Go for Ruler 01," David's voice responded.

"Be advised. South, Wentworth Avenue is flooded and impassable. Looks like a water-main burst. Over."

"Solid copy, Ruler. Will update maps accordingly. Are you withdrawing? Over." Lovecraft looked around and saw that there was a ladder to a nearby rooftop in an alley to his right.

"Negative. I have rooftop access and will use that to reach Hilliard Apartments, over."

"Roger that. Some of the roof bridges got blown down in the storm. Be careful. Sandstone out." Lovecraft took his hand away from his head and motioned for Aaron to follow him. He did and found himself over at the ladder his leader noticed; he wrapped his left hand around one of the rungs. It was old and rusted, certainly not meeting the typical safety guidelines, but that was how every piece of metal was in the Flood Zone. Contractors had to worry more about tetanus than getting shot…most of the time.

"Seems sturdy enough. Catch me if I fall," Aaron said, pushing his gun onto his side.

"Oh, and get crushed by fifty pounds of gear on top of your two-hundred pounds? I think I'll have a better chance of dragging you than catching you," Lovecraft chuckled, looking down both ways of the alley.

"You're so considerate," Aaron started, ascending the ladder, "So far so good." An old, metallic waning echoed through the alleyway, as he got to the top. However, as he reached the top, his foot struck an old rung in the wrong spot and broke it off.

"Ah, you fuckin' piece of shit," Aaron swore, as he held on for dear life.

"You alright?" Lovecraft asked, not breaking his concentration on the alleyway.

"Yeah! Yeah, I'm good. Just shit my pants a little bit." Aaron pulled himself up onto the roof and had his rifle in his hands soon after. Lovecraft followed, as he watched and luckily got up the derelict tool without further incident.

"Let's hope that's all the excitement we get today," he said, pulling his own rifle into his hands.

"Agreed." Both stood up from their crouched position and looked to the right of the ladder where they found a sheet metal bridge that was, somehow, still standing. It was strange, from this high up, they could see the bones of the old city. The skyscrapers that only stood to fall down, the uncompleted construction sites, the flooded parks and restaurants, even a school whose playground was just barely visible above the flood waters. Lovecraft was so mesmerized by this that his eyes barely registered the rainwater dripping down the front of his helmet. Aaron's breath could be seen coming through the front of his balaclava, as he too looked at the dead city.

"Let's go," Lovecraft soon said, turning around. Aaron didn't say a word, as he followed his boss across the rickety bridge. The rain drowned out all other sound.

William walked down the wet streets of the Flood Zone in a pair of holey jeans and worn-out hoodie. He was soaked in rainwater, to the point that it dripped down the front of his hood and hit him in the face. In his hand, he carried a bag of white powder; no cops meant drugs could be carried out in the open. He had just spent the last of his meager paycheck and it would be so worth it. He wiped the snot from his nose and ducked into a nearby doorway.

It led him to a flight of water-damaged stairs that he quickly ascended. Two floors up, he pulled out a set of keys that had been left in the front office, and let himself into apartment 209: the place he and his girlfriend, Argentina, were squatting. He ran a hand through his blonde hair.

"Baby, I'm home! I got the good stuff!" he announced, smiling. Not hearing a response, he kicked off his shoes and walked further into the apartment. To his right, was a kitchen with an old refrigerator, and to his left, was a long hallway leading to the bedroom; he currently stood in the living room.

"Ari are you home yet?!" he asked, without hearing another response. Disappointment filled his heart, as he wiped his nose again. He sat the bag on the kitchen counter and just barely noticed a black blur move out from behind the refrigerator, before the leather palm of a tactical glove covered his mouth.

"No, she's not, but you are," Aaron said, thrusting a needle into the man's neck, "My stuff's better anyway." William watched as the world around him suddenly began to spin, and before he knew it, he was waking up in his bed; stripped naked and unable to feel anything below his collarbone. Day had turned to night, which left him with only a little bit of streetlight to look around.

"Hell of a drug, isn't it?" an unknown voice said from the bottom of the bed. He craned his neck forward to look toward the voice's origin, and found that he couldn't move the rest of his body.

"What did you do to me?!" he asked, looking at a man wearing camouflage and a black shirt.

"We gave you what you wanted; however, our narcotics have a terrible tendency to cause paralysis," Lovecraft responded, leaning against the door frame. Aaron was out in the hallway.

"What the hell do you want? I can't feel my fingers," he started to cry.

"Oh, don't be a pussy, it's only temporary. As for what I want, I'd like know when your girlfriend gets home."

"Why?"

"Don't be stupid with me, bitch. You and I both know why I have business with her. Would you like to try again?"

"I still don't know what you're talking about! What the fuck is wrong with you?!" Lovecraft sighed and rubbed his brow, before standing up to go over to the nightstand. He pulled a picture of Argentina out off of the piece of furniture and held it in front of William's face.

"If you truly don't know what I'm talking about, would kindly explain why you are sleeping with a wanted criminal?" William stayed silent, fear in his eyes.

"I'll ask you one more time," Lovecraft said, unfolding his knife and pointed it toward his captive's mouth, "When does Argentina get home? You best talk this time, else...you'll feel what it's like to remove a molar the old-fashioned way." A tear fell from William's right eye, causing Lovecraft to smile.

Argentina's red heels clicked down the soaked sidewalk; her umbrella having more than a few holes in it. She had just gotten off work a lot later than expected, thanks to someone spilling beer in her hair, which no amount of soap could get the smell out. She was tired, frustrated, and in need, since she could already feel the pin pricks around her neck. Her dark eyes widened in gratitude as she saw the door to her and William's apartment. She almost jogged her way up the stairs, since she knew that inside was an opportunity to take off her shoes and send herself to cloud nine.

Almost knocking the door off its hinges, Argentina flew through the doorway and into the small apartment where she saw that it was a quarter after one. Her eyes fell to the counter and started glistening once she saw the bag of white powder sitting there. Smiling, she pulled a piece of paper from her purse and put a little cocaine on the counter. She took a hit of it quickly and couldn't help but notice that her head started to spin a little bit as she got high. She smiled at this new sensation; her mind in too many places at once to be concerned about it. She dropped her umbrella and purse on the counter to turn around toward the hallway.

"Baby, are you here?!" she asked, pulling her sweatshirt off, "I noticed what you brought home, and I really appreciate it." Her eyebrow rose when she didn't get an immediate response, "Hey! You better not be sleeping when I'm like this!" She unzipped her skirt and let it fall to the floor. She entered the room and saw that William's back was bare and his face was buried in the pillow; a position he had never slept in before.

"William?" she asked, pushing him over. Her eyes widened as he flopped over like a dead fish, with his mouth duct taped.

"Oh God! Baby, are you alright?!" she screamed, reaching into the drawer where her machine pistol was. All William could do was moan, as his eyes caught a glimpse of the black figure that had injected him with the narcotic. He started to moan louder and flicked his eyes more rapidly behind Argentina. She turned and brought the machine pistol to bear on Aaron's form; the nine-millimeter rounds passing through him and hitting the refrigerator.

Aaron looked down and, in a distortion, meant to hide his voice, said, "Holograms. What would you do without them?" In the blink of an eye, he disappeared, but Argentina couldn't get a chance to wonder what happened, as her head started pounding and the world around her started to distort, just like Aaron's voice.

"Laced cocaine. Nasty trick," a voice said to her left, and when she turned to confront it, she saw that Aaron was now the one laying where William was. Without thinking, she screamed and brought her weapon to bear on the person on the bed; unknowingly blowing away William, whose blood now covered the sheets, walls, ceiling, and Argentina's arms, as well as her breasts. The image faded away and William came into view; his face ripped in half by the weapon.

"No!" she screamed upon seeing this horrifying image. She jumped up to her feet and plunged into the darkness of the apartment; just running anywhere that wasn't there. The hallucinating woman almost ripped the door off its hinges, as she left and found herself face to face with Lovecraft, whose night vision made him look like a man with four green eyes. Argentina pointed her gun at him and ripped apart the hallway, as he ducked into a small corridor; pieces of wood and mildewed plaster falling around him.

Argentina stopped shooting to look behind her where Aaron stood; his four night-vision lenses were red. She pointed at him and fired, as he ducked inside a room without a door.

"Die you fu—" She was cut off, as a much louder shot rang from behind her, and ripped through her shoulder. She felt the warmth of her own blood running down her arm, but otherwise, felt fine. Turning around again, she sought to kill Lovecraft, who looked a lot like Aaron now, but was stopped when a heavier, .308 caliber round, tore through her midsection. Its round was much faster than Lovecraft's 5.56. Thus, it over penetrated and was sent down the hall. It could have hit Lovecraft, but he was already in cover.

Argentina hissed in pain as she started bleeding profusely from her abdominals; no matter how much cocaine she had in her system, these rounds would not go ignored. They were selfish like that. Bearing her teeth, she turned back to Aaron, only to have her machine gun shot out of her hand, as well as having three of her fingers removed, her hand mutilated.

"Give it up, Argentina! You. Are. Beaten," Aaron yelled, as she screamed in pain whilst holding her hand.

"Surrender while you still have your life!" Lovecraft yelled from behind her. The two men pushed from their respective covers and now stood toe to toe with the woman who leered at them like a wounded animal. Her eyes darted around rapidly and found a window to her right, Lovecraft's left and Aaron's right, and had already made her decision upon seeing it. Lovecraft saw her look at it and already knew what she was about to do, so he started lowering his rifle right as she took off. The sound of glass shattering and a single shot echoed through the hall.

Outside, Michael Dumont and his four-man team had been drawn to the Hilliard Apartments by the sound of gunfire. They arrived just in time to see Argentina fall from a first-story window and try to crawl away; her left knee having been blown out by Lovecraft's last shot.

"Holy fuck," Michael's medic swore, as he ran to the injured woman. His two other men had their rifles pointed toward the building. Yet, they weren't ready when another shot rang out and buried itself in the pavement in front of their medic, who fell backward to avoid it. Michael pointed his AKM toward the window now, but was astonished when another Contractor climbed out of the window and landed in front of them.

Lovecraft's face deadpanned as he gave each of them a once over; they were all wearing flecktarn and looked like they were about to piss themselves.

"Find your own goddamn bounty, fucking vultures," he said, as Aaron jumped down behind him. Lovecraft immediately picked out Michael as the team leader, since his night vision was the only one that didn't look like the Soviets took them to Afghanistan. Aaron went over to Argentina and wire-tied her hands, before tending to her wounds.

"Who the fuck are you guys supposed to be?" Lovecraft asked, pushing his night vision up. Michael immediately recognized him.

"Wow, I didn't think we'd run into you out here, Ruler. I couldn't even recognize you with all that shit on your face." Rolling his eyes, Lovecraft motioned for him to answer.

"I'm, er...we're from the Luft Company based in Germany, call sign: Panther," he said, showing that he was as green as an apple.

"Right..." if Lovecraft deadpanned any harder, his face would have sunk into the ground, "...why are you here? The Flood Zone's off limits at night, unless you're a Contractor with an active mission."

"Well, we do have an active mission, but it's probably best if we don't go around saying it, else more people will want a cut."

"Kid, did you not get enough childish secrets told to you in high school, or are you bullshitting me? No job, in this shit hole, is worth that much." Michael felt his ego nosedive, as he knew the truth behind Lovecraft's words, but it's what kept his team together, so he had to prove him wrong.

"Oh yeah? Well, have you ever heard of Menagerie Alexandre?" he asked with a sly grin. For a split millisecond, Lovecraft's world stopped as he heard Kara's real name, *So that's his big mission.* Aaron stopped working for a moment at the mention of the name, but continued when he saw how calm his boss was.

"Of course, I've heard of her. She's an international arms dealer wanted in Europe. In fact, I think her photo's on my computer somewhere."

The younger Contractor nodded, "Well, here's the deal. Her bounty just skyrocketed to over five-hundred million dollars, and this was the last place she was seen before she disappeared, so I figured," he added with a cocky voice, "this would be the best place to look." Lovecraft pursed his lips and looked between each one of the four men; they all looked barely in their twenties and were so full of youth and vigor that he knew they were no match for Kara. The thing about the arms dealer was that she was impossibly smart; to fight her would like be like playing a game of chess, while trying to find a mouse that had the brain capacity of a human. However, it is to be said that Kara was not a soldier and the closest she ever got to being one was when she was on the range with them; yet, the woman had outsmarted several Special Forces teams before and even killed some of them. She was as sly as a serpent and these four meant nothing to her; she'd probably play with them instead of devouring them.

"Okay," Lovecraft looked around, catching a glimpse of Aaron pulling Argentina to her feet, "have you found her yet?"

Michael's face became downcast, "Unfortunately, we haven't found anything, but I have it on good notion that she's still here in the city and I've heard that she may have dyed her hair."

"Lovecraft," Aaron suddenly said, looking at his watch. Lovecraft turned toward his teammate with a questioning look.

"Ten minutes until the Blackhawks stop making runs."

"Roger that." Lovecraft turned back to Michael.

"Who told you she's still here?" Michael shrugged his shoulders; his expression trying to stay neutral.

"Some merc named Jamie. Allegedly, he works for her, but I'm taking that with a grain of salt. Everybody just wants a slice, you know?" Lovecraft's face hardened a bit upon hearing the name.

"Yeah, I know. We need to be going and I suggest you guys do too; don't want to have to walk out of here, believe me." Michael opened his mouth a bit to speak, but stopped halfway before nodding and turning around. After this, the two groups separated and before long, Aaron and Lovecraft were aboard a police Blackhawk that was cutting its way through the downpour. Lovecraft reached into his pocket and withdrew the flip phone he used to call Kara and dialed it.

The warm sun danced across Kara's pale skin as she sat on top of a seaside cliff; the waves crashing beneath her and the warm winds blowing through her copious amount of hair. The place she sat was a particular restaurant on the Mediterranean side of France that was known for its seafood. Two powerful arms encircled her midsection, but before she could look to see who it was, her eyes abruptly opened to a dark room.

Her eyes fell onto a bedside table and saw that it was almost three in the morning. She also saw that her second phone was ringing off the hook. Grimacing with a green flame in her eyes, she pushed past her red, satin sheets and grabbed the phone.

Opening it, she put it to her ear and said, "Lovecraft, you better have a damn good reason I should not kick your—"

"Your new mercenary's selling you out." Kara closed her mouth, her eyelids lowered, and her green eyes hardened to the point their green was more blued.

"Oh, I see. How did you find out?"

"Met a new group of Contractors in the Flood Zone. They specifically used Jamie's name." Kara went quiet for a moment and sat on the side of her bed; she was pissed.

"Goodnight, Lovecraft."

"Let me know how it goes," With that said, Lovecraft hung up and allowed Kara to contact Sam on her actual phone. She waited rather impatiently; tapping on her bare thigh until she heard the line open.

"Ma'am, are you alright?"

"Sam, I am just peachy," she began, her voice low and deep, "Lovecraft just called me. We have a problem." Kara took the time to relay the message she received from Lovecraft and after Sammy hung up, she got up and went in the bathroom to take a shower. After this, Kara pulled out a pair of black yoga pants, a red T-shirt, and a black trench coat with gold buttons and stitching. Her hair was such a dark green that it went well with dark colors, especially black. The coat went to the top of her thigh and her shoes were a pair of low-rise heels, also colored in black. The cherry on top was her red lipstick that made her lips look like a candy apple.

Kara pressed her lips together and ran her hands through her long hair before turning toward the door. She opened it and walked down the oak stairs that led her to the front room of Lugers and Leggings; the guns on the wall glistening from the blue neon lights located on the shelves they sat on. Kara turned to the left, walked past the counter and into the small room that Jamie had retrieved the revolver from earlier. She swiped her hand over a seemingly vacant space on the wall and heard a chime before the lock was disengaged.

This area was her office and just from looking in, one could tell that she was a lot richer than she appeared. From wall to wall, there were cedar cabinets that had been handmade in Lebanon. Inside, they were filled with specialty items that were only offered to long time customers – this was where Lovecraft's CZ99 had sat before Kara gave it to him. In the center of the room, whose floor was covered in red carpet, was an ebony desk that was custom made in Brazil. Behind the plush, black chair at said desk was a particularly large cabinet that featured two display cases.

The first, and lowest of the two, contained her grandfather's hat, gloves, and a picture of the two of them when Kara was little. The rest of his uniform was back in France with her mother – whom she had not spoken to in a long time.

The second display was of Kara's personal weapon: a gold-plated AK-74 that she had pried from the dead hands of a war child in Chechnya. It was an old rifle, so old that it may have been used in Afghanistan during the 1980s, but Kara would never know, since the serial numbers had been scratched off before she found it.

The gun had also been rebuilt with titanium-gold alloy parts, thus destroying any semblance this weapon had to its former self. Strangely, it was rather poetic how this 'new' gun was just a vessel; and passed the gold exterior; passed the old, cracked wood furniture that she still used; the soul of an old warrior continued to twist and twirl. It curled around the firearm like a molten piece of iron and had a bewitching effect on any who saw it; all except for Kara: its creator. Yes, Kara had breathed new life into a broken and decaying weapon that she found in the hands of a broken and decaying child. She always found this ironic: mankind can breathe life into lifeless things, but can't breathe life into something that was once alive. After all, mankind's only answer to death was to say it was a problem for tomorrow, not today, which was then the excuse for tomorrow as well.

Kara walked past her desk, ran her hand over the display, and reached down into a drawer on the right side. She pulled out a large pistol that was painted jet black, but inlaid with gold for its accents. She took a seat in her chair and set the firearm on the top of the desk, while pushing a full magazine up her sleeve. A match was struck and the flame was soon cupped by her hand, as it was pushed into the head of a cigarette; Kara's red lips reflecting the flame. Putting her feet up on the desk, she shook the match out and blew a large cloud of smoke from her mouth after taking the cigarette out. She then ejected the full magazine and swapped it for an empty one; there was still a round loaded in the chamber. Kara shifted the gun around in her hand, feeling its weight, before there was a knock at her door.

"Come in," she commanded, setting the gun on her lap. The door opened with a slight squeak, as a tired Jamie walked in with Sam behind him. Shutting the door behind him, Sam stayed inside the room and blocked the entrance. Kara smirked at her turncoat employee and took great amusement in how lethargic he was; it would make him slow and stupid.

"Have I done something wrong, ma'am?" he asked, wiping his eyes. Kara's smirk grew bigger at the question, and she debated between getting this over with quickly or if she wanted to have a bit of fun with him. She chose the latter.

"Oh goodness, no," Kara laughed inside herself as she lied, "Jamie, it just seemed like a good time for you and me to get to know each other better. After all, I can't just openly talk about myself in broad daylight." There was a tightening in the man's chest as he saw an opportunity to get even more information about her; maybe even a genuine confession that Kara was indeed Menagerie Alexandre. He'd have to keep himself squared away to not reveal his hand, like a poker game, but it was too late; Kara had seen his reaction and knew what he wanted.

She brought her finger to her chin, "Now, where should I start?" she looked around for a moment, until she looked down at her pistol, as if she had forgotten it was there, "Perfect. Do you know what this is?" Jamie looked at the pistol for a moment, somehow noticing it for the first time, and looked like his brain hit a brick wall.

"It's a Colt 1911," he replied, unsure of himself. Kara laughed at this and circled the air with this golden, extended barrel.

"No, this is a very special pistol, in fact, it's so special, that nowadays, you probably wouldn't be able to find one. This is a LAR Grizzly, and it's chambered in 45 Winchester magnum." Kara pointed toward the name imprinted on the slide with her cigarette, before filling the room with even more smoke, "I got this as a reward in India; I sold faulty weapons to militants working out of Pakistan… I wonder what happened to the guy who bought my stuff after the two countries reunited." Jamie had noticed this before. Kara seemed to have a terrible tendency to get lost in her own thoughts; her memory being something akin to a vast ocean. Of what, he did not know, but if he were to venture a guess, it would involve a lot of blood, money, and brass casings.

"Are you saying that you've sold arms illegally?" Jamie asked, deciding to go straight to the point. If he let this go on any longer, he would be here clear into the afternoon with Kara's rambling. However, he started to rethink asking her this, when she pointed her pistol at him.

"And why would you assume that, Jamie?" she asked, smirking playfully. His mouth suddenly went dry and his composure threatened to slip away into a desolate wasteland. He tried to backtrack in a stammering apology, but was stunned when Kara started laughing.

"I'm just fucking with you," she pulled the magazine free and showed it to him, "See? It's not even loaded. Now, to answer your question, yes, I am an illegal arms dealer." Kara had decided that she had enough of this game, her attention span wasn't that impressive when it came to certain things, "And you…you're a fucking moron." Jamie thought his ears were playing tricks on him, but he found that they were truthful when Kara picked up her pistol again and shot him with the one round that was still in the chamber. A pink mist filled the air around Jamie's shoulder, as he tumbled onto the floor; his adrenaline trying to carry him over to the door where Sam stood with his Glock. His scalp was suddenly set ablaze with pain as Kara grabbed his dreadlocks and slammed his head into one of her cabinets.

"What the hell?!" he asked, as the room started spinning. There was a throbbing in his head that made him even more delirious, until he felt something hard pressed into his chest, just below his gunshot wound.

"What the hell, indeed." Kara grabbed Jamie's collar and pulled him up to where her pistol was mere inches away from his nose, "Listen to me, you piece of horse shit, I know that you've been running your mouth to a bunch of European mercenaries, and I have a bit of advice for you." Kara was going to relish this moment. If there was one thing that she had come to find satisfying, it was when she could see the fear in a traitor's eyes.

"In Chechnya, the Muslims called me the 'Queen of Black Gold.' They came to loathe that name when they found that none of their weapons worked. You too will come to loathe that name." She stood up and looked at him for a moment, before shooting him in the right leg. Jamie howled in pain as the fires of hate started to ignite within his eyes, and it only increased once he saw his former boss smirking at him.

"Oh, are you mad? I think he's mad, Sam. They're so cute when they're angry, you can almost see the pathetic will to live inside of them," Kara mocked him. Sure, she had stopped playing with him a long time ago, but it didn't mean that she couldn't have fun with him. In her previous experiences, taunting and mocking the individual also proved to weaken their resolve, thus making information and other key facts slip out. Yet, what slipped out was something that she could have never imagined.

"The Master will gut you, bitch!" Kara's very soul stiffened as her mind recalled the news report involving the Japanese Prime Minister. She immediately pointed toward Sam and then to Jamie. Sam already knew what she meant and put his gun away, before picking up the wheezing man and dragging him out of the room. Kara put out her cigarette and turned to look at the blood on the carpet. She would have to call her cleaner.

As the day matured into dawn, the temperatures came to reflect the time of year and this made Lovecraft dawn his wool coat again. It was the same ritual as the previous morning. He would stand on the roof of his compound and just watch the sun rise until it was time to start his day. However, he heard the door open and assumed it was Aaron, but when he heard high heels, it narrowed down who it could be.

"Still staring at the big glowing ball?" Kara's French accent asked, before her image came into view next to him. Lovecraft had been up since five and had only gotten back some 20 minutes before that; thus, his ability to fully participate in a conversation was rather lacking. It was a common case of lethargy displayed in those who felt that when they slept, they didn't really sleep.

"Helps wake me up, why are you here? You know it's not a good idea for you to be here when the 'German Inquisition' is looking for you." Lovecraft had loathed his encounter with Michael Dumont and his inebriated band, Luft Company. The one that pissed him off the most though, was, surprisingly, not Dumont, but the medic that tried to help Argentina. His name, being the only German on the supposedly German company, was Karl Heinkel; a real bastardization of a medic.

Kara shrugged her shoulders, "This 'German Inquisition' or Luft Company, as I hear they're called, do not scare me. Believe me, the dogs in Afghanistan and Pakistan were more intimidating than them."

"Yes, but dogs can't carry guns," Lovecraft objected, "What did you find out, or did you shoot first?" Kara knew exactly what he was talking about and took a moment to sit down, with her legs hanging off the edge. She had quite some time to think about this conversation, so what she was about to say would come naturally to her.

"There is a movement…happening in the Flood Zone. A guy calling himself the Master showed up about six months ago, and is waging war against the gangs, drug dealers, and the police—"

"Sounds like a typical crime boss to me," Lovecraft interjected. Kara shook her head.

"The things that Jamie told me last night sounded like I was watching some shitty sci-fi movie from the turn of the century. He described him as a man: tall, strong, but the other half is metal, like a genuine cyborg. Yet, he's not finished, like, there are still wires and shit everywhere, and he can barely speak." Kara shook her head. Even hearing it the second time didn't make it seem real; if she ran a blood test on Jamie, she wouldn't have been surprised to find him as high as a kite. She knew this wouldn't be possible, since he had routine drug tests and his license would be revoked if anything came up.

"Sounds like bullshit to me. The world's failing and stagnating because there's no innovation; yet, people are saying that a space man is walking around like God. It's unbelievable. It also sounds like people are so desperate in the Flood Zone that they've put their hopes into fantasies." It was a sad truth and Lovecraft could relate to it. People want nothing more than to believe there is something more, something bigger than themselves, and will go so far to find it that they will believe anything. When the chips are down, people turn gullible and lose their self-control.

"It is bullshit, but I must say, it's not the worst story I've ever heard. There was one time that these Burmese soldiers tried to convince me that that the Titanoboa still existed, and they lived in the darkest parts of the forest… In the course of this conversation, I ended up being the 12th cousin of Marie Antoinette as well," Kara said, standing up again. Lovecraft had to chuckle at this. If there was one thing that everybody enjoyed, it was Kara's stories of when she traveled. The time she went to India, her dealings in Nepal, and when she supplied Israeli rebels in Palestine, were some of Lovecraft's favorites.

"It was quite the interesting conversation; almost made the money I lost on that venture worth it." Kara's soul stiffened at the thought; she felt like a piece of ice which was not helped by the temperature. "Speaking of which," she tried to recover, "you got me up really early this morning…and it was so early that I didn't get to put on my makeup, eat breakfast, have a cup of coffee." Lovecraft could see where this was going.

"So I was thinking, since I helped you find your fugitive, you could take me somewhere as payment?" Kara smiled, as she put her arms behind her back, fingers crossed. Lovecraft deadpanned and looked at his watch. He had seen this coming a mile away and was prepared.

"You do know that I have to go to work in 15 minutes and since Luft is running around, it would not be a good idea for us to be seen together." Kara's mouth went dry, as her fingers slowly unwove themselves. She felt the all-familiar crushing reality that she lived in and first felt anger and then despair, but a woman could not show her emotions so easily. A blush erupted across her face as she began stuttering; she felt dumb.

"Of course. I'm sorry. Well, I have to go, but I'll be in touch, and call if you need anything?"

"You know we will." Kara grimaced at the word 'we,' and nodded before opening the door and walking down the stairs. It was a short drive back to Lugers and Leggings, which was thankfully closed on Mondays, and an even shorter walk to her apartment, on top of the store. She quietly shut the door and rested her forehead on it, muttering, "I suck at this."

The day passed, and while Lovecraft tried to focus all of his attention on his tasks, the information Kara gave him that morning kept him up clear into the night. He searched social media, news networks, surveillance, the police database, and even called some of the different Contracting groups, short of the Union itself. None of them had heard of anything relating to this 'Master.' This left him with a massive headache and useless computer page. It was almost 12:30 A.M. and he came up nothing; he needed a break.

Lovecraft stood up, threw on a shirt, and headed outside, after taking a few aspirins. The night air made his coat almost jump over his shoulders; the holographic apparitions looked deceptively warm as they advertised their various wares over loudspeaker. Taking a breath, he looked to his second-favorite thinking spot, a vacant bus stops right outside the compound, and found that there was some humongous monstrosity sitting on in. Lovecraft looked up and down the deserted streets before pulling a pack of cigarettes from his coat pocket. Fishing one free, he clicked his lighter open and let the warm flame ignite the end. After this, he pulled it free from his mouth and strode toward the bench.

Eyeing the strange blob sitting on the metal, he was surprised to find that it wore a titanium helmet with metal-glass visor sticking up toward the sky. In fact, the strange being was a man, a huge man who wore the biggest parka he had ever seen. His legs, although being clad in baggy cargo pants that were colored in an off-blue, were the size of tree trunks and had his body not been covered, Lovecraft would have felt as though he was David and this man was Goliath. Yet, the man seemed to be still, and gave him reason to believe he had frozen to death out here.

"They stop running the buses through here after midnight," Lovecraft said, puffing his cigarette. He only half-believed that the man was still alive, but was surprised when the helmet moved up and revealed a scruffy black beard with a dusting of white. He looked from the right to the left before his gaze on fell on Lovecraft. His blue eyes were cold as ice and his face was like that of chiseled stone; lips were chapped and damaged from years in the cold.

"May I sit?" Lovecraft asked once the man made no move to speak. He nodded and Lovecraft sat next to him; both of them sitting in silence for a long time. It was not that neither of them didn't have anything to say, but they just didn't know how to bridge the subject. It was a common problem, but Lovecraft knew just what to start with. After all, this was where he thought and pondered things.

"Where are you from, Contractor?" Lovecraft asked, pulling the cigarette from his lips and turning toward the man. The name got his attention and his lips started to part. He kind of reminded Lovecraft of an imposing giant that had trouble speaking because of a mental deficiency, but he knew this to not be the case.

"I'm from the Russian Federation, and I just got here 30 minutes ago," he replied, with a surprisingly soft accent. To say that Lovecraft was surprised would have been a lie; he had recognized the helmet as an eastern design, but to assume that he was Russian just off this would have been rude. It was like saying, all Asians were the same just because they looked vaguely similar.

"Why are you sitting here?" the Russian asked, "If it's true that the buses are not working right now, why would you sit here?" Lovecraft laughed inside his head. To the common person, he was just a weirdo who liked to sit in the cold whilst smoking a cigarette. However, his reasoning wasn't all that strange.

"I come out here to think and ponder my thoughts. It was a particularly long day today, so why not make it longer?" The man shrugged his shoulders and could see his point. It was not a bad thing to lose some sleep at times; kept your body working and your mind on its toes.

"It's not the worst reason I could have heard," the man outreached his hand which was clad in a thick glove, "Lieutenant Abram Sokolov, Spetsnaz support gunner and counter-terrorism specialist." Lovecraft accepted his gloved hand into his own and held it for a moment.

"Lovecraft, unfortunately, I have no fancy titles. I'm just good at what I do." He withdrew his hand and eased back into his sitting position. His cigarette had burned down to the filter and as he threw it into the street, he noticed the look on Abram's face. It was the look of a reserved man who just met the most famous person in his work field.

"Your reputation precedes you, Mr. Lovecraft."

"Please, just Lovecraft. I feel old when people use mister."

"Of course. It's quite funny, when one applies for a contracting visa, you can hear the guards talking about you and the feats you have accomplished. You have a lot of admirers for being so young." Lovecraft felt his head harden like a steel cage, and his eyes dilated. He felt as stiff as a piece of rod iron; an anger began building within him as he thought of the people who would praise him for his work.

"You have no idea how bad that makes me feel." Abram turned his full attention onto the man sitting next to him. His face was screwed up into an incredulous look, and for a second, thought Lovecraft was crazy, but he also had an inkling that his judgment had read him wrong. Could the best Contractor in Chicago really be this…selfless?

"Why? There is no reason to feel bad. If a man has admirers, then it means he is trustworthy." Lovecraft knew he'd say this. He had this conversation with Aaron, Kara, Pamela, even Aaron's sister, Amanda, when they were involved romantically, but he had come to find out that most people did not think the way he did. Thus, he would spell it out for Abram just as he had spelled it out for everyone else.

"Do people admire me for the people I save, the ones I protect every day? Or is it that they admire me for my ability to kill people? If it is for the latter, then I want nothing to do with them, because they are the ones whom I kill. They just don't know it yet." Lovecraft stood up and gestured to the piercing skyscrapers and neon holograms, "The people who call me 'Protector' are more valuable than the ones who call me 'Dominator.'" Abram could not help but feel his spirit moved by his noble words. He sought to keep his composure; however, Abram did allow himself to stand up. The Russian seemed to dwarf Lovecraft; he had to be just a little under seven-feet tall.

"I find your words to be genuine, but I have to ask. Would you protect them from me, should the need arise?" Lovecraft looked into his cold eyes and found that there was a flicker of warmth. Could his words have stirred a fire in the frozen man? Abram mistook Lovecraft's surprise as fear for a second, but recognized that it was not, once his eyes hardened with determination.

"Should the need arise, no body armor would save you from me. Kevlar, steel, ceramic, Nano-weave, would all be torn and melted away by my wrath." Abram knew this kind of determination. He had been next to it almost every day of his life.

"You remind me of my commander, the one who I still call 'Brother.' However, there is one difference between the two of you." Lovecraft waited for the man to tell him his faults and why his commander was better. It was both nice and annoying to see that this would turn out like so many other conversations before it. Lovecraft felt like his teacher had suddenly risen from the dead just to chastise him.

"My commander has the heart of a bear; noble, yet unruly and filled with fury. You…have the heart of a lion; noble and content with the rule of law. Your fury is measured to only the amount that is fair." For a second, Lovecraft believed that this man was not a Contractor, but a Russian street gypsy that had come here, stowed away on a ship or plane. He had half a mind to laugh in his face, but figured that him being a gypsy was just as farfetched as what he had just told Lovecraft.

"Fair enough," was what Lovecraft decided to say before switching topics, "What's the next step for you, Abram?" The Russian looked up and down the street once more. His suitcases and bags still at his feet.

"I'm supposed to get my Contractor's license tomorrow, and then I suppose I'll be assigned to a team, considering that I'm without one." Lovecraft had already assumed Abram was here in the country alone, which was kind of shocking, considering that when a foreign company sent a team in, they were a 'team,' not an individual. While thinking this, he fished a gold coin out of his pocket and handed it to Abram, who accepted it with a stunned and bewildered look on his face.

Pointing down the street, Lovecraft said, "Two blocks down, there's a bar that's open twenty-four hours. The neon sign reads 'Lady Finger.' Go inside and hand that coin to a woman named, 'Emily'; she'll give you a place to stay." Another thing involving Emily came into Lovecraft's head, "Oh yeah, if you end up making some small talk with her, tell her that she owes me for cleanup. Trust me, she'll know what it means." Abram nodded, even though he had a feeling that it would get him in trouble with the woman. Lovecraft hit him on the arm and started to walk back to the compound.

"Good luck, Contractor," Lovecraft said, before disappearing back into the warm confines of his building.

Chapter 4

Russian Bazaar

Days passed and as February 19th rounded the corner, Lovecraft became increasingly more frustrated with the fact that this 'Master' was a ghost. He had been looking for evidence for a week and had nothing, positively nothing that could lead him anywhere. This, naturally, led to another headache and another thought of buying stock in Tylenol; unfortunately, the stock market had been in free-fall for the last 20 years, which only added to Lovecraft's luck. See, to a common person, Lovecraft would probably have been the luckiest man alive. Hell, there was even a time he got shot in the head and it ricocheted off his helmet and killed another bad guy behind him. Isn't life grand?

Outside of work, however, Lovecraft would always be up shit's creek without arms; forget the paddle. He had almost no social life, and the few people he kept in contact with were almost exclusively men. There were some women, sure, and he was most definitely not a virgin, but it said a lot when the international arms dealer (in some places, terrorist), Menagerie 'Kara' Alexander, was the only woman he could hold a decent conversation with. It also didn't help that she was the only person in his age bracket who was female. Kara was surprisingly young, at 29 years of age. It was like he skipped from graduating high school to be a fulltime grandpa; he even had the irritable attitude of one. It was quite fitting that this period of self-loathing was interrupted by Aaron announcing, "Yo, Kara's here."

Lovecraft took a breath and exhaled it into his hands before nodding. He was not very interested in talking to really anyone right now, but Kara was a friend and he took care of his friends. Quietly getting up from his desk, he went to greet the eccentric French woman, who did not disappoint, when he saw a bright smile that looked like the sun. He questioned why he left his room. Kara, for her part, stopped smiling, and put her arms behind her back which was covered in a red, leather jacket.

"How goes the search?" she asked, hoping for good news.

"I think it would be easier to find a nude strip club in a convent," Lovecraft said, leaning against the wall, as Aaron laughed in his seat.

"I know a few, if you'd like a referral," she said, her smile returning. Lovecraft looked at her if she had just added instead of subtracted. His mind gridlocked with possible responses.

"Why do you know about them?" he eventually asked, noticing a small briefcase on the floor next to Kara's right foot. It was not a good sign.

"A girl has needs," she replied, in a jest that was just a bit too serious.

"You're fuckin' me," Aaron said, believing her just a little too much. Kara looked down at her black cargo pants and checked her belt. Lovecraft rolled his eyes and covered half his face with his left hand before saying, "Why are you here? I could have sworn I told you to stay away so long as Luft is here." Kara apparently had enough of her fun.

"Simple. I'm sure you've heard of the Bazaar?" she asked, with a flick of the hand. Lovecraft grimaced and Aaron rubbed the back of his neck. The Bazaar, as it had come to be known in the few years, was the only technical settlement in the Flood Zone that was designated 'civilized.' Although 'civilized' was just a hopeful term that helped get people to move there, in reality, there were very few people who lived there who weren't traders. The traders sold goods and other junk to Contractors, but more specifically, the Scavengers. These people were tasked with going deeper into the Flood Zone in order to find necessary supplies that were too expensive to just buy. The only problem Aaron and Lovecraft had, was that they were allowed to be armed, which they should, given how bad the area was, and lot of them were paranoid. Especially of other people they didn't know.

"No, we started doing this job last week," Lovecraft said sarcastically. Kara's reaction was a playful smirk. She had gotten used to Lovecraft's sarcasm a long time ago.

"Well, then, I'm sure you know that Lugers and Leggings has an off shoot there called, 'Amaranth'; which is supplied by shipments from L and L. Well, it just so happens that my merc guards got called to another job and can't protect my shipment, so I need some extra help." Kara reached down to her briefcase and set it on the table with a surprisingly loud clunk. She flipped its tabs open and reached inside. Aaron and Lovecraft watched as she withdrew something that looked like packaged crackers. However, when she threw it into Aaron's hands, it felt like she threw him a brick. He threw it between his hands before tearing it open. He dumped what had to be one hundred, brand new, hundred-dollar bills onto the table, half of what they made in a year.

"You don't spare any expense, do you, Kara?" Aaron asked, rolling the packaging up and tossing it into a trash can. Lovecraft shook his head. The payment was eccentric and ridiculous, but when you had as much money as

Kara and only one source of income, her gun stores, you would probably do anything to not lose money.

"No, I don't. Besides, I know how much you guys hate going to the Bazaar, so I thought I'd make it worth your while." She shut the briefcase and held it in front of her legs, "I really don't feel like carrying this heavy thing back to my place, so will you take the job?" Lovecraft's mood had improved since he first stepped out of his room, and when he looked at Aaron, both of them already knew the answer.

The roaring engine of an old Humvee echoed off the steel and metal buildings, shaking windows and turning certain holograms fuzzy for but a moment. Aaron was sitting in his rightful place, the driver's seat, while Lovecraft sat next to him, and Kara sat behind both of them. The town car they had used the previous week was retrieved by David and his band of Israeli Contractors. All in all said, the town car was more armored than the Humvee, but it was due to this heavy armor that it lacked the two attributes that kept the military artifact around: space and armament. It could hold around five people, plus a few more in its cramped spaces, and featured a 50-caliber machine gun on its roof.

The town car only sat two people and featured nothing in the way of armament. It was quite literally built to keep whoever was inside, safe. Lovecraft liked to attribute it more to a titanium coffin, since both were bulletproof. He pulled his MK. 18 assault rifle from between his legs and pulled its bolt back to see if he had remembered to charge it. After he determined that he was ready to go, Lovecraft wiped the sweat from his brow and popped the ear cups open on his headset; who knew that the first 80-degree day would come in late February? He could feel the sweat beneath the section of shirt where his plate carrier sat, and grimaced once more when he felt the sweat beneath his kneepads.

"Would you like an ACOG for that?" Kara asked, gesturing toward Lovecraft's rifle. An ACOG was 3.5 to four times optic made by Trijicon, and had been the U.S. Military's go-to-optic for the last 45, or so, years.

"I'm selling them for half off right now. Only six hundred," Kara added, trying to seem like that was a good deal. Lovecraft shook his head and rolled his eyes at the woman.

"Don't I spend enough money at your store? Also, why are you here?" Lovecraft asked. They had just barely left for the Bazaar when Kara had popped up from the back seat and scared the shit out of them; almost got her head blown off too. There was a new hole in the roof as evidence of this, which Lovecraft took partial responsibility for, since he had neglected a very important rule with Kara: don't lose sight of Kara. This rule was a part of a bigger rule that simply stated: Don't let Kara wander around. The rule was spawned from the many times Aaron and Lovecraft found her where she should not be. Some of these places were: the men's restroom, Pamela's guest bedroom, the garage, the sewer, hell, one time, they found her 'exploring' the back of Lovecraft's closet. Needless to say, he almost shot her when she popped her head out from between the shirts the next morning. Kara was a handful and if she were an animal, she'd definitely be a special needs animal, simply for how close you had to watch her.

"Hey, I have to get back to the store some time. Plus, I want to make sure that you don't fuck up. I'm gonna laugh at you if you do," Kara replied, twirling her braid around.

"You do know that if we fuck up, we're probably going to die, right?" Aaron asked, turning down a street that looked like it was sweating. The holograms displayed the current temperature and dew point; the latter was above 70.

"Yep, so don't make me laugh at you. How the hell are you not sweating? You're wearing all black."

"I am sweating. My nipples have never been more wet." Kara's face turned to stone as she looked toward Aaron's J.P.C. Her mind had come to a dead stop and only the image that Aaron put into her mind was there. Aaron smirked underneath his balaclava; he knew that would shut her up.

The rest of the ride was rather uneventful. As they traveled north, the humidity seemed to dissipate a little, but the dry heat was still there. It baked the cement, cooked the buildings, and made the holograms look like they were fuzzy T.V. screens. They passed a block where they saw a team of Contractors sitting outside of a bar; a glass of water in one hand and a beer in the other. They had stripped off most of their gear and were left with only their basic essentials. After all, they were probably hired to guard the place. A hoard of medical drones flew down the streets and alleys, looking for anybody stupid enough to not drink water in this mess.

"Alert, a heat advisory is in effect. Please take proper action to ensure you are hydrated. Thank you for your cooperation," a loudspeaker announced, its origins unknown, other than it was somewhere high. Lovecraft couldn't help but wonder just how many snipers had their eyes on this exact street.

At any one time, there were around 50 to 100 snipers on active duty in Chicago; the ones off duty numbered far above that. It was kind of funny to think about, but where Hollywood had the paparazzi, whose camera lenses captured images of America's biggest pussies, Chicago had sniper teams, whose big guns would make Hollywood shit it's pants. It was hilarious. The rhythmic chopping of helicopter blades were suddenly heard overhead and were soon followed by a strange helicopter that looked like a piece of carved glass: jagged yet symmetrical. Its colors were that of a dark purple, with a large 'S+' painted on its side. A loudspeaker screamed to life from its underbelly, *"In 2044, America became the laughingstock of the free world. NATO dissolved and we were left to defend ourselves. Yet, when the rest of the world abandoned us, we were the last ones standing. Now, it is our job to fix this sad and weary world. Join Switchboard! Help us fight for the glory of the human race, and for America's dignity! Switchboard Robotics, putting the 'in' back in 'innovation.'"*

Lovecraft rolled his eyes at this propaganda. It was all nonsense, yet if Switchboard Robotics had anything going for them, it was that half of all artificial life in the United States (robots, A.I., and drones) were manufactured by them. They had turned up shortly after 2044 and used this same propaganda to gather workers, and in just a few years, America had itself a new billion-dollar company. Honestly, the propaganda would have been funny, if it wasn't so damn effective.

"You think they'll ever achieve that goal?" Aaron asked, turning away from the street.

"Let's hope not. If they do, then that's all we'll ever hear about. If they don't, then that's their problem. Switchboard has never helped us or the people we fight to protect; all they do, all day, is spout their idealistic bullshit, like the Democrats did in the early 2000s," Lovecraft said, before Kara leaned in through the seats again.

"If you want an example of what it would be like, I can refer you Berlin, in the year 1939. Strangely enough, France and that version of Germany aren't that different anymore." She sat back in her seat and pulled a pack of cigarettes from her pocket. It was a pack of Marlboros, her favorites, but everybody's least favorite. Pulling the newly lit cigarette from her lips, she said, "The world's fucked. It's been fucked worse than some back-alley whore and now, the only people standing in the way of the Totalitarians are the Contractors." Lovecraft pursed his lips and wanted to tell Kara that she was wrong, that there were others who would stand up and fight. He would be wrong though. The military was decrepit and underfunded, politicians were utterly useless, which was nothing new, and most of the charities didn't have the manpower to help people, as well as protect themselves. This was where the Contractors came in; they could do everything typical guards could do and more. They were versatile, but expensive.

They stopped by Lugers and Leggings so Kara could grab some of her stuff, and pulled around the building where there were two, seven-ton trucks sitting – one after the other. The two Contractors pulled in front of the lead truck and once the Humvee was turned off, they got out and found Sam standing outside.

"Seven tons?" Lovecraft asked, slinging his assault rifle, "Wouldn't a trailer be more discreet?"

Sam laughed, "Trailers are more expensive, plus, it's not *that* discreet when we have a military vehicle leading the way." Sam was dressed in his typical slacks and blazer with a white, buttoned-up shirt. He kind of looked like a bouncer at a strip club that also had friends in the Secret Service.

"Yeah, I guess. Then again, we are going to the Bazaar, so it'll fit right in." Lovecraft heard a metal door open and close, "I can hear the sounds of royalty already." The three men turned toward the noise and saw Kara walking toward them; high heels on her feet, cargo pants decorating her legs, and her coat over that. There was a chaffed, leather strap across her breasts that lead to the abused wood and pristine gold of her Kalashnikov; it sparkled like glitter.

"Are we ready?" she asked, reaching into her pocket to pull her sunglasses free. Sam looked at Aaron and he looked at Lovecraft, who just rolled his eyes at Kara.

"Yes, we are. Luckily, I know that coat is made out of Nano Weave and not actual wool. Although, if you pass out due to heatstroke, I'm not helping you." Kara reached out her hand and cupped Lovecraft's cheek, "It's always nice to know that you care about me." He rolled his eyes as he pushed her hand away; it smelled of old wood (probably from her rifle) and, strangely enough, mint. He wiped his cheek with his gloved hand before saying, "Okay! Everyone to your trucks, we're leading the way!" He put his own sunglasses on and shared a fist bump with Aaron before climbing atop the Humvee. He jumped in the hole and rested his right arm on the 50-cal. He turned around and gave a thumbs up to Kara and Sam, who replied in return. The truck behind them was being driven by a few more of Kara's men and they were waiting for her and Sam to start driving. Lovecraft hit the top of the Humvee twice; that was the cue for Aaron to start driving. They pulled out of the lot and before long, they were on one of the many highways that would lead to the Flood Zone.

The world around them seemed to move at the speed of light, as it shrunk and the cars around them began to disappear. Sweeper Drones began to appear, with their primary function being the elimination of contraband coming out of the Flood Zone. Their little red eyes were scanning vehicles leaving the area. In doing this, they had full x-ray vision, allowing them to see just who was inside and whether or not their paperwork cleared. A strange, hyperactive buzzing noise could soon be heard and when Lovecraft turned to his left, he saw three, Police Assault Drones, racing toward the Flood Zone. They were followed by a large V.T.O.L. transport that also belonged to the police.

After the V.T.O.L. disappeared from view, they passed a large, pink hologram that took shape of a woman dressed in equally pink underwear. It was equipped with a loudspeaker that said, *"Mary's Mind. We know what the ladies like."* They passed another one that was of a woman with big eyelashes, purple lipstick, and had some type of electric extensions in her hair, *"Kenzie's Kosmetics, for when crazy needs to be beautiful."* Lovecraft watched all these pass away as the smaller, submerged skyscrapers of the Flood Zone appeared. His gaze shifted across the horizon, until it landed back on the road where he saw the checkpoint coming up. He pushed a hand inside the admin pouch on his carrier and fished out his Contractor's license. Aaron had his held in his right hand, while his left kept the vehicle on track, his eyes dancing across the white highways.

Lovecraft looked behind them and saw that Kara already had her paperwork plastered to the window with her hand; the other sending another thumbs up to Lovecraft. He returned the gesture and soon enough, they were on the other side of the checkpoint.

They were surrounded with boarded up, water-damaged buildings that could only exist to rot away. The air, although being declared safe, smelled of mold and mildew. When Aaron and Lovecraft first arrived in the Flood Zone all of two years ago, seems like an eternity now, it took them a full two days to get used to the putrid stench.

Kara had to go through the same treatment, since Lugers and Leggings sat almost a mile away from the Flood Zone. Just like Lovecraft and Aaron, she could remember the burning in her lungs, the water in her eyes, and the snot in her throat. Hell, she could have sworn her urine smelled of the rot as she got up from the toilet seat. The air was safe, sure, but even mustard gas leaves evidence of its existence.

"Ma'am," Sam said, pulling Kara from her thoughts. She turned toward him with an eyebrow cocked.

"What's Lovecraft's first name?" he then asked. Kara felt the bubbling sensation of laughter in her loins and before she knew it, an amused smile formed on her face. Lovecraft was a very interesting, and popular, topic for people to ask Kara about; although there were only a handful of people that knew she and Lovecraft were connected. It was like she was the *Big Bad Wolf* and Lovecraft was an invisible spectator holding her leash.

"The question you should be asking, Sammy, is, 'What is Lovecraft's real name?'" Sam looked at her for a moment, before turning his eyes back to the road.

"That's not his real name?" Kara burst into laughter at this question. She really couldn't understand why anybody would think his real name was 'Lovecraft.' If that were the case, then he would have no first name.

"Of course not. Although, I have a feeling you'd have an easier time finding the lost ark than you would his real name." Kara found this topic fascinating. It was her favorite pastime besides guns and anything that involved peanut butter.

"So you don't know his real name?" Two medical drones flew out from underneath the highway, with red and blue lights flashing.

"Nope," her French accent coming out strong, "I've asked him countless times, but he always says it's his real name." Her right hand suddenly shot up and its black-tipped fingers curled into a fist, "And that's why I will not rest until I figure out just who Lovecraft really is!" Sam just looked at her from the corner of his eye and made a mental note to never ask her again; he kind of wished he never asked in the first place.

After that, it did not take them long to make it to the Bazaar, and quite an impression it made, time after time. All around them, the destroyed houses had been torn down and replaced with small shanties made out of metal and plywood. It was not to be said that they all were shanties, but that's what the majority of the housing was. The stores, however, were a different situation entirely. They were all set up in once-lavish buildings that had been restored to some semblance of livability. Amaranth, Kara's secondary shop in the Bazaar, was one such place. It lived in the bones of an old Texas Roadhouse, a restaurant chain that went out of business in 2044.

The people around them watched the convoy drive through Main Street; they parted like a Biblical sea. Lovecraft looked around and saw the tanned faces with bloodshot eyes. Their clothes were tattered, and some were stained with paint or other substances that were a testament to their hard lives. Among them stood their fair share of Contractors: simple wandering bands that patrolled the Flood Zone and used this as a safe haven. Abram was one of these Contractors and while Lovecraft failed to see him, the Russian noticed him immediately. He was filled with the same excitement that any person is when they see someone familiar, and Abram didn't have that many familiar people around him. Yet, he let the convoy pass and focused on his soup for the time being. If he should see Lovecraft again, he would, without a doubt, greet him.

Aaron slowly came to a stop in front of Amaranth, and the trucks pulled in behind him; a woman with her hair dyed purple stood in front of the shop. She wore a black dress that was cut well below her breasts and the left side of the skirt was cut all the way to her waist. It only had one sleeve that was opposite the cut in the skirt. Her exposed arm was covered in a tattoo sleeve that appeared to have her skin torn away; there was machinery underneath. This design went all the way to her fingers which were coated in red fingernail polish.

Almost as soon as the trucks stopped, Kara jumped out of her seat and ran toward the woman; the ground she ran on was covered in gravel and broken asphalt, needless to say, her skill in heels was remarkable. She threw herself at the shocked woman and embraced her, yelling, "Bevs!" Lovecraft jumped from the top of the Humvee, as Aaron turned the engine off and got out. Both men put their rifles on their backs.

Beverly Simpson was her name and she was the manager of Amaranth. She was Kara's only other friend outside of Aaron and Lovecraft, which wasn't that hard to tell, since they both had an affinity for tattoos, unique hair colors, and firearms. However, Beverly couldn't help but be flustered when Kara showed up out of the blue; she was, after all, her boss, and controlled her paycheck. It was quite an interesting turn of events when a meeting in a bar turns into a business agreement, and suddenly, you wake up, over a million-dollars richer. Beverly still had trouble keeping up sometimes, but at least she wasn't blowing all her money on drugs anymore.

"Kara, you crazy bitch, what are you doing here, and why are you wearing heels?!" she asked, finally returning the embrace.

Kara laughed at her friend, "Hey, we have a business image to keep up." She let go and put her hands on her hips, "Plus, I wanted to see how things were going before we gave you the new stuff." Lovecraft and Aaron walked up to the woman and listened to them for a bit, as they talked about the activity inside Amaranth.

It was fairly popular with the locals, and for good reason. The Bazaar was more or less cut off from the rest of the world, except for the one road they worked tirelessly to protect. Thus, other places had to ship their weapons to the Bazaar through various middlemen and often times lost money, just trying to get them there. It was for this reason that gun prices were 15 times the national average, but Amaranth's were not. Two years ago, Kara was Menagerie Alexandre, and still an international arms dealer. However, now that Lovecraft held her in one place, she was like the store houses of Gilgamesh to anyone who needed a gun. The woman had stockpiled so many weapons over her career that she could almost give them away and that was why Amaranth was able to sell at such a low price. She was bleeding firearms into the Cyber Market and kept her own prices low by buying the existing stock of failed competitors; Chicago was her wet dream and she was going to milk it for as long as she could. The *Great Devourer* was an appropriate nickname for her style of business and it was just something that the weakened American dealers could not compete with, because, while the world collapsed around them in 2044, Kara was selling old Communist tanks in Sierra Leone and supplying the Israelis with cutting edge, Chinese radar. Most manufacturers were broke by the end of the year, but she was a billionaire in nine months.

"Wow, you two are a sight for sore eyes," Beverly said, finally noticing Lovecraft and Aaron. Both of them chuckled at the younger woman.

"Yeah, we don't get out too often," Aaron replied in jest. Beverly smirked at him and shook her head.

"Of course you don't." The sarcasm was almost dripping from her lips and Lovecraft had to smile at this. They had only met Beverly a handful of times and all of those were on business. This was generally a good idea, since the Bazaar wasn't a place for people to stay after hours. It was a classic example of life giving something, but also taking it away.

"So how are things, Bevs?" Lovecraft asked. Beverly sighed at his question and he already knew it was going to be bad, but what he didn't expect was for her blue eyes to tear up a bit. However, she was a woman who did not like to show such weakness easily, or rather, she couldn't, thanks to the business she was in. She ran a hand through her hair and tried to pass off, wiping her eyes as allergies.

"Boy, could they be better, but we'll talk about that in due time. Right now, I have to take inventory. There's some food inside if you're hungry," she said, excusing herself. Kara and she walked to the very last truck and would work their way up from there. Lovecraft looked to Aaron, who only offered him a shrug, before they went inside and made themselves two sandwiches each. It was about an hour later when Kara and Beverly joined them in the small break room; their bodies flying to the remaining food without hesitation. Kara had set her Kalashnikov next to the stained, oak door and helped Beverly set the table. The latter's hands were shaking. Lovecraft sipped on a cup of water as he watched the two women eat; he had been drinking coffee all morning and needed to flush his system.

Beverly took ginger bites of her sandwich and appeared to have a hard time swallowing; she was apparently nervous. Lovecraft noticed this, but his past experience dictated that he make her feel more comfortable than she currently was.

"Are you sick, Bevs?" Lovecraft asked, before taking another drink. She appeared to be lost in thought, since she looked up and acted like Lovecraft was a ghost. A set of coffee-stained teeth appeared from her mouth and looked a little goofy, since she was trying to conceal some of her missing molars. It was a smile that Lovecraft could see through easily, thanks to how many times he had seen one just like it; a sickening memory of his own mother filled his mind like a migraine.

"I'm fine, Lovecraft. Just a little stressed is all," the 36-year-old woman said, rubbing her neck. He nodded his head at her admission and reclined back in his chair; his right arm was placed on the back of the chair.

"So how is the good old Bazaar? The same tunnel shit being washed up around here?" Aaron asked, resting his hand on his helmet and balaclava which he had placed on the table earlier.

Beverly nodded, "Same shit, different day."

The tunnels they were referring to were old metro tunnels that had been built a little over ten years ago. Most were blocked off by large metal gates on the escalators and large hermetic doors on the actual lines. However, some were partially flooded and only had the rusted gates to keep people out. Needless to say, they weren't effective and people, particularly of the criminal variety, liked to squat down there.

"We started sending Scavers further into the Flood Zone last week, and my…" Beverly immediately stopped talking; her eyes wide and mouth still open. This is what Lovecraft had been waiting for; thus, he immediately stopped reclining in his chair. He folded his gloved hands on the table and asked, "Bevs, why are you so upset?"

Suddenly, Beverly felt as if the awkward spotlight on her intensified and when she looked around, she saw that everyone was now looking at her. She looked back and forth before she put her head into her hands and stared at the table for a moment.

"My boyfriend was out with the Scavers when we suddenly lost contact with them. That was…" her voice caught for a second, and Kara started rubbing her back, "That was three days ago, and we still haven't heard anything." It was with this that Beverly broke down and Kara had to hold onto her as she sobbed. Lovecraft looked at Aaron in bewilderment, but all he offered was a shrug. She started to murmur into Kara's coat and as she came up for breath, she said something that made the whole table freeze, "…I'm pregnant and scared." Kara's green eyes fluttered as she became like steel; her back as straight as a power pole. Aaron had moved his drink to his lips, but set it back down once his ears had heard the news. Lovecraft had twitched at first, but then relaxed and let his hand relax across his mouth.

Kara was the first to speak, although it started as a nervous laugh, "I'm sorry, could you repeat that?" Beverly pulled her face away and realized what she had let slip out; she didn't know what to say…but Kara did.

"Oh. My. God. You're pregnant!" Kara almost yelled, loud enough for building to shake.

"Kara, not so loud," Aaron chided.

"Okay, sure, but she's pregnant. Like, she has a human growing inside of her!" In all his years, Lovecraft had never met someone who could switch between being as preppy as a cheerleader, to something that could earn her the nickname, *'Le Loup Vert'* or 'The Green Wolf.' It was quite interesting, as well as entertaining.

"Kara, please. You're embarrassing me," Beverly protested, with a huge blush on her face. It was with this that Kara tore off into a tirade of reasons why Beverly shouldn't be embarrassed, but happy that she has accomplished, in her opinion, one of the greatest things a woman could do. Lovecraft watched with same amount of annoyance he felt toward the hologram outside his window. He had to get back in control whether Beverly was pregnant or not.

He cleared his throat to garner both women's attention, "So your boyfriend goes missing. Where did he go?"

"Weiss Memorial Hospital, it's next to the old waterfront." Lovecraft looked at her like she was crazy. Everything along the old waterfront was flooded to the point that they required a boat to reach them. Not to mention that the water was filled with raw sewage which made it toxic. The only way somebody could live there now was if they shored it up and pumped the remaining water out, although they'd have to do it by hand, since Bazaar was the only place in the Flood Zone that had electricity. Sure, there were some places that still had it, but those were multistory buildings that were run off of generators that had been untouched.

"Did they take a boat there?" he then asked after considering this. However, she would shock him when her head started to shake.

"The water, it's receded in that place. Nobody knows why, but one of our advanced scouts noticed it and when Danny's team arrived, they could walk through, on *dry* land." When Aaron heard this, he looked to Lovecraft in alarm. If the water was truly receding, then it meant the Flood Zone might not be its namesake anymore. Lovecraft, however, wasn't so sure this was the truth; Scavers had a tendency to stretch facts and tell lies all in the name of producing hope and resentment for those that lived in the hospitable part of the city.

"What about power? Did they find any buildings with electricity over there?" Lovecraft asked. Now it was time for Beverly to look at him like he was crazy.

"Lovecraft don't mistake my pain for vanity. There is no power near the waterfront; just ghosts. There is a reason the signs label the place a 'Dead Zone,' you know?" Lovecraft apologized for apparent sarcasm and stood up from the table. He looked to Kara and reached for a pouch on his lower back and pulled a two-wave radio from there. He handed it to Kara, who looked at him in bewilderment.

"We'll keep in contact as much as we can. However, if you don't hear from us for 30 minutes, come running," he instructed, pulling his assault rifle from his back.

"What are you doing?" Beverly asked, suddenly lost as to what was going on.

Aaron joined Lovecraft as he turned back to the door, "I have a great many questions for your Scaver, and it appears that the only way to attain answers for my many questions is to go and find him. We'll see you soon." Beverly clutched the strap of her dress and just stared at the two men. She would never admit it, but the fact that they stunned her, shook her to the core and made her a little sick. That could have also been the pregnancy though.

"Ruler, right?" Kara asked, watching as they were about to leave. Lovecraft stepped out of Aaron's way and allowed him to leave.

"That's right, Lycan." Kara's mouth twisted into a sly smirk that showed her K9s. Lovecraft turned back to the door, opened it, and climbed inside of the Humvee. His helmet was thrown onto his head almost immediately after sitting down. Aaron had already gotten the Humvee started, and pulled out once he saw that Lovecraft was in place.

"Tell me, L.C., do you really think the water is receding?" Aaron asked, pulling up to a gate that would lead them north. It was quickly opened, and they were able to proceed further into the Flood Zone.

Lovecraft shook his head, "I think it's just the ramblings of a crazed Scaver who isn't ready to be a dad."

"But what if it isn't? If the water were to really recede, then we would be able exert a lot more force on the Flood Zone, maybe even pacify it." This last phrase caught Lovecraft's attention and tickled the suspicious part of his brain. In a lot of ways, Aaron was like him, but he did not readily go for the hopeful outcome. At points, Aaron was even more of a realist than Lovecraft, which made people brand him as a pessimist. However, he tried to temper this by being more jovial than Lovecraft could ever be. This meant only one thing: something was wrong.

"What's up? It's not like you to think that a possibility," Aaron shrugged his shoulders.

"It's nothing, I just miss my family. Last week was Mollie's birthday, and I missed it…again." Mollie was Aaron's middle child and was the only one of the three kids that didn't have blonde hair. She was the one who looked most like her dad.

Lovecraft hated having these conversations, because it always felt like Aaron was forcing himself to do this, "Don't worry, come March, we'll have a week off and a chance to go home. Everybody needs time off." Aaron nodded in affirmation before swerving past a fallen billboard. What was on the other side stunned Aaron and Lovecraft.

It was dry. The street, the buildings, the sidewalks, the poles; everything was dry. There were still watermarks on them, but the Humvee was able to proceed all the way to the hospital.

Lovecraft shook himself free of his paralysis and lifted his hand to his ear, "Lycan, this is Ruler, radio check. Over."

"Loud and clear, Ruler," Kara's voice came with just a hint of static, "That was fast, you must have gotten lucky in finding a bridge."

Lovecraft shook his head because he still couldn't believe what he was seeing, "Nope. No bridge and no fucking water either. Damn, place is so dry that I'm getting thirsty just looking at it."

Back at Amaranth, Kara thought the line had messed up somewhere, but she knew that was false, "You're kidding."

"If I were, I'd tell you about it when we got back. We're coming up on the hospital. I'll keep you updated, Ruler out." Lovecraft took his hand away from his head and got out of the Humvee; his right hand clasped firmly around the pistol grip of his MK.18. Aaron did much the same, only he held his battle rifle in both hands, as they walked to the first set of sliding doors.

There was nothing off about them. The glass had been broken a long time ago, and now allowed one to just walk right in. The second set was much the same, only this set was stuck half open; the glass coated the floor like dew on a spring morning. It crunched under the boots of both men; its jagged edges unable to penetrate the heavy rubber soles. The darkness enveloped them to the point that it was like a black wall that reached clear to the ceiling. Even when they put their night vision on, where green lasers told of where their guns were pointing, it was still so dark that the only thing the goggles did was paint the outlines of objects in green. Hospital beds lined the hallways directly behind the reception area and old I.V. bags littered the water-damaged tile. It smelled of mold, mildew, medicine, and shit, all at the same time.

"Jesus," Aaron muttered, as he moved down the hallway, gun pointed forward, "Hard to believe it's February and not October; this place is giving me the creeps." The whole place had a tip of eerie ambiance that made the ears ring. It was like the whole place was filled with white noise and the only other sound to relieve its madness was the crunching of glass. However, even that ran out and it was replaced with bits of tile, wood, plaster and plastic; all strange and differing echoes that made the ambience only simmer in the back of one's mind. Then, as if it were an Old Testament prophet, their boots made a wet, sticky slap on the particle board. Aaron looked at Lovecraft with his red, night-vision lenses and Lovecraft looked at him with his green. Both pushed their goggles up and turned on their flashlights; the deep color of red filled the floor in front of them. There was a long line that appeared to be evidence of something being dragged around the corner.

"Shit," Lovecraft muttered in a low whisper. He reached up to his ear again and started to speak, "Lycan, we got a lot of blood here. Probable wounded, how copy?" he waited for Kara to respond, while Aaron crouched down and watched the corner. He waited, and waited. He even shook his head and thought that his nerves were altering his perception of time. However, this was proved false when Aaron looked back at him, and cocked an eyebrow that was just barely visible in his flashlight.

"Lycan, this is Ruler Zero One, how do you copy, over?" Lovecraft began to wait again, only he would cut it short when all he heard was the open line's static.

"It was working before we entered," Aaron said, standing up.

"I know, which is worrisome." Lovecraft checked his watch and found that it had only been 17 minutes and he knew that Kara would think something was wrong once 30 had passed.

"Put your night vision back on," Lovecraft ordered, turning out his light, "Somebody got attacked in here. It best to keep the element of surprise in our favor." Aaron turned his own light off and returned his night vision to his eyes. Lovecraft nodded to him before both of them started to follow the blood; Aaron in the front, Lovecraft in the back. They came to a flight of stairs that had flies buzzing around it. They began their descent.

Outside, heavy boots thudded across the abused asphalt, as Abram brushed his hand over the hood of Lovecraft's Humvee. It was still warm. His eyes of ice traced the hood and went up to the hospital. He had volunteered to go with the Scavers, he wanted to provide extra firepower should they require it, but his team leader wouldn't allow it. "Scavers aren't worth it," he told him, "Hell, none of these people ain't worth two bullets, much less your hundred-round box. The only one in this shitty place worth anything is that fine ass arms dealer with the purple hair...what I wouldn't do to have her oil my rifle." Abram shook his head clear and slammed his fist into the steel hood. His white teeth shone from beneath his beard. He had snuck away. That's right. He had snuck away on the count that he had to take a piss, but it would probably be the longest piss he had ever taken.

Abram took his hand off the hood of the Humvee and used his strong arms to lift his P.K.M. light-machine gun; its powerful 7.62x54R cartridges held in a green, metal box beneath it. His legs carried his massive form up the stairs and through the same doors that Aaron and Lovecraft had entered already. Abram held his weapon at the hip and did this in order to not fatigue himself too early; holding it to one's shoulder was incredibly cumbersome and unwieldy. Doing so would cause a lack of dexterity and would put great strain on one's arms, thus limiting accuracy and exchanging it for pain. He reached up to his helmet and flipped on a small flashlight that was mounted over where his ear was. He proceeded further in.

Lovecraft and Aaron followed the blood down to the basement where the darkness was like a fine fog. If it weren't so ludicrous, Aaron would have tried to cut it with a knife. The smells down there were even more powerful than upstairs; yet, there was something missing. It was something that needed to be there to make the story they were told believable.

"Okay..." Aaron began checking a nearby corner, "if these guys were Scavers, who are normally armed, why do I not smell gunpowder?"

Lovecraft also noticed this missing detail and even went so far as to look for shell casings on the floor; he found nothing, "I thought I was losing my fucking mind. I'm glad you noticed that too." The two of them jumped as something moved in the darkness and knocked a set of rusted tools over. They pointed their guns at it and from what they saw in their night vision, they could tell that it was just a rat. However, what captured their attention wasn't the small rodent, but the flies buzzing around the bloody corpse at the end of the room.

The two men pushed the distance to the body and put their night vision up. Lovecraft pulled out a smaller flashlight from his belt and shined it on the body. What he got, in return, was the lovely image of a badly decomposed body whose face had been smashed to the point that its teeth were caved in; some had even flown onto the floor.

"Jesus," Lovecraft muttered, moving the beam of light over to the body's right hand, where he found that it was still wrapped tightly around the pistol grip of an AR-15.

"Is it our guy?" Aaron asked, using the flashlight on his gun to look around. Lovecraft started prying the man's fingers open to inspect the rifle.

"I have no clue. I was hoping that either he would be alive or Kara would be able to send us a picture of him, but since something is jamming our comms, that *isn't* going to happen," Lovecraft said, letting his sling catch his rifle, as he played with the other one. He pulled the bolt back and was surprised when a live round was ejected onto the floor. He then ejected the magazine and, from his own experiences, found it weighed enough to be full.

"This guy never even fired a shot," Lovecraft commented, before looking at Aaron.

"Maybe he ran off. Cowards typically have more ammo on them than the brave guys do." Lovecraft looked down at the body and furrowed his brow. It made sense, but that theory presented its own possibilities.

"Sure, but that leaves another question: What was he running from?" Aaron shrugged his shoulders as his boss threw the magazine down on the chest of the body. However, the room was suddenly filled with blue light, as the body made a deep vibrating sound.

Flying, holographic fish swam through the walls, blue trees had taken the place of flooded boilers, and strange, holographic anomalies filled the empty space. Lovecraft dropped the dead guy's gun and picked up his own, as Aaron fell in behind him; holographic butterflies left behind with every step. Lovecraft's head twitched as his headset suddenly crackled to life; *Für Elise* started to play.

"What do you hear?" Aaron asked, eyes not breaking away from the sight in front of him.

"*Für Elise*, you?"

"A song that was played at my wedding, Millie must be thinking about me." Lovecraft looked around before disconnecting his headset. He let out a sigh when the music stopped. The last thing he did before telling Aaron to do the same was to pop the ear cups of his headset out; they were connected to the rails on the side of his helmet so they stayed in place.

"Any ideas?" Lovecraft asked.

"Holo Mine?"

"I thought the same thing." Lovecraft pointed his gun at the body and sent three rounds into its torso. There was a spark and some smoke before the images faded away.

The Holo Mine was a high-tech landmine that was meant more for diversion and disorientation than it was to just destroy. The one Aaron and Lovecraft had just stumbled upon was either broken or defective, since a working one could alter the environment seamlessly, and took specialized equipment to detect. Lovecraft and Aaron's headsets were one such piece of equipment, and they had a 90-percent accuracy rating.

"What a weird song choice. To think that mine would play a song from my wedding right after I told you that I miss home."

Lovecraft looked at Aaron and shook his head, "I'm not the most superstitious Contractor out there, but that is weird. Fuck, even the fact it played *Für Elise* is weird, considering it was in a horror novel I read recently." The way the headsets worked was when the Holo Mine detonated, it would expel electromagnetic particles that would then be rearranged to copy lighting and images. The headsets would pick up on these and interpret their signals as a randomized song. Essentially, music was an alarm.

"I think this place just got a whole lot creepier," Aaron muttered, looking around, "What do we do? Pull out, wait for backup, or do we press on and see if anybody is alive down here?" Lovecraft looked around at the black abyss around him and gave the blued stairs only one glance. He made decisions rather quickly.

"We're going further in. We're already here and even if we do have more people, it'll just be us who can detect the mines." Lovecraft put his flashlight away and used the one on the front of his rifle; night vision was pointless now that he had fired his weapon, plus the Holo Mine had an internet uplink that notified its owner upon activation. Aaron nodded to Lovecraft and they continued into the darkness.

Meanwhile, Kara clicked her fingers on the hardwood table at Amaranth and anxiously waited for Lovecraft, or Aaron, to contact her. She had three minutes left before she should begin to worry, but they always checked in a lot sooner than that. Kara tried to distract herself by playing with her phone, reading the news, and even balancing a pencil between her nose and lips; this one made Beverly look at her like she was crazy. Her purple haired counterpart had taken to reading Dmitry Glukhovsky's *Futu.re*; reading was her choice of distraction and even went so far as to declare that, "Reading is better than sex," – it clearly was not.

Kara took notice of her thoughts and wondered if it was too soon to start asking about names. She played with the idea like putty before making her decision, "Have you thought about names yet?" Beverly turned to her friend and looked at her over her bifocals; her hands closing the book around its marker.

"Umm, well, we, er, *I* don't know the gender yet, but I was thinking of naming a boy, Daniel, after his father," Beverly said, her voice cracking like a virgin.

Kara's nose crinkled into a look of confusion, "What do you mean by, *'I'*?"

Beverly bit her lip at the question and rested her hand on her collar, "I never said I had the chance to tell James I was pregnant."

Abram's head ducked underneath the lip of the basement's ceiling; the building around him clearly not built for someone of his great stature. He had been wandering around the first floor, trying to find any sign of where Lovecraft or Aaron might have gone, but they were extremely good at covering their tracks. However, the thing that gave it away was a bloody boot print in the direction of the stairs; the amount of blood was cause for concern, but it would have to wait, considering Abram was all by himself. His boots crunched along the concrete floor and kicked up dust and iron oxide. His flashlight fell upon the same body Aaron and Lovecraft had found a few minutes ago; the fresh holes and smell of gunpowder making Abram wonder why they had shot the body. He pointed his machine gun in front of him and took a moment longer to inspect the body before pushing forward. However, he did not notice that Aaron had draped a sheet over another Holo Mine in order to nullify its proximity sensors. This only worked to an extent though.

The mine triggered the way it was supposed to this time, and copied the area around him to the exact atom. There was no sound, no light, no smell; it just worked as silently as air; however, even air could be found.

Abram stopped when the flashlight-mounted helmet started to flicker, like it was dying. Yet, like Lovecraft's and Aaron's headsets, this was a warning and not an anomaly. Russia had fallen behind in the technological arms race, even further than the United States. To Abram, America looked like Heaven compared to his country that was still stuck in the early 21st century; however, Russia had survived due to its brutal winters and its ability to kick the crutches out from under their opponents. Thus, they created a new class of soldier, a new scourge to the western world, the *Virusnyy* or Virus. They had one job in the Russian military: destroy technology. After all, soldiers could not keep warm if their heaters would not work.

Abram checked his surroundings with the blinking light and when he saw that it was clear, he set his weapon on the floor and reached into his belt. He pulled a strange, circular ball from it and pressed a large, red button on the top of it. When it turned blue, he tossed it onto the floor and put a hand in front of his face. It rolled for a bit before it exploded into a blue mess of tangled electricity; an electromagnetic pulse ripping through the room and ripping the Holo Mine's facade to pieces. Abram turned around to see the smoldering mine covered by a burnt piece of fabric. He picked up his gun once again and continued to traverse the abyss.

Two sets of circular light danced over the concrete walls that had once been painted a light blue. Aaron and Lovecraft were the one responsible for the light and were now approaching a large glass cubicle; their boots stained with blood.

"What the fuck is this supposed to be?" Aaron asked, pointing toward the glass with his gun.

Lovecraft looked at the cubicle and saw that there were two small, porcelain tables inside. There was a white door on the right side, which was lined with thick, black rubber, and a large drain in the floor underneath of it. Bags of medication still hung in the rooms, but it, thankfully, looked deserted.

"I think it's a quarantine room." He moved closer to the box and found a metal sign on the floor, it confirmed his theory, "It looks like they brought contagious people here and either helped them or put them out of their misery. It's kind of spooky to think about how this was where the zombie apocalypse was supposed to start."

Aaron rolled his eyes at Lovecraft's joke, "I think you watch too many movies when we get home. There's no way a—"

Aaron stopped, as they heard glass suddenly shatter, and both men jerked their rifles up to meet whatever had done it. They waited, counting to three, before they both pushed toward the sound. Their lights found a pool of blood, one of many, only this one did not accompany a body, only bloody streaks belonged to this one. A maintenance cart had been rolled into the glass, a blood stain on it as well. Aaron and Lovecraft followed the streaks with their flashlights, and it led them to a pair of white doors. It disappeared underneath and it became apparent that something had just dragged a body deeper inside. Lovecraft flexed his shoulders uncomfortably and Aaron cracked his neck, before they each put a hand on one of the doors. In half a breath, they pushed the doors open, moved inside, and found themselves in another quarantine area. However, while the other one was deserted, this one presented the first signs of confrontation. The walls were littered with impact holes, the air was so thick with gunpowder that it was almost suffocating, and the floor was littered with blood and the sparking husks of robots.

The two men stepped into the room carefully, with Lovecraft noticing that these were the same series of robots that had shot at them previously.

Aaron knelt down next to one, "Weird, same series as the sniper on the highway. Think there's any connection there?"

"Probably. Get their serial numbers, we'll find out just who they belong to."

Lovecraft continued following the blood trail, while Aaron pulled out his phone and started taking pictures of the robots. The shortened barrel of his rifle perfectly cleared the corner; the trail bended itself around, however, it would see no action as the only thing he found was yet another dead body. The white of his ribs stuck out from underneath his shredded clothing; his body having been sat up in an awkward sitting position on the wall.

"Jesus," Lovecraft muttered, fishing for his own phone.

Aaron heard this and asked, "What is it?"

"Nothing beautiful," he said, pointing his phone to the mutilated corpse. The camera clicked and he returned it to his pocket before standing up. Lovecraft walked over to Aaron, but on his way back, he noticed a problem: there was only one entrance and exit.

"Aaron, guns up now. We're not alone in here," Lovecraft commanded, taking his rifle and swinging it around from left to right. Aaron got behind him and did the same; a metallic hand at his boot slowly flexing.

"Confirm? Is there only one way out of here?" Aaron asked, not noticing. Lovecraft didn't notice either, and took a step away from Aaron.

"If there isn't, it's hidden. I didn't move any of the—" Lovecraft stopped talking, as he heard Aaron yell. He turned around to see his friend fall on the floor, with a robotic arm clasped around his ankle. Lovecraft moved the barrel of his gun over to the robot and send three rounds into its visor, but he could not kill it before a light popping sound came from Aaron's leg.

"Shit!" Aaron cursed, sitting up and shooting two more of the robots as they got up. Lovecraft turned around and was stopped by a metal hand grabbing his carbine. The robot's other hand punched him in the chest, smashing Lovecraft's ceramic plate, cracking his ribs. For the second it took him to fall to the floor, he knew what it was like for Rocky Balboa to fight Ivan Drago, only Ivan Drago's punching force was around two-thousand P.S.I.; these Worker Bots were in the neighborhood of three-thousand to four-thousand.

The pain in his chest was excruciating and to the point he could feel pieces of his bones moving around. Yet, he pulled his pistol free and sent four rounds of the special, Depleted-Uranium Core cartridge into the robot – two in the chest and two in the head. Lovecraft had to roll out of the way or risk being crushed by the three-hundred-pound, steel amalgamation. Aaron killed another one of the machines before he heard the sickening click of his rifle. His standard cartridges were powerful enough to handle these hardened robots without a problem, but they were incredibly inefficient when compared to his armor piercers.

He ejected the magazine as fast as he could, his eyes focused on the robot striding toward him. However, he didn't think for a moment that he would suddenly start being dragged toward the door. He looked behind himself in shock, hand on his pistol, before he recognized that Lovecraft had grabbed the back of his plate carrier and had his gun in the other hand. When his boss switched his weapon over to fully automatic, he was thankful for his hearing protection, as Lovecraft peppered the robots with a full 30 rounds which were coming out at a full 900 rounds per minute.

The weaker 5.56 cartridges did little more than stun the machines, but it did buy time enough for Aaron to reload his gun. He only managed to kill one, however, before the doors closed and he was slid behind a gurney. Aaron watched as Lovecraft limped over to an overturned desk and fell down behind it; his breathing labored and a line of blood running down his chin.

"You alright, L.C.?" Aaron asked, grabbing his gun and pointing it toward the door.

"I'll be fine," Lovecraft coughed, slamming a new magazine into his carbine. Aaron nodded and they both turned toward the door and watched it with strained eyes; their holographic sights glowing angry red.

As time droned on, however, nothing came, and another song started streaming through their headsets: it was a grating violin that sounded like it was being stroked with a razor blade. Somehow, though, it was able to harmonize with itself.

"What the fuck is that?" Aaron asked, turning back to the darkness. Lovecraft turned around as well, and felt static electricity flow through the ground. He could feel it getting stronger to the point that it was affecting his injuries; the music was getting louder as well. His eyes suddenly caught a glimpse of something. It was white and humanoid, but it was not white like a race. No. It looked fake, not real, like whoever this was had their skin made of white rubber.

The image suddenly flashed again. It looked like a woman with a strange metal crown. It flashed again. She was getting closer now. It flashed again, and for the first time, Lovecraft got a decent glimpse of this strange woman's face.

The crown she wore was more like a helmet that was delicately pieced together with finely cut steel. The steel was cut in such a way that its individual pieces would look like strange Asian symbols; this also left several holes in the surface of the helmet that lead to darkness. A long, steel plate came from the helmet, covered her forehead down to her eyelids. A single plate of metal connected itself to this plate and covered the bridge of her perfect nose. Finally, the spines of the crown were pushed back and in line with her white hair; yet, there were two spines that were bent, broken, and pushed forward, like two little horns that were so close to forming a halo, but couldn't quite make it. A pink rabbit hung from the left one.

Lovecraft pointed his gun toward the darkness and fired off three rounds. He heard the rounds impact the woman, before a robotic arm with five fingers grabbed him by the throat and lifted him a foot off the ground. The strength behind the metal arm was like an industrial press, but that was not what alarmed Lovecraft; it was that the arm was attached to the woman's body with muscle tissue. Two smoldering, purple eyes gazed right into Lovecraft's soul. They glowed in the shadow of her crown. He looked down as shots rang out, her jaw was covered in no skin, no muscle, no bone, no lower lip; it was just a metal mandible with steel teeth just barely visible beneath her grey upper lip. Her plate-skin had apparently been sheared off at some point.

Aaron's armor-piercing cartridges thudded and ricocheted off her skin, tearing her white dress. Her head jerked over toward him; purple eyes softening to a lavender blue, and this gave Lovecraft just enough time to grab a cylindrical stick off his belt. He jabbed it between her breasts and clicked the button on its tip.

Electricity shot from the stick and as Lovecraft was dropped to the floor, the woman let out a scream that would have sounded normal, had there not been so much static tied to it. The shock bolt was also affecting her artificial voice box, since her cries started shorting out.

"Lovecraft run!" a familiar voice shouted from down the hallway. Lovecraft looked up and saw the massive form of Abram standing there, machine gun on his hip, and E.M.P. grenade in his offhand.

"Aaron, let's go!" Lovecraft commanded, moving away from the stunned abomination. He helped him up and both started hobbling over to Abram; the Shock Bolt burned out. A line of electricity traveled down the length of the woman's body and was finally absorbed into her feet which were no more that sharp, metal, high heels. Her eyes saw the world around her in a fuzzy grey, as the word 'rebooting' appeared in large, capital letters. The Shock Bolt had shorted out her censors, voice box, and even left her immobilized, but in 15 seconds, everything would be as good as new.

However, the room started spinning, as a volley of heavy rounds hit her and sent her to the floor. Abram's machine gun spit the heavy 7.62x54R bullets at a fire rate of 650 rounds per minute. The added punch to the bullets were more than enough to overwhelm the strange character before him. Yet, he didn't fail to notice that the rounds, although breaking her skin and causing her to bleed, were being stopped by something harder inside of her. *What the fuck is she made out of? No, it can't be. Are... Are her bones made out of metal?* Abram asked himself, before his thoughts were confirmed by the fact that a round ricocheted off of her back. This was something the old Russian had never seen before – it was something that *nobody* had ever seen before. He started looking around for different ways to hurt her and possibly break through her crazy armor. While still keeping her pinned, his eyes spotted the rusted husk of an old gas line. He quickly shot it open and pulled an E.M.P. grenade from his belt.

He stopped firing and twisted the top of the grenade, making an audible ticking sound come from the device. He threw it into the room and started to run off the stairs as fast as his legs would carry him; the thought of being thrown up the stairs like Jonah was thrown up from the fish ever present in his mind.

The woman's systems rebooted at almost the same time as Abram threw the grenade. She got to her feet and looked at the grenade. Breath filled her fleshy lungs and, as the world filled with fire around her, she let out a scream that cracked the cement beneath her feet, ripped tile from the walls, broke glass, made Abram's ears ring through his hearing protection, and even shook the dilapidated pipes off the ceiling, which buried her under their weight, as the grenade went off.

The explosion, true to Abram's belief, damn near threw him up the stairs. Luckily, he had made it just in time and only had to suffer the discomfort of being thrown, face first, into a desk. The helmet he wore took most of the blow and when he opened his eyes, he was greeted with the sight of an old AKM being pointed in his face. It was just like home.

"Hey, who the fuck are you?!" came a voice laced with adolescent naivety. Abram put his hands up before carefully reaching for his I.D. This proved to be a waste of time, considering the moment he grabbed it; the kid's head exploded into a mess of skull and pink mist. Stunned, he looked past the now-dead kid and saw Lovecraft hiding underneath a nearby cubicle. He put a finger up to his mouth and then motioned for Abram to come over. The Russian complied and crawled over to him, sliding behind the cubicle before they were spotted again.

"What the hell is going on?!" he asked in pseudo whisper. Lovecraft helped him push his machine gun further into cover and pointed through the cubicle with his thumb.

"Wolverines. They're a gang that has ties to Juarez, and they must have come running once they heard all the commotion. I just saved you from getting your penis tacked to a wall," Lovecraft explained. Abram looked to him and saw that he had cuts around his neck and had two more lines of blood flowing from his lips; he was in bad shape. He heard some rustling behind Lovecraft and saw, for the first time, his companion, Aaron Castellanos. He had a makeshift splint stuck in his boot and featured three white spots on his plate carrier; they were powdered lead from him getting shot, luckily his body armor ate it.

"Are we in a position to fight?" Abram asked, semi-hoping for some miracle. This hope was dead before it even got off the ground, thanks to Lovecraft shaking his head.

"No. I've got a least three broken ribs and internal bleeding. Aaron's ankle is broken, and he also has broken ribs from getting shot; we can fight, but if we can't walk, then we're about as fucked as France in World War Two." Abram looked between the two men just before he heard two others run in; they were arguing in Spanish.

"They're arguing about whether or not they heard a shot," Aaron said, lazily pointing his weapon over Abram's back. Abram let out a hushed breath and looked at his equipment. The box connected to his machine gun still had around 50 rounds left and he had three more 100-round boxes left on his plate carrier and belt. If all else failed, his nine-millimeter still had a full magazine and two in reserve. Each could hold 17 bullets a piece.

He got up into the crouched position and said, "I think you need a miracle. Unfortunately, I'm not God, but I have enough bullets to put the fear of God into them. I will clear a path." Lovecraft looked to Aaron, who shrugged his pained shoulders; both of them knew that they were in no position to stop them. Instead, Lovecraft reached onto his belt and pulled out a fragmentation grenade.

Handing it to Abram, he said, "In case it doesn't go as planned, *don't* get captured."

The Russian nodded and stuck the grenade into a pouch on his belt. He got up from the floor and saw that the two men had their backs turned to him. Flashbacks to Syria filled his mind, as he hoisted his machine gun and slowly walked toward them; his boots trying to be as quiet as they could possibly be. They spoke in a language he didn't understand, and fought for things that no sane human being could possibly get behind. Yes, this was just like Syria.

Abram took aim and in half a second, shot the first one, three times. His point of aim shifted, and he did the same to the other. Both of them fell forward, with eviscerated heads and broken necks. Bullets tore through the concrete floor in front of him and caused him to look up to a balcony another floor up. He pointed his gun up to the balcony and watched, as the high caliber rounds caused the white tiles to explode, concrete to crack, and the shooter to drop for dear life. He yelled out something unintelligible and garnered the attention of his comrades, before Abram lowered his aim and tore through the balcony. Blood splattered the wall behind the concrete structure, as the voices of five other men were impossibly heard.

Lovecraft watched as Abram tore through the first three and when he saw the head of the next one explode, he knew it was time.

He turned to Aaron, "Time to go. Think you can use the 50?"

"I can stand just fine, fuck these guys." He dropped his battle rifle and let his sling catch it before pulling his Sig free from its holster. Lovecraft helped him up; putting his arm over his shoulders, he started to help him walk away. They walked about halfway down the line of cubicles, before bullets started to tear through the particle board, one of them snaking its way past Aaron and hitting Lovecraft in his right forearm. Lovecraft grit his bloody teeth and let out a strained grunt, as Aaron looked across the room and shot the attacker in the head.

"Lovecraft!" Abram's Russian accent called out, "Keep moving!" Lovecraft looked to him and saw that he was sliding a fresh box into his PKM; his left bicep, which was still covered by his blue fatigue, was bleeding. If he could, he would have grit his teeth even harder, as he pushed through the pain and started walking toward the door again. He grabbed his own pistol with his injured arm and turned ever so slightly and sent three rounds into a Wolverine that had just shown up to kill Abram.

As the man fell, the Russian pushed the belt of bullets into the feed tray of his machine gun and closed the hatch. He covered Lovecraft and Aaron, as they made it outside by cutting down two, assault-rifle toting, Wolverines, and one that had a sniper rifle. However, while he was doing this, one of his attackers got too close and grabbed the overheated barrel of his machine gun. The man screamed in pain, but started a small tug of war with Abram. Blood splattered from his left shoulder as a round passed right through it and imbedded itself into the floor; there was another sniper. In hindsight, he would count this as being lucky, since the other guy fighting over his gun probably moved his head out of the line of sight; yet, this didn't make the windedness and stamina drain of being shot any better. He looked into the hate-filled eyes of his attacker and knew that he had to win; anything less would not be good enough.

Another round cracked and Abram was surprised when it was not him in pain this time, but the man he was fighting with. He looked to the door and saw Aaron sitting next to the doorframe, with his SCAR 17 tucked into his shoulder; barrel smoking. He felt the weight shift at the end of his barrel and saw that the man, who had previously been holding the barrel away from his body, had collapsed to his knees, thanks to a large hole in his left ankle. The barrel was in line with his head now and Abram wasted no time in making it pop like a balloon. He then set his sights on the sniper who shot him and tore apart the balcony with concentrated fire; a hand rolled down to the ground floor.

"Abram, it's time to go!" Lovecraft yelled, with a strange, green-haired woman standing behind him. The large shoulder, somehow, heard his name over the gunfire and started walking toward the door. He kept suppressing the enemies inside, until he got close enough to the door, where a feminine hand touched his shoulder. He turned to see a strange woman with evergreen hair and a black trench coat. Her right, gloved hand was clutched around the pistol grip of a gold plated, AK-74 Kalashnikov.

"You've done enough, honey. It's my turn," she said in the faintest French accent he had ever heard. Her eyes, although only getting a glimpse of them, terrified him. They were about as cold as green could get, and reminded him of the Siberian winters where he lived. They seemed so familiar that he thought that he had been out hunting and had come face to face with a...*wolf*. She swung her assault rifle up to her shoulder and as the formerly pinned down Wolverines started to stir, one of them poked their head out. A round was fired, but what caught the attention of everybody in the room was how there was no pink mist, but an eruption of white fire.

Kara started peppering the back of the balcony with these unique, White Phosphorus Rounds, and the screams of burning people filled the room. White Phosphorus Rounds, or W.P.I. rounds, were the kings of anti-personal, small arms ammunition. When fired, they immediately ignited with white fire that would not burn out until there was nothing left to burn; however, the biggest problems with them were: they could not be used at point-blank range, and they could not be used past one-hundred yards, else the white phosphorus would just burn away. Thus, there was a 'sweet spot' where these rounds were like an acid-spitting flamethrower that would eat through *anything* flammable. This was where Kara stood.

The scent of burning flesh filled the room, as Kara let out small bursts into the back rooms that caught old medicine on fire and suffocated anybody inside. One unlucky Wolverine actually got close enough that Kara couldn't shoot him; he quickly found out what it was like to be knocked on your ass by a girl and then he also found out what it was like to have your head crushed by the buttstock of a rifle. It wasn't fun.

The last one to die was a woman who looked to be in her mid-twenties; she was lit on fire and, in her panic, ran around the corner she was hiding behind. Kara took her as threat and covered her with more white phosphorus, to the point she looked like the flame on a candle; she fell into a puddle of liquid fire and stopped moving soon after.

The battle was over. Bodies burned, walls burned, and every Contractor lived. Lovecraft watched the fire spread onto the floor and smelled the sickly stench of burning people. Abram let out a sigh as his adrenaline started to wear off and his wounds started to make themselves known; he put his machine gun on his back anyway. Aaron sat in the doorway and looked at the overcast sky; the humidity was gone, but a new heat had just been made. He pulled his helmet and balaclava off; inside the helmet was a picture of his wife and three kids: Margret, Mollie, and Martha. He pushed it away from the door as if protecting them. Kara lowered her rifle after killing the woman and looked around to the burning rooms. Flashbacks of the French Coup, Afghanistan,

71

Singapore, Iran, and her grandfather's cremation all entered her mind. With one hand, she lifted her rifle to where the barrel was pointed to the ceiling; dustcover touching her shoulder, and walked back to Lovecraft.

"We're done here," she said, in broken English, "Getting you all back before you collapse is what we need to focus on now." Lovecraft nodded and let her pass. He then unsnapped his helmet and took it off. He held it in his right hand, as he held his carbine in the other, while he followed Kara out of the building. The French woman helped Aaron to his feet and Abram made sure to watch behind them as they left. He would drive them back to the Bazaar after much protest from Kara; and even drove them out of the Bazaar the next day.

The wind rippled through Kara's hair and made her extremely long braid whip about wildly, as the rest formed a unique halo around her head like that of a king cobra. They drove passed the Kenzie's Kosmetics hologram once again. She had her arms rested on the 50-caliber machine gun's top and watched as the sun rose above the metallic city. Beverly had accepted the fact that she would never see her boyfriend again and was now putting a lot more effort into the store and her unborn child. Everything was going back to normal.

Pipes dripped, unhindered by human intervention, as smoke filled the basement in Weiss Memorial. The floor was covered in the rusted pipes that had buried the hybrid woman; only one metal arm and her crowned head were visible. The hissing sound of machinery moved through the room and floated around the metal arm. Her metallic index and middle fingers started to flex and twitch. Eyelids jerked open to reveal blood-red eyes, as her hand clasped into a fist.

Chapter 5
Are You Afraid of the Dark?

February froze into March, and as the last snow of the season fell, Lovecraft, Aaron, and Abram were sidelined in their compound. They were all stiff and sore, but that's why God made painkillers, and if Lovecraft thought he should buy stock in aspirin – he almost damn near swore to buy it now. It was in these thoughts that Lovecraft found himself, as he sat at his desk. It was hard to believe that it had been almost two days since they nearly got killed along the waterfront. However, it was abundantly clear that one thing hadn't happened yet, and that one thing was about to burst through the front door of the compound and wreak havoc.

"I'm back!" Kara's French accent echoed through the hallway. Lovecraft buried his face in his hands; Abram damn near opened his stitches as he jumped so much, and Aaron groaned as he was woken up. Kara walked further into the room, mouth covered by a scarf. Her arms carried a large, wooden crate that she quickly sat on the kitchen table with a pained grunt. She pulled the scarf from her face and set it next to the crate. She threw her gloves into the same spot, before she turned to the hallway. She walked past the first room where Abram was busy cleaning his machine gun. His hands were covered in carbon and he had already gone through two rags that were currently sitting on the same bench the machine gun was. He let out an annoyed groan and a hand flew to his bandaged shoulder; he was trying his best to not hurt himself even further.

"Are you alright?" Kara asked, taking a step into the makeshift bedroom. Abram turned around and wiped his hands with a surprisingly clean towel. He opened his mouth to speak, but found his tongue unable to form words, when he saw the mess the back of Kara's hair had become. She gave him a quizzical look as his mouth slowly shut; his own mind trying to process just what he was seeing.

"Your hair," finally came from his lungs, and motioned toward a cracked mirror with his hand. Kara glanced over to a mirror and watched, as her own expression deflated like a balloon. She ran a hand through her hair and almost pulled it out of her braid that she had lazily put it through this morning.

"Better?" she asked, hands on her hips.

"Better, and yes, I am okay. Is there something else you needed?"

Kara smirked at his awkwardness, "Is there a crowbar in here?"

Abram looked around the room until his eyes caught the sight of the tool Kara needed. It was of the red variety and hard to miss.

The room Abram now inhabited was less of a room and more of a storage shed. Previously, Lovecraft and Aaron had used it as a place to store tools, loose ammunition, old electronics, and, strangely enough, an old workbench. When Abram inquired as to its origin, Lovecraft said that it belonged to a female Contractor named Pamela, and once she moved out, the two men had no use for a third workbench, thus they put it in storage. Since then, Abram had adopted it, and now used it for whatever he needed. Yesterday, it served as a place to build replacements for the grenades he used. Today, it was for gun cleaning.

The modestly old Russian bent down and grabbed the tool. He carefully handed it to her and for a moment, became aware of his own height. Kara certainly wasn't short when it came to being compared to women, in fact, some might say that she was a 'giant' among women, when she stood at a full five-feet eleven-inches, and almost broke six-foot, two in her normal heels. However, when she was compared to Abram, who almost broke the seven-foot mark, she looked like she was fresh out of high school. Yet, when she took the crowbar from his grasp, he couldn't help but feel that she surpassed him in all other aspects. She was a truly terrifying woman.

"Thank you, Abram," she said, leaving his room not as a fluttering girl, but a woman with clenched fists and solid ground underneath her snow boots. Abram looked at the hand that held the prying tool and couldn't help but hear his wife's voice saying the same phrase. He was quickly pulled from this by the sound of another door opening and closing. He turned back around and went back to cleaning his weapon.

Kara was standing in the main room of the compound, popping the top of the crate open with the crowbar. She heard the same door that Abram did and when she looked toward the sound, she saw Lovecraft walking toward her. His right arm was wrapped in thick gauze and she could just barely see more of it poking up from the collar of his shirt. The fact that he was wearing a pair of black jeans told the story of how they were off duty and wouldn't be seeing action any time soon.

"What are you doing?" he asked, sending a hand to his bandaged chest, before walking further into the room.

Kara popped the last corner of the crate and opened it, "We got the shipment of ammo you ordered last month, and I brought it here." She reached inside of the container and pulled a one-hundred round box of 5.56 caliber ammunition from it.

Setting it down the table, she then said, "There're five-thousand rounds in here, and the 7.62 is on its way, but there's a shortage thanks to our friends on the Southern Border." Kara pulled her Marlboros from her pocket and put one in her mouth, "I'll let you know when it gets here."

The 'friends' Kara was referring to, were the Contractors stationed on the U.S.-Mexico border. These Contractors worked directly with the U.S. Border Patrol, and were currently engaged in a violent drug war with the Pena De Muerte Cartel. Pamela was one of these Contractors. The main warzone was Juarez: Mexico's Afghanistan.

"Great," Lovecraft said, before another door opened and they saw Aaron limping forward on a pair of crutches. He had dark circles under eyes, chapped lips, and stubble that Kara thought would make Lovecraft jealous. His clothes were very much like Lovecraft's, although they smelled much nicer, thanks to Kara's detergent.

"You alright? I thought you were going to be out of commission for the rest of the day," Lovecraft asked, concerned that his friend had gotten up when he shouldn't have.

Aaron shook his head, "Dude, I am still on enough Percocet to put down a small, fluffy animal." His words were slurred and fell off at the end, "But, I just got a call from Barons."

"Barons? Why the hell did he call you and not me?!" Lovecraft asked, only to get a shrug from his friend. Kara folded her hands in front of herself, as she waited for Aaron to continue.

"I really didn't think to ask him... He called right after Kara came back and—" Kara had to jump behind him, as he started to fall backward; she barely made. "You have really pretty eyes."

Kara turned to Lovecraft, and rolled her eyes and said, "It figures that he'd have to be high as fuck to start complimenting me." Lovecraft wasn't as amused as Kara, in fact, she was rather impressed by the scowl that had engraved itself on his face.

"Focus, Aaron. What did Barons want?"

"He said that he wanted to see you and had read your report, even the redacted parts... I think I should stay here," Aaron admitted, trying to put as much weight on his crutches as possible.

Lovecraft nodded and Kara helped Aaron back to his room. The leader of this group of Contractors, excluding Kara, who was a civilian, took a seat at the table and ran his hands over his face. He felt the stubble that had almost turned into a full beard, the length of his bangs, the annoying oil of his skin, and lastly, the sleep beneath his eyelids. Just like yesterday, he hadn't planned on doing anything today, especially going to see that fat slob Barons, but peace was expensive. He heard Aaron's door shut, which was then followed by the soft thud of a pair of rubber, snow boots coming toward him.

"Christ, how much Percocet is he on?" Kara asked, her accent butchering the drug's name.

"He's not on Percocet," Lovecraft admitted, pulling his hands away from his face.

"What?"

"He's hopped up on morphine. I just tell him it's Percocet so he'll take it." Kara was immediately dumbfounded by what she heard. I took her a moment to respond to what Lovecraft said.

"Um, alright. Two questions: first, how does he not know that you're lying to him and second, what does he have against morphine?"

"He's never actually seen Percocet, or doesn't remember what it looks like, and I really couldn't say what he has against morphine. Whenever I ask him, he just says, 'It reminds me too much of my mom.' If I try to push further, he just changes the subject and won't look at me. I guess, in the grand scheme of things, it doesn't matter." Lovecraft stood up and touched his ribs, as he let out a sharp breath, "I'm going to have to go talk to Barons. You can take care of yourself, right?" Kara's brow fell before she turned to look at Aaron's semi-closed door.

She then turned to Lovecraft and said, "I can, but I'm coming with you." Lovecraft's face deadpanned. He blinked once, then twice, and finally on the third, he spoke, "Why?" There was irritation in his voice. Kara looked over her shoulder to see Abram still cleaning his gun. She then thrust her hand forward and gently poked Lovecraft in the ribs; a sharp, snake-like hiss leaving his lips.

"Aaron can't walk ten feet without falling asleep. You can walk, but at the slightest sign of use, your muscles are killing your injured ribs. Not to mention that your arm is still fucked up as hell, so you can only drive with one hand. Me poking your ribs should have been enough of an explanation of why I'm going with you." Lovecraft's annoyed scowl returned to his face as he took his hand away from his chest. He hated it when Kara was right, and he hated it more when he couldn't figure out a decent comeback.

"What about Aaron? Sure you don't want to rub his feet?" Lovecraft chided.

"Please, I know for a fact that he hasn't had a shower in days; that's just gross. We can let Abram rub his feet."

"I heard that!" Abram yelled from his room, swearing at her in Russian. Kara smirked at this, before turning back to Lovecraft.

"I think he'll fit in."

"Yeah, I'll cover that later. Are you armed?" Kara nodded, before grabbing the bottom of her coat which wasn't buttoned like its top portion, and pulled it to the side, revealing her Grizzly sitting inside a black, plastic holster. The gold accents even sparkled without light.

"Always." Lovecraft nodded and walked over to Abram's room, "Abram, I gotta leave. Think you can keep Aaron from wandering down the street without his pants?"

Abram chuckled, "So long as he doesn't think of shooting me; I think I can manage." The old Russian turned toward the window and confirmed that it was caked in a thick layer of frosted ice, "By the way, I would recommend taking the heaviest coat you own. I feel sorry for the poor motherfuckers who have to scrape their car windows." He pointed his thumb toward the window and Lovecraft nodded. He moved as fast as his healing body would allow him, and grabbed a pair of heavier boots, a pair of thick leather gloves, his shemagh, and finally, a bigger overcoat. Once again, he tried to put them on as quickly as he could, but he left the belt of his coat loose in order to ease his pain a touch. After that, he returned to the kitchen where he joined Kara, and the both of them headed down the stairs which were covered in at least four inches of snow, and into Kara's old Honda. Like her personality, the car was a very bold, burnished bronze; while the steering wheel was covered in a fuzzy, pink skin. A pair of shotgun shells hung from the rearview mirror, as well as rubberized French flag. The rear windshield only featured one sticker which read, *"I always get head."* This was being underscored by a 50-caliber sniper rifle which had a small heart carved out of its white form. Needless to say, she liked aggressive things. Hell, even her car had an illegal turbo booster on it that Lovecraft had reluctantly looked over, in exchange for a 50-percent discount on ammo for the six months, after she bought it, and a one-hundred dollar VISA gift card. It was the best set of spareribs Lovecraft had ever eaten.

"Please tell me you're not going to use the turbo charger in this," Lovecraft stated, putting his seatbelt on.

"Oh no, why would I do that?" She put the car in drive, "I can't have the old man shitting his pants and ruining my upholstery."

Lovecraft looked at the shitty black leather he now sat on and couldn't even begin to count the cracks and the fuzzy, yellow padding underneath them, "Sure, you bitch."

"Hey, free country. I reserve the right to be a bitch if I so choose." Lovecraft looked at her and *smirked* at her. Even though she knew this was a surefire way to get on Lovecraft's good side, it still made her smile. They pulled away from the frigid sidewalk and went into the storm.

Snow fell in droves and perfectly framed the holograms that danced around the city like frozen poltergeists. The streets were strangely deserted and reminded one of the post-apocalyptic disaster movies that were popular in the early 2000s. The snow created a heavy, white mist that was just a prelude to the inevitable whiteout that would happen as the storm got worse. Kara tried to drive as slow as she possibly could; the streets were very slick and the possibility that they were going to get stuck made the hair on her neck stand on ends. She cursed the road crews, even though she knew that there was only so much they could do, and even the streets were heated to prevent icing; they couldn't hold up under such cold snow.

"They said that this was just the start of a bigger blizzard that had been blowing through the northern parts of Lake Superior yesterday," Kara said, trying to distract herself from her anxiety.

"You know what that means, right?" Lovecraft asked in response.

Kara was slightly caught off guard and replied, "Umm, maybe?"

"Means wet snow. When I was growing up in Omaha, that's usually the kind of snow we got, considering Omaha, Nebraska, and Council Bluffs, Iowa, are parallel to each other, with only the Missouri River to separate them. Shit's heavier than the ammo crate you carried in." Kara gave him a sideways glance that she hoped showed her wonderment; although, he probably didn't even see it, considering he was looking down at his feet and then back out to white-grey world.

"You never talk about it, Nebraska," she pointed out, trying to see if she could learn anything about him.

"What's there to tell? I grew up in the biggest city in the state, and bounced around the Midwest with Aaron, after we got our Contractor's licenses. Of course, any further detail would be lost on you, considering you grew up on the other side of the planet."

Kara turned and smirked at him for a moment, "Try me, you've got nothing better to do."

Lovecraft gave her a dirty look, "I grew up on a bunch of hilly earth that had water on one side and endless flatland on the other; at least, until you got to Colorado. Really, Menagerie, there's not much to tell."

"Sounds a lot like Bordeaux to me, minus the part about Colorado. I can still smell the English Channel in my dreams sometimes. Jesus, I can even hear my dad telling me not to get to close, so I wouldn't go tumbling into the water. What about you? Do you dream of home?"

Lovecraft pursed his lips and cracked his fingers, "Whether I'm asleep or not, I think about it too much." Kara turned down another snow-packed street and had to go around two wrecked cars that had been abandoned by their owners; too damn cold to worry about shit like that.

"Why is that?" she asked, her accent breaking into her voice again. Lovecraft shrugged his shoulders; his eyes being blinded by the unplowed streets.

"Who knows? Sometimes, I can smell the stockyards, to the point that I think it's coming through my window, and other times, I can feel the coarse fabric of a shitty school uniform on my arms and legs."

"You went to a school that required uniforms?"

"Yeah, why?"

It was Kara's turn to shrug, "Don't know, I mean, I can see why you wear a tee shirt with your combat gear now." Lovecraft stroked his chin at the thought. It had really never occurred to him that his use of a tee shirt could be attributed to his school uniform. It was an interesting theory that could be explored later.

"I don't think that's why, I just like to be flexible." Lovecraft reached into his coat pocket and pulled out his sunglasses, "Wake me when we get there." Kara nodded, as he slipped the glasses onto his head, covering his eyes. He reclined the seat back and let his eyes close. Sleep was almost immediate.

Rain and white light was all that Lovecraft saw. It was like he had suddenly drifted up to a glamorized version of heaven where everything was paved in white gold. He looked down and saw that he was clothed in his old school uniform; buttoned-up shirt with no tie, sleeves too small for his unusually large biceps. The shirt was tucked into the belted waist of his pants; his boots were not school-approved, but after what he had done, they couldn't exactly say no. Wait, what had he done? He suddenly jerked himself around, as he heard the echo of the bell which marked twelve-thirty. Lovecraft's eyes went wide. He remembered this bell. He remembered this place. He remembered this day – but couldn't remember why.

Suddenly, as if a lesser instinct took over him, he started sprinting forward, his footsteps echoing off the wall and draining them of their brightness. The old cinder blocks formed, the triple-paned windows became transparent, the green trees, the sand in the playground glowed from the sun, and the flashing lights of police cruisers blinded the senses. There was no sound. It was like Lovecraft's ears were stuffed with some substance that even put his hearing protection to shame. He ran past the lockers, the wood doors, and the stairwell where a cop in a bomb suit stood. Their movements were in slow motion, but

Lovecraft could run without feeling tired. He didn't know why he was running, he didn't know why the police were there, he didn't know why he was so scared.

He stopped, suddenly, when his feet carried him to the only open door he had found. The white light had retreated around the corner of the door frame and blinded anyone from seeing inside. Everyone, but Lovecraft. He covered his eyes and let out a loud scream that no one heard. In the dark of his eyelids, he felt rough lips touch his chapped ones. He felt semi-strong arms wrap around his torso. Fingers danced in his palm. Premature breasts pushed into his bare back and then bare thighs straddling his waist. Suddenly, in this world where noise was swallowed, he heard something that made his ears ring, "You'll always protect me. I know you will, because you're my soldier."

Lovecraft collapsed to his knees and cried enough tears that they started to form a puddle. He remembered what happened that day, he remembered who had done it, he remembered everything; yet, there was still something missing. "The name! What was the goddamned name?! Her name, for fuck's sake, why can't I remember her—"

Lovecraft was awoken by Kara calling his name and her hand flicking his head. He jumped back in his seat and looked around, before taking his sunglasses off. Kara was just about to ask if he was alright, until she saw a line of water flow from his eye and fall onto his shoulder.

"Lovecraft, are you crying?" Lovecraft immediately wiped his face and looked up at the ceiling.

"No, the damn roof must have a leak in it or something. Are we here?" Kara was about to open her mouth to protest, but decided to just agree with him. Her eyes widened, as he all but leaped out of her car like a damn cat and was across the sidewalk in no time at all. He had either forgotten about his injuries or they had healed miraculously.

"Are you coming?" Lovecraft asked, noticing her staring. Kara shook herself free from the trance and pulled the keys from the ignition. She gave a quick glance up to the roof of her car; it was completely dry. She opened the door and stepped out into the frigid, snow-laced wind, and felt the moisture drain from her lips. It was much colder than the forecast had originally predicted, and from the way her hands felt in her heavy gloves, it had to be well below zero. She looked to the sidewalk where Lovecraft stood, and felt the warm sensation of relief when she saw that the defrosters were working; she wouldn't have to worry about falling on her ass today. Kara quickly joined Lovecraft on the sidewalk and followed him inside of the Police Headquarters.

The waiting room was as deserted as the streets, and made Lovecraft even wonder if Barons was here. The thought of Barons calling Aaron and then not be here made Lovecraft's expression sour.

Kara noticed this and asked, "What's up?"

"Nothing, just a bad prediction. Hand me your gun and we can get this over with," Lovecraft said, pulling his own pistol from the confines of his coat. Kara shifted the bottom of her coat around and pulled her Grizzly free. She handed the firearm to Lovecraft and he went to the robot behind the kiosk. He set the pistols on the counter and pulled his Contractor's license from his wallet. He set that in between the firearms and only then did the robot take notice. It grabbed the blue card, set it down, and then typed on its keyboard so fast, that that it sounded like it was breaking. Upon finishing, the robot opened the desk drawer and fastened two trigger stops to the guards on the pistols. Lovecraft put his pistol away and threw Kara hers. The French woman looked at the strange, black oval fitted inside the trigger guard and was already formulating a way to remove it.

"Chief Barons is up in his office. Thank you for your visit, Contractor," the robot said in a pseudo-male voice. Lovecraft breathed a sigh of relief and nodded; his feet turning him to the stairs where Aaron and he had seen the technician up in the ceiling. Kara followed and saw that there were black cables hanging from the ceiling; they must have been doing maintenance.

It didn't take them long to arrive at Barons' office; although, it took Lovecraft longer than it usually did, since Kara drew a lot of attention, thanks to her unusually tall stature and flirty looks. If it had been men, Kara could have just satisfied them with a few words and kept walking, but no, most of them were women, who *loved* to talk to women who were obviously more attractive than them, just to show that this was their territory. Unfortunately for them, Kara was a hawk, and they were just sparrows. No woman could intimidate this 29-year-old gunrunner; she had been everywhere and had seen everything. Thus, she was smarter than all of them combined, which was evident by their dumbfounded looks. If he wasn't in such a hurry, Lovecraft would have been rather amused by these women, who were all in their early 40s to late 50s, getting their knowledge refuted by someone who was ten to 20 years younger.

The eternity ended sooner than Lovecraft had predicted, and when Kara walked up to him, he somewhat expected there to be another person behind him. However, when she put a hand on her hip and smirked at him, he knew that she was done. He turned around and went through the door to the hallway where Barons' office was.

He knocked on the door and when he was told to come inside, he held the door open for Kara. She smirked at him in a way that mocked his etiquette and walked inside. Lovecraft ducked inside just in time to see Barons' stunned expression. He hadn't seen Kara since they had originally found her and hoped he never would again. He had been eating a bowl of chicken-noodle soup, which fell back into the bowl, as his mouth dropped.

Kara smiled and waved at him, "Long time no see, huh?" Barons sputtered as Lovecraft shut the door; his mouth felt like jelly, as he reached for a napkin.

Lovecraft stepped forward, "Now, Barons, it is not nice to spit in front of a lady." Kara mocked him again with a roll of the eyes.

"A lady? Sure. Although, last time I checked, criminals didn't get the luxury of rights." He threw his spoon into the bowl and grabbed a cigar from his desk. *Pre-cut?* Lovecraft asked himself, as he watched Barons press it into a black spot on the desk, *I knew he was a bitch, but come on.* The black spot lit the cigar to its full potential and Kara was singing about her being hurt by Barons' words, when in reality, she couldn't give a shit in the least.

"Shall we begin?" Barons asked, puffing on his cigar. Lovecraft nodded and motioned for Kara to stand next to the door, should anyone try and come in.

Satisfied, Barons continued, "I just finished reading your report, and I will say that I, at first, thought you had sent me a screenplay from *Blade Runner*. My second thought was that you had finally gone mad and it was the darkness that broke the camel's back. Are you afraid of the dark, Lovecraft?"

"You wish," Lovecraft scoffed, "You wouldn't have to pay me so much." He let out a sigh and rubbed his brow, "When I was down there, I thought I had started hallucinating; I only realized that it was real when the stupid bitch grabbed me by the neck. I assume you saw the whole report, even the redacted parts?"

"Redacted parts? Almost the whole damn report was covered in black ink. My guys down in Intel thought our computers had fucked up." He shuffled through the papers on his desk, until he pulled Lovecraft's report free. He skimmed it for a few moments before locking eyes with Lovecraft.

"L.C., I'm going to ask you this once. What exactly did you see down in that basement?" Kara, who hadn't the slightest clue as to what the two men were talking about, looked at Lovecraft with the same interest that Barons did.

"I saw…a woman, and she could very well be the best lie I've ever seen, or is the scariest truth that has ever been presented."

The wind howled through the cyber-clade streets and carried snow clear back to the clouds, as Kara's four-door tore through the snow-covered streets; the plows were doing a really sucky job apparently.

"So run it by me again." Lovecraft thrust his head back into the seat's rest. "You go down into that hospital's basement, get jumped by a bunch of robots, and then got fucked up by Motoko Kusanagi on steroids; only for Abram and me to save your ass?" Man, did she have a way with words.

Lovecraft nodded, "Yes, for the third fuckin' time. That is what happened." Kara gave his frustrated expression a playful smirk.

"Hold on, explain it one mor—"

"Oh my God, fuck off." Kara let out a sharp chuckle, as Lovecraft turned his attention to the world outside. He watched the holographic sprites shift around in particularized frigidity that seemed as though they could feel the cold. They suddenly rounded a corner and Lovecraft's view changed from the holographic images of animals and people to the creepy animatronic mannequins of a department store called, 'Death Barbie.' It was clearly made for a certain class of teenagers. He watched the animatronics as they struck various poses and before long, his mind started to show him images of the *cyborg* that assaulted him. His eyes put her unfinished and broken face on the first, the second, and third; to say that her plight was not the least bit intriguing was an understatement.

However, once he was done daydreaming, he noticed a key detail that made his eyes go wide in alarm.

"Uh, you do know we're going the wrong way, right?" Lovecraft asked, turning his attention back to Kara, who was tapping a strange rhythm on her steering wheel.

"That's a stunning observation, Captain Obvious." Sometimes, her accent really pissed Lovecraft off.

"Big talk coming from someone who has 17 words for surrender. Where the hell are we going?"

Giving him a dirty look, she said, "We're going back to my place for a moment so I can shower, change my clothes, and we can stop for lunch, if an asshole like you would appreciate that."

Lovecraft looked to the deserted streets and wondered who would be crazy enough to actually go out and eat in this storm, "That'd be great." Kara let her lips form a smile, which she shot at him, and continued her way through the snow-caked city.

As they approached Lugers and Leggings, Kara suddenly let off the gas and started tapping her breaks. Lovecraft's left hand shot out and grabbed the dash, keeping the seat belt from killing his ribs. The green-haired woman bit her lip as they slid to a stop, not a breath's length away from a five-foot snow drift; the storm was getting worse.

"Well, that was exciting!" Kara breathed, as Lovecraft undid his seatbelt and held his chest.

"If 'exciting' is your word for 'hurts like a son of a bitch,' then I'll agree."

Kara chuckled at him and grabbed his shoulder, "Are you alright?" He nodded and held up his index finger.

She gave him a brief reprieve before asking, "You ready to march to Berlin?"

"Ready? No. Can I? Yes. Do I want to? Hell no."

"That's the spirit!" she said, opening the car door and blasting Lovecraft with frozen air. Even though multiple layers covered his body, he started shivering, even after she turned the car off and shut the door. He swore under his breath and pulled the lever on his own door and stepped outside. The walk to the front door reminded him of Luke Skywalker in *The Empire Strikes Back*, and while there was no man-eating, horned gorilla, the cold might as well have been one. Lovecraft looked past the blowing snow that stung his eyes and saw Kara shove her hands into the pockets of her trench coat; her brisk pace tearing through the heavy snow like a plow. For a moment, he wondered if she was actually cold or if she was just doing that because she could think of nothing better to do with her hands; she had said once before that her half-Russian blood kept her warm. It was bullshit, but there were times that it seemed more truthful than a nonfiction novel.

She had the collar of her trench coat raised behind her head like a hood; it was her signature style that made her look like Charlize Theron in *Atomic Blonde*. She would always get mad when he called her 'Theron,' saying, "Unlike her, I would make a great damn spy, and I wouldn't have to fuck another French chick to do it." He always laughed at this, since they both felt that the movie was a quite good for what it was; yet, they still made fun of it.

The wind tore down the street, howling in a language all its own, and pushed Lovecraft's thoughts away by throwing Kara's extremely long braid into his mouth. She obviously didn't feel it, since it was so long and there were many other things to clog her senses with. The wind was so intense that she stopped moving and planted her boots, whilst covering her face with her, now free, hands. Lovecraft took a moment to pull a piece of green hair, which was nearly two feet long, from his teeth. It tasted of fragranced soap and frozen water.

When she started moving again, Lovecraft noticed that her hair and shoulders were being overtaken by snowflakes and wondered if leaving the car was such a good idea; superior Russian genes or not, Kara had to be freezing.

He looked past her and saw that they were very close to her shop and, seizing the initiative, Lovecraft starting walking faster than her, catching up to her and putting an arm around her waist. Kara looked up at him in bewilderment, and felt herself start moving faster than her numb body could have ever carried her. She blushed like a virgin and had to look down the street for a moment before she started looking for her keys. Lovecraft saw this and just assumed that he was a lot warmer than he initially theorized; his boots came to a stop at the front door of Lugers and Leggings.

Kara shoved the key into the door and after putting a little elbow grease into it, got the door to open. Both of them almost fell inside of the shop; the snow was so deep around the door.

"Thanks for the help," Kara said, giving Lovecraft a thumbs up. Her hand was red and shaking, but she otherwise seemed okay. Lovecraft nodded to her and started to shed his protective clothing. Kara did the same after a while of awkwardly swaying in place; she seemed to be *very* flustered. Lovecraft didn't seem to notice this, however, and only looked at her once his boots had been set aside. He now wore a grey sweatshirt with dark jeans and Kara wore a white T-shirt, which was rather low cut for the weather, and a pair of black skinny jeans which the white T-shirt was tucked into. She offered to lead the way, but he declined for a moment, saying that he had to go to the bathroom. Of course, there was a snide joke about him being an old man and the need for diapers, but she eventually went upstairs.

Lovecraft didn't actually need to go to the bathroom; he was just trying to get Kara out of the room. He clutched his injured ribs with his hand and sat on the floor, back to the counter. When he pulled Kara close to him, it was so cold that his whole body had gone numb. Now, he realized that he had pulled her right into his wounds and now, it hurt like hell. No, hell felt like a sauna compared to this; this felt like an Abyss, like a hole was ripped into him. He let out a few strained grunts and shut his eyes once, then twice, and finally on the third time, he felt the pain subsiding. God, he felt nauseous, but even that was going away to the point that when he stood up, the room didn't feel as wobbly.

He held his ribs all the way up the stairs which were lined in hard AstroTurf – like they were ancient artifacts from the 80s. He dropped his hand from his torso, as he got to the door and where he heard the water running. Opening the door, he felt a sense of familiarity, as he stepped inside of Kara's Spartan apartment. The walls were painted a light gray and featured very few items in the way of personal decoration. To his left was a small kitchen area that was really meant for only one person, and to his right was her glass television that had a game console hooked up to it. The poor thing was coated in so much dust, that it looked as though it were a second skin. Directly in line with the front door, and being flanked by two white bookshelves, was Kara's bedroom door which was pushed open. Lovecraft stepped inside and from the direction of the water, he could tell that the bathroom was located off the bedroom. He walked into her bedroom, thankfully the bathroom door was shut, and took a moment to admire the American flag hanging over the headboard of Kara's bed. It was pinned to the wall by its top, with the stars on the left and the stripes on the right. There was an old, wooden chair in the left corner; it had an MK14 marksman rifle sitting on it. Lovecraft noticed this weapon was the first in a long line of AR-15s, M4A1s, AKMs, and several pistols lying on the carpet next to the bed. He surmised that when somebody lived this close to where they worked, there was no way for them to not bring work home.

He turned his head to the right and looked at the white, heavenly light and quickly looked away; his eyes trying to recover from the slight pain. It was as he waited for it to pass that he looked to the floor and saw Kara's red underwear strewn across the right side of the room.

A hand was sent to Lovecraft's brow as he muttered, "Jesus, Kara." He left after seeing this and made a mental note to never go inside Kara's bedroom again. He walked back out to the living room and sat down on the couch. His injuries thanked him immediately, as he grabbed the remote and turned on the news. He was greeted by the allegedly slutty news anchor who looked rather pissed today; it was a nice look for her. She talked about the weather mostly, but did refer some of the petty crimes that had happened last night, and Lovecraft wanted to fall asleep; she was *so* boring. This woman could do nothing but sound like a broken record and her voice was so squeaky that he wanted to strangle her. Seriously, whenever she said anything, it sounded like *nagging*.

"Why are you grinding your teeth?" Kara asked, her hair wrapped up in a towel even though she had already gotten dressed. Startled for a second, Lovecraft jerked his head toward her and saw that she was dressed in a white buttoned-up and a pair of black skinny jeans.

"Because this woman should find a different career that doesn't involve talking, like, at all." Kara chuckled and rolled her eyes.

She turned around and let her green hair fall free, "Hey, if she's half of what I hear about her, I think she'd be right at home making porn." Lovecraft turned off the television and reluctantly stood up. He moved over to Kara, but something caught his eye from a nearby window. She started to move into her bedroom, but Lovecraft grabbed her arm and stopped her; his eyes glued to the whitewashed world. Kara's heart jumped in her chest, as he surprised her, and when she turned around, his gaze somewhat unsettled her.

"What is it?" she asked, limply pulling her arm free. The only response Lovecraft offered was to put a finger to his lips, before he slowly walked to the window. He pushed the curtains to the point that there was a small slit and peered into the white world.

Outside, he saw five other Contractors clad in white camouflage and specialized winter gear. Balaclavas covered their faces and reflective goggles covered in their eyes in all colors of the rainbow. Behind them drove a large, armored plow that was pushing the snow to one side. Lovecraft could tell from just the way their leader walked that it was the Luft Company. How close they were to their ultimate goal alarmed him; it was a cruel coincidence that made his wounds hurt.

Deep down, Lovecraft cared for Kara, because in the last two years, he had seen that she was human and when not left to her own devices, could be a decent person. He would never admit this to anybody but himself, but Kara never used to act the way she does now. The first year was filled with dirty looks, cold shoulders, and a bad attitude that rarely brought anything wonderful. He didn't know why she suddenly started acting better, but he could say life was better when she was like this.

The other side of Lovecraft's affection for Kara was her tactical advantage. He had *the* Emerald Wolf in his back pocket and while she was a ruthless, merciless, killing machine that could probably kill the Terminator by crushing his skull, she was a master of logistics. Lugers and Leggings started out as a small gun store south of Lincoln Park, now, the net worth of the store and its subsidiaries was well above five-hundred-thousand dollars. She had built this in under two years, by being the most savage business woman to arrive in Chicago; the store was built on, repaired by, and lived in with the blood money of one-hundred countries; and in a fallen nation – it represented a *massive* amount of power. This is why Lovecraft allowed her an immeasurable amount of freedom. If Kara was selling guns to the bad guys, she could talk to them and then relay that information to Lovecraft; plus, there were other perks that the leader of Ruler kept between Aaron and himself. Kara was a woman of many dark secrets, most of which she brought with her, and Lovecraft had free reign to use them, should the situation deem it necessary.

"Who are they?" Kara asked, craning her neck to get a better look. Lovecraft let the curtain shut which earned him an annoyed scoff that he promptly ignored.

"I hate it when you do that."

"Yeah, well sue me later. That was Luft Company; apparently, they took the shit job this time around." A faint glimmer of alarm and excitement sparkled in Kara's irises, as she looked back to the window and then back to him.

"Should we ambush them now?! We can probably kill every single one of them before they even fire a shot. Then you can pass it off as a gang attack!" Kara was way too happy about what she just suggested; however, Kara had a certain type of humor that one could only pick up after having worked with her for a considerable amount of time. It was high-pitched and overly excited.

"You're hilarious. So funny, in fact, I forgot to laugh...or even smirk."

"At least I thought it was funny."

"You have to get some real friends."

"Real friends would have turned me in."

"Point taken." Lovecraft turned to the door and started walking toward it, "Let's go. We need to get out of here before your car gets buried and I have no interest in spending the night here."

"Hey, wait!" Kara yelled after him, but he was already gone. He moved surprisingly fast for being as injured as he was. Kara turned to look at the dusty game console and then the rest of her pristinely clean apartment. *Is my place too dirty?* she asked herself, thinking of Lovecraft having no interest in staying there.

"Kara! Let's go, or I'm going to snag your keys and drive myself home!" Lovecraft yelled up to her. This spurred her into motion, as she jumped around the area, grabbing her shoes, keys, coat, scarf, gloves, and her purse.

"Coming!" she shouted; however, as she was about to walk over the threshold, she felt the hairs on the back of her neck stiffen and when she turned to look at the window, she saw that the shade was crooked.

"Damn it, L.C." She quickly walked over the window and straightened it before nearly sprinting out of the building. Yet, Michael, the team leader of Luft Company's main squad, noticed the window shift suddenly and saw that it was the Lugers and Leggings building. A gun store that had been surprisingly closed on the Wednesday they tried to investigate it. He made a mental note of it and vowed that he would be back here again.

The ride back was much quieter than the previous one. Kara bit her lip, as she tried to focus on the road as much as she could; the storm had gotten worse, which she thought was impossible, and had now covered several streets in large drifts that the road crews were hurriedly trying to knock down. However, they could only move so quickly, and this left the streets covered in four inches of snow.

"You know, I am very surprised this thing is going so well," Lovecraft commented, startling Kara a bit. The younger woman gave him an unsteady, open-mouthed smile that was the saddest attempt at hiding uneasiness he had ever seen.

"I'm glad you are a man of great faith," she responded with a shaky voice; her mind trying not to think of the fact her car had only about an inch of clearance. "So I wanted to ask you about Abram. Are you going to let him join?"

Lovecraft shrugged, "Don't know, he saved our lives, sure, and reaped the rewards for that," Lovecraft was referring to the significant bonus Abram had received from Barons for saving his best team, "but I'm not sure that a place on my team is one of those rewards."

"It could be. There's no reason that he shouldn't be given a fair chance, especially given his skillset. A Spetsnaz Virus Unit is nothing to sneeze or laugh at."

"I'm well aware, but it doesn't mean that I'm just going to throw him into my team and expect him to do well. We will wait and see."

Kara nodded, "That's fine, but don't forget that he saw whatever that thing was down in the hospital. I'm just saying that if you don't want things to get out of hand, it might be in your best interest to keep him close to the chest."

Lovecraft had thought of this before she had mentioned it, and what she had said had only reinforced the snare that he was in. He neither enjoyed nor cared that he had to make the decision, but then again, he didn't really have an option. Kara gave Lovecraft a few sideways glances and let out a sigh through her nose.

"I only pointed that out because it's what I would do. I almost got killed early on in my career because my dumbass let pride get the better of me."

"You gonna lecture me about doing my job, Kara? If my memory serves, I caught you by accident, so I must not be totally stupid."

"You got fuckin' lucky, damn it! If only God didn't decide to shit on me that day, I wouldn't be sitting here!" Kara let out a comical growl, as she gripped the steering wheel with both hands and Lovecraft started to chuckle.

The rest of the ride, thankfully, went without a hitch, and when they pulled up to the compound, Lovecraft thanked God because he was starving. The snow was coming down a bit slower now and even allowed some of Chicago's maintenance drones to come out of hiding. They would go around to the various buildings and break ice off the various Holographic projectors; the Holograms appearing across the city like the gradual appearance of stars in the night sky.

Lovecraft checked his watch and saw that it a quarter after five. He was somewhat surprised that he had spent the entire day running around with Kara, but it didn't bother him. After all, the seasons were about to change; he always seemed to lose track of time during this event. The tall man stepped out into the frigid air for what seemed like the umpteenth time today, and was glad that this was the last time hopefully. He took solace in the white, glowing light that streamed through the windows, like sheets of cotton.

The outside world had been darkened by the overcast skies and soon, neon streams of pink, green, red, yellow, and most of all, blue, erupted across the tall skyscrapers. Television-windows started playing their advertisements and propaganda, while the streetlights flickered to light with ambient buzzing. Kara watched and loved how the light rippled off her car's beautiful exterior and took a moment to look up at the world that had suddenly woken up from its slumber. Large, colored spotlights danced across the dark clouds and highlighted every single snowflake. Wires crisscrossed the buildings and more so beneath the two people's feet, gently humming with energy. A snowplow, complete with a holographic warning circle, drove down a street that intersected Lovecraft's, and flashed its blue secondary light all over the neighborhood.

Lovecraft turned to Kara and asked, "You coming inside?"

She shook her head, "No, I better get back home before it decides to start coming down again. I'd hate it if my car got snowed in while I was inside." Lovecraft understood her plight and after saying their goodbyes, he went inside, while Kara drove back down to her apartment.

It took two days for the weather to moderate and while the snow left the first day, the cold only left on the second. This gave Lovecraft an opportunity to stand on the roof and watch the sun rise, although he had to wear his wool coat. His mind was still preoccupied with the words that Kara had spoken in the days prior; it was funny, with all the mess that was the 'Master' case, the problem that he was mulling over now was what to do with Abram. However, as with most things in life, he would need to make a decision when he really didn't want to.

"You know that coat will not protect you from catching a cold." Lovecraft turned around and saw Abram standing behind him with his own heavy parka, making him appear even bigger than he was. "The common cold has killed more men than bullets, my friend, I've seen it."

Lovecraft chuckled, "As have I; trust me, my immune system is as strong as an oak. Did you need something?"

"This team, Ruler, how does one officially join?"

"Most don't."

"Why not?"

Lovecraft reached inside of his coat and pulled out his cigarettes, "Because it is very hard for anybody to impress me." He saw Abram's brow furrow, "Let me ask you something, do you know how long I've been doing this? Contracting?"

"I would assume that you've been doing this since 2044."

Lovecraft shook his head, "I've been in this business since I was 16 years old; hell, Aaron and I went to the same school, and that's where I trained him in the art of war. When 2044 rolled around, it just legalized our jobs." Abram was stunned. Lovecraft had been doing this job before it was even legal and potentially fought off the law. It was almost unbelievable to think about a 16-year-old kid fighting and killing criminals, but when it came from Lovecraft's mouth, it carried such a weight that no crane could hold it up. "So, tell me, Abram. What makes you think that you deserve a place on Ruler? What do you fight for that would put our interests in alignment?"

Abram already knew the honest answer, "I fight because I was rejected."

Lovecraft's head jumped back, "What did you say?"

"I said, 'I fight because I was rejected.' I was sent here because my life took a turn and my country was afraid I would fuck up. Please, don't think of me saying this as animosity toward my country; I love my country, but now, I must prove to myself that I am still worthy." Lovecraft could see the burning passion in the old Russian's eyes; they were the eyes of truth that used to burn into his soul at night. He shook those thoughts from his mind eye and undid the button of his coat to show Abram his plate carrier.

Pointing to a Velcro patch of the American Flag, he asked, "Do you see this?"

Abram nodded.

"Some once said that, 'Home is where the heart is.' Well, my home has tried to hunt me down like a dog; yet, I still wear its flag. This country has room for outcasts; those betrayed by their country, it graciously accepts those who wish for a better life. The question is, are you ready to accept her help?" As expected of Lovecraft, he asked all the impossible questions that would be hard for anyone to swallow. Abram thought of his daughters back in Russia and how his death here would be pointless; because, in the grand scheme of things, he was not fighting an enemy of Russia. He was fighting evil in a distant land where flags, accents, and morals didn't matter. He could end this all right now and just accept the paycheck, accept the discomfort, accept that such a decision would lead him to the bottle again, and accept that fighting for the people was 'just business,' as his commander put it.

"Sir, my county gave me an ultimatum: leave or become a Contractor. As such, this city, Chicago, is the graveyard of my military career. My rank means nothing here and in Russia, it means nothing. However, this country has shown me, a discarded carcass of a Special Forces Soldier, more hospitality and respect than anybody in my home country ever has. I guess, what I'm saying is, I'd rather die for the people of this country, before I die for the fools in the Russian Army." Abram had not noticed, until now, that his brow was covered in chilled sweat and it made him wonder just how long he had wanted to say that.

Lovecraft had allowed his cigarette to burn down to the filter with barely any use. His lips were slightly parted, as he suddenly shook himself back to life; taking the filter and flicking it into the snow. He buttoned up his coat and walked in line with Abram.

He put a hand on Abram's right shoulder, "Citizenship is not so easily handed out, but you can *keep* the room, *Ruler 03.*"

Abram froze and thought, for a moment, he was having a heart attack at the age of 38. However, he knew this to be untrue, by the fact he didn't feel weak. Lovecraft took his hand off the taller man and walked to the door. He opened it and slammed it shut. On the cue of Lovecraft leaving, Abram looked down and smiled at his clenched fist; it was a short and simple celebration.

Interlude 1

"You can call me evil as many times as you want, but the fact of the matter is – you bought guns from me too." – Menagerie 'Kara' Alexandre

NOTE: Interlude 01, and all other interludes like it, are from an interview I had with Menagerie, some 20 years after the events that take place in this novel. Please note that her official name is Kara and, Menagerie, while being her true name, is just a 'nickname.' Also, Menagerie has stated that while her language may be extreme, it is necessary to describe the nature of the events that she and Ruler were thrust into.

"I started Lugers and Leggings at the end of my first year in America." Kara began, her greyish-green hair framing her soft and slightly wrinkled face, as she sat in front of me, "It was ambitious, but for the first time in my extensive expeditions, it was almost like it was certain. However, I never thought in a million years, that Lovecraft or anyone else would approve. Turns out, they did."

Kara took a sip of her coffee and switched subjects, "Lovecraft was always a mystery in those days. Yet, he always helped me whenever I needed something. It was strange, since I was a criminal, but I eventually grew into it. That was where I discovered that I was just like anybody else. I wasn't special, and neither was anybody else."

That's remarkable, did it just happen like that or did you have some outside help?

Kara nodded, "Both, honestly. When you have men and women like Lovecraft, Aaron, Pamela, and Monica, they start teaching you whether or not you want them to. Needless to say, when I ran away from France, I was immediately taken in by a family that wanted me and wasn't going to take no for an answer."

That's really nice, what did you think when you personally got involved with the Master Case? Also, who is Monica?

Kara leaned back in her chair, "That Lovecraft had finally lost his marbles, but given what I saw and the things that happened, I was inclined to give him the benefit of the doubt. You see, at the time, I don't even think that Lovecraft was able to fully comprehend how deep this would go, or how deep it actually went. It was hard for all of them and it was only about to get worse.

"When Ruler was so preoccupied with the Master, it seemed like the world itself tried to pull them in every direction, this was the killer of many Contracting teams. However, my heart still bleeds for poor Ying; that girl had no past, no present, and no future. I guess, Lovecraft was right in the end though." Kara took a moment to drink and then started again on the subject of my second question, "Monica is my second in command when it comes to leading my men; although, she usually stays in the U.A.E. She was the one who raised me after I ran away; think of a teacher who also doubles as a soldier. It's quite exciting!"

You said that it, I'm paraphrasing here, it got bad for Ruler, and Lovecraft in particular; how bad was it?

Kara just stared at me for a second, and smirked in such a way that it could only be described as her own.

Part 2: Beijing's Ruthless Pit Viper

"A thing is not necessarily true because a man dies for it." – Oscar Wilde

Chapter 6
Communist

March rains poured from the thunder whose lightning ripped across the Springfield skyline. American flags whipped wildly around their stationary flag poles, as the rain surged through the holograms, refracted their light, and made them appear as dull as an old T.V. People, like the water, flooded the sidewalks, with umbrellas in hand. They were of various colors and some were even transparent. However, these people were much like the ones in Chicago – they were lost.

Contractors and police shared the streets with them; their roving patrols and talk would make a drill sergeant self-conscious. They carried their assault rifles, machine guns, and even their submachine guns with loose, gloved hands. For some of them, one could actually see their faces, but for most, they were covered with black, sometimes camouflage, balaclavas. The reason for them was, in a shallow term, so these men didn't bring 'work' home. After all, it's a lot harder for the local drug lord to find your family if they can't even see your face.

The rain fell on two concrete buildings; one was immaculately clean and adorned with flags. The other as the sight of a terrorist attack and was covered in black soot, rubble, and weeds. Rain streamed down crystal-clear windows, while it also ran like waterfalls through the rebar floors. Inside of the prettier building, two men with wrinkled hands shook and sat across from each other at a synthetic table. Their food arrived and as they ate, they began to discuss things that most should not hear. The ruined concrete building stood approximately 750 yards away; atop the roof lay a flat, grey tarp. Water traveled down the side of the tarp that was facing the building's pristine brother, and ran down the length of a long, black barrel adorned with a suppressor. A narrow hand with thin fingers was wrapped around its grip; the index finger running parallel with the trigger guard.

The radio crackled to life in the sniper's ear and asked, "Ying, check in," the voice that called out to the sniper was of an Asian dialect.

The tarp shifted some and revealed the head of a woman, whose black hair was cut in the style of a pixie, "Ying Li, checking in. I have eyes on the target. Am I clear to fire?"

"Stand by," she was ordered, "The strike team's on the roof, but need confirmation that he actually is the one. Do you see a black briefcase?" Ying moved her sniper rifle just a bit to where the scope was delicately drawing lines across the floor. She found the mentioned container underneath the man on the right.

"Rodger, male, with the red tie, to my right," she said slowly and precisely; her finger pulling back to rest on the trigger.

The radio crackled again, "Acknowledged. Disable them so our team can secure the package. Kei out." Ying's left eye slowly shut, and she held her breath; the beating of her pulse filling her ears. She delicately squeezed the trigger and let out another breath, before seeing her target's neck explode with red syrup. They both fell to the floor and as soon as the thud was heard, their security jumped into action, trying to help. The one that was trying to help the man who owned the briefcase suddenly crumpled to the floor; blood pouring from the hole in his head. The one who was trying to help the other man cursed and pulled his Glock free from his belt; he stopped moving once a bullet blew out his front teeth and severed his spinal cord.

Ying jerked the bolt back on her JS762, ejecting the large casing of the 7.62x54R, and used the area between her thumb and index finger to push it forward and down. She steadied her breath and looked for the next target that would be stupid enough to try and help these dying old men. However, one would never come as the strike team rappelled down from the roof, dressed in jet black, carrying QBZ-95-1 assault rifles, and sporting the Chinese flag on their shoulders.

The glass windows fell, as the remaining civilians who had not taken cover ducked behind overturned tables. Bullets and blood marred the walls as the remaining security, as their heads were filled with two holes each. Kie, whose head wasn't covered by a helmet, was the last to rope in, and he was also the one to pick up the briefcase. He put his boot on the head of the last man who was choking and pointed his pistol at him.

"Look at how pathetic your country has become. You used to rule the world and now, you can't even protect yourselves," he said, before shooting him. Looking at his men, Kie motioned toward the windows with his head. They walked back over to the windows, the metal exoskeletons they wore clanging like bells, and jumped from the building. The shock absorbers that were built into the metal skeletons took the fall and even split the concrete.

They would run to the street where they got in their cars, one of which Ying drove, and fled from the scene.

Back in Chicago, a black skillet crackled, and the scent of bacon, eggs, and peppers mingled with the scent of hazelnut coffee. The sound of the room was dominated by a woman with red-highlighted black hair, greedily shoveling food into her mouth whilst talking. She was dressed in a black T-shirt and matching cargo pants; her jacket was hung up next to the door. Lovecraft sat across from her and kept glancing between her shoveling a whole egg into her mouth and reports Barons sent to him last night.

Her name was Marlene, and she was the sniper a top the building in the Flood Zone the day that Aaron and he went to get Argentina. She was an old Afghan War veteran and had a mouth on her that would make a king cobra cry. She was also the team leader of Eclipse, one of Ruler's friendly rivals and allies.

"So I was like, 'Barons, if you want somebody to go on fucking guard duty all day, have one of our dipshit errand boys do it. I'm not going to waste my damn time looking over a fucking road that's as dry as the Queen of England's pussy.' Do you know what he said?" Lovecraft shrugged his shoulders and looked at the piece of paper Abram had. It simply read, "Swear words used," and had over 25 tally marks on it.

"He said that the use of such language in his office was 'frowned upon.' So I told him he could kiss my ass and that he could only order me around when he started paying me better. He took exception to that." The four of them, including Aaron, who was in the kitchen, started laughing.

"I bet he did," Lovecraft said, "So what brought you here anyway, Marlene? It better not have been to get free food, because I will kick your ass out with the homeless people."

"Sure, like you'd kick a hot piece of ass like me out with the homeless." Marlene was surprisingly well-known for her looks and curves, but she knew it, which was the worst part.

"Don't tempt me."

"Fine. I honestly came here to see the new spice you added to your team." She flexed her hand toward Abram, "After all, it's not every day that you let somebody else into your reclusive team. It was more like Team Hermit, instead of Ruler."

Lovecraft cocked an eyebrow, "Sorry, Marlene, you can be hot, but hot and funny is a stretch, especially for you. Seeing Abram is most definitely not the only reason you came down here to see us on your day off, either."

Marlene crickled her nose and crossed her arms, "You know, Lovecraft, I really, really fuckin' hate how perceptive you can be. Like, if I could take your

101

innate ability to guess things right without reading the question beforehand, I would strap it to a chair and electrocute that motherfucker."

"You're welcome to try, but I can guarantee you one thing: you would wake up in the chair." If someone were to say that Lovecraft was intimidated by Marlene, he would laugh in their face, while also calling them a 'dumbass.' He knew how people like her worked and it was a whole lot more sad than it was annoying. To put in a generalized term: Marlene was a 'one-trick pony.' Being a sniper was *all* she could do. It bothered her far more than anybody else realized, anybody except for Lovecraft, who tried to not broach the subject for fear of getting too involved.

Marlene smirked at Lovecraft answer, "Okay, well, the Cheytac's been acting up on me again. The stupid bitch keeps jamming."

"It's still jamming?" Lovecraft asked, surprised. His mind wandered to the image of the Cheytac M200 sniper rifle that Marlene used. Yes, it was old, yes, it was rusting in some areas, but it was a bolt action rifle; it shouldn't be as unreliable as it had been recently.

"Yep, for the third time in the last two weeks. I took it to the range and all I could get outta her was a click. I ejected round after round, but I could never get one to go off. I even tried *more* expensive .408 C.T.; damn near had a heart attack at the cash register. I'll probably just end up bringing her down to have Kara's people look at her, since I'm at a loss as to what could be the problem." Lovecraft's expression soured.

"Sorry to tell you this, Marlene, but Kara's in California right now, on business. She'll be back on Wednesday."

She growled in annoyance, "But that's a whole damn week." She ran her hands through her hair in annoyance, "Means I'm going to have you use that fuckin' .300 Win Mag for another five days."

"My heart bleeds for you," Aaron yelled in, as Lovecraft's phone rang. Marlene threw her middle finger toward the kitchen, as Lovecraft answered. A few yes's and no's were said, before he took the phone away from his ear and slipped it into his combat pants.

"That was Barons. We finally got a hit on those robots that attacked us in the hospital."

"That's the best start we've had since February," Aaron said.

Lovecraft nodded, "Get your gear ready, we're going to see what they found." He then turned to Marlene, who took the words right out of his mouth.

"I get it. It's time for me to leave. Welp, if you guys need me, I'll be either trying to fix a broken gun, watching holographic porn, or sleeping. The latter sounds the best actually."

The three of them watched, as she walked out of the building. The sound of a motorcycle soon followed, and this was the alarm that told them to get ready.

Water streamed down Ying's body like the rains she had been subjected to. However, all she felt was *pain*. It was the kind of numbing pain that made it feel as though one's very nerves had been crushed, and from the looks of the long, red lines across her tattooed back – the feeling was more than superficial. The world around her was an inferno of pain that the hot-shower water could never cleanse. Blood ran from her lip and the bite marks on her neck; her inferno of pain was dominated by sexual violence that the *Red Flag* turned its back on. After all, *everything* was for the *glory* of China, the state, even her *pain* was. She bit her tongue as she cleaned her privates; they were just as red as her back and they even bled at points. Ying could see herself in the glass box that the shower formed and had to bite back tears, as she saw the five stars of the Chinese flag tattooed on her left shoulder; the only tattoo she was forced to get was her brand. After all, a *sow* was all she was destined to be. A sow soldier, a sow bodyguard, and a breeding bitch was all her uses.

A voice rang out from the other room that shook her to her core and almost made her yelp, "Ying!" Kie's voice came, as he put his pants on, a cane being kicked under the bed, "There's a convoy being sent to Chicago in an hour. I put you on the security detail, try not to fuck it up."

"Yes, s-sir," she said, before she heard the door shut. The young Chinese woman sank to her knees and let the water fall on her, as she curled into the fetal position. She let herself cry; it was something she did a lot.

15 minutes later, she was out of shower and pulling her thick, black cargo pants over her slender legs. A verbal expression could not begin to describe how thankful she was when the pants didn't immediately start to hurt. It was also a blessing that the term 'Going Commando' wasn't just an urban legend. She gasped as she slipped her black synthetic shirt over her torso and tucked into her pants. It strangled her sore breasts and constantly rubbed her back; if not for her modesty, she would have taken it off and just worn her plate carrier. Speaking of, her carrier was unique when compared to many others, because hers featured a plastic holster that let her pistol hang off her chest. She checked the time and saw that she would have to leave in 15 minutes. In a panicked manner, she grabbed her radio, magazines, submachine gun, helmet, and her boots before moving over to a small station next to the bed. She put her feet into the two holes that were cut for them and the machine suddenly came to life. It strapped a harness just above her waist which lead down to the metal skeleton that now hugged her legs and was secured to her boots. She stepped out once the red lights on its side turned green. Her hands flew to a small

console on the harness and once there, she flipped the last of the safeties to 'off,' before running out of the apartment.

Barons' office smelled of cigar smoke as Lovecraft, Aaron, and Abram stood and listened to what the police chief had to tell them. The robots that attacked at the hospital and the cemetery had been hacked; that was pretty obvious, even to the blind and deaf. However, when Barons said they were affiliated with Switchboard Robotics, that was alarming.

"I'm having a hard time believing that somebody broke Switchboard's code. I mean, they were workbots, sure, but isn't this 'Super Code' damn near impossible to crack?" Aaron asked, crossing his arms.

"Supposedly, that's why I want you to go down to Switchboard and ask them just what it would take for someone to break in." Barons turned his chair toward the window and folded his hands in his lap, "Phantom cyborgs, ultra-hackers, and killer robots; this story just keeps getting better and better."

"I would pray that it doesn't. Our plate is already too full to be screwing around with anything else," Lovecraft said, standing up from his chair. "All we need is some jackass to show up and blow up a school or some shit. Then we'd be well and truly fucked."

"My police officers can deal with that. You just focus on finding this phantom Master." Lovecraft nodded to his back and led his men out of the room.

Hurriedly, they flew down the stairs, past the waiting room, and almost threw the door into someone's face, as they went to their Humvee. Aaron bit into the end of a cigarette as he grabbed the keys. Unlocking the door, he had a sudden feeling that he was being watched. Putting his hand on his pistol, he turned around and saw an alley behind him. What he saw in the alleyway, stunned him.

"Hey, Lovecraft," he called to his friend, "get a load of this." He motioned toward the alleyway with his head. Lovecraft closed his door and went over to where Aaron stood. Abram, who was already inside, stuck his head out the gunner's port. Lovecraft's eyebrows rose when he saw the strange, prune-haired woman that he had helped a month ago.

She stood there, with her hands behind her back, wearing a pair of very tattered shorts and an old, pink T-shirt. The woman timidly started to shuffle toward them and when she came to Lovecraft, an eternity later, she pulled a brand new Medkit from behind her back and dropped it into his hand. She smiled at the stunned man before turning to walk down the street.

When she disappeared behind a building, Abram asked, "Friend of yours?"

"Barely. Aaron and I found her beaten to a pulp inside the police station. We treated her wounds and left; I guess her problem was worked out to some degree." Lovecraft opened the Humvee and threw the Medkit inside of it.

"You know that's probably stolen, right?" Aaron asked.

"All the more reason we should get out of here."

The ride to Switchboard's Chicago branch was uneventful as usual. The sidewalks were crowded with people of various colors, the holograms moved at differing speeds, and the tall, black buildings with recessed windows still looked more like prisons than apartments. Yes, that was the theme of this new world that had been created out of the ashes of America; it never changed. Lovecraft still wondered if this is what eternity felt like. If this is what it was, he wanted no part of it.

The Switchboard Building, as it was known, was located on what little waterfront the city of Chicago still possessed. Well, it still owned all of it, but most of it was the Flood Zone which was deemed unusable. The building itself was held in place by a large foundation that bloomed into a multi-floor bubble where a traditional skyscraper was twisted like a spring out of its top. The overall height of the building was around 1700 to 1800 feet high.

"You know, I always heard that American architecture was overly complicated. I now know that this true," Abram said, as Aaron found a parking spot. The three men got out of the vehicle and walked through the front door.

The inside was just as immaculate as the outside. Large, blue lights hung from cables and, had it not been daytime, would have shown light on Switchboard's technological achievements, such as Nano Weave Body Armor, the JRK-35 Arachnid Tank, and the HG-S Strider Robot which was a joint project between Hanging Gardens, a company specializing in Artificial Intelligence, Switchboard, and the U.S. State Department. The goal was to make a frontline combatant and they achieved just that. Such was evident when one stopped the three men.

The bot was rather short, probably on the taller side of five feet, and it carried and 6.8-caliber carbine in its metal fingers. It's most prominent features were its triangular head and its single red eye.

It pointed over to a teller's booth, "All weapons and phones are to be deposited at the front desk where you can retrieve them later." Lovecraft reached into his plate carrier and pulled his Contractor's license out. He held it up for the bot to see.

"My apologies, Contractor. I was not informed of your immediate arrival." It pointed its metal hand toward a long hallway that was intended for Switchboard staff, "If you'll please follow me, I believe that Head Engineer

Burrow is waiting for you." Lovecraft nodded and motioned for his comrades to follow him.

Their weapons clattered on their backs as they moved threw a hexagonal, metal hallway. Electronic signs ran text across the top of the walls.

"You are entering a Restricted Area. Authorized personnel only," a female voice echoed. In each corridor, there were armed guards in full gear that featured a red visor. Their armor was as black as Aaron's and their hands were firmly clutched around their 6.8-caliber rifles. Lovecraft glanced at them and saw that their barrels had been replaced with Tungsten-Titanium Alloy barrels; a costly upgrade that only had one purpose: to allow for the use of White Phosphorus Ammunition. This was highly illegal for a company who only held a basic military charter which only catered to the buying of fully automatic weapons. Lovecraft kept his mouth shut, however, and put it to the back of his mind. Maybe he could revisit it later when everything wasn't so fucking chaotic.

The three men stepped through a sliding door where they found a man with salt and pepper hair standing behind a desk. He turned toward them with a smirk, his cheeks as flat as a sidewalk.

"Thank you, Dotty." The robot nodded and stepped out of the doorway. Lovecraft immediately hated this place when the door slid shut with a loud thud; it didn't help that, from this guy's stupid smirk, he knew he was going to be a prick.

"I'm happy to see that you made it, Lovecraft," he said, gesturing to the seat in front of the desk.

No, you aren't, Lovecraft thought, as he sat in the chair. Abram leaned up against the wall next to the door, while Aaron pulled the other chair back and sat across from the Russian.

"I take it that Barons told you why we had to barge in like this?" Lovecraft asked, resting his rifle against his leg, barrel up.

"The gist of it, yes, and when he told me the model of the unit that had attacked you, I had to look it up; they were so old."

Lovecraft raised his eyebrows, "Old? They had only been out for two years."

The head engineer folded his hands in front of him like an old Roman Senator, "Technology is advancing, Contractor." Lovecraft tried to not flinch at the name, "Six months ago, we created a code so complex, that it took our most advanced Artificial Intelligence two minutes to decipher it. Four months later, we created one that took it *five* minutes. Soon, we will have A.I. so advanced, that it can crack these codes in seconds. However, for someone to hack a Switchboard code is something I've never heard of."

Bullshit, Lovecraft thought, *You people hack into your own networks all the time. It's the reason you keep making better code. God, this guy has the biggest boner for himself, it's fuckin' disgusting.'*

Lovecraft thought all these things with a face as hard as stone and eyes – harder than titanium. If this were a poker game, not even a single person could have dreamed of knowing his hand.

"Okay, it did happen though. Somebody cracked the *Da Vinci Code* and now I need to know something. What would it take to break into Cyber-Fort Knox?"

Burrows leaned back in his chair and looked at the ceiling with a straight mouth, "You would need an advanced A.I. that could scan the entire network, copy the standard procedures of the firewall, isolate a weakness, while also cloaking itself so that the system doesn't detect an intruder. Even if you had all those things, the system is still locked up by a randomly generated password that the system itself knows; you'd have to have the Administrator give the *'Skeleton Key'* to the system. This would then let you inside to where you could manipulate the code."

"Sounds like a pain in the ass," Abram commented.

"It is, and we have to use it every time a new set of code is written."

This statement piqued Lovecraft's interest, "You said that new code is being written and sent out rapidly these days. Could somebody have stolen this *'Skeleton Key'*?"

Burrows shook his head, "Not likely. The person who holds the Skeleton Key isn't even a real person. Our O.S. Class A.I., 'Sarathun,' who runs the whole building, is the keeper of the Skeleton Key."

"Is there a chance this 'Sarathun' has been hacked?" Aaron asked. If a man could turn as white as the salt flats of Bolivia, Head Engineer Burrows just did it.

"No," he only half said, "That's impossible. Utterly impossible. If a would-be hacker ever got close, the A.I. would crush them with its own countermeasures. It was made to be like a human, where it could have a natural sense of its own space and detect anomalies much faster than any human reflex could."

Lovecraft nodded and found that the engineer had told them everything he needed to know.

He stood up from his chair, saying, "I appreciate the inconvenience. Seeing as this has gotten us nowhere, I'm sorry for wasting your time." He turned to Aaron and Abram, "Back to the Humvee. We'll have to look elsewhere."

Burrows ran a hand through his short hair, "D-Dotty will show you the way back." The robot suddenly appeared at the door and instructed the Contractors to follow her. They were led through the Restricted Area and soon found themselves back in the stunning lobby. All of them left the building and piled into the Humvee.

When they hit the highway, Lovecraft finally spoke, "The man's a liar."

"Oh yeah? What gave that away: his demeanor that started off all calm and benevolent or the fact that when he saw that you weren't a complete idiot, his tongue started to swell up?" Abram asked, with a humored smirk.

"Both, honestly. When your company, even if you are just a small branch, is put in the crosshairs of the law, you don't act like all is fine with the world; because it's not. Secondly, when he started to spout technical nonsense, I realized that he's just a sucker fish and somebody is spoon-feeding him the bullshit. It's a classic example of a technique that every Contractor should learn. If you ask educated questions, even semi-educated ones, a lie will fall through, because no *whole* lie can exist with a *whole* truth. However, half-truths are technically *true* and that's why the best *liars* arm themselves with the *truth*," Lovecraft said, thinking of Kara.

"Kara and other illegal arms dealers are a great example of people who use the truth to reinforce their lies. Hell, the reason why nobody could ever bust the great Menagerie Alexandre was because she always told the best *White Lies*. Should ask Kara about it sometime; she could tell you how to work the system so well that you'd never be put in jail even if you murdered someone," Aaron said to Abram, smirking at the thought of yet another one of Kara's stories.

"I'm sure I will. Speaking of Kara, why do you let her travel when she's your responsibility?" Abram asked.

"Because she's 29 years old and thus, is old enough to know that if she does anything stupid, that I will find her and kick her ass. Besides, she's a Contracting Dealer and the majority of her business is done internationally. I can't deprive her of income." Abram nodded and figured that if Lovecraft could find a way to trust the arms dealer, he could too. Lovecraft, personally, didn't like trusting Kara with such things, but she hadn't screwed him yet and, once again, he couldn't legally ban her from leaving the city. Taking off his gloves, he grabbed his cigarettes and as he lit one, he felt that even though the warmth of March flowed through the streets, he could have sworn that it had turned into the *coldest* city on earth.

Chilled raindrops clung to the armored truck's windshield like oversized dew. The windshield belonged to the first truck in a four-vehicle convoy; an envoy heading to Chicago's infamous Bazaar. Ying sat in the passenger seat of this truck and grit her teeth, as she leaned back against the seat, her ass and back writhing from position to position.

"Are you okay?" the driver asked in Chinese.

"Fine, just a little uncomfortable is all," Ying said, quickly trying to just focus on the tall trees passing by them. However, the driver had other plans, and extended his hand toward her. She turned just as the pain was starting to go numb and was rather surprised by his hand.

"Do you not shake?" he asked, starting to move his fingers back. However, Ying was quicker than he thought, and grabbed his hand; her tight leather sleeve slipping from under the neck of her glove. He looked down and saw that her skin was almost as black as the leather and gloves she wore.

"Ying Li," she introduced herself, thankful that her hands felt like the only thing on her body that wasn't hurting.

The driver smirked, "Sun, and if I tell you anymore, my wife may just skewer me." He then pointed at Ying, "You're the Snow Leopard guarding us, aren't you?"

Ying was taken aback by how bold he was and how good his intuition was. When it came to Chinese Contractors, one could not tell the difference between ex-Chinese Military, Current Military, or the Snow Leopards. However, it appeared that there was enough of a difference that Sun could tell just by looking at her.

"That's a bold assumption from someone I've never met before, how do you know I'm one?"

He held up two fingers, "First, I haven't met you, so I can only assume you came from a different section. Second, the tattoo on your arm tells me that you've been given special privileges." Ying looked down and saw that her sleeve had come untucked and quickly moved to push it back inside her glove. She started to fear that Sun would tell Kei about her wardrobe mishap.

Her fears were dashed, however, when Sun declared, "I think it's cool though. The fact that you guys are given so much freedom is inspiring." He smiled at her as he said the last phrase, and all she could do was offer a friendly smirk. She just couldn't get how he could see her as free when she felt like she was in a cage – like a falcon with a broken wing.

Sun turned back to the road and saw the sunrays break through the cloud in front of them; a flock of blackbirds evacuating the deep forest. They splashed through the puddles that lined the street and found the rain again, when they saw the tall skyscrapers of Chicago jutting up above the tree line. Sun carefully watched the road through the swiping of the windshield wipers and Ying sought to hold her attention out the window. Her eyes tried in vain to hold onto the trees as they flashed by like film reel. Ying saw families, children, men, women, machinery, and weapons in the stilled frame. Great cities rose and fell in the blink of an eye between these many frames, and were a testament to the imagination of a child she kept hidden away. Hidden, for fear that they too, would be snatched away. However, it was in this concentration that one simple thing tended to drag one back to reality and the simple thing that brought Ying to her senses was a faint, shimmering distortion between the trees.

Ying sat up in her seat, the pain in her rear end seeming to disappear for the moment, and watching the man-shaped distortion vanish into thin air.

"What is it?" Sun asked in a serious tone, his foot ready to hit the gas. Ying looked back toward the woodland and then shook her head. She was tired and it was probably just her exhausted mind trying to tell her so. However, when she turned back to Sun to tell him everything was alright, her face fell, and her eyes widened as she saw a dark, robotic figure pop up from a ditch. A long, Bakelite tube was thrown over the robot's shoulder, with a nasty tandem warhead pointing out of it.

Ying felt her breath go cold, as Sun failed to see it in time, and she had to grab the wheel.

She grabbed the wheel and jerked toward her body, yelling, "R.P.G.!" The vehicle jerked violently, as a sound rivaling thunder ripped through the area; the rocket flying from the tube and skidding across the street. With half of its stabilizing fins torn off, the rocket lifted off the pavement and whipped into the cab of the second truck, barely missing Ying's.

Chunks of burning metal, shrapnel, molten copper, and smoke exploded with such a force, that it rang ears through hearing protection. Ying's truck swerved off the road and down the embankment, crashing into a clump of fallen branches. Gunfire started to rhythmically pop on the street, as the Chinese security teams started to return fire at the R.P.G. gunner. More robots joined the fight and the Chinese quickly realized that they were massively outnumbered. Another R.P.G. whistled through the air and planted itself inside a Chinese soldier; the detonation turning him into mist and shaking the truck. The shockwave made Ying come to a bloody spot on her left eyebrow where her head hit the dash. Dazed, she saw two of everything, as her heavy arms grabbed her JS-2 submachine gun off the glassy floor. Her mind was so numb that she didn't notice that her left hand's pinky and ring fingers were broken.

She held her head with that hand, as she steadied her vision; she definitely had a concussion.

"Sun...you good?" she asked in a withdrawn voice, "Sun?" Looking to her left, her dark eyes finally focused, when she saw Sun sitting next to her, a piece of metal sticking from his chest. A stream of air was forced from her mouth; blowing bloody, sweat-matted airway from her mouth. Her eyes inspected the piece of metal and found that it was not just a large piece of shrapnel; it was a

110

blade. It was about the length of a typical sword blade, but there was no guard or handle. All there was a cylindrical end that was obviously a magnet by the pieces of steel clinging to it.

Ying was so focused on the end of the sword that her eyes barely caught the background move. Her eyes traced the strange outline, until she realized that whomever or whatever it was, still had a grasp on the sword. Ying held her breath, as she quickly realized that it had not realized that she wasn't dead; the gunfire apparently masking her delirious voice.

As hard as it was to see just what was on the hood of the crashed truck, Ying could just tell that the invisible figure was a humanoid. Its head was looking at the clouds that were sending a chilled mist down to the ground. Looking down to her submachine gun, Ying started to slowly raise it up toward the figure, but was stopped when an explosion rocked the vehicle and showered whoever this was with black, soot-covered dirt. His cloaking apparently had automatic fail-safe, since the dirt caused it to fade away and give Ying her first glimpse of her attacker; she nearly pissed her pants.

He had no face. In fact, his head was more like a chromed helmet. He was naked, save for a pair of black boxers, and his back had long, steel vertebrae protruding from silicone skin; he looked like a grotesque dinosaur. His left hand, which was entirely robotic save for a flap of fake skin on the back of it, reached up to his 'face' and grabbed its chromed front. Ying watched, with horror-widened eyes, as the front suddenly depressurized and was pulled off. She started to shake, as her ears heard him groan in a half-human, half-computerized tone; he pulled a syringe from a pouch fastened to his arm and started to inject it into that arm. Half of Ying couldn't believe what her eyes were watching, but the other half was vehemently aware that she was in danger. While the attacker was busy, she slowly removed her right hand from her weapon and grabbed the door handle. It broke off with a sharp snap, as she pulled it.

She held the broken piece in her shaking hand and then immediately felt the feeling of eyes on her. Turning back to the robotic man on the hood of the truck, she saw that his yellow eyes were now staring at her.

"Shit," she breathed, before throwing her gun up. She pulled the trigger and watched, as three bullets pierced his rubbery skin. He wailed in pain before suddenly disappearing; the next thing Ying knew; she was pulled through the windshield by his silhouette and thrown into the woods. She flew through the air at an unimaginable height; the humid air burning her eyes as she crashed through copious amounts of branches. Ying suddenly couldn't breathe when she hit a particularly thick branch and fell straight down.

The exoskeleton wrapped around her legs kept them from breaking, as she crashed onto her feet and then planted her back into the ground. This all happened in one motion and, had she not been gasping for breath, one would have thought that she had died instantly. Blood clung to her sweat and mud-matted hair; the strands of black splayed out behind her head like a pool of liquid. Her eyes stared at the monochrome sky, as her cut-up face stung like it was attacked by a million fishhooks. Ying's lungs burned, her chest hurt worse than it had previously, and her legs, oh my God, they might well have been broken; they hurt so *bad*. The once tight leather shirt she wore had been torn apart by the branches which had literally worn away parts of the shirt that had not just been blatantly torn off. Her pants were much the same and the only thing that had really made it through the impromptu flight was her plate carrier, but even that was currently killing her.

Memories, emotions, facts, and fallacies all passed in front of her eyes, as she suddenly heard herself crying. Here she was, yet again, on the ground; crying was her only lot in life. It was all that she was good for. The fact that she was one of the best snipers in the Snow Leopards meant nothing. After all, she was trained as the *reaper*, not the *savior*.

"Ying, stand up. Even death needs life because without life, there can be no death." Ying heard her mother's voice echo through her mind and while it really didn't say anything, her mind already knew what it said. She felt as if her eyes had just opened and for the moment, she felt strong enough to push herself off the ground.

Removing her plate carrier, she threw it into a nearby shrub. It wouldn't help her anyway, since she could just be stabbed where there was no armor. The next thing she threw away was her right shirt sleeve, since it could barely be considered a sleeve anymore. After this, she reached for her pistol, but when her fingers felt hollow plastic, her heart sank. Apparently, her submachine gun wasn't the only weapon that she had lost. Cursing under her breath, she grabbed a red, rubber cord on the harness her exo-legs were attached to, and pulled it as hard as her weakened state would allow. Safety locks on the belt, her knees, and her boots released at the same time. Gravity took over and brought the metal apparatus to the ground.

With her legs now free, Ying reached into a set of small sheaths strapped to her left leg. The knives themselves were no bigger than a common throwing knife, but the two major things that told why they were not typical were the grenade pins protruding from the back and their unique, scarlet blades. Ying had seen enough 'last man standing' movies to know how this would work and it was kind of funny how calm that made her.

She heard a tree creak in the direction of the highway; her head simply turning toward it. She could see nothing but the sparse mist out in the distance, but the eyes didn't need to see what the mind already knew. Ying was being watched.

Slowly, she panned her view around the misty forest and when she heard an unseen bush shake, she hooked three fingers into the first three pins and pulled them free. The last two were left in, as their three brothers hummed to life with scarlet blades. Ying stood and listened after doing this. Surprisingly, she heard no further movement. Deciding that her hunter was rather patient, Ying picked up a stick that was about as thick as the pipes in gas lines, and started to walk in Chicago's general direction.

Her injured legs were too sore to support her body weight while she walked; the stick proving to be the only way she was getting out of this quickly. If something happened to it, however, crawling would be her only other option.

Slowly, and painfully, the short, Chinese woman trudged through the woodland; her speed just as lame as her legs felt. It was embarrassing just how much hope she had to put in this stick. *I guess this is how Moses felt whenever he used his staff to perform miracles.* Ying thought to herself, the slight amusement helping to ease her pain for a moment.

However, the stick fell to the ground as she heard the trees behind her crack and snap; the branches falling just behind her boots. Ying didn't turn around; her hand sliding down to one of the knives that she hadn't pulled the pins out of. With the sure grip, she turned around and immediately ducked, as a long blade was thrust above her head; several pieces of black hair falling to the leaves. She grabbed his outstretched arm, his camouflage fading, and swung herself behind him. She thrust her knife into his lower back, twisted it, and pulled it out. She repeats this several times, tearing fake skin from his metal bones and covering the ground in oily blood. The robotic man yelled in pain, as he turned around and shook Ying off.

He grabbed her by the armpits and threw her into a tree with a large truck. Her back accordioned around the truck, eliciting a pained groan from her as she rolled onto the wooden floor. She got up on her hands and knees; her body feeling as though it were on fire. She heard him moving toward her. Ying looked down at the knife still in her hand; the silver pin shining bright enough to show through the tears in her eyes.

Pulling the pin free, she spoke in broken English, "Hey, motherfucker. Still think I am prey?"

She heard the metallic song of a sharpened blade rub against rougher metal; he would come to take her life soon.

"I am no beast," he said in his own broken voice, "What I hunt is for sport; it's nothing personal." He moved closer to her whilst raising his sword above his head.

"It's just very unfortunate that filth like you had to be killed. I would have preferred that you killed yourself. That way, you wouldn't have been such a pain in the ass." He brought the weapon down, but was surprised when Ying's knife was thrust into the arm.

Feeling his own version of pain, he stepped back, just as the knife began to heat up. He realized what this strange weapon was doing too late. An explosion erupted from the edged weapon, covering him in thermite, and blowing his arm clear into the sky. It landed past the tree line, as he wailed in pain.

"I'm a pain in ass?" Ying asked, pulling two more knives from their sheaths, "You haven't seen anything yet." Having said this, she threw them at the metal man, sticking them into his collar bone. She took her final armed one and threw it at his feet; the dirt growing very hot. The explosions rocked the area and their concussions deafened Ying, as she rolled down another embankment. It was there, at the bottom of his small hill that she waited. She then waited some more and even more after that. The Chinese soldier waited until her almost-broken body screamed for her to leave. Maybe then, she could find somewhere more comfortable.

She picked up another stick, which was flimsier than the first, and fought to get up. The fog had rolled in by this point, and as Ying stood up, her scratched and cut-up face turned around to look at this strange and mysterious world. After she had taken in her surroundings, the leaves started to crutch beneath her boots.

Chapter 7
Foreigner

Thick, black smoke flew into the clear sky, as the bodies of robots and Chinese soldiers littered the street like paper. Police, as well as fire and rescue, were swarming around the area; men with High-Vis vests walked around the wreckage and searched for evidence. The incident had shut down a large portion of Interstate 55 and was backing up traffic all the way to Peoria. Those commuters that could actually get through were given a firsthand look at the grizzly sight, as well as police and Contractors armed with M4 Carbines and AK-47 assault rifles.

One such person was a little girl, who looked to be about the age of 12, watching a bloody body bag getting loaded into the back of an ambulance. Her mom's car slowly pulled down the road, but not before disappearing behind Aaron's form. He stood in the middle of the street, tactical gear on, and sleeves rolled up over his large arms. His gun was lazily resting in his hands as he watched the cars go by. Breath came through his balaclava and rose to hang around his night vision which was pushed back. He turned to Abram who was lent up against one of the burned-out trucks.

"We need to call Lovecraft."

"Agreed."

A thin, sharp blade was pressed to Lovecraft's neck and then slowly drug up to his chin. The shaving cream it collected was warm and helped him relax; something he very rarely was able to do.

"You know, L.C.," his female barber began, "you should let me do this more often. This scruff of yours gets pretty gnarly."

"Yeah, I'll do it more often when we trade jobs, Connie," Lovecraft said in jest.

She brought the razor back and repeated the process she just completed, "Sure. Can you imagine me carrying around a big gun all day with these toothpicks?" Lovecraft looked at the young barber, who was just barely 20, and looked at her scrawny frame, small shoulders, flat chest, and narrow hips.

"Well, you're skinny enough to not have to require special gear."

Connie pursed her lips, "Thanks, I guess."

"Hey, if you're not going to be satisfied with my answer, then I could go on all day about how much of a washboard you are."

She glanced at her chest, "You know, some people would consider that sexual harassment."

"Yeah, and the two females I talk with most of the time would call you a pussy and that you need to 'woman up.'" Connie rolled her eyes at this and continued her work. She knew the two women Lovecraft had referenced were Marlene and Kara, with the latter being somewhat regular, thanks to the fact that her job required her to look fancy at all time. Plus, they also offered waxing services that she had to take advantage of as well. Connie truly had a high-maintenance clientele, but she couldn't forget that no matter *how* busy she felt, she would never be as busy as the ones she served. Such was evident when Lovecraft's phone rang right as she was finishing up.

He sighed as he reached into his pocket, "It was supposed to be a day off for me today. Thus, I'm either going to have to shove my foot up Aaron's ass, or the second 9/11 happened."

"Both sound equally unpleasant," Connie commented, putting the stuff away. From the corner of her eye, the young barber watched, as Lovecraft put the phone to his ear and didn't say a word. He just listened. After what seemed like barely a minute, Lovecraft put the phone back in his pocket, pulled his wallet out, grabbed some money, and slapped it on the front desk. Like a flash, he was out the door and when Connie went to get her tip, she almost choked, as she saw over forty dollars sitting in her hands. Lovecraft stopped by the compound, where he grabbed his combat pants and the rest of his gear, before making his way to Interstate 55.

As he pulled up on the current crime scene, Lovecraft put his helmet on, right as one of the burned-out trucks was being towed away. He got out of the armored car and started to walk toward the Humvee; his MK. 18 swinging slightly as it hung from his back.

The police were directing traffic in the lanes that were lucky enough to still be open, and even more of their drones were hovering above the woodland. Armed police robots stood guard next to the heavily armored ambulances and the fire trucks were busily trying to make room; some even pulling off the road. Aaron waved his gloved hand toward Lovecraft and Abram jumped down from the hood.

"Okay, gentlemen, give me the 411 on exactly what the hell I'm looking at," Lovecraft ordered, putting his hands on his hips.

Aaron cleared his throat, "Essentially, a Chinese convoy got hit a few hours after leaving from Springfield. From the wreckage, I'm sure that you can see

116

they had more than a few rocket-propelled grenades. As of yet, there are no survivors."

"Civilian witnesses?"

"No. Apparently, this convoy was one of the last things on I-55 before they closed it for the night. Damn, population crisis is fucking up all kinds of logistics." Springfield and Peoria were facing an overpopulation problem. Thus, they shut down a portion of Interstate 55 at night. The purpose was to keep people from spilling over and into Chicago, which was low on space thanks to the Flood Zone. It was a stupid plan; if they really didn't want overcrowding to be a problem, then all Chicago would have to do is raise the taxes to the sky – unfortunately, they were already higher than the heavens.

"I've never heard of any Chinese Contractors working in Chicago or Springfield. Who are they?"

Abram spoke up this time, "They're like me. Pseudo-military Contractors that have ties back to their origin country. Although, I have a feeling that China is more involved with their international resources than Russia. Bastards still get a solid paycheck."

Lovecraft looked back at him, "They still get funded by their state? Doesn't sound sketchy at all." The other men nodded in agreement as another gun truck pulled up behind theirs. The three of them watched, as David and his band of Israeli Operators piled out of it.

Lovecraft smirked, "David, you son of a bitch, where have you been?"

David laughed at his words and said, "Oh, we have been everywhere since that day at the checkpoint. Shit, the only place we haven't been is Mary's pants." Religious jokes were something of David's specialty.

Lovecraft chuckled, "I'll bet. What brings you here to our corner of hell? I imagine it wasn't for sightseeing."

David shook his head, "Nah, we've come with news. There's a survivor at Wilson-Clark Hospital, just got that over the radio."

"No shit?"

David shook his head and Lovecraft turned toward his men, "Time to go, guys. Need to get to that hospital and find out just what the hell is going on."

Wilson-Clark was about as busy as one could imagine, with the current state of Chicago. Doctors, nurses, and paramedics practically ran back and forth through the overcrowded halls, as Lovecraft, Aaron, and Abram pushed their way through. They had left their primary weapons at the front desk, a pain in the ass that was almost worth it when they witnessed the fat receptionist trying to lift Abram's machine gun, and were allowed to keep their pistols. Lovecraft had gotten the room number shortly after depositing their weapons and after a short elevator ride, now found themselves walking toward a room with large windows looking inside.

Security cameras followed their every move and armed security guards were positioned at each end of the hallway. Outside of the windowed room stood a tall woman in a white lab coat. Her lips were painted with such a red that it stained the filter of the cigarette between them. Her developed bust and slim figure gave off a mature sensation that was only further magnified by her blonde hair that was slicked back and out of her face. Her nose was buried in the electronic clipboard she held in her left hand.

The three men walked up to her and in a dry tone that was caused by the cigarette, she said, "I was wondering when you guys would show up. Typically, you Contractors would have been here 15 minutes ago, what gives?"

"Shit hit the fan. Need to find people to shovel it before tending to the fan." Lovecraft turned to the room and saw an Asian woman in a hospital gown, "Name's Lovecraft, I'm an Operator for the city of Chicago."

"Doctor Erin Magnolia, and I'll assume you're here for her," she surmised, pointing a painted nail toward Ying.

Lovecraft nodded and asked, "Who is she?"

Magnolia tapped the screen of her clipboard, "First name: Ying, last name: Li. She's 29 years old and was born in a small province just outside of Beijing." Magnolia took a rather long pause, "I'm sorry, a lot of this stuff is covered in black ink. She belongs to the Snow Leopard Commando Unit and is known for her marksmanship, while also being trained in V.I.P. protection, essentially a bodyguard, and has some training in logistics management."

"Marksmanship? You mean, like a sniper?" Abram asked, running a hand through his beard.

"I would assume so, but then again, such specificity is your profession, not mine."

Lovecraft stepped back into the conversation and got it back on track, "What has she said?"

Magnolia pursed her lips, "She just says the same thing and personally, she's getting really frustrated with the fact that we can't understand her."

"She can't speak English?"

"No, she can speak it fluently, and rather beautifully, I might add, but when describing what happened, she doesn't necessarily know how to word it. We brought in a translator and the only thing he could come up with was a literal interpretation: 'Invisible robotic man.'"

Lovecraft looked at Aaron and Abram, before turning back to Magnolia, "If it's possible, I'd like to speak to her."

"That'd be fine, but I'd like you to look at few things before you go in there." Magnolia handed her clipboard over to Lovecraft and pointed to a series of five pictures; the first featuring the marks across her back being highlighted against the various other injures. The second were the grotesque marks around her genitals. The next two were of each individual breast and the bruises present there. The final one was of a bruise on her lower right cheek that had been covered by her hair.

"These don't look very new, Doctor," Lovecraft observed, handing the machine back to her.

"They are not. Recent, yes, but new, no. We found similar marks on her arms and legs. When we asked her how they got there, she wouldn't say." Magnolia took a puff of her cigarette, "I'm no fool, I've been in this profession for over 20 years, and I can tell you right now, that somebody sexually abused this girl. Whether it was consensual isn't the issue; it's the fact that she was beat hard enough to mark, is what pisses me off."

Lovecraft looked into the room and saw the relatively small woman looking at the tops of the buildings through her window. He could just barely see the bruise on her right cheek from his point of view.

"I agree with you, and I'm willing to bet this girl is a gold mine of evidence against someone in the Chinese military. Have they asked about her yet?"

"No, I think you and the Israelis are the only people who know that she's here."

"Good, see that it stays that way. Direct message those pictures to me and then send them to the chief of police. I'll be coming back tomorrow and, with your permission, I'd like to take her with me."

A hint of surprise filled Magnolia's eyes, "W-Well, I guess I'll see. The extent of her injuries varies, but the worst is her broken fingers. I'll give you an update when you arrive tomorrow." Lovecraft nodded and motioned for his teammates to follow him.

"Wait, are you still going to talk to her?"

Lovecraft turned back around, "Unfortunately, given the new circumstances, I can't spare the time. I will be back tomorrow." With that said, Lovecraft and company walked away and after they had disappeared, Magnolia scratched her forehead with her thumb, and then took a much longer drag of her cigarette.

As the three men began to push their way through the crowd once again, Abram was mulling over a thought that had come to him during their conversation.

"Lovecraft, while we have a moment. I'd like to discuss something about the Chinese woman."

"Speak."

"Her name was Ying Li, and while you may not recognize the name, it rang a bell for me."

"How so?"

"Well, back in Russia, we've been having an off and on border dispute with China, since there were minerals discovered in a section of the Altai Mountain Range. Fast forward a few years since then, and roughly six months since I got here, and there was a terrorist attack in one of the border towns. Damn near leveled the whole town and when we arrived, there was clear evidence of Chinese involvement. One of the terrorists even went so far as to call one of his financers, 'Ruthless.' I did some research before coming here and I learned that this 'Ruthless' was something of a ghost-tier sniper; real nasty business. There were also some allegations that it was also not a man but a woman."

"And so you have a hunch that Ying could be your collaborator?" Aaron asked, pushing a doctor out of his way.

"I'm not going to jump to conclusions, but I would at least like to look into this further. If she is the sniper, then she could lead us to the person who directly assisted those savages."

"I'll keep it in mind, Abram, but remember, whether she is your criminal or not, the evidence doesn't lie. She's being beat to a pulp and it's not by her enemies." Abram's mouth formed a perfect line and nodded to nobody in particular. This was truly some shit they stepped in.

The day flew past so fast that, Lovecraft soon realized that it was nighttime, and as the clock ticked to 11, he realized that he was *still* sitting at his computer. The *Chinese Incident*, as it came to be called, had only compounded a day that Lovecraft had underestimated when looking at his metaphorical to-do list the day prior. Yes, when Lovecraft had thought about crunching numbers for tomorrow's paychecks, he completely forgot that he also had to maintain Abram's equipment which involved getting things sourced in from Russia. Typically, he would just ask Kara and then leave it to her, but now that she was in California, it had been a pain in the ass.

This was the reason for him sitting in front of a computer, completely numb to time. He looked over at his phone and knew that he needed to call Barons, but then again, it was already too late to talk to him. Upon putting this out of his mind, Lovecraft turned off his monitor and got up from his chair. He turned his bed down and just as he was about climb in, his phone rang. Lovecraft stared at the wall above his bed and then slowly turned toward his phone. It was then and there that he contemplated suicide, for there was only *one* person who would call him this late.

Slowly, he walked back over to the phone and immediately saw Kara's name, as well as the picture he put for her. Naturally, it was her flipping off the camera whilst cleaning her A.K. It was an interesting day.

Lovecraft reluctantly answered it and was greeted with a muffled, "What's up?" Kara was apparently eating something.

"Kara…what are you eating?" There was a slight pause as Lovecraft heard something get stabbed into something squishy.

"The local MegaMart had a sale on cookie dough. I bought like 15 tubs and I'm on my fifth."

"That's not healthy."

"Neither are the crackheads living down the street from my hotel; L.A.'s so great – totally would raise my kids here."

"Oh, of course, I also heard that Charles Manson was a cool neighbor." Lovecraft looked at the clock, "Was there something you needed?"

"I can't sleep."

"Could the four tubs—"

"It's five now."

"*Five* tubs of cookie dough be the problem?"

"No, I started eating them when I realized I couldn't sleep."

Lovecraft rubbed his forehead, "Where, in the space of logic, would that be a good idea?"

"…"

"Kara?"

"I was bored, okay?"

Lovecraft deadpanned, "Goodnight, Kara." He hung up the phone and threw it onto his bed. He laid down and shut his eyes, only to open them a few seconds later. He let out a long sigh of frustration.

Time ticked forward, and as the sun slowly rose above the horizon, Ying was being helped out of bed with the aid of Doctor Magnolia and another nurse. Her legs didn't hurt as bad as she thought they would, and, after resting her weight on her helpers for a bit, was able to stand on her own. After she assured them that she was okay, Magnolia handed her a pair of jeans and blue sweater. She stepped into her hospital bathroom and changed into them; it was also here that Ying realized that she had lost everything yesterday.

Her money was gone. Her guns were gone. Her clothes were gone. Her allies were gone, and for her failure, would probably be stripped of her rank. She sat on the toilet and prayed that it would all work out, that the beatings wouldn't last for too long. Ying was interrupted by a knock on the door and Magnolia asking her if she was okay. She replied in the affirmative and opened the door for her.

"Wow, they're a little big, but it still looks cute," Magnolia said, smoothing out the wrinkles on the Chinese woman's sleeves. Ying gave her thanks and both of them looked to the door once they heard a knock. The nurse that had assisted Magnolia returned and said that someone named 'Lovecraft' had come for Ying.

Suddenly filled with questions, Ying turned to Magnolia and raised her eyebrows.

The only satisfaction she offered was, "Come, I'll explain when we get there." She slowly started walking out the door and Ying was quick to follow, considering that she had no idea what was going on.

The two women walked through the cold labyrinth and as Ying walked through the door to Magnolia's office, her eyes saw a small bag full of clothes and a man standing in front of her desk, with his back turned to them. Like a small dog, her eyes went wide, as she saw that he was taller than her by almost two feet. Kie would have also looked like a dwarf compared to him; this man was both taller and had more muscle than her commanding officer.

He turned around and allowed Ying to see his face for the first time. His hair was strewn about on top and the sides looked as though they had been freshly shaved the previous day. She discovered that his facial hair was a different story, when she noticed the shadow of thin hair covering his lower and upper jaws. She examined his body and saw that his plate carrier was, in fact, carrying a metal plate. From this, she surmised that he wasn't a fool; he knew the profession that they occupied, and he wasn't going to let chance take over. The black T-shirt he wore underneath it did give her some concern, however, considering that she could feel the cold through her window this morning. She silently wondered where his coat could be if his helmet was the only thing he held in his hands.

"Ying, this is Lovecraft, he's the commander of Ruler here in Chicago." Lovecraft extended his hand and Ying tried her best not to give him a limp-wristed shake, but failed. "And you will be staying with his team for the time being." Ying's head jerked toward her doctor and then slowly back to Lovecraft; her hand falling free.

"I, um, do I get a say in this?" she timidly asked.

This time, Lovecraft answered, and his voice made her jump a bit, "Unfortunately, you don't. Due to the events that caused your hospitalization, we can't let you leave the city, and we also can't leave you to your own devices. It's for your own safety."

"But I can protect myself," she protested. However, Lovecraft was smart and knew the personal arrogance that each Contractor held. He pulled his phone from his pocket and showed her pictures of herself the day she was found.

"*Barely,*" he said. For Ying, his words only multiplied the fact that it was the first time she had seen the pictures. She looked at her soggy, bloody form that was curled up in a drainage tube. She couldn't keep her hands from shaking when she saw how bad her face really looked; her hair looking like it was covered in reddish-brown mousse.

Lovecraft pulled his phone away and put it away, "I just saw that picture this morning and I'm still wondering how in the hell you didn't bleed out. I got this from the Medical Contractor that stabilized you and even he couldn't believe that you were alive." He turned to Magnolia, who had lit a cigarette by this point, and asked, "Am I free to take her?"

"Whenever you like." Lovecraft nodded and motioned with his head for Ying to follow him. The younger woman watched as he began walking out the door and thought about crying for a moment, before the bag of clothes was dropped into her arms and the thought was erased from her mind. She looked up and saw Magnolia standing in front of her. The woman told her a few sayings of encouragement before ushering her out the door.

Now Ying was thrust into the annoying game of trying to keep up with Lovecraft; the man seemed to walk like the roadrunner in this one American cartoon she had seen. Lying in bed for a day really hadn't done her much good either; her sore legs were screaming their protests. She eventually made it to the front lobby, her body thanking her for the moment of breath, and from there, she watched Lovecraft throw his helmet onto his head. He picked up his MK. 18 from the front desk and threw its sling over his body. Two frag grenades were also placed on the counter, which he slipped onto his belt. He situated the sling into a more comfortable position on his plate carrier, and then motioned for Ying to step toward the reception desk. Somewhat surprised, she reluctantly stepped forward, and was stunned when they placed her knife in front of her; the last one she had to defend herself.

Running her hand gently across the handle, Ying picked up the weapon and admired the mere idea of its survival. There was something else too, and when her eyes met her Contractor's license, she reached for it excitedly. However, her hand coward in surprise, when Lovecraft's own gloved version covered over it. She looked at him and he looked at her, as he slowly slid it across the Bakelite surface. He slipped it into the front of his plate carrier, and that's when Ying realized that she wasn't a Contractor – she was a prisoner.

This fact in her mind made the drive extremely awkward for her. Lovecraft seemed as though he didn't care. It seemed as though he had completely forgotten that she was in the seat next to him. This made her itch her head uncomfortably, as she tried to not be the 'quiet prisoner.' She had dealt with them before and, needless to say, it didn't go well, for the simple fact that silence never won you anything. Thus, she looked at Lovecraft and searched for anything that could spur a conversation; it was like lighting a fire on a cold night. Now that was a memory she didn't need to be thinking about.

"Aren't you cold?" she asked, choosing to hit on the fact he was wearing a T-shirt. Lovecraft glanced at her and saw that her small frame was still slightly shaking.

"Nope, but I can tell that you haven't been here long." He pointed to her slightly shaking arms, "How fresh off the boat are you, Firefly?"

Ying watched him turn on the heat for her, "Firefly?"

"It's what your name means in your native language." He watched Ying's brow furrow in slight surprise, "Judging from that look on your face, I'm now a lot smarter than you initially thought."

Ying's cheeks gained a reddened hue, as she started to sputter, "N-No… I've only been here a month."

Lovecraft continued to press, "Oh yeah? How was the ride?"

"Crowded." Lovecraft nodded and slowly turned down an adjacent street. Ying looked out her window and watched the citizens of Chicago go about their daily lives. She watched a woman slap her boyfriend, a robot trying to sell people cheap fish, two police officers casually talking next to a granite pillar, and a group of three Contractors knocking on a door before kicking it in. The graffiti lining the steel and concrete walls was a mixture of English, Spanish, and Japanese; it was rather unsettling, but nothing Ying hadn't seen before. The thing that *did* cause her some concern was that the sun had been shining all day – until now. Her need to investigate this strange occurrence led her to push her face closer to the window and when she looked up, Ying realized that the sun was being blocked by the black stone-metal works of downtown Chicago. The shade had turned into the type of darkness that had wrapped around every corner, every sign, every person, and every shadow. She looked down an alleyway and, past the slight steam coming from a sewer, found that it was so dark that it looked like it was blocked off by a wall.

"Careful," Lovecraft suddenly said, startling her, "staring into the abyss might alert something to your presence." Ying glanced back at the alleyway before it disappeared from sight. She saw somebody walk down that alleyway just before it disappeared and she wondered if there was any truth to Lovecraft's words, or if it was mere superstition meant to scare her.

She put it out of her mind and decided to bring it up later, "Where are we going?"

"The police station; I'm going to ask you some questions." Ying's face fell and her body slouched in her seat.

"Great."

The rest of the drive was rather quiet when compared to this interaction. Ying had come to find out that Lovecraft wasn't the most talkative person she had ever met. This led her to wonder, now that she sat in this dark interrogation room, what he could possibly want to ask her. It was as she thought about this that the buzzer sounded, and the heavy, reinforced door opened. Lovecraft's heavy boots carried him into the room, with a cup of coffee in one hand and a manila file in the other. He grabbed the chair in front of her and pulled it out before sitting down; his coffee was set on the table while he opened the folder. He laid it out in front of himself and then pulled out his phone where he started a voice-recording application.

He tiredly rubbed his face and let out a heavy breath, "Okay, let's get this started. My name is Lovecraft, commander of Team 2501. Designation: Ruler." Ying found it rather odd that Lovecraft hadn't used his full name, but before she could ask, she suddenly found herself on the spot.

"Please state your name and rank," Lovecraft ordered, looking down at the manila folder.

Ying took a moment to search for her words, "Second Lieutenant, Ying Li."

"You are a member of China's Snow Leopard Commando Unit, correct?"

"Yes."

"Alright, it says here that your primary talent is marksmanship, with your longest confirmed kill being over a mile from your position. I'm sure you know that all of this is easily obtainable information when I run your Contractor's license. However, your additional job is V.I.P. protection, a *very* unique and priceless skill when it comes to your current occupation. Tell me, Major Kei, what's he like?" Lovecraft noticed her slightly flinch at the name and while she didn't notice, he intended to make her notice.

"He's a strong leader," Ying said, with an obnoxious power in her voice, "He cares for his men and has never known defeat. He's a true hero of the Chinese military."

"You said, 'He cares for his men.' What about his women?" Lovecraft countered her answer, scribbling something down inside the file. Ying tried to read what he wrote down, but she struggled with reading some English words, and when they were written in cursive, she couldn't read it at all.

"I don't know what you mean."

"Does he treat his female soldiers as well as his male ones? I'm not stupid enough to believe that there's no difference between male and females. They are two different things. Hell, if there are two genders, then one has to be inherently different than the other, otherwise one would be redundant."

"He treats me well." For the first time, he looked up at her and reclined back in his chair. He looked down at his scribbling and then back to her.

"Okay," he tapped his phone twice and shut off the voice recording, "the next series of questions will be off the record and will discuss the events that took place on March 15th, yesterday. Ying, what was the cargo you were carrying and where was it going?"

"I don't know what we were carrying, but we were bound for your Bazaar."

"So are you telling me you willingly, willingly meaning voluntarily – of your own free will, chose to partake into a mission that you knew nothing about. Ying Li, you are a *Contractor*, one of Operator level at that, thanks to your current military status of course. However, if what you have just told me is true, then do you just not care? Is there a reason to follow so blindly?" Lovecraft witnessed her fingers recoil into her palms, "If there is no reason, then you have got to be the stupidest person I've ever met."

Ying looked like she was about to cry, "What is your point?" Lovecraft knew better though; he was in her head and her persona was in his mental hands.

"The point? The point is that I have a very hard time believing that a soldier of your caliber just says, 'Yes' to anything. The way you describe it; you're a slave than a soldier." Lovecraft reached beneath the table and brought his pistol into view. "Speaking of being a slave, how is Master Kei?"

"Excuse me?"

"Master, is that not what you call an owner of something? From what I understand, Kei own many parts of you." Lovecraft produced three holographic pictures and threw them in front of Ying, "Like your head, your back, and your vagina. Although, that last one could be a red herring, considering that you could be on your period. Although, I don't think it's supposed to be that bruised."

"Where did you get these?! And just who do you think you are to insinuate such things about my commanding officer!" Ying spat, pushing the photos away.

"You can drop the act now, Second Lieutenant. You know who I am. You've known from the moment you laid eyes on me that I am who I am." Lovecraft leaned across the table, his chair creaking as he got close to Ying, "You knew the moment that you saw me, that you had fucked up, and your *beloved* Major, who beats, molests, and tortures you, would have your ass. Maybe you wouldn't be able to walk right for a week, maybe a month, maybe he'd break your jaw this time so you couldn't speak. After all, he already beat your unborn child to death."

Ying jerked her head over to look at Lovecraft, all her rage was the most amusing thing he had ever seen. He took his pistol and jammed it into the palm of her right hand.

Pulling the hammer back, he said, "Now here's a test. If you shoot me right now, all this information dies with me and with you, but if you do not, then you are admitting defeat and are willing to give over vital information concerning your intentions in the United States." The same defiant rage filled Ying's eyes anew, as her finger curled around the stiff trigger.

"Who the fuck are you?" she venomously spat.

Lovecraft's face was like chiseled stone, "A man who's *done* with your shit." A click echoed through the room. It was cold, menacing click that made Ying's heart drop and her stomach churn like a swollen river.

Lovecraft placed a gloved hand on the top of the pistol and lowered it, "Like I'd really give you a loaded gun." The last thing Ying remembered before blacking out were carbon-fiber knuckles.

Chapter 8
When You Spoke, I Listened

Three days passed since Ying's interrogation. She had woken up a few hours after Lovecraft had knocked her out. From there, she found herself in a strange room with a white, cinderblock wall directly opposite the door. There was a recessed, four-paned window in the white cinderblock wall and even though there was a bunk bed in the room, Ying chose to sleep with her head against the window pane, her back against the wall, and her legs up on the window sill. The young Chinese woman didn't know why she found this to be the most comfortable place in the room, but if she were allowed to take solace in one thing, it was the fact that this was the *only* place in the room that felt comfortable – felt safe.

Thus, this was the room that she cocooned herself inside; like a recluse, she only left the room to eat. She never ate with Lovecraft or any of his other comrades. She would just simply open the door and, like a ghost, stroll into the kitchen, grab her food, and walk back to the room. She would slowly eat whatever was given to her and listen to the merry laughter of the three men as they told stories, called each other names, and laughed at each other's bad and good fortunes. It reminded her of the nights when her dad would sit her by the fire while his friends and he would say vulgar things to each other. Her mother would have had a heart attack if she ever found out, but that was their little secret. Now those times seemed so, so far away.

She became a shut-in for three whole days, and it was on the night of the third that it changed. Ying had only been given a small amount of clothing from Magnolia, two outfits to be exact, so she would need to wash the one she had worn for these three days. She used the plastic bag she had been given to store the dirty clothes, while she wore the clean ones, and for the first time in three days, she opened the door to her room.

Ying looked toward the kitchen and saw that, excluding the red glow of the exit sign, it was a wall of pitch black. She looked down the opposite end of the hallway and her heart sank, as she saw soft, orange light running through the crack of Lovecraft's door which was slightly ajar. This could possibly lead them into a confrontation and as much as she wanted to recoil back into her room, she *needed* clean clothes. So she took in a soft breath and began slowly creeping through the hall. As she got closer and closer to the door, she kept telling herself that she couldn't look inside the room, for fear that it would give her away somehow. However, her natural curiosity was more of a reflex than a conscious action. The sniper soon found herself looking through the slightly ajar door and what she saw was somewhat surprising.

The tall man was standing with his back turned to the door, with his combat pants and black T-shirt. Ying's eyes caught sight of a holographic clock and she saw that it already well past one o'clock and Lovecraft still hadn't changed his clothes. When she heard the sharp ting of metal hitting each other, she looked past him and saw that he had his M4 pulled apart.

It was as he inspected the lower receiver, that he suddenly asked, "Is there something you want, Ying?"

The sniper was dumbfounded, and she was beginning to think this man had eyes in the back of his head.

"I-It's nothing, I just saw the light and my curiosity got the better of me."

"I bet it did, but that doesn't mean there isn't something you'd like to ask me. After all, it was your curiosity that made you look in here to begin with," Lovecraft said, turning toward her and wiping his hands.

A frown spread across Ying's face, as she submitted to the fact that Lovecraft was right yet again. It was annoying, but very interesting how he could seemingly know things just by listening to the smallest clue.

"How did you know about my lie?"

"I didn't."

"What?"

"I didn't know that you were trying to trick me, I just expected that you would. Then you tried being friendly and that told me all I needed to know. Your very training hung you." Ying took a slight moment to consider what he had just said; her finger scratching her lip.

"Why did you expect it?"

"Because you're not the first abused woman to lie to me. You're also not the first to lie to me in order to protect their abuser." Ying hid half her face behind the door as a weak pang of shame filled her chest. It was soul-crushing to know that she had been violated over and over again, and did nothing to stop it. What would other women think of her? What would a guy think of her? It made her very soul sink into the floor.

"Why didn't you just call my bluff when you recognized it?" she then asked.

"There was no point to do that. If I had, you would've just shut up like a box and getting inside your head would have been impossible. Think about it, if I hadn't raked you over the metaphorical coals, would you still be trying to defend your superior?" Her eyes widened in surprise for a moment, before being sent to the floor in order to search their owner's thoughts. It was a sudden and stunning realization for Ying that in these three days, she had not thought once about Kei. She had only thought of the circumstances around him and how that, while she was in that room, he wasn't there. That meant she was safe. This brought her to her next moment of euphoria, as she noticed that she had slept the moment her head hit the pillow. There was no pain that kept her up for hours. There was no waking up in the middle of the night to expel bloody urine. The aftertaste of semen was gone from her mouth and her head didn't hurt from the hair being pulled free. She looked up from the floor and back down the hallway; she didn't see Kei. She turned down the opposite end and he wasn't there either. For the first time in a decade, Ying's tense shoulders relaxed and sent shivers down her whole body. A toothless smile formed on her face before she even knew what she was doing.

Lovecraft's voice saying her name woke her up from her fantasy, "Huh?"

"I asked what you were doing up?"

"Oh, I was going to do laundry. I saw the washer and dryer down at the end of the hallway, so I decided that I should do that." She cursed herself for how awkward she sounded.

"At one in the morning?" Ying pursed her lips and let her eyes dart across the room a few times.

"Okay, then. Well, you should know that we're going to the range tomorrow with some other Contractors. You're welcome to come," Lovecraft said, beginning to put his weapon back together.

"I thought I was a prisoner," Ying admitted.

"Technically, you are. But I know that if you try and run, other Contractors will come for you and maybe even the Chinese will rip you apart. If you'd like to run, be my guest. After all, we're the only ones keeping you safe."

Ying frowned, "Wouldn't shooting you with your own gun be more likely than running away?"

"No."

Ying was taken aback by how quick his answer was, "A-And why's that?"

"Because I'm faster than you."

"How are you so sure?"

"Because, unlike Major Kei, I'm not a pushover." Ying's eyes widened when he said this. Now, her mind was thrown into a sea of interrogatives where most of them dealt with the phrases, 'Who is this guy?' and, 'Why does he seem to not feel fear?' She couldn't believe that he didn't seem the least bit concerned about Kei. It seemed like he thought of her commanding officer as more of a pest than an actual threat. She looked next to his bed and saw a beat-up flyswatter. The connection made her skin tingle.

"So, will you go?" Lovecraft suddenly asked.

"I, um, I'll think about it," Ying struggled, trying to sort out her thoughts.

"Good. By the way, the showers are next to the laundry room. No offense, but I can smell you from here," Lovecraft said, snapping his rifle together. Ying blushed at his admittance and nodded to no one, as she disappeared into the dark hallway.

Flashing lights, a loud bass, and scantily clad women were all aspects of Divine Retreat; one of the most prominent strip clubs in downtown Los Angeles. Here, one could find satisfaction for even the most complex of vices, but that wasn't what brought Kara to this place. No, the thing that brought her here was much bigger than her need for pleasure, and that was taking care of her business. Thus, she sat at the small bar, the black nail of her index finger lightly scratching the finish, and watched as a certain stripper pulled the top of her micro bikini off and swung around the pole like Tarzan. It was rather impressive actually. A beer slid its way down the bar and ended up in front of Kara's bound-up bosom; the gold buttons of her coat turning various metallic colors as the lights changed.

She looked toward the direction that the beer came from and saw a short blonde, with big breasts, holographic tattoos, and way too much makeup, heading her way. The look she gave her told her that a conversation was about to be had and the French woman knew she was going to need a cigarette by the end of the night to restore any lost brain cells.

"The drink's on the house, Contractor," she said, in the most ridiculous southern accent Kara had ever heard. It sounded as though she only knew how to say those exact words right and then anything else would devolve into another, off-the-wall accent.

Kara grabbed the drink and took a big gulp of it, "I'm not a Contractor, and your beer tastes like piss-water."

The stripper's face was filled with a mixture of shock and alarm. The shock, Kara assumed, was from her French accent, and the alarm was from the fact that she just gave a random customer a *free* beer.

"W-Well, could've fooled me. That demeanor you have is a very common trait with most Contractors." Kara turned away from her and looked around the room, where she saw a few men in combat gear sitting next to a group of naked women. She wasn't impressed and turned back to…whoever this stupid bitch was.

Kara pulled a Lugers and Leggings card from her coat pocket and slid it over to the stripper and told her, "Take this to Romanov and tell him I'll be waiting."

The shorter woman gave her a look of annoyance at being told what to do, "I'm sorry, but Romanov is not here."

"Then find someone who is," Kara said sternly, scratching four, long, white lines in the bar. She watched the stripper step around the bar and disappear around a corner. Kara's hand was tightly wrapped around the beer bottle, which she only just noticed, and when she looked at it again, she realized that there was still over half its contents left. She looked at the ceiling and wished someone would just shoot her. She dumped the bottle onto the dirty, black carpet and contemplated throwing it behind her, in the hopes of hitting somebody in the head; now that would be entertaining. However, the sound of a pair of shoes sloshing in the mess she just made brought her back to this rather annoying reality.

She turned around and she saw two, tall, white men who were dressed in black suits. They were rather overly dressed for the debauched procession that was taking place behind them, and Kara thought it was rather funny. The third man to reveal himself was much shorter than the other two, and had his hand on the stripper's waist.

"Are you the one asking for my boss?" he asked in a Bostonian dialect.

"I don't know, who's your boss?" A look of frustration spread across one of the guard's face and moved toward her, but was stopped by his short leader. Kara took note of this and made sure to relax the muscles in her right arm, should this get ugly.

"Heh, Romanov," the shorter man replied to her question. Upon her ears hearing the name, Kara stood up from her stool and looked at the greasy man. God, he had to be at least a whole head shorter than her.

"Then we do have something to talk about," she said, throwing her long braid onto her back. The man smiled with surprisingly white teeth; Kara's purple reflection flashing on and off in his sunglasses. He turned around and, with the stripper who Kara would later come to know as Betty, began walking to a backroom. The two bouncers accompanied Kara, as she followed them, and kept an extra close eye on her as she stepped through a metal detector. However, they were stunned to the point that they stopped her when the machine didn't go off.

"What? I have a nickel allergy," Kara lied. Beneath her coat was her signature Grizzly and all her ammunition, but for some reason, it had not tripped the detector. Both of them looked to their boss and after he waved her through, they allowed her to enter the room.

Inside were two plush, pink couches that made Kara grimace. She didn't know what happened in this room, but something told her that she would need to wash this current outfit twice.

"I understand that your name is Kara?" the man asked, sitting on the couch farthest from the door. Betty sat next to him and looked a little uncomfortable, until he started playing with her left breast.

"You are correct," Kara replied, paying his action no mind.

"Fantastic, my name is Lark, but most people call me 'Boston.' From the accent, naturally."

"Fascinating," Kara said, sarcastically.

"It is, isn't it? To think that my parents gave me such a beautiful name and over the years, that name has boiled down to just my place of origin. It's a tragedy that even Shakespeare couldn't rival."

It was official, this guy was as full of himself as Romanov was. "Look," Kara began, setting her hands on her black denim thighs, "while I would love to get into a philosophical discussion about names. Especially while you fondle Miss Silicon Dreams over there. I have business to attend to, and that business involves money. More specifically, money that your boss owes me. So pay me and I'll leave, so you two can fuck." Kara's hard, green eyes moved from the man to the guard behind him; his hands wrapped around a Glock pistol that was pointed toward the floor. The other guard was behind her blocking the door, and she figured that he looked much the same.

Lark smiled at her and said, "But of course." He knocked on the table in front of them a few times and suddenly, the guard standing behind him moved to a closet located in the backroom. Kara watched as he opened the door and pulled a naked woman out of it. Her arms were bound with rope and her eyes were covered by a black blindfold. She had a ball gag in her mouth and sent a wad of spit onto the floor, as she was thrown on the floor.

Kara snorted with a slightly amused smirk, "What the fuck is this? Sorry, guys, but I'm not gay."

"Oh no, you are misunderstanding. *This* is Romanov's payment." Kara's face deadpanned as her head slightly shook in anger.

"She doesn't look like a million dollars to me," she said, her voice cracking in agitation.

"That's where you're wrong, Kara. This is the daughter of a famous celebrity and she will sell for much more than one million." Kara looked at him and saw nothing but pure rage, until she took a breath. She listened to her pulse beating in her ears and through its singing did she hear what she truly felt for this man. It was a black, sticky goo, very much like that of the tar that coats a smoker's lungs. Its name was *hate* and she knew it very well.

She let out a sigh whilst undoing the buttons on her coat, "This could have gone so well, but you tried to screw me."

"No, Ma'am, this is mu—"

"Shut up, you little fucking toad. It is rude when you do not allow the guest to speak. I will now state my counteroffer." Kara pulled her pistol free and shot the captive in the head. Chaos enveloped the room as she fell over, and Kara took her next step beautifully, as she moved her pistol to the other side of the room and shot the guard in the head. She then rolled off the couch as the other guard shot at her; his bullet missed her and hit Lark in the knee. Kara was now on the floor and took the opportunity to shoot the guard in the foot, causing him to drop to a knee, and then pulled a combat knife from her belt and drove it vertically through his chin.

She pulled her knife free, coating her hand, as well as beginning of her sleeve, in his blood. Three more shots cracked through the room and pushed Kara forward, as three equal amounts of pain rippled through her back. However, when she turned around, the lead, along with the copper jackets, fell from her coat and covered the floor. Betty's hands started to shake when she saw that her shots had done nothing besides dirtying Kara's clothes.

"Really?" Kara asked, pointing the golden barrel of her pistol at the stripper.

"Wait—" Betty was silenced by the sound of Kara's pistol going off; her lifeless body slumping over.

"I didn't like you anyway," Kara smirked before turning to Lark, who was curled up on the couch.

"How the fuck did you get in here armed?!" he yelled. She laughed at him and held up the bottom of her coat.

"Nano weave, Boston. Have you heard of it?" She knelt down next to him and pushed her Grizzly's long, gold compensator into his cheek, "It's some of the most expensive body armor on the market, and its invention spawned a new wave of metal detecting technology, because the technology interwoven into the armor can render traditional metal detectors *useless*." She stood up and asked, "Romanov, where can I find him?"

"How the fuc-AAH!" he wailed, as Kara shot him in the shoulder, his blood dripping from the black and gold pistol.

"Where the fuck is Romanov?! I want an answer, you little fucking cock, or I might just rip yours off!"

"I don't know where he is," Lark answered crying. Kara's eyes widened in anger, as she lowered her pistol and shot him in the groin. He let out an even higher-pitched scream, as he was pulled to his knees, his head at Kara's waist. She rubbed the barrel of her gun into his half-bald head.

"Last chance, asshole. Life or death, choose wisely."

"2-2950 South Fisher Avenue. T-That's where he lives," he responded through labored breathing. With the answer in hand, Kara's shoulders finally relaxed, but she didn't let go of his collar. Instead, she lifted him up closer to her face.

"See? Was that so hard?" she asked, holstering her pistol. Lark shook his head and breathed a sigh of relief, now that he was out of imminent danger.

"Are you gonna take me to the hospital now?" Kara smiled at him before the sound of fabric tearing and liquid falling on the floor filled the room. Lark looked down and saw that Kara had plunged her knife in to his belly, all the way to the hilt.

"Sure, the hospital of God," she replied, twisting the knife all the way to the side. She then jerked it out of him, causing his body to fall face down in front of her. Kara used his jacket to clean the meaty chunks from her knife's top serration, before putting it back in its sheath. She looked around the once-peaceful room and then looked at her blood-stained hands. Kara fetched a tissue from her coat pocket and tried in vain to clean the thick liquid from her palms, finally settling for slipping them into her leather gloves in order to hide them. After this, she bid the room adieu and opened the door. Immediately, she turned around and shut it; the music in the club having drowned out the noise of the various gun shots. She let the knob go slowly and composed herself before turning around. Kara looked to the door and her eyes immediately widened, when she saw a tall man with dark, slicked hair. It was Romanov.

He saw Kara as well, and immediately told the two bouncers at the front door to grab her before fleeing back out the door. The two men rushed Kara and almost damn near tore apart half the building doing it. The action certainly made the patrons take their eyes off the naked females and guided them onto the only clothed one in the building. Kara furrowed her brow and rolled her eyes, as she pulled her knife once again.

She ducked underneath the grabbing arms and ran her knife over the right bouncer's belly, before stabbing the left in his side. Kara was now behind both of them and used her left hand to pull the knife out of the one, only to drive it into the nape of the other. Screaming resounded through the room, as the Contractors jumped into action, pointing their M4s at Kara. The French arms dealer noticed this and wrapped her left arm around the last guard and used him as a shield. She pulled out her pistol and shot the last remaining round in its magazine, the heavy Winchester magnum cartridge forming a large hole in one of the Contractor's faces. One of his Contractors yelled his friend's name, apparently, he was the leader of whatever Californian group this was, and hurled a plethora of obscenities toward Kara. Needless to say, she was not impressed, even after they started to shoot her meat shield.

Judging from the fact that they were trying to shoot through a human body with the 5.56 caliber round, which could barely smash a cinder block, told Kara that they weren't very experienced with their firearms. She guessed that they were the most basic forms of Contractors, but basic still meant they were a threat.

Kara put her empty pistol away and fished through her now-dead captive's waistband and found his Glock 19 right where she had seen the others'. She pointed it toward the Contractors and fired off three rounds. These were eaten by body armor before the fourth was lodged in a neck. Kara continued shooting, but only managed to keep them pinned into one area of the club. She heard something fall next to her and when she looked down, she saw an old, soviet-era grenade roll its way past her boot. Her eyes widened as she dropped her shield.

"Shit!" she yelled, diving behind the bar – covering herself with her coat. The explosion ripped through the bar and deafened everyone who was not wearing ear protection. Kara was covered in blackwood chips, ceramic tile, and the left side of her coat looked more like a piece of netting than a coat. Her green hair looked like it was sprinkled with snow as she coughed, her left ear was ringing painfully, but it would survive. Her left foot was about as lucky. It was still attached, thank God, but the glass shrapnel had more or less ripped apart the leather and her skin underneath. It throbbed like a damn marching band. She attempted to pick herself back up, her bloody left arm visible through her wholly sleeve, but stopped, when a steel-toed boot came crashing into her ribs. She didn't even get out a gasp, as two powerful hands wrapped themselves around her neck.

Hoisted into the air, Kara was thrown into the liquor shelves, taking them down with her. She tried to look up at her attacker, but couldn't, since he bent down and immediately punched her in the face. Kara felt the blood flow from her eyebrow, as she was then tossed into the small crater that the grenade had left behind. His hands returned to her neck and she looked up into his burning eyes.

"Die, you French cunt. You killed my best friend and I'm gonna make sure you never see yours again." Kara could feel the tingle of relaxation in the back of her head, her muscles were starting to feel weaker. She choked and sputtered, as his grip grew even tighter. The heel of her kicking feet caught the lip of the crater and with a sudden burst of energy, pushed herself forward, knocking the man off balance. This, in turn, caused him to lose his grip, thus making him collapse on top of Kara, who promptly rolled over to where she was straddling his chest.

The next thing she did was punch him in the face so hard, that she broke his nose in one swing. The man wailed as he reached for his knife. Pulling it free, he sought to plunge it deep into Kara's chest. Instead, she caught the blade with her hand and watched, as the blade tore through her palm and came out the back of her hand – splattering her face with her own blood. She grit her teeth angrily and grabbed the handle with her free hand. Slowly, she pulled the blade from her hand and used all her strength to bend the man's hand back toward himself.

"Do me a favor and kill yourself," Kara said, inching the knife closer and closer to his chin. The man started to kick violently, his knees hitting Kara in the back every time. He also punched Kara in the face, splitting her lip. He hit her again as the blade started to cut his skin; the hair around Kara's face was beginning to catch her blood and became matted like that of an abused animal. He threw his third and final punch, but Kara leaned back and pulled the knife away from him, before her body recoiled back and shoved the knife through his jaw.

Kara rested on her haunches after this and looked up toward the black ceiling, before she heard a glass fall from the table. She turned toward the noise and saw the petrified forms of the remaining three Contractors. The gun dealer looked at each of their pale, sweaty faces as she stood up. Shifting her body weight off her injured foot, she pulled her pistol out once more. The three of them were much smaller than their skewered comrade who was still twitching a bit. Kara dropped the magazine of her pistol, stowed it in her coat pocket, and winced and slapped in the new magazine inside using the hand that was stabbed. While she did this, one of the Contractors reached for his rifle, but fell over with a loud thud, as Kara sent her pistol's slide forward and shot him in the head. She then pointed her weapon at the two survivors who aptly directed their attention back to her. She watched their wide, frightened eyes dancing in the changing light, as their jaws were clenched so hard their teeth would crack. Kara focused her pistol on the one closer to her before, in the blink of an eye, switched to the one farthest away and shot him in the head. She then shot the one closest. She did this so fast that the two bodies made one thud as they hit the floor.

Putting her pistol away, Kara went over to one of the dead bodies and fished a roll of gauze from his Medkit and wove it tightly around her hand, before taking her coat off. She then used the same roll to wrap her arm. After this was done, she looked at her foot and furrowed her brow; there wasn't much she could do, since taking her boot off wasn't the best idea. With no other option presenting itself, Kara threw the gauze away and then grabbed a syringe that was filled with painkillers. She filled herself clear to the eyeballs with the colorless cocktail before turning to the door.

She limped her way out of the club and into the humid, Californian air. Kara's eyes were stuck in a thousand-yard stare as a bead of blood dripped from the tip of her nose and splattered on the sidewalk. Suddenly, she grabbed her pistol and pointed it to her right. Like the lightning streaking across the black clouds, she emptied her five remaining rounds into the darkness. A loud thud, followed by the clatter of something metal, echoed off the club's walls, as a red puddle snaked its way into the neon light. The pink light transitioned to a deep, Valentine's Day red and silhouetted Kara, like a figure-shaped hole in a red piece of paper.

Kara inched her thumb forward and dropped her pistol's magazine for the second time. She replaced it with her third and final magazine, before putting back in its holster. Thunder rippled through the area, as Kara began to walk in the direction of the person she just shot; her coat blowing in the wind as it threw trash and leaf litter to and fro.

From the first step into his club that night, Romanov had been on the run. The thought had never occurred to him, in a million years, that Kara would chase him all the way to California. Yes, he stole her money, but nowadays, people didn't care and that's what he was counting on. What kind of crazy bitch flies halfway across the country just for money? It was unheard of; money just wasn't *that* valuable anymore. Especially if it was stolen; nine times out of ten, the amount lost couldn't begin to cover the work that went into bringing it back. This was why Romanov was so confused, frustrated, and scared out of his pants, as he drove down the back streets. Lugers and Leggings wouldn't lose shit when it came to this, but for some reason, this psycho came after it and is now killing everything between it and she. Romanov pulled into the driveway of a lavish, two-story house in the suburbs of L.A. Pushing the button to turn his car off, he ran across the driveway and up to the front door.

He damn near pulled the door off its hinges, saying, "Honey, I'm back! Is everything alright?!" A sharp crack echoed through the front room and a searing pain ripped through his left thigh.

"Ah, God!" he cried, collapsing inside the doorway.

"Please, if you're going to cry out to somebody," Kara put her feet up on the dining-room table, "I would highly recommend the only god in this room, *me*." Romanov looked up and saw the bloody and beaten French woman sitting at the dining-room table. Her pistol was lazily pointing at him, its golden barrel smoking from the round it just fired. A strained moan alerted him to another presence in the room, and when he looked, he found his wife and son bound with duct tape. Frantically, he started to call his wife and son's name. Kara waited patiently before pointing her pistol at the kid's head, getting his father's attention.

She chuckled at the look on his face, "Where's my money?"

"My men gave it to you," he said angrily.

She pushed the barrel closer to his son's head, "No, your men tried to give me a stray bitch in the hopes that it would appease me. Now, would you like to tell me the truth now?"

"I don't k—" Kara shot her gun past the kid's face and blew a hole into the wall next to him. He cried as he fell back into his mother; Romanov screaming his name, as well as throwing more obscenities Kara's way.

"Don't bullshit me, Romanov, I am not in the mood. It's your fucking money, no? You should know where your damn money is. Otherwise, you could just give me my guns back," Kara said, still holding the one side of his family at gunpoint. Romanov's breathing began to get even more labored, as his leg went numb, save for a constant and rhythmic throb.

"I don't have them," he mumbled, his sweaty face dripping onto the floor.

Kara turned to him and with a voice as cold as the grave, asked, "Excuse me?"

"Um…"

"That's what I thought you said," Kara pointed her pistol to his wife, "Who did you sell them to? Tell me the truth, or your son is going to live his whole life without his mother, and it will be all your fault."

Romanov set his forehead on the floor and said, "A Chinese Contracting Unit. They were based in Sacramento before they uprooted to Springfield."

"What was their leader's name?" Kara asked, quietly.

"What?"

"What was his goddamn name?"

Romanov shook his head, "Kei. They called him Major Kei." He started to describe what he looked like to a blank-faced Kara; her mind trying to believe the words that were just told to her. The pain in her body suddenly felt numb, as she stood up and caused Romanov to stop mid-sentence.

"You just fucked up really, really bad, Romanov. You fucked up so bad, I'm not going to kill you or your family anymore. No, you need all the help you can get, but then again, I'm willing to bet all the money you stole from me, that you and your family will be hanging from bamboo within a week." Romanov watched, as she got up from her seat and walked past him. She apologized for the mess and walked out the door, after tossing a knife to Romanov so he could cut his family free. Kara walked down the sidewalk and headed in the direction of her hotel; her newfound focus ebbing away the pain in her body.

Ying woke up to bright, white light flooding the window in which she slept; past dreams, reality, and her late-night talk with Lovecraft, all swirling around like a purple tornado in her head. She wiped the crude from her right eye and then moved to her left, before sliding from her windowsill. She hooked her fingers together and reached for the ceiling; she stopped once she heard her shoulders pop. Ying looked around the room and got her bearings, as her memories returned to her. She remembered her conversation with Lovecraft and also remembered that she would need to change into her secondary outfit for today.

The young woman set about doing just that, by grabbing the plastic bag Magnolia had packed for her. The first thing she searched for was underwear and when she found them, Ying was surprised that they were actually her size. Ying had an unusual problem in China when it came to buying underwear; everything was just a bit too small. In a part of the world where women were slim and flat-chested, Ying was the exact opposite, with various curves that most women in the east would die for, and a line of lean muscle that, thanks to her military training, made her look 'normal,' until she tried to lift something. After she lifted something, well, the men started to believe her, when she said that she could curl 60 pounds. Needless to say, shopping for underwear in America would be easier than she thought. Ying quickly put the underwear on after her inspection and found that the main attraction of her clothing was a black tank top and a pair of black cargo pants. Magnolia had included a tan belt with the socks, which Ying laced through her pants' belt loops, after she tucked her shirt in. The last things to make it onto her body were her socks and the white sneakers she had been gifted. Standing up, Ying took a few lazy strides across the room in order to judge the feel, and when she found them satisfactory, she went over to the door and hesitated once she reached for the knob.

Ying looked toward her hand and then back to the door; her mind reinserting the fact that she wouldn't be returning to her room today, directly into her synapses. She contemplated falling back into the same routine of going out, grabbing food, and going back in. Like a hamster running around a wheel. Her ears suddenly heard her grab the knob and turn it; she had already made the decision without making it.

She opened the door and walked into the white-washed hallway where she heard the Russian talking in his booming, accented voice. Casually, she walked into the room, with her tattoos on display for the first time. However, the three men glanced at her and then went back to their food and stories. Normally, Ying would have been a little pissed that they had treated her like a wild animal, but she wasn't stupid. She hadn't given them any reason to treat her like a human.

Ying calmly walked behind Abram, who was sitting next to her food, and made him stop talking once he heard the chair being pulled back. Aaron and Abram both focused their attention on her as she sat down; the extra attention causing her to awkwardly grab her silverware. Lovecraft was the only one to not look at her; his nose buried deep in his data pad.

"You were saying, Abram?" Lovecraft asked, grabbing his coffee and putting it to his lips.

"Er, yes. Well, my wife filed for divorce shortly before my arrival," Abram continued, drawing the attention back onto him and giving Ying an opportunity to breathe before she choked.

"No shit?" Aaron asked.

Abram shook his head, "Said that I'm always going away and leaving her to take care of our kids. She also felt the need to insinuate that I didn't want to be a part of their lives, but one also has to realize that the only reason she was able to afford her mink coats was because of my job."

"Not trying to be insensitive, but it sounds like she had a lover to me," Lovecraft commented, swiping past a story about Congress.

"Don't worry, I already know she did, that's why I got custody of my children."

"Who watches them now?" Aaron asked.

Abram chuckled a bit, "That's the good thing about having nine kids. Your whole house is a colony." A voice piped up amongst them and surprised them.

"They just live by themselves when you're gone?" Ying asked, looking at Abram incredulously. The big man was almost so surprised that he almost forgot to answer.

"No, that was a joke. The eldest is very mature for her age, and she knows that I can't be around all the time to watch the little ones, so she helps me out when I have to leave. But they still stay with my parents. I hope to one day bring them closer to me," Abram explained, still somewhat surprised that Ying was being so talkative. Lovecraft watched the exchange and set his data pad down.

He motioned toward Ying with his hand, "I think it's time you met her. Gentlemen, this is Second Lieutenant, Ying Li, of the Chinese Snow Leopards. Yes, I know that she is technically a prisoner, but while she is staying with us, we will treat her with the same respect and dignity that we would give a guest."

Aaron and Abram both looked at her for a moment and Aaron was the first to extend a hand toward her, "Aaron Castellanos, not your typical Contractor, but one, nonetheless. I assume you can speak good English?" Ying noticed that Aaron seemed to have a twinkle of friendliness to his eyes; something that Lovecraft seemed to lack.

Ying accepted his hand with her opposite, "Immaculate, English."

Aaron smirked, "Good, because I don't know shit when it comes to Chinese." It was as Aaron laughed at himself, that Abram extended a hand to her.

"Abram Sokolov, I'm a Lieutenant in the Russian Spetsnaz's Third Viral Unit." Ying accepted his hand as well, and softly smiled at him. She tried to give him her best, even though she knew that he was technically her enemy. How many Russians had she killed? God, she just couldn't begin to estimate the number, and it hurt her because she remembered every one of their faces; the unique personal relationship that a sniper held with their target was a deep ocean that could swallow even God himself.

Lovecraft watched as Ying got lost in thought upon seeing Abram and decided that he would need to get them back on track.

"So, as you all know, we're going shooting with Marlene and the rest of Eclipse today. Well, Ying is going to come with us." Lovecraft raised a hand when he saw their faces stiffen, "And before you object, let me just say that whether it is a shooting range or our compound, Ying would have the same access to firearms no matter what. At the very least, if she comes with us, there will always be at least one eye on her." Abram and Aaron both looked at each other before Aaron, the younger of the two, spoke.

"As long as somebody watches her, I can live with it. After all, it's not the sketchiest thing we've ever done when holding somebody." Abram nodded in agreement.

"Personally, I would feel safer if we just locked her in her room, but I'm willing to trust your judgment, since it seems to be pretty spot on most of the time."

Abram leaned back in his chair and was just about ready to get up, when Lovecraft said, "Just a moment, there's one more thing and it relates to the Master Case." Abram immediately stopped and looked at Lovecraft. He calmly sat back down and folded his hands in front of his face.

Lovecraft tapped the screen of his data pad a few times and brought up a selection of photographs. He then formed a cone with his hand in the center of the screen, spread his fingers out across its surface, and then did a throwing motion toward the television. The television suddenly came on and the pictures filled its screen, allowing everybody to see them in a higher quality. Ying looked as though she had just seen magic performed, and wondered if Lovecraft was actually a reincarnation of Merlin. She had little time to dwell on this thought, however, because the images placed on it filled her with a mixture of fear and anger.

Lovecraft took a laser pointer from his pocket and pointed it to the first picture which was of a woman being crucified in her living room.

"This was taken about a week ago, in an apartment that borders the Flood Zone. The victim's name is Mary Magdalene, 40 years old, divorced, lives alone." Lovecraft circled the crucifix, "She's also an atheist."

Aaron snorted, "Her name is Mary Magdalene? It's too bad that David's not here to tell a witty joke." Ying cocked an eyebrow at him, "He's our Jewish friend."

As Ying nodded, Abram asked, "Grizzly scene, but how does this involve the Master?" Lovecraft switched to the next picture which was actually surveillance camera footage of from a nearby gas station. The four of them watched intently as the victim walked down the sidewalk and disappeared out of frame, as the video cut to a different area; nothing out of place, nothing abnormal to be found. Lovecraft lit up a cigarette as the woman unlocked the sliding door to her apartment with a keycard, her dark form disappearing behind the heavy, metal door. That was where it ended. Abram and Ying's heads immediately flew back in surprise; their gazes turning back to Lovecraft. Aaron looked at the screen with intrigue.

"I don't get it," Abram admitted.

"Of course you wouldn't, Russia's the fifth when it comes to technological advancement. Noticing this minute of a detail is next to impossible for somebody who doesn't work with much technology," Aaron said, motioning to the video. He rewound it and cut to the part where she stepped through the doorway.

"Now I want you to count how many seconds tick by before the door closes," Aaron instructed, making the video play. Abram started to count and was surprised to find that the door stayed open a full three seconds longer than it needed to.

"It stays open for an extra three seconds."

Aaron chuckled, "Now you're getting it. However, it still doesn't rule out a malfunction, L.C."

Lovecraft rubbed his head, "I was waiting for you and the school children to get finished." He switched to the next clip that showed the same apartment entrance, only it was blacked out and the woman's figure was white. "This is F.L.I.R. video of the area at the same time. The police had a recon drone patrolling the area due to a raid happening in the Flood Zone." He allowed the video to play and the two foreigners were amazed when they saw a second, white figure duck into the building right after the woman. The figure was inside the building in a matter of seconds, to the point that if you didn't immediately see it, you might've missed it.

"Now that is a sight to behold," Aaron said, stretching his arms out, "Active Camo in an infancy stage."

"Active Camo?" Abram asked.

"It's a type of hyper camouflage that bends light. Imagine Predator or the Halo videogames and that's what it's like. However, it's only been around for about five years, and to say that it's not perfect is…an understatement."

"What do you mean?"

Lovecraft stuck his cigarette in a nearby ashtray, "It's so unrefined that it confirms that our attacker is undoubtedly male or, at least, built male. You see, camouflage suits need to be custom made for the user and are about as skintight as a dive suit. Thus, you can't wear definite shapes. This is also the reason why we can rule the female gender out."

"Wait, I don't get it. Why can't women use camouflage suits?" Ying asked, her mind swimming.

"I never said they couldn't, but the easiest way to explain it is men are flatter than women." Lovecraft flicked his eyes down to her chest and then back up to her. She looked down and, like a light bulb flickering on, her brow arced.

"I really don't know what I expected," Ying quietly muttered.

"Neither do I," Lovecraft said, dismissing the conversation.

After it ended, Abram quickly asked, "So it has a problem projecting itself across shapes or just certain ones?"

"The easiest way to tell what it will and will not cover is by taking a protractor to whatever it is. If you can get an even angle out of it, then it won't work. It's easier for it to cover a piece of tile than a piece of bent rebar. It's the reason it's typically seen in use by male operators and not female ones. Female figures are more exaggerated than a male's, thus it's easier for males to use," Aaron explained.

Lovecraft further simplified what he said with, "Its enemy is abundance. If there are too many things for it to process and cover, it'll start to tear and fail." He picked his cigarette back up and put it to his lips, "The only thing that makes no sense is why this random woman got killed. It just makes no damn sense." They all nodded at this fact; it was a random, brutal murder that was carried out, and for seemingly no reason.

Aaron was the first speak up, "We should stop by the crime scene later. After all, it wouldn't be the first time the police missed something that we didn't. However, I believe we are needed in other places." Lovecraft nodded, knowing that if they didn't leave right now, they would be late. Aaron, Abram, and Ying, all excused themselves from the table; the Chinese woman following the two men through a metal door that would lead to the garage. Lovecraft sat there for a moment longer and looked at the picture of the woman, his mind trying to find a purpose in all that blood and gore. He sighed, as no answer presented itself, and tapped the screen of his data pad twice. The image faded to black, as he stood up from the table and pushed his phone and wallet into the pockets of his combat pants.

The drive to the shooting range was a quiet one, but the air was filled with a certain kind of enthusiasm that could only be produced by a young mind seeing modern-day Chicago. They passed by the twisting architecture of the Switchboard building, the monolithic super-structure of the Contractor's Union, and the metallic Super-Skyscrapers that made One World Trade appear as an ant. All this was seen as Susume Hirasawa's *Island Door* was played.

Ying couldn't take her eyes away from any of these things. Chicago was so much *bigger* and refined than Springfield that it should have been the capital instead. The technology here was nothing new, but the sheer quantity of it was shocking. Even China, excluding Beijing, didn't come close to this, and Lovecraft, Aaron, even Abram at points, glanced at it once and then hardly looked back. It was…stunning, that these men didn't care that she would have paid her weight in gold for a chance to glimpse this heavenly view and breathe its air, but then again, these men didn't grow up like she did.

Like a snap of the fingers, the ride was over, and she found herself a little sad that it was over. It was a funny thing when a simple car ride was so interesting that you don't want it to end. However, there were other things that needed to be done.

When Ying got out of the Humvee, she was introduced to the arsenal of weapons that Ruler used, as well as being introduced to Marlene and the other Contractors of Eclipse. They all voiced their concerns about having her present, but still treated her with dignity. Ying took note of their Kryptek Typhon camouflage, a type of layered camouflage that looked like black snakeskin, and then compared them to the mismatched armors and camouflages of Ruler. She would later find out that Eclipse, as the name would suggest, primarily worked at night, where Ruler did everything, so a structured uniform wasn't necessary.

Ying was surprised when she found that even these Contractors were pretty friendly, even though every other word out of the one with the red-and-black hair was a curse word. Ying enjoyed the atmosphere, even though it gave off the 'Favorite Zoo Animal' vibe. Oh well, better to be the best than the one that gets euthanized. The topic of conversation quickly changed to that of Ying's various tattoos, especially the one that covered her entire left arm in black. She explained to them that the Chinese symbols, seemingly etched into her black arm using her natural skin color, meant 'faith' in her language. They all agreed that, at the very least, it was remarkably creative. However, while they were admiring her body art, they also noticed that Ying was starting to form goose bumps from the wind and one of the Eclipse members handed her a grey sweatshirt from inside the truck. After she thanked him, Ying zipped it up to her chin and they all went back to the point of why they came here.

The young Chinese Operator got to witness Ruler running joint drills with Eclipse, and even got to shoot one of their Vector .308 rifles, with someone watching her every move of course. She was a good shot, naturally, and even got an impressed look from Marlene, when she hit three, upper-mass shots in a row, at a distance of 500 yards... with only an Eotech sight. This sight was meant for close quarters and offered little to no magnification. However, when Marlene fetched her Cheytac from the back of their truck, Ying felt her pulse quicken in anticipation.

"Guess what, Lovecraft. Beverly fixed it," Marlene announced, hefting the 31-pound rifle onto the wooden table. This was a good explanation for the big, .408 Cheytac rounds she had slipped inside the M.O.L.L.E. webbing on her plate carrier. Ying couldn't help but notice that Marlene looked winded from just the short journey back to the table.

"Great, what was wrong with it?" Lovecraft asked.

"You'll never believe this, but the tip of the firing pin sheared off in such a way that it could still strike, just not consistently."

"Just the tip?" Aaron chided her with a smirk on his face.

She smirked at him with predatory eyes, "Always just the tip." Everyone laughed, including Ying, who simply chuckled. Dirty jokes weren't really her thing, but she did appreciate them to an extent. Marlene laughed with them, as she grabbed a magazine and pushed it into her sniper rifle's magwell. She unlocked the bolt-action and chambered a round before taking her place behind the rifle. There was a target set up at over two-thousand yards away; a distance that most rifles couldn't even dream of reaching. One of her teammates got on the spotter scope next to her and called the shot. Everyone secured their hearing protection to their heads; an idea already formulating in his head by the time Marlene fired her first round. The target was too far for the naked eye to see so they were relying on the spotter.

"Low. Come up one and left two," he called. Marlene grimaced behind the rifle. She had been trying to hit this target the first time consistently, but had

146

only managed it a handful of times. She adjusted her aim and hit it with the second shot.

Behind her, Lovecraft had withdrawn his wallet and was currently taking out 200 dollars.

"What are you doing?" Aaron asked.

"Betting."

Aaron looked at his friend incredulously, "On?" Lovecraft looked up from his billfold and saw that everyone had their attention focused on him now; the smell of gunpowder permeating the air.

"Two hundred dollars," Lovecraft began, "says that Ying is a better shot than you." The whole area went mute as eyes widened. Ying's mouth was bent like a wire as she looked at Lovecraft; she couldn't believe what he just said.

Aaron's expression was the first one to change and with it, he said, "I'm staying out of this." However, Lovecraft knew that his smirk meant that he was deeply interested in how this would turn out.

Abram was just as interested. Yet, he bet the same amount against her. This made Aaron shake his head; he had learned a long time ago to never bet against Lovecraft. Every time he bet against his boss, and best friend, he rarely won. In fact, he could count his victories on one hand. While this exchange took place, Marlene took it in stride and rechambered the rifle for Ying. She then motioned toward it with her head and the timid woman walked up to it.

The second her small hand touched the textured pistol grip; it was like the world had been swallowed around her. She unzipped her jacket and threw it off her shoulders before pulling the magazine free. She set it off to the side and pulled the bolt back, ejecting the live round. Everyone looked at her in confusion, as they saw her put its end between her lips like a cigarette; her left hand reaching up to adjust the scope. When she had it to her liking, Ying pulled the bullet from her mouth and fed it into the rifle's open bolt; she closed it soon after and held her breath. The shot cracked out the end of the barrel and pushed the 31-pound rifle into Ying's shoulder; her small frame taking it in stride while her eye neither blinked nor watered. She reclined back and smiled at everyone before she took her hearing protection off. The spotter turned to everyone, his face visibly impressed, and said, "Target hit, it was a headshot."

Breaking Benjamin's *Red Cold River* played softly inside the small, Los Angeles hotel room, as Kara pushed herself up and down. She grit her teeth as she pushed on the hand that got stabbed; her eyes hidden behind a mess of sweaty, green hair. She was brazenly dressed in only a pair of black panties, since she would be bathing immediately after this; her defined back muscles rippled beneath fresh welts and old scar tissue. There were the marks left by a whip as it tore flesh; she received that in France. There were puncture marks; those were from glass shards in Iraq. The deep divot in her right side was another one from France, and the large burn mark that covered the nape of her neck, and all the way down between her shoulder blades; that was from her dad. It were these scars that told a story; a story of black spider-webs circling, crisscrossing, weaving, and binding their past. The lights were off in her room and the pink lights from the Californian strip clubs and brothels flooded her area; turning her pale skin pink and the bumps of her scars into black crevasses.

Kara huffed as she hit 50 and rolled onto her side; her back hitting the bathtub. She stood up on bare feet characterized with black nails; the bruises on her front creating holes just as black in her pink appearance. It had been over a day since her shootout in the strip club, but the marks to her face were still present. Yet, her eyes, even though one was blackened, were as sly as a cat. Her lips were as soft as cotton, and her whole body gave off an air of sex that it could be anything but slutty. It was too sultry and commanding to be that of a whore; not even an expensive one could compare to the way she looked, and one was damn sure that she looked better than any actress. These were the three aspects of Kara's life: guns, sex, and pain. The *guns* were her livelihood and passion. The *sex* was her victory speech; a gift to herself for making it one more day. The *pain* was her past, the black chains sprawling across her back that sought to take it all away.

Kara stood up and grabbed her Marlboros off the sink and lit one, before waving the match out. She tossed the stick into the trash where it joined a few tissues, several bloody bandages, and a couple of used condoms. The arms dealer stood there, bare chested, looking out on the street, as the pink turned to white. She smelled of sweat, blood, and cigarette smoke, as her green eyes watched the prostitutes trying to invite strangers to play. When she first arrived, she had wondered why there was a vertical window in the bathroom, but now, she believed the answer presented itself. She watched as two Contractors stopped in front of the brothel and in a matter of seconds, they were inside. The white intensified as Kara took the last drag from her cigarette, flicking the butt into the sink. She turned around to the bathtub, which she had already filled with water, and grabbed two bags of ice sitting next to one of its legs. She dumped both bags into the water and then dropped her panties to the floor. Kara stepped into the ice water and gasped as she sank into the arctic water.

She rested her neck against the lip of the tub; the white light coming from the window making her appear as a black silhouette. She sucked in air, and in one movement, fully submerged herself. The green-haired vixen came back up and gasped for air; her body gradually going numb. This bath was not meant to cleanse her or to make her smell better; it was to take away the pain of her injuries. The cuts on her face stung and some even bled a bit, but none marred her image. Her body was almost numb, save for the tops of her breasts, her shoulders, and her arms which were resting on the tub's sides. It was at the point that she couldn't feel her toes and was beginning to lose feeling in her privates, when she heard a knock on her door.

"Enter," she commanded. The door squeaked open and then shut; a pair of footsteps echoing across the hardwood floors of the bedroom. Kara's green eyes turned toward the bathroom door and watched a short, flat-chested woman, dressed in a suit and tie, wander her way into the room. Her white face was framed by layered, blood-red hair, and her eyes were hidden behind the lenses of her glasses; the white light blocking them out. Her name was Monica Chevrolet, Kara's personal bodyguard.

"Good evening, Ma'am," she greeted, in a French accent much thicker than Kara's.

The weapons dealer clicked her tongue in response, "I suppose it is a good evening, but if it was truly a 'good evening,' I wouldn't be taking an ice bath."

"I suppose saying, 'I told you so' wouldn't allow me to get my paycheck faster, would it?"

"No, but it will get your tongue cut out." Kara stood up and this action got some droplets of water on Monica's glasses. Her bodyguard stepped back and pulled a white cloth from her jacket pocket. Having stepped back into the darkness, Monica pulled her glasses off and cleaned them. Two eyes like sapphires danced in the darkened room before being hidden behind the glare of her glasses once again. In the time it took her to clean them, Kara had covered her nakedness with a white bathrobe; although, it was loosely tied and barely covered her breasts. To Monica, the way that Kara seemed unconcerned with whom saw her naked kind of reminded her of the ancient queens throughout history. Those women would have servants around them 24/7 in order to cater to their every need and this did not exclude bathing. It was for this reason that most of them felt no shame when being seen naked. Kara, on the other hand, rarely used Monica for anything, so she simply deduced that she was either born with an unnaturally high form of confidence, or she had an abnormal sense of maturity that found nudity to be normal. After all, everyone was naked underneath their clothes.

"The Chinese will come for us," Kara suddenly said, turning one of the circular lamps on. Her prediction pulled Monica from her musings and caused her to turn toward her stead. She watched her grab a bottle of bourbon laying on the bedside table and unscrewed its lid. She took a drink straight from the bottle. It was a gift from her lover whom she had met more than a few hours prior.

"Isn't it a little late to be drinking?" Monica asked, referencing the fact the clock read a quarter to 12. Kara held up her index finger, signaling for her to wait, and walked into the bathroom once again. She spit the alcohol into the sink and dumped the rest of the bottle as well.

"So not only was he a big fuckin' creep, he couldn't buy good bourbon either. Thank God, he doesn't know my real name," Kara muttered under her breath, "You don't seem to be too concerned, Mon."

"Whether it's the P.R.C., Colombian F.A.R.C., or the French Conglomerate's G.I.G.N., I have no doubt we will win. After all, they can't destroy what they can't find." Monica focused her attention on the now-empty bottle, "Was he good for anything?"

Kara already knew the question she was asking and side-eyed her before slowly shaking her head, "20-year-olds can't do *anything* right."

Monica frowned and nodded just as slowly, "Satisfied?"

"Nope."

She also understood that and then asked, "What was the story behind the injuries?" Kara left the bottle in sink and turned around. She braced her rear end against the counter and folded her arms.

"Dirt bike accident," Kara smirked, "He believed it too. Although, he was staring at my tits when I told him, so I doubt he even heard it." Monica closed her eyes and shook her head in amusement.

Kara's face fell a little bit after the answer, "Monica, contact the others and tell them to be on high alert. We're leaving tomorrow."

"Of course, Ma'am."

"Also tell them to be ready for anything and that every suspicious person should have a gun pointed at them," Kara added, walking back into the bedroom. Monica nodded, but made no move to leave.

Kara turned to her, "You have permission to get out of my room now."

"With all due respect, Ma'am, it would put my mind at ease if I kept guard," Monica explained.

Kara shook her head, "You're not going to stay in here because I am not getting dressed till morning. Why? Because I'm tired, and in order to not be tired, I need sleep. I cannot sleep knowing that you are in here, one bed sheet away. Clear?" she asked in French.

"But what if the unthinkable happens and I can't get to you?" Monica countered in French as well. Kara backed away, turned toward the bed, and slipped the robe off her shoulders.

"Monica, get out of my room." Seeing that there would be no changing her mind, Monica conceded and opened the door.

"Wake me up at seven," Kara commanded, giving her the last order. Monica nodded and closed the door.

She stepped out into the brightly lit hallway and looked both ways. To her right, she saw a maid gently folding towels for a vacant room, and on her left, there was a tall, tanned man talking on his cellphone. Her eyes met theirs and when she nodded, they immediately went back to what they were doing. Monica then entered her room across the hall and shut the door.

Inside, she set the alarm for six o'clock and pulled her tie free; she felt like she had just unwound a noose. She threw her jacket on the bed and unbuttoned the top two buttons of her shirt. She took a quick shower after this and simply put her shirt and slacks back on. Monica moved back over to her bed, water still dripping from her hair, and grabbed her suitcase from underneath of it. Opening it up, Monica pulled a tan-plate carrier out of it. She slipped it over her head and then grabbed her holster. She fastened that to her leg and cocked her pistol, before slipping that inside the synthetic apparatus. The last thing she pulled from it was her M4 carbine. She checked her Eotech holographic sight and also pull-checked its ammunition, before she pulled the bolt back and chambered a round. Turning around, Monica sat down and braced her back against the door, her rifle held in her hands. This was how she fell asleep.

Chapter 9
The Legion of Grey Men

Pots and pans banged together, as forks and knives scrapped last bits from ceramic plates. Ying scrapped the last bits of her third helping into her mouth, and she was finally satisfied. She set the plate down and closed her eyes, as she sighed lazily. Aaron and Abram looked at each other; they had just recently, very recently, discovered that Ying had an unusually large appetite that directly contradicted her 125-pound frame. Aaron grimaced at the thought of having to buy more food the longer she stayed there.

Through all of this, there was yet another thing that was interesting at this table. It was the now-cold plate of food where Lovecraft usually sat. The three of them had noticed right away when he wasn't already out here, but now, Aaron began to get concerned. He quickly dried his hands and began his march toward Lovecraft's room. When he arrived, he took ahold of the doorknob and opened it, only to find Lovecraft not there. Aaron blinked a few times before turning in the direction of the laundry area, which was also the direction of the roof. On cue, Lovecraft rounded the corner and was walking at such a brisk pace that his boots seemed heavier than they were.

"Lovecraft, something happened, didn't it?" Aaron surmised, as his friend blew past him. He walked in and said, "Everybody, weapons." Abram stood up and immediately jogged to his room. Lovecraft turned to Aaron as Ying stood up, "Something very bad happened." He then pulled a pair of wire handcuffs from his belt and turned to their Chinese counterpart, "Ying."

Back in Los Angeles, Kara had just got off the phone with Lovecraft and was currently slipping a pair of black yoga pants around her waist. She was still sore, unsurprisingly, and this brought a plethora of colorful words to her red lips, as she put her bra on. After this, Kara slipped a black Metallica tee shirt over herself and then pulled a leather jacket over that. She frowned as she put a finger through one of the bullet holes in her trench coat. This meant she was going to have to get it repaired and, unfortunately, Nano weave was anything but cheap. She huffed as she folded it and stuffed it inside of her suitcase. The last thing she did was to wrap her tac belt around her waist and to clip her drop leg holster around her upper thigh. She slipped her Grizzly inside of it soon after; her airbrushed nails sparkling just like its gold accents.

Outside of the hotel, an Asian man in an expensive suit walked down a dirty and damp alleyway. Five stars were tattooed on his right hand and as he walked, a homeless man watched him curiously. He tried to get out of the sight of any prying eyes, and pulled out a silver phone.

He hit a certain contact and said, "Inform the Major, I have found the root of our problem. Current location: 2436 Tack road. She's on—"

"Excuse me, sir. Do you have the time?" a voice asked him from behind.

"What?" he asked in Chinese, before the soft crack of a suppressed nine-millimeter made him drop to the ground. A pool of blood spun around his head like the remains of a dying star. The homeless man stood over him with a silver Beretta M9 and shot him in the gut two more times, before shooting the phone as well. He pulled off the dirty raincoat, the perfect camouflage for the urban jungle, and revealed that he was wearing another tan-plate carrier just like Monica's. He had a holster strapped to his hip and no patches, flags, or even a name attached to his gear. The man turned around and pulled his own phone out and dialed Monica's number. As it rang, he holstered his weapon and pulled his M4A1 from a nearby trash can.

The red-headed, head of security, stood outside of Kara's door and waited patiently for her ward to emerge. The maid from last night was back again and this time, was emptying garbage cans. The man from last night was there only in spirit, since he was currently in his room, but the door was fully open.

Monica's phone suddenly rang and startled everyone except its owner, who casually grabbed it from her pocket and put it to her ear. There were no words said. She pulled it away from her ear and returned it to her pants pocket. She pushed her glasses up the bridge of her nose and rolled her M4 over to her front. She pulled its bolt back in order to check to see if she had a round chambered and then pressed the forward assist to make sure it closed. After this, Monica formed a fist with her gloved left hand and hit Kara's door three, distinct times.

Kara looked at the door and sighed, as she pulled her cigarettes from her jacket pocket, "So that's how they want to do this." She grabbed a match and lit the cigarette, before pulling her pistol out to check its chamber. She found it was loaded and then returned it to her holster, before standing up to grab her suitcase.

Outside, Monica's signal had alerted the maid and the direct result was her pulling the trash bag out of her cart and then pulled another tan-plate carrier from underneath it. She quickly stripped out of her uniform, leaving herself in just a white tank top and a pair of grey slacks, and slipped her body armor over her head. A Glock pistol was then pulled from the bottom of the bin, as well as a tan baseball cap.

The man from the other end of the hallway suddenly emerged from his room, with his torso covered in body armor, as well as a Nexter, Famas F2 in his hands. The door behind Monica opened and the three of them turned to see Kara standing there.

"Ready?" Monica asked. Kara nodded and the three of them formed a cone around her, Monica at the front, the maid to her right, and the man to her left. They started to walk at brisk pace, their shoes making a haphazard marching sound. They all piled into the elevator.

"Last chance to check weapons and ammo," Monica said, just before they hit the ground floor. Her two comrades quickly ejected their magazines and then returned them to their weapons just before the doors opened.

They thrust themselves onto a marble platform and then down a set of bronzed stairs that shimmered in the light of the chandeliers. A woman clad in a mink coat screamed, as she saw them rushing down the stairs with their firearms. The security guards started to draw their guns, but stopped, once two men, dressed in black suits, pulled G36C carbines out of their briefcases. The handle of the briefcases had, in fact, been the rifle's carry handle. They pointed their red lasers at their hearts and ordered them to get on the floor. Monica led Kara and the rest out the door, just as the guards touched their faces to the marble.

Outside, the air was dry, salty, and hot, as they jumped down the concrete stairs; hearts going 90 miles per hour. Civilians screamed, as they saw them running toward them with weapons drawn. It were these people that they pushed out of the way, as they made it to the street. An old, silver Toyota came screeching to a halt, as their shoes came to the end of the curb. Sammy was driving it.

"Get in!" he yelled, moving over to the passenger seat. Monica turned to her comrades, as Kara got in the back seat.

"You two," she ordered, "Go with Lawrence." They nodded and started running over to the alleyway, as Monica climbed into the driver's seat; Vinny grabbed her M4 and held it close to his chest – ready to fire at anything in front of them. Monica shut her door and then threw the car into reverse, before pulling onto the street and driving away. The two men in suits hopped inside a different car and followed them.

As they sped through the city, they dawned a headset each, with Kara being the leader. She gave the order to be extremely vigilant and to keep all radio chatter to a minimum; they didn't need to be inundated with useless speech.

Monica and Vinny were both trying to keep as low a profile as they could. Yet, getting out of the state was going to be a problem.

"What's the plan here, Kara?" Monica suddenly asked, getting through the green light.

Kara made sure to keep looking once in a while, "Utah. Cross the border into Utah and from there, we can get a flight back to Chicago."

"That's a long stretch, ma'am. How can we make it without taking contact?" Sammy asked.

"By trying it," Kara answered, "Besides, I have the distinct feeling that our beloved Major Kei doesn't treat fuckups very well. Thus, these men will want to deal with us as quickly as they can. Plus, I don't think he knows that Lovecraft has his sniper," she mumbled this last part.

"What was that?" Monica asked.

"Nothing, it's a situation to be discussed when we are out of our current one." Kara turned around again and saw her men, the ones in the black suits, pull down a different street, and, as much as Kara didn't want to admit it, this made her pulse quicken. They continued to drive without them, and as they approached the city limits, their journey started to stall.

"You've got to be fuckin' kidding me," Monica swore, as she fluttered the brakes. The car set at the beginning of a massive, seven-lane onramp that would allow them to get on the Interstate. However, all seven lanes were currently stopped at the checkpoints and backed up for at least three blocks. Police and social service drones flew around the backup like curious bees; their zipping about doing nothing to help one's nerves.

"Here's the deal," a voice suddenly spoke over the radio, "a vehicle broke down in the far-right lane and emergency crews are trying to get it sorted. However, it could be a while."

Monica slumped in her seat, "Great, just what I wanted to do today; what a pain in the balls." Silence fell after her complaint and the three of them proceeded to use every mirror and every angle to watch for the enemy. Kara looked to her left and saw a woman messing with the front of a pink stroller; apparently her kid was being fussy. Next to her stood a man busily talking on his phone.

Kara then turned to her right and was treated to the sight of another homeless man digging in the trash.

"Sniper team in position," cracked over the radio rather suddenly.

Monica put a hand up to her ear, "Affirmative." Kara kept watching the smoldering world behind them. In one of the far-left lanes, there was massive, white-and-brown Pit bull, barking his lousy head off, but it was muffled by the sound of a Blackhawk helicopter flying over them. A slight movement at the front clued Kara into the fact that Vinny had just slipped his sunglasses onto his head. She turned around and her eyes locked onto an old Ford; the driver having one hand on the steering wheel and the other one hidden from view. Kara took note of how he would every once and a while talk to himself.

She slowly turned away and reached up to her headset, "Blue Fusion, two lanes right, three cars behind us." Vinny and Monica both rolled their windows down. Vinny brought Monica's rifle up to his shoulder; barrel semi-pointed toward the window, while Monica pulled her Five Seven pistol from her holster with a hollow click. Kara pulled her pistol free of its holster and moved over to the left side of the backseat.

"Green Camry, four lanes left, two cars behind you," another voice said over the radio. Monica shifted her view, as Kara put her legs up on the seat and made herself as small as she possibly could. Monica's eyes saw the silhouette of a QBZ-95 type rifle, and her hand immediately flew up to her ear

"Gun! Gun in the Camry," Monica took her pistol into both hands.

"What are rules here?" another unknown voice asked.

"We must be engaged to engage," Kara replied.

Another voice came over the radio and asked, "Permission to blow cover and set up a perimeter?"

"Negative, maintain cover. If they move, then you move." Monica and Vinny took a tan scarf out of their pockets and tied them around their heads, effectively covering their faces.

"Ma'am, your lane is starting to clear. If something's coming, it's coming now." Sammy and Monica put a hand on the door handle, ready to storm out the minute anything happened.

"Remember how to say, 'Don't shoot me,' in Chinese?" Sammy asked, chuckling.

"Very funny," Monica replied. The three of them watched the two cars; their hearts pounding in their ears. Vinny wiped the sweat from his brow and flicked it onto the floorboards.

The car doors opened up randomly and, as if they were lightning, Monica and Vinny were out of their seats. Both of them pushed to separate cars, as six men in Multicam pants, tan-plate carriers, and equally tan hats, jumped out of a nearby S.U.V. Their faces were covered with balaclavas and their carriers featured no insignia. They pointed their M4A1 and Famas rifles at the men inside the green Camry.

Another four men jumped out of a nearby van and surrounded the Ford Fusion, as Monica joined them, with pistol pointing toward the driver. Kara looked to either side of the street and smirked when she saw the woman, who previously had been messing with her stroller, pull a HK MP7 from it. The man that was on his phone also joined her with a concealed pistol. They joined the rest and forced two civilians, who had gotten out of their cars in the confusion, to the ground, tying their hands behind their backs with wire ties.

"Stop, stop, stop," Monica commanded in Chinese, "Peace. Peace. Drop the rifle." Vinny heard her over the radio and glanced over to her, with his rifle still pointed at the men in the Camry. The men in Monica's car uncertain and threatened glance.

"Hey, do you want to die? Drop the guns. Drop them and everybody goes home." Their leader didn't respond and just kept looking around; his QBZ still clutched with an iron grip. He made his decision by slightly pulling his arms up and it was in this same moment that his right eye disappeared, and the back of his head erupted. Monica shifted her aim and set two rounds through the windshield, as her comrade sent two rounds through it as well. Two heads in the back seat simultaneously flew back, as the car was riddled with bullets.

Vinny held his gaze close to the men in his car and slowly shook his head when they made no move. He slowly started to turn around, but was back on them in a flash when he heard door open further. He put four bullets into the window, killing those men while his backup killed the men in the backseat. Monica peered inside the car once the shooting stopped and grabbed a cellphone just before they heard the sound of screeching tires. Everybody turned and pointed their guns toward the end of the block, just in time to see an S.U.V. barely clear the corner. It turned toward them and went even faster, as it began being riddled with bullets. An impressively loud shot echoed through the buildings and the bullet impacted the S.U.V.'s hood, covering the windshield in fluid and white smoke. Kara's men recognized it as the Sniper Team's 50-caliber Hecate rifle.

The vehicle rolled to a stop in front of another alleyway where the maid from the hotel stood in the back of an old, white pickup. A black barrel stuck out above the cab and the wood buttstock of a PKM was buried in her shoulder. She pulled the trigger all the way back into its recess, tracers of hot fire ripped through the door, windows, and the occupants. The driver's side door fell off before she stopped firing, and with it came the mangled, butchered body of the driver. She stopped after seeing this and tapped the roof of the cab.

Hearing the signal, Lawrence, the same man who killed the Asian man in the alley, hit the gas and joined his comrades on the road. Kara's men packed inside their respective vehicles and got in line behind their boss's car, which Monica and Vinny nearly threw themselves inside; they were moving so fast.

"This is about to be on every news outlet in the country," one of the men said on the radio. Monica smirked as she pushed through the checkpoint; the guards having fled long before.

She scoffed into her radio, "You shitting me? This won't make even make the news in San Antonio." Monica then pulled the captured phone from her pocket and handed it to Kara, "Here, ma'am, a souvenir." Kara grabbed it with calloused fingers and her lips curled into a smile. She had the good Major by the balls, and he didn't even know it yet.

"Wait and hope, Mr. Kei," Kara muttered in her native language. Their convoy sped toward the Californian border; the world getting more pristine as they approached it.

A chilled wind rippled through Lovecraft's hair, as he sat atop the compound that Ruler called home. The grey clouds above him reflected his mind, as he held a half-empty glass of bourbon in his hand. He had just returned with the rest of his team, including Ying, from the Police Department, where they had spent the last four hours interrogating the Chinese sniper once again. He had asked her about Romanov, the orders she was given, and Kei's plan. However, the moron was mum on all subjects and it eventually went nowhere. Needless to say, Lovecraft was frustrated, and Ying wasn't his favorite person in the world right now. He suddenly heard the rooftop door squeak open, pulling him from his annoyed musings.

"I thought I'd find you up here," Aaron said, beer in hand.

"You act like I'm Houdini."

"Well, back in the day, you were. Don't tell me you can't remember the days when Pamela would be at an utter loss as to where you went. Oh, and let's not also forget the times that you were at school for first roll call and then weren't seen for the rest of the day. Where did you even go during that time anyway?" Aaron asked, putting his back against an air conditioner.

Lovecraft kind of chuckled, "The woman in the office. God, what was her name? She would always go to the bathroom at the same time every morning, so I just walked out. After that, I would go to the library and drink free coffee while reading."

"You are still the only person I know who skipped school, yet didn't skip school."

"I'm also the only person you know who fucked the married P.E. teacher." Aaron laughed, shaking his head and rolling his eyes. Until this point, he had forgotten about that.

"True," he let this conversation run its course before switching to the reason that brought him here, "So what's next?"

"What do you mean?"

"What do we do next? Do we prepare to take on Kei and potentially start a war with the Chinese, or do we hand Ying over to the feds and have her tried for treason?" Lovecraft frowned and dumped his drink onto the ground below. He stood up and set his glass on a nearby air duct.

"Neither, we're going to have to go to the Governor tomorrow, but Kara will also be back that same day."

"You're intending for her to use the Legion of Grey Men against them, aren't you?"

"The Legion is already stateside, and more are on their way. Romanov and, to a lesser extent, Kei, stole from the wrong woman. You can almost hear the war drums and can feel the heat from Kara's rage."

"How do we know that the city will not be caught in the crossfire?" Aaron asked, crossing his arms.

"Simple, we keep Ying a secret as long as we can. In the end, no matter what cards Kei holds, we have him by the balls. For now though, we focus on the Master. He is our one, true goal."

"Fine with me, but…what happens if Ying is found to be alive and with us?" Lovecraft took a moment and shoved his hands inside his pockets. The chilled winds making his bare arms flinch.

"Then we focus on the Chinese and humiliate them."

"Humiliate?"

"Beat them so far into the dirt that they forget what the sun looks like. That's how you beat an arrogant Communist." Lovecraft walked past him and headed toward the door. Ying, who had been listening in on their conversation, quickly went back down the stairs and retreated back into her room.

She shut the door and climbed into the window; the bright light turning her left side white and her right-side gray. Her hands found the last Praxis Knife she possessed and stared into its red blade. Ying rolled its handle between her fingers a couple times, before her eyes gently shifted to the pin that was still in the bottom of it. She contemplated just pulling the pin and holding it close to her chest, maybe that would just end all of this – revert it back to the way things were. After all, it wasn't so bad, was it? An old ashtray crashed to the floor. Startled, Ying turned toward the noise and were met with a pair of eyes very similar to her own.

"Of course, Ying. I'm not so bad, am I?" Kei asked, before crashing his lips into hers. She screamed into her mouth, as her wounds opened again, and the pain shot through her like she had just stepped on a mine. She could feel her bones breaking, muscles tearing, eyes swelling shut. Ying could taste her bloody tears and her numb privates once more; it was too familiar. However, there was one thing she noticed during this, it was faint, like a glimmer of imaginary sunshine, but she was adamantly aware of her own hands and how they were unrestrained. She felt each of the five fingers on her right-hand curl into a fist like they were old, rusty hinges on a long-lost door. Her fist flew through the air and as it was about to make contact with Kei, the dream faded, and Ying woke up in the same windowsill.

Raindrops were pelting the window as she hastily checked her surroundings; the clock telling her that it was around nine and that she had been asleep for over five hours. She put her hand through her hair and just left her hand on her head, trying to make sense of what she had just seen and done.

"You alright?" came from her door. Scared, she jerked her head up and saw Abram looking at her; his bearded face half concealed by the door.

Breathing in relief, she said, "I'm fine." Abram nodded and disappeared into the dark hallway; his heavy footsteps leading to an opening, and a closing, of a door. Ying looked down at the floor after he left and found that her knife had slipped from her hands. She picked it up and in its, blade she searched for memories long buried.

She remembered her mom, her dad, and her little brother. Ying remembered their rice farm in Beijing, and she remembered those humid summers and cold winters. She remembered when her dad would sit with her by the fire. She remembered when her mom dressed her up for her birthday and made her feel like an empress. Ying remembered when she used to play with her brother by the creek and they would swear like the sailors they pretended to be.

She flipped it over to opposite side and remembered the day she was stolen. She remembered watching the violation of her mother, the execution of her father, and the beating of her brother. They wrapped barbed wire around their necks and pulled it so tight that it almost beheaded them before they were buried in graves with no marker. Ying remembered watching their farm go up in flames, as she hauled off in a military truck; the humiliation and sting of heat only added to her tears. The last things she remembered before putting a vice grip around the knife were the first words, Kei's first words, to her, "Memories, emotion, *all* is now mine."

"Liar," Ying muttered in Chinese, running her fingers over the blade's edge. She didn't know why she suddenly felt this fire within her chest, nor did she know why it had taken so long to surface, but now, she understood what she had been given by being taken into Lovecraft's care: a chance to be more than a pawn.

Ying jumped down from her perch, walked across the room, and into the hallway. She found herself in front of Lovecraft's door yet again, and she felt the familiar signs of her nerves as she stood there. However, she sucked in a breath and exhaled through her nose before knocking on the door.

"Enter," Lovecraft's voice beckoned from the inside. Ying took ahold of the doorknob and let herself in. The soft light colored her skin in orange and the cigarette smoke burned her nostrils; Lovecraft was to her immediate right, typing an email on his computer.

"What is it?" he asked, turning in his chair.

Ying licked her bottom lip, "It's about my commanding officer...Major Kei Ming. I want to help take him down."

"Yeah? And why should I believe you?" he turned back to his computer and used a pencil to scribble something down on paper. He wrote it in cursive, meaning Ying had no chance of reading what it was. The question that Lovecraft asked her was so cold that it cut straight to the core and stung worse than anything she had ever felt in life, but something told her this was the first step. The first in many to clean her blighted path.

"They call me *Ruthless*, and it is a nickname I do not deny. I am the scourge of the Russian border." She waited to see if her admission would have any effect on Lovecraft, but he either already knew or he didn't care. She got the feeling that it was a little bit of both.

"However, I didn't join the military willingly."

Lovecraft put his pencil down, "Conscription is nothing new, Ying. Shit happens and, unfortunately, China stepped in a big pile of it."

Ying shook her head, "I wasn't conscripted, at least, not in the traditional sense."

"And just what are you insinuating, Ying?" Lovecraft asked, turning to her once again. Ying spied a chair on the opposite side of the room and grabbed it. Sitting in front of Lovecraft, she began, "In 2037, I was 14 years old, and that same year, I was kidnapped by the Chinese military. The government wanted a fresh batch of recruits for the S.L.C.U.; ones that could be molded into perfect killing machines that could feel nothing. After all, how can you feel remorse when you've forgotten what it is? Enter kids like me. They kidnapped 500 children and put them into the most brutal training regime imaginable; so brutal, that some died, and only 12 remained. Seven boys and four girls survived and were officially enlisted; we were as cold and as unthinking as a grave. They had killed our parents and siblings, covered them with a shroud of accident, and stripped away our humanity; the boys, tempered with vice until they became like animals. The girls were tempered with pain and molestation. Kei was one of these kids, as well, and while others torment stopped once they were put in their squads, I wasn't so lucky."

"I take it that's when you got pregnant," Lovecraft surmised in his naturally stoic voice.

Ying kind of flinched at this and wringed her hands like a towel, "Yeah, it wasn't that long of an event though, so I try not to think about it."

"I'm sorry," Lovecraft continued writing, "Can you prove any of this?" She nodded and then put her hands on her knees; she couldn't help but think that her story had little effect on him.

Lovecraft put his pencil down and said, "In the last few hours, I have been implored by many to remove this threat from U.S. soil. However, that is not so simple for us right now."

Ying looked at him incredulously, "So you're just not going to do anything?!"

"Don't put words into my mouth, woman, or you may just find yours being slapped." Ying sat back in her seat like a puppy. "What I mean is we are very few, and we cannot do everything. So I need some incentive to put my main case on the back burner for yours." Ying's face fell as she realized what he meant. Lovecraft was a man of reason and if he didn't have a clear reason for doing something, then it would never happen.

"I don't have anything I can give you, unless…" she looked down at her belt buckle.

"Don't you even think about it. I'm not some bitch in heat like your major. Plus…you wouldn't be that much fun anyway."

Ying was slightly taken aback, "What's that supposed to mean?"

Lovecraft had to chuckle a bit, she was so close yet so far away, "It means that sex with you must be the most boring thing imaginable. Please, Ying, do you really think a guy like me would get off to a cheap thrill like you? I'm not 16."

"I am not some fucking cheap thrill!!" she said, getting more pissed off.

"Oh yeah? Then quit letting Kei fuck you like you are," Lovecraft leaned in close to her with venom in his words, "I am not stupid, Ying. Somehow, you keep forgetting this. Here, he can't fuck you physically, but mentally, you still think you're an object on the level of a dog park. You're just there to be walked and shit on. You walked in here with a lot of confidence, Ying, but can you walk up to Kei with the same confidence?"

Ying's face fell and started to look at her hands, as she thought about his question. She wanted to cry when she found that she really didn't know if she could. Her head was a mess and she was getting progressively more exhausted; her nerves were wearing her down. However, it was in this relaxed state that her mind brought back another memory that had been scrubbed away. Her mom picked her up after she had fallen down and told her in a stern, yet gentle voice, *"Ying, big girls don't cry."* With this, Ying realized how much she had truly forgotten, and how much she had truly forsaken her parents. She furrowed her brow and then looked back up at Lovecraft.

"I... I don't have any way to pay you in by traditional means. As you can see, I don't have that many things anymore, and my pay is more of a formality, but what I can offer is my help. Either way, I was trained as Special Forces, and have the necessary skills to do that job and do it well. Plus, this 'Master Case' has piqued my interest and I believe that it may have something to do with how I ended up in your care to begin with."

Lovecraft was impressed with Ying's offer, "Alright, let me straighten that out for you. How about I keep you out of prison and in exchange, you help us with this section of the Master Case? After that, you would be free to leave and start a new life if you want to."

"And you promise to deal with Kei?"

"Of course, but not immediately. If you're asking me to do this, then you are agreeing to follow my lead and to treat me as your new commanding officer. With that, I intend to stay out of the fight with Kei until it is absolutely necessary for us to respond. God willing, Kei stays down in Springfield and never learns that you survived."

"Why is that so important?"

"Don't be stupid, Ying, if he finds out that you're alive and tracks you down to here, it will mean open season for all of us. We'd have to find a place to hide you while trying to figure out how best to counterattack, and it would just be a shit show."

Ying's shoulders fell, but she couldn't argue his point. Given the current situation, she was more of a refugee than a prisoner, but at the same time, she was more of a civilian than a soldier. She had no gun, no ammunition, no gear, and no orders. The only thing she had was her knife and wits. She knew that while trusting Lovecraft was basically trusting the enemy, a lighter version of Stockholm syndrome, she had to reason that she wasn't exactly the good guy here. Ying pursed her lips and forced her right hand into a fist and then released it. She then held it out toward Lovecraft, who accepted it.

"Tell me, Lovecraft, have you ever failed a promise?"

Lovecraft furrowed his brow as dull, dark memories filled his consciousness, "One time and never again."

The next day dawned and black storm clouds rippled, with lightning above the tall skyscrapers who lazily blinked their red lights toward God. Holographic advertisements and severe thunderstorm warnings sizzled in the rain, as their projected light was refracted one too many times. The heavy torrent pelted the window where Ying's head resided; her lower half covered in a thin blanket. Her arms were crossed, and her back was braced up with a pillow; all anonymous gifts from Abram after she had fallen asleep. Her brow suddenly furrowed in resistance, as a particularly loud drop hit the window; her eyes barely opening as her head rose. The whole room was blurry and unrecognizable, before she rubbed the sleep from her eyes; the unfamiliar blanket and pillow coming into the view of her senses. Ying looked at it with confused curiosity and rubbed it between her fingers; it stuck to her pajama pants like Velcro. Letting it fall back to its place, she stretched out with a loud groan and felt her shoulders and hips pop; yet another sign that she was getting old.

Swinging her legs over the ledge, she rolled her neck and felt that pop multiple times. The blue carpet she stepped onto looked like it was straight out of the 90s, but it was really something she hadn't noticed, and so long as her bare feet didn't get cold, she really didn't care. Ying slowly grabbed her clothes, a simple, black tee shirt and black jeans, and also grabbed her toothbrush and toothpaste.

A loud stretch of thunder rocked the clouds, air, and the building, as Ying opened her bedroom door. She hobbled down the hallway and met Aaron who was walking toward the kitchen with a coffee mug in his hand.

"Good morning," he greeted, watching the woman act like a zombie. She half-muttered something in Chinese and kept walking toward the bathroom. Aaron watched, as she disappeared behind the door and turned the water on. If Aaron was skeptical about her not being a morning person, then this exchange just shot that notion in the head. He continued his trek to the kitchen and started to prepare breakfast. Lovecraft was sitting at his usual seat and had his CZ99 pulled apart in front of him. He was busily cleaning it, while occasionally looking up at the muted T.V. which was tuned into the news.

He heard the sound of rain intensify and when he looked to the source, he found that Abram was dressed in his combat gear, standing in the doorway, watching the rain. To be honest, it was the first time that morning that Aaron had noticed the rain; he had been distracted and was a little behind.

"Maybe we'll get a tornado," Aaron commented, walking over to the fridge.

Lovecraft scoffed, "This early in the year? I'd eat my own tongue."

"Come on, Bro, you remember that time when we were in Indiana and we had one in late February?"

"God, that was a fucking shit show. Never in my life, even in Nebraska, have I ever seen one that early," Lovecraft redirected his voice to Abram, "You ever been in a tornado, Abram?"

The Russian turned toward him and said, "No, I've had my fair share of bad storms, but this is a spectacle. Although, it's not as cold as Siberia during a storm." It was after he said this that they heard one of the bathroom doors shut and Ying trotted her way into the room, almost tripping over her own shoelaces as she sat down to Lovecraft's right – back turned to the kitchen. She put her head face down on the table and exhaled.

"Good morning, Ying," Lovecraft greeted the mass of wet hair.

"It's not even morning though," she whined. Lovecraft looked at the clock and smirked, when he saw that it was only seven o'clock.

"Well, Ying, A.M. does signify morning," Lovecraft said, snapping his pistol back together. She rolled her head on the table in response to his words. It was after this that Aaron got breakfast ready and it was discovered that the easiest way to wake the young woman was to bribe her with food. The four of them ate their fill and it was as they picked their teeth clean that Lovecraft briefed everyone on what would be happening today.

"Kara's coming back today," Lovecraft began, "and the Legion are already here, and more are entering the country. This was all because of a deal with Karl Romanov, a Lithuanian national, where Kara sold him guns that were then donated to the Chinese Snow Leopards. Mind you, that this was all done without paying Kara, or Lugers and Leggings. Because of this, the idea that we can simply hide from the Chinese is not as solid as we once thought, and as much as we'd like to think otherwise, Ruler is not capable of taking on Ying's former allies in a head on fight. Thus, against my better judgment, we are taking Kara with us to Springfield, where we will meet Barons and Governor Fairhill. There, we will try and formulate a plan to deal with the Chinese, should the veil lift and we are suddenly thrust into the crosshairs." Lovecraft took a final sip from his coffee, "Are there any questions?"

Aaron flexed his hand forward, "Are you sure it's a good idea to bring Ying? There's a high possibility that the Chinese could not only see her, but recognize her."

"I know, but if we hide her well enough, it may negate that possibility. However, we need to take a lot of comfort in the fact that you and Abram will be armed, and so will Kara and the Legion."

Abram was the next to raise his hand, "I'm Russian, and this means that I've had experience with Communist tactics. How do we know that the Governor and his staff haven't already been tainted?"

Ying answered this question, "We've only started operating in Springfield recently, and didn't have time to start infiltrating the local government. Now, is there a possibility that they could have done it after I disappeared; absolutely. Yet, you have to remember that they lost a lot of men with that convoy, plus all the revenue that it would have generated."

"Speaking of," Aaron chimed, "what were you guys transporting anyway?"

Ying blushed a bit and ran a lock of hair behind her ear, "Some, uh, *acquired* firearms." The three men looked at each other and then back at Ying, who tried to sink into her chair.

"Let's…leave that out when talking to Kara," Lovecraft said, standing up, "Get the Humvee set up and make sure we're good to go." They all stood up, except for Ying, who really didn't know what she was supposed to be doing.

Lovecraft noticed this and turned to her, "Ying, go with Aaron and he'll get you set up with a vest." The Chinese woman turned to Aaron, who nodded to her. She followed him into his room where there were clothes thrown onto the bed, a picture of his family on the nightstand, and a rather impressive collection of Playboy magazines in the corner. He pushed an old ammo box back to its brothers and opened his closet. For a moment, Ying thought that he was digging for gold, since it was taking so long, but just as that thought finished, he pulled a *really* old plate carrier from the recesses of his collection; the damn thing was even colored in the old MARPAT camouflage to boot. He handed the carrier to her, her atrophied arms getting shocked at first.

"You alright?" he asked, not ready to let go of it.

Ying shook her head, "Yeah, it's just, I uh…" she let out a frustrated sigh before taking it from him and slipped it over her head. Her drive was rather admirable, although not impressive. Yet, that had its own sort of charm.

"I gotta get my gear ready now. Go help Abram in the garage, God knows he could use it." Aaron reached underneath his bed and pulled his MK. 17 from it. Ying turned and left his room. She walked out to the kitchen before hearing a pair of feet running after her. She turned around and saw Aaron coming toward her with a black umbrella in his hand.

"Here," he said, offering it, "no sense in getting wet for no reason, is there?" Ying smirked at him and shook her head. She took the item from him and deployed it before stepping out into the downpour.

The compound's garage was actually only a few steps from the front door, since it was integrated into the main building. It featured two, large, blue doors that were only doors in a sense because they were completely holographic, yet one couldn't walk through them if they were activated. It was the first in the world of 'Force Fields.' Abram was inside of the bay closest to the door and had the hood of the Humvee open. He was checking the oil when he heard the rain tapping on Ying's umbrella, beckoning his attention. He returned the stick to its rightful place and turned toward her.

"What's up?" he asked. Ying relayed Aaron's instructions and Abram felt his shoulders lighten. While he was still on the fence about Ying, he wouldn't deny the fact that managing, organizing, and working in this garage alone was hard work.

"That's actually music to my ears." He turned to the far wall behind the Humvee and pointed to a pallet lying on the concrete floor that had several boxes of ammo on it, "You see those boxes over there?" Ying nodded.

"That's ammunition for the 50," he pointed to the M3 machine gun on top of the truck, "and it needs to be loaded back into the truck. Be careful though, they're rather heavy."

Ying folded her umbrella and set it against the Humvee, "Don't worry, I can manage." She walked over to the pallet and took one of the 30-pound boxes and felt its weight before she stacked another on top of it. Ying carried this over and then stowed it in the back of the truck. Abram watched and was rather surprised that the scrawny woman proved that she was much stronger than her frame gave off. This jolted him back to his own work and before long, the two fell into a rhythm, until Lovecraft and Aaron showed up.

Lovecraft was dressed in his typical Crye/5.11 combat gear and held his helmet in his right hand, as his rifle was on his back. His upper half was semi-soaked from the rain, although he appeared to not care.

Aaron was dressed in his all-black Crye gear and wore his skull-decaled balaclava underneath his helmet. His battle rifle was resting on his shoulder, as Ying loaded the last two boxes into the truck; her eyes caught an old, olive-drab jacket that had been crumpled up and thrown underneath a seat.

She grabbed it and asked, "Whose is this?" The three men directed their attention to it and gave it a once over. Abram was the first to give his answer and it was just a simple shake of the head. Aaron knew who it belonged to immediately, but let Lovecraft answer, since he was already halfway through his sentence.

"That's Pamela's. She was wondering where that went," he replied, crossing his arms.

"Who's Pamela?" Ying asked, although her accent butchered the name.

Aaron answered this time, "Old friend of ours who's stationed in Juarez right now; everybody knows her as 'Black Lightning.'"

"Why do they call her that?"

"It's um...a long story." Aaron replied, as Lovecraft walked around the truck. He opened the passenger door and climbed inside, pushing his rifle around to his front and, after unhooking its sling, pushed its barrel into the floor mat.

"Abram, if everything's ready, get in. You're driving today," Lovecraft ordered. Abram nodded and grabbed his PKM from the top of a nearby toolbox. He handed it off to Aaron, who stowed it away in the back, and climbed into the driver's seat. Aaron got in the seat behind Lovecraft, and Ying slid into the one behind Abram.

"If you want, Ying, you can take the jacket. I doubt Pamela would really want it now," Lovecraft offered. Ying looked down at the old piece of fabric held in her arms and started to put it on with a shrug of her shoulders. She noticed that there were three holes in its back that vaguely reminded her of bullet holes and some black stains around them. However, she didn't ask how those were made, for fear of learning a bit too much about this jacket. She zipped it up to her chin and then looked around as the truck turned over and they started to pull forward.

She looked at Aaron and asked, "Why the mask?"

"It protects my family." Ying understood and turned back to her window. Yet, it seemed the silence would not be allowed to reign peacefully. Lovecraft pulled his phone from his pocket and plugged it into a jack that was fed into the dash. He touched its screen a few times and adjusted the volume before Metallica's *Sanitarium* started playing. This was the theme to their tour through downtown Chicago, where the images of the semi-cyber age shown in all their glory. As they got closer to Lincoln Park, the metal and concrete started to taper away, and was replaced with more traditional brick structures that were flanked by large industrial warehouses and factories. The people walked around with jackets and their chins buried into their breasts; their umbrellas soaked to the steel rods. More thunder tore through the black sky, as Abram turned down a right-hand street.

"How do you think Kara is?" Aaron suddenly asked.

Lovecraft turned the music off and replied, "In pain, which means she's probably pissed."

"I thought she was already pissed," Abram added.

"Well, getting robbed is enough to get Kara moody and, uh, some people act like they're dying when they get sick or injured. Kara is the exact opposite and gets very…malicious when she's hurt," Lovecraft explained, as he saw the sign of Lugers and Leggings come into view.

"Right, I'm just going to give her a wide berth," Abram said, pulling over.

Aaron laughed, "I don't think you understand, Abram, even if you try and avoid Kara's kill zone, you're still in it." Ying listened to all of this and felt her hands shaking; maybe she shouldn't have gotten up this morning. She opened her door and stepped out into the rain; the jacket holding up better than she thought it would. Lovecraft shut his door; the rain running off his helmet like a waterfall, and motioned for all of them to head inside with him.

Ying stepped inside the building and was immediately floored by just how much better the building looked from the inside. She had known that it was a

168

gun store just from the name, but she never imagined that it would look so *elegant*. From the tube lights clinging to the shelves, to the pink drapes, Ying couldn't help but feel that this place was 'put together.' Icky Blossoms's *Babes* was quietly playing on the speakers, as Aaron came in last.

"Looks a little bit wet out there," a soft, French accent said sarcastically. The voice garnered everyone's attention and when Ying first laid eyes on Kara, she was floored yet again. Standing behind the counter was a woman with radiant white skin, emerald eyes, and twisted, stormy evergreen hair that went down to her thighs. She was very tall, making Ying feel like she was only 14 again, and was rather busty, making Ying feel a little more comfortable. She wore a Lugers and Leggings tee shirt that featured the business's main logo in green, a simple L&L on the left sleeve, and an American flag on the right one. Its end draped around a pair of black skinny jeans. Ying also noticed that her left hand was wrapped up in thick bandages.

Her evaluation was suddenly interrupted when Kara asked, "Speechless? I get that a lot." She pointed at Ying with a fingernail that was airbrushed in cobalt, "You're the little marksman that embarrassed Marlene, aren't you?"

Ying was flabbergasted, "Um, embarrassed?"

"Yep, according to her, a small, Chinese sniper showed her up by hitting a shot she could never hit, in one go." Ying really didn't know how to take all this. She had just done as she was told and now, it seemed like it was a bad thing. Kara could read this all over her face and let out a sigh. She pulled her pistol out and unloaded it.

"And here I thought you would be a bit more feral," Kara said, ejecting the cartridge.

Ying's eyes widened in alarm, "You were gonna shoot me?!"

"It's nothing personal, I just can't afford to not be cautious. Especially, since your former friends tried to kill me back in California." Kara lifted her chin and looked at Ying more closely, "I guess you're okay, though. Right, Lovecraft?" He nodded in affirmation and then strode further into the room.

"We ready, Kara?" Lovecraft asked, looking at a selection of B.C.M. parts.

"Almost, I just have some stuff to take care of in the warehouse before we can go. Oh yeah," Kara pulled a black-and-gold cane from behind the counter and started toward Lovecraft, her foot not exactly healed yet, "you should probably say hi before you go." Lovecraft looked at her like she was crazy, a verdict that was still out to this day, until she motioned toward the stairs with her head. Lovecraft followed her gaze until he saw Monica standing there, a smirk on her face.

"Long time no see, L.C.," she said, meeting him at the landing.

"I thought I had enough troublemakers to deal with," he said, smirking at her. She laughed at him before moving forward to hug him.

"How are you?" she asked, after pulling away. Lovecraft let her go and told her that he was tired and stressed, but that was usually the life of a Contractor. Aaron came up to her and she hugged him as well, before introducing herself to Abram and Ying. Kara watched all this before beckoning them to follow her outside. Monica handed Kara an umbrella before grabbing one for herself; everyone else declined one since they were used to working in the rain. Their boots sloshed through the miniature rivers forming behind Kara's store. The warehouse was directly in line with Lugers and Leggings, and as Lovecraft was crossing the short distance, he looked down the left side of the street. A pair of yellow galoshes splashed in line with him and when he stopped, this female figure stopped. She was dressed in a yellow raincoat, with raven hair spilling from its hood.

"Hey," Aaron said, bumping into him, "what's up?"

The woman disappeared and Lovecraft's reality returned to normal, "Nothing." He started walking again and Monica held the door open for them. Abram and Ying entered after them and Monica was the last.

The warehouse was dark and smelled of Cosmoline. Flashes from several plasma cutters illuminated the room, as men and women cursed. Wooden crates filled with guns from Russia, Cambodia, Serbia, Germany, and even the Czech Republic, were stacked onto palettes, where they were labeled with an abbreviation which stood for their destination. Most were labeled with the abbreviations for the southwestern states. A more detailed shipping manifest was strapped to the topmost crate and then they started to secure it for transport. The men who were using the plasma cutters had now switched to blow torches and were now working on mounting a DSHK machine gun to the bed of a black truck. There was a white one sitting next to it, with a PKM machine gun mounted to it.

"Damn, Kara, you preparing for war?" Aaron asked, watching one of the Legion crack open a box of Nexter Famas.

"In some sense, yes. While most of my inventory in here is being shipped out, I've started importing a lot of ordnance in the name of self-preservation. I can't afford to be too cautious." She then turned to Lovecraft, "Don't worry, it's specifically for self-defense." He nodded in approval. Kara then took a moment to look around and get her bearings for just where everything had been moved.

"Okay, so I bet you guys were wondering why I need to check on some things, well, just follow me and see." She led the way to a small group of black crates that were covered in Cyrillic script.

Abram ran his hand over one and said, "It's been awhile since I've seen these." Kara beamed with pride and ordered Monica to open one for the rest to see. Her subordinate whistled and was thrown a crowbar which she aptly used to pry the wooden box open.

Shiny brass gleamed in the dim light, while the bullet's white heads almost glowed in the dark.

Lovecraft ran a gloved hand over the rounds, "I take it the A.T.F. didn't care, or did you smuggle this in?"

Kara chuckled, "You're out of the loop, Lovecraft. White Phosphorous is legal now, well, it always has been, since the U.N. collapsed and everybody stopped giving a damn about Geneva, anyway, the U.S. finally pulled the stick out of its ass and I can now legally sell this to Contractors, but Contractors only." She gave another proud smile before it fell into a line, "You guys could at least say something."

"Chicken," Lovecraft responded.

Everybody looked at him and Kara simply asked in a confused tone, "What?"

"You said, 'say something,' so I said something. Where's my 20 bucks?" The green-haired bombshell shut her eyes and let out a big sigh before hobbling her way back to the door.

"Let's just go. I need a cigarette." Everybody watched her open the door and also watched it close behind her.

"Why is she walking like that?" Ying asked, noticing that Kara was suddenly walking even worse than before.

Lovecraft put a hand on her shoulder, "Because, she has been infected with the 'Pose of Defeat.'" He smirked, before stepping away from her to chase after Kara. Aaron shook his head and the rest of them followed suit in tailing their respective leaders.

Ruler's Humvee sped down I-55, with Kara's car behind them and another Technical behind her car. Monica was driving Kara's car for her and had its wipers on full blast in an effort to at least see something. It didn't help that the wind had started blowing even harder since they left; there were leaves and branches already covering the street.

Monica pulled her radio from her plate carrier and held its button down, "Can't see a fuckin' thing."

Aaron's voice responded, "Same. The storm's getting worse. Luckily, we haven't seen too much crap blocking the road." Kara started touching the thick wrapping around her hand and was quickly nudged in the shoulder by Monica.

"Stop it," she commanded, "I don't want to re-bandage it when we get to Springfield." Kara pulled her hands away from one another and kind of chuckled a bit.

"You know, I'm not a kid anymore, Monica." she said, looking at her hands in comparison.

"Of course, ma'am. You'll be turning 30 years old here in the next few weeks, and I know that because every year you get older, my Crow's Feet get worse." Kara laughed at her bodyguard; it helped to keep her mind off the dull pain in her hand and foot.

"Speaking of you turning 30 soon, have you been seeing anybody recently?" Monica asked next. Kara directed her attention to the outside world and suddenly found it more interesting than the conversation.

"No," she reluctantly replied.

"And why not?"

Kara threw her head back into the seat and sighed, "Because the last guy I went out with brought his damn kids, and he wasn't the first one to do that, and I'm sick of it."

"Well, at your age, finding somebody who hasn't been with someone already is next to impossible. What's so bad about kids?"

"Nothing specifically. I just find them annoying and it's just something I don't want to deal with right now. Like, I want to have a hot romance, not suddenly become celibate because I have to take care of some other hoe's kid. If I wanted to do that, I'd have started a daycare, not a gun store."

Monica side-eyed Kara with a smirk; a knowing one that could only appear on a mother's face. Although, Monica was neither married, nor had any kids.

"Uh-huh, so not only is there somebody, but you're smitten with them. Now the only question is, who is it?" she asked, putting a finger to her chin.

Kara glared at her, "Monica, I will fuck you up. Then you'll have to re-bandage my hand with broken glasses and a black eye." God, Monica loved it when she was right.

Meanwhile, Abram was silently wishing for a pair of binoculars so he could see through this onslaught. There were several emergency vehicles parked alongside the Interstate, and there were also several crashed vehicles as well.

"Do you think they'll shut down 55?" Aaron asked, looking at his watch.

"Probably, that fucking Communist has been a pussy ever since they put him in office. Oh well, we have our pass, we'll get through no matter what," Lovecraft assured them.

Ying was confused by his words, "Communist?"

"It's an expression," Aaron explained, "The current governor is a Liberal. Worst part is, he's from way back during the Obama Administration, and he's a shitty, lame duck governor. Yet, he likes to throw his weight around, because he can."

"Why don't you just remove him then?"

"Because this is a free country and everybody has power here," Aaron motioned toward his gun, "should they choose to take it." The cab suddenly filled with cigarette smoke and tickled the back of Ying's throat. She looked to the front and saw that Lovecraft was the owner of the smoke; the fire clashing against the blackened sky. Lovecraft then reached out and opened the glove box and handed Ying a fabric half-mask.

"Here, this is your cover," he said, handing it to her. She held it in her hands and slipped it over her head; her face from the nose down was now unrecognizable. Ying turned her attention to the road and through the water and leaf litter, saw the tire tracks that began her journey slowly being washed away.

Their footsteps echoed through the ornate and robust Capitol Building, as Ruler and company traversed the inner halls that lead to the Governor's office. Their guns clattered against their armor and left watermarks on the floor that quickly morphed into the bigger footprints. They were walking slower than normal, since Kara was forced to hobble along with the aid of her cane; the wannabe crutch frustrating Kara with the shame of slowing everybody down. They came to a pair of sliding metal doors that had the 'Governor's Office' scrawled above it in holographic script.

Lovecraft turned to Ying, "If any of these guys in here touch you, you have my permission to defend yourself." Ying nodded and steeled herself, as he stepped up to the door. Lovecraft hit the door several times and waited for it to open. It opened with an automatic wane and they were treated to the sight of a clean, equally robust interior, with a single black man sitting behind a desk, while his guards stood around him. Lovecraft entered first and he was then followed by his team, including Ying, and was then followed by Kara and her men. The Governor watched them from behind his glasses as they came in, and watched as Kara helped herself to an ornate and high-quality couch that honestly wasn't as comfortable as it seemed.

"Lovecraft, I thought you wouldn't make it due to the nature of this storm. There's a flood warning for your part of the state," he said, standing from his oak desk. He extended his hand and was immediately met by Lovecraft's gloved one.

"Sorry to disappoint you, Jeremiah, but a storm doesn't scare us," Lovecraft stated, withdrawing his hand.

The Governor snorted and turned to Kara, "And what are you doing here?" Kara scoffed and Lovecraft just looked at him.

"Do you even do anything besides preach your anti-gun policy and subjugate minorities?" Kara started to chuckle, "No, of course you don't. Hell, I guess reading a little piece of paper is too much for your narrow-minded and prejudiced brain. You're worse than a Catholic priest."

Kara's words lit a fire in the governor's eyes, "Now just a minute—"

He was interrupted by Lovecraft, asking, "Are you serious? Did you even read a single word of the report I sent to you?"

"Well, of course I did, but it didn't mention—" he was cut off yet again, when Lovecraft pulled a physical copy of the report and slapped it against this chest. The guard closest to him tried to grab Lovecraft, but was stopped, when Aaron shoved the barrel of his rifle into his side and then stood in front of him when he recoiled.

"Seriously, Jeremiah, I would *highly* encourage you to read it; you know, so the Governor has some idea of what's going on in his state," Lovecraft hissed. The Governor looked down at the paper and slowly removed it from his chest, as Lovecraft stepped back. They all waited for him to read it and in no time, he set it down on his desk.

"I'm terribly sorry, Kara. I didn't know," he apologized, only to make Kara scoff again.

"I didn't come here looking for an apology, I came here wondering what you're going to do. If you haven't noticed, I got my ass beat by a bunch of Commie-loving dipshits."

"Well, yes, I noticed that. But, you see, it's hard to feel sorry for you if you use such belligerent language." Everybody, including Ying, looked at him, and Kara was the one to tell him what everybody was thinking.

"Your job is to guarantee my safety. As for my language, I will start cleaning it up when bastards like you stop telling me what to do." The Governor was stunned with her and struggled to retort.

Lovecraft stepped behind Kara and got his attention, "Jeremiah, unfortunately, the rules demand that when dealing with matters pertaining to national security, I must report them to my governmental superior, and then I must report it to my contracting agency. I have done this, and I would be willing to assume that the only reason Barons has not shown up yet is due to the weather and if that is the case, then he will not be showing up at all. Thus, the decision is up to you on how I proceed." The Governor looked at Lovecraft and then turned back to the report and gave it another onceover.

"Lovecraft, how can you be certain that these atrocities have been committed? Do you have any proof? Any solid evidence?" Lovecraft could have punched him in the face for just how much evidence of it had happened in his city; yet, he still didn't notice. However, he smirked and turned to Ying; yet, he didn't present her, for another thought popped into his head. Governor Jeremiah was being a little *too* oblivious to this problem. Lovecraft turned back to him and pulled few more papers from his carrier and presented his rock-solid evidence. The Governor took the papers from him and quickly read through them; his expression changing to that of a tired parent.

"Lovecraft, while I appreciate all the hard work," he handed them back to him, "these cases have already been settled."

"What?"

"Yes, most of these were perpetrated by a radical street gang calling themselves, 'The Family.' Apparently, they are based out of California, which would explain why Miss Alexandre was attacked." He turned to the woman with a satisfied smile, until he saw her hard eyes piercing through his soul.

"Hey, motherfucker…when you try telling a lie to my face, make sure you're actually a good liar. Now who actually committed all those murders?" Kara chuckled, "I'm curious how much Chinese dick you had to suck in order to not get yourself whacked. Hmm, you probably enjoyed it thou—"

"Kara, enough," Lovecraft commanded, stuffing the papers back into his carrier. The arms dealer looked at him in surprise, but followed his orders, nonetheless.

"It's nice to see that you do have your dog on some type of leash," Governor Jeremiah commented.

Lovecraft retorted with, "Weird, I don't see a leash on you." The Governor turned to him in astonishment, before he was suddenly pushed up against the desk by Lovecraft's body. His eyes looked into Lovecraft's dark, cold eyes, and he could smell his breath.

"Believe me, Governor," he said, "the next time I see you, it will be in handcuffs and I will have a Federal Search Warrant."

"Are you threatening me, Contractor?" Lovecraft backed away and motioned for his allies to follow him.

"No, it's just to remind you that even you are not above the law…or me." He turned around and opened the door for himself. Aaron walked up to it and held it for everybody, as they started walking out.

"You need a new couch," Kara gave her parting words, "it's so hard it might break your fragile ass." She walked out with Monica and the rest of her men, as the Governor stepped into the doorframe.

"Lovecraft, if you ever make such remarks in my presence again, I will have you turned over to the authorities!" he yelled after them. The man this was directed to turned around and met his gaze with a deadpan expression, "Tell somebody who cares." With that having been said, he continued walking and, before long, came outside to calm, clear skies and red, setting sunlight.

Chapter 10

Is There Something in the Dark?

A refreshing breeze blew through neon streets and swirled through Kara's hair, as she rested her head on her knees. She watched the superstructures of downtown Chicago breathe like bioluminescent fish, from the vantage point that Lovecraft usually used to watch the sun. They had just returned from Springfield a few hours prior and had a big meal that seemed to raise everyone's spirits, including her own. However, she abandoned the merry making early in favor of being alone for a bit, and this was where it lead her.

She watched those beautiful buildings with muddied thoughts; a terrible weight on her shoulders as she processed everything that had happened. It was like a disease had taken hold of half her heart, half her mind, and half her body. Kara could not possibly form words for these feelings, but they were immensely similar to regret; yet, she had nothing to regret. The door opened rather abruptly and shocked her being back to life from its hibernation. She turned and saw Lovecraft standing behind her, with his black overcoat fixed around his body.

"You know, I can kind of see why you like it up here so much," Kara said.

Lovecraft took a few steps forward, "Oh yeah?"

She nodded, "It gets your mind working, lets you focus on the trials of the day, and helps you sort through them. Is that why you came up here?"

Lovecraft's mouth formed an almost-perfect line, as he threw a blanket onto Kara's head, "No, it was to make sure you didn't catch a cold." The younger woman struggled with the piece of fabric, as Lovecraft sat down and braced his back against an air conditioner; his boots pointed directly at Kara.

She pulled the blanket off her head and draped it around her shoulders just in time for Lovecraft to ask her, "So what are you having trouble thinking about?"

She looked at him quizzically, "Pardon?"

He cocked an eyebrow, "You said that this was a place that helps you think. Well, what can't you think about, Miss Goldfish?" Kara didn't know what it was about being one-on-one with Lovecraft that made her head suddenly go blank and her heart race. Well, she did, but that was a private thought only meant to be unlocked in her dreams. Whatever it was, it blindfolded her to the insult until much later.

"I don't know," she said, shrugging her shoulders, "I just feel like this whole ordeal is my fault. Like, if I wasn't so stupid and gave Romanov those guns before he paid me, then the stakes wouldn't be so dire. America's made me softer than I used to be."

Lovecraft took a moment to pull his cigarettes from his pocket, a new brand called 'H&P's,' and lit it shortly after putting it in his mouth, "Well you know that I'm not going to take you under my wing and tell you that it was nobody's fault, teachers get off on that shit, but in the grand scheme of things, *something* is always *somebody's* fault. Sorry, Kara, but in order to not make you believe a lie, *this is your fault*." His words cut deep into her chest, but she did not look away from him. Kara would not allow herself to look away and fall further into despair, like most people would. No, she would take this guilt, carry it, and use it as a weapon against a repeat scenario. This led her to pulling out her Marlboros and earning a judgmental comment from Lovecraft.

With an amused smirk, she put the filter between her lips and said, "Hey, give me a light." Lovecraft grabbed his lighter again and struck it beneath the rolled tobacco. However, no flame came out. He shook it a bit and struck it again; yet, got the same result.

He sighed, "Just my fuckin' luck."

Kara chuckled, as he threw the worthless object off the roof, "Having some trouble getting it up?" Lovecraft turned to her with a dead expression and stood up only to sit down right next to her.

"Hold still, you ass," he commanded, and guided the tip of his cigarette to Kara's; an act that not only surprised her, but impressed her. She took a mental note to never underestimate just how bold Lovecraft could be, or to forget the sight of his face so close to hers. However, the cigarette lit too quickly for her liking and all too soon, Lovecraft was back up against the A.C. unit.

"It figures that your shitty brand would suck the life out of my lighter," he said, crossing his arms.

"Nah, I'm just a hotter fire than your lighter; sucked all of its oxygen away." Lovecraft visibly cringed at her overconfidence before she asked, "So what's next, Ruler Actual?"

"Back to the Master and try and get somewhere."

Kara frowned, "You're not going after the Chinese?"

"No, we can't. At least, not yet." He sighed again, "We have to get to a resting point with this assassination case. We've been going on a month without finding anything. Luckily, Ying has agreed to help us in exchange for the hunting down of her former allies."

"Well, just don't forget about your friends, L.C., you'll be weaker without us after all," Kara stated.

"Kara, if you're my friend, then I'm screwed."

She laughed a bit, "Sounds pleasurable if you ask me." She took a moment to laugh at her own joke, "Seriously, though, you could have worse friends, Lovecraft." The older man was immediately reminded of Joan of Arc and Edmond Dantes when she pointed this out.

"I guess you're right."

It was after he said this that they heard the squeak of the door again and Aaron came walking toward them, asking, "Hey, are you guys makin' out?" Both of them turned toward him and watched him sluggishly move in.

"Aaron, you're drunk," Lovecraft responded, standing up and flicking his cigarette away. Kara smirked as she stood up and folded the blanket around her arms.

He nodded in agreement with Lovecraft, "I am, but I'm sober enough to recognize it. By the way, Ying drank a whole bottle of vodka and is as sober as a priest; at this point, I'm convinced she a terminator. There's no way a normal human can have a bottomless stomach and liver."

Lovecraft groaned, "I was hoping to have that at Christmas."

"Yeah," Aaron said, "Anyway, it was getting pretty late, so I started kicking people out and that's why I'm here. Kara, Monica and Lawrence are ready to go." The woman in question shook her head and thanked him, before handing the blanket back to Lovecraft. Aaron was the first to walk back down the stairs, which wasn't a good idea, but he made it without injury.

"I've never actually seen Aaron drink before," Kara commented, after not hearing him crash down the stairs.

Lovecraft shook his head, "That's because he's a lightweight; always has been. I've always made the joke to him that his alcohol content is right at the limit normally and if he drinks anymore, its instant drunkenness. He then proceeds to call me an asshole, but doesn't drink after that."

Kara laughed a bit before she started walking to the door, "Oh yeah, I forgot to say, thank you for not calling me a dog earlier today. It means something to me that you don't see me as a tool like everybody else you're involved with."

Lovecraft nodded, even though he hadn't really thought much about it. The Governor's 'leash' comment had been out of line and what he said pissed everybody off, but he really didn't expect to get thanked for standing up for her.

"Well, leashes are for slaves, and as much as Jeremiah would like to deny it, there's an amendment against that. It's part of the reason why you have the pseudo freedom you do," Lovecraft said, draping the blanket around his arm and shoving his hands into his pockets.

Kara smirked and turned back to the door, "America's been too good to me; I'm moving to Iran." Lovecraft huffed out a laugh as she walked back down the stairs. He turned his head back toward the city and followed the neon buildings up to the sky where he saw the moon shining even brighter.

The next day, Ying woke up like she had since coming to Ruler's compound, with a red mark on her head from the window and her feet still asleep. Yet, if people found out that she was actually sleeping better than she had in years, they wouldn't believe it. She stretched her arms out and heard the same pops, before she jumped down and landed on wobbly feet, as the room started spinning slightly. Ying watched it in surprise, as the memory of last night's dinner came back to her; especially the memory of Abram and her sharing that bottle of vodka. She chuckled a bit and it was at this point that she realized the spinning had stopped. Looking to and fro, she shrugged her shoulders before grabbing her clothes and toiletries. She exited the room with neither a headache nor nausea, which could not be said about Aaron.

"I feel terrible," Aaron declared, resting his head on the table.

Abram was working in the kitchen in his stead and yelled in, "Come on, Aaron, you had two beers, what the hell is wrong with you?"

Lovecraft laughed loudly, "I told you he's a lightweight. Mister one-and-done is what I used to call him."

"You guys are so loud," Aaron chided, as Ying walked in, with water still dripping from her longer hair.

"Did one of you guys take my towel?" she asked, sitting down across from Lovecraft. Aaron and Abram shook their heads, but Lovecraft looked as if he just had an epiphany.

"That was probably the towel I used as a rag this morning," he admitted, standing up.

As he went into the kitchen and grabbed her another towel, Aaron asked, "How in the hell do you not have a hangover?"

She looked at him with a quizzical look before asking, "How do you have one? You only drank two beers." Abram's laugh returned with the smell of food from the kitchen, Lovecraft soon followed and dropped a new towel on Ying's head. She gave her thanks and started to towel off the water that hadn't already dried.

"You know, Aaron, I'm only being loud because I know you can just shoot yourself up and get rid of that hangover," Lovecraft teased. Aaron grumbled as he fished a syringe out of his pocket and started preparing it.

Ying looked at it with wide-eyed curiosity, "There's medicine for hangovers?"

"Welcome to the land of modern medicine," Aaron said, as he shot it into his arm and felt the burning fire start through his veins. He flicked his tongue like a snake, as the taste of mercury tainted his mouth. After this subsided, he voiced his disgust and Abram brought the food, a common Russian dish, and set it out for all of them. He made sure to make enough for Ying, and they all ate their fill, until Lovecraft garnered their attention.

"Okay, gentlemen and lady, with the results of our trip to Springfield yesterday, we will be returning to the Master for the foreseeable future. Thus, the incident with the Chinese will be set aside, until a reasonable and large-enough opening has been presented to us. Now, I know that this may discourage some of you and I understand this, but the reality of the situation is that the Chinese could swoop in and knock us out at any moment. This is the reason we need to lay low for a while. Now, are there any questions?"

Aaron raised his hand and started to speak, "What is our plan of action in the meantime? Like, what's the game plan should something actually come up?"

"If something should come up, we will switch back over and proceed with the help of the Legion. Barons will also supply a police presence and then our main goals would be the apprehension of Major Kei, the gathering of evidence, and legal action against other Chinese sects in the United States, but that third one could be handled by the State Department and the F.B.I." Satisfied, Aaron let his hand fall and was soon replaced by Abram's.

"What would happen to Ying as a result? I can't imagine that the authorities, especially the F.B.I., would like to let someone with anti-U.S. ties go freely."

"Ying has, as was previously stated, agreed to aid us in both the Master case and the Chinese problem. As such, these would, without a doubt, aid her in getting lighter repercussions. Especially, when presenting evidence, that she was kidnapped and forced into the Chinese military. Now, if there are no further questions, then I would like to discuss what we are doing today." Lovecraft waited for a moment and when he saw that no one rushed to speak, he began.

"Okay, so as most of you may have noticed, this case concerning the Japanese Prime Minister has stalled, and since there are no foreseeable leads besides Miss Magdalene's case, it means we missed something." Lovecraft touched his data pad and drew a holographic card from it. He threw it into the center of the table and a holographic image of a hospital Ying had never seen before, "When we went to Weiss Memorial, we were attacked by an unknown assailant in the basement. However, we were never able to find anything short of that, until recently." Lovecraft manipulated the image and pointed to the basement they had been in previously, "While we were in Springfield, the police continued to search the building, but had to withdraw due to the weather. After that, the building flooded, but when they went back, they found that the building, including the basement, was completely dry. Long story short, they started excavating the basement and they found a large tunnel that was half-flooded and blocked off by a bunch of metal crap."

"It sounds like you guys have something bigger than rats in your sewer system," Ying commented.

Aaron scoffed, "Yeah, tell that to my leg. So do you think there's some hidden tunnel system in the Flood Zone that nobody's ever seen before?"

"There's one way to find out," Lovecraft said, swiping away the hospital and having replaced by a holographic map of the Flood Zone that was colored in red, "So nobody's ever seen this place before, well, I can't think of a better place to look for something that doesn't exist, than a Restricted Zone."

Aaron sighed, "Good thing I'm up to date on my shots. When are we leaving?"

"As soon as we get geared up. We'll be heading to Police Headquarters and boarding a Blackhawk there. Make sure Ying gets kitted up and instruct her if she needs it, and make damn sure you have everything, should shit hit the fan. It's better to have it and not need it, than vice versa. We leave in under ten minutes, get going." Everyone stood up and started going to their respective places. Ying grabbed her knife and then went to Aaron's room where she was given an old, but more modern, plate carrier, and was also given a radio and a Medkit. He then slipped his balaclava on and then placed his helmet over that. He tested his night vision, making himself look like a red-eyed spider, and then grabbed his battle rifle off his bed. He instructed Ying to follow him, as he pointed the Belgian rifle toward the ceiling; its barrel barely clearing. She heard Lovecraft's door open and close, before Aaron led her to the garage, where he proceeded toward a black cabinet.

He dug into his collar and pulled out his dog tags that had a luminescent blue light on them. He waved them in front of the cabinet and the lock disengaged immediately. When the doors opened, it smelled of must and Cosmoline, as Aaron reached inside and withdrew an old Colt M4 that looked like it was straight out of the 1980s; it was even rusted in spots.

"You know how to use an American weapon?" Aaron asked. Ying stated that she could and was then handed the old carbine that still had its irremovable carry handle. After that, he pulled a Beretta M9 from the locker and handed that to her; she slipped this into her holster before she was allowed to grab the ammunition from the cabinet. It took her some time, but when she was fully outfitted, Aaron locked the cabinet back up and the others joined them.

The ride to Police Headquarters was actually much shorter than Ying remembered, and it also seemed like they were rushed through the building as well. It seemed as though Ying had just climbed into the Humvee and now, she was being whipped around inside of a helicopter. She sat with her assault rifle between her legs, directly across from Lovecraft, who had his eyes fixated on the modern ruin that was the Flood Zone. Abram sat next to him and Aaron next to him; their eyes seemed to be filled with an intense yet vague sense of disdain for what they were looking at.

"So why do they call it a Restricted Zone?" Ying suddenly asked, breaking the monotony of the helicopter blades cutting the air.

"It's a part of the Flood Zone that was hit especially hard by the storm," Lovecraft explained, "They're places that people could never resettle due to just how dangerous they are. For instance, the one we are heading to right now, harbors a shit-ton of soil erosion – making the ground highly unstable. So watch your step." The small compartment fell into relative silence once again; the only thing being the obvious machine noise from the aerial vehicle. It was eerie. Ying mulled over Lovecraft's explanation and doubted her choice to help him; what good would it be if she got killed before she could see justice served? Alas, Ying pushed this from her mind and tried to resign herself to the current mission. However, she just couldn't help but feel that this strange and perverse black cloud that seemed to hang over Lovecraft, and the rest of Ruler, was getting thicker and seemed to be consuming her as well. Ying shook her head in an effort to clear her mind; she had learned, long ago, that such thoughts could be a fatal error in her line of work.

"Something wrong, Ying?" Aaron asked.

"I'm fine, just nerves. You guys won't pull a fast one on me and shoot me in the back, will you?"

Abram scoffed, "We should be the ones asking you that." The conversation went no further, as the pilot informed them that they would be landing. Lovecraft ordered them to get ready and in a matter of moments, a large, gravel-covered roof appeared in front of the door. Lovecraft was the first one out of the helicopter and once he jumped from the levitating vehicle, he made sure the roof was stable before commanding the rest of his team out. Abram was the next one out, Aaron followed him, and Ying was the last. Once she landed, Lovecraft waved the chopper off and then pulled a map out of his pants pocket. He unfolded it to reveal that there were lines drawn over their current position.

All of them crowded around him and he explained to them that they would be using the rooftops to traverse this dangerous plane; an idea that Ying grimaced at, but discarded, because there was no other option. Lovecraft pointed to her and Aaron, and stated that they would be proceeding across this rooftop and pushing toward an old subway line that should be completely submerged; their goal was to confirm if it was truly flooded. Both nodded and then their leader turned to Abram and said that he would be coming with him to investigate an anomaly in the Old Maps; whatever those were, Ying just took it as the literal 'Old Maps.'

After he got done speaking to Abram, Lovecraft and the other three stood and offered one last order, but it was probably the most important one, "We should be the only ones in this area. Thus, anybody found here is an enemy and should be killed. There is no time and no backup for prisoners." All of them acknowledged their orders and started turning in their respective directions. A wild wind whipped through the area, as Ying began walking, and brought partly cloudy skies to watch over them, as Aaron started across a sheet-metal bridge.

Two people trudged across the old and decrepit roofs; one dressed in black and the other dressed in olive drab. One whose gun was an example of a modern marvel, while the other's was an example of modern relic. Aaron and Ying kept looking to either side of the rooftop and they would be lying if they said they felt safe up there.

"Talk about sky lining like a motherfucker. Don't you snipers get off on this type of shit?" Aaron asked, vaulting down onto a lower roof.

"If the enemy is sky lining, it's always a good thing, although it usually doesn't amount to much. We just kill the one sky lining and, hey, there's a free kill we didn't have to work for," Ying explained, jumping down to the same roof. The two of them took a few steps and were suddenly almost thrown to the gravel, as the area started to shake, throwing a few rusted window guards into the muddied canyons below. Aaron and Ying waited for a few moments before standing up, they immediately decided that staying in this area was not the best idea. They double timed it to a different set of buildings that seemed to be a little more stable than the ones they were currently on.

Meanwhile, Lovecraft and Abram were inside of an abandoned high rise, when the tremor hit them. This brought forth Abram's concern about being buried underneath a building, which Lovecraft shared, but they continued traversing the building, since this was the only sure way to get to their destination. They found themselves inside of a dirty and dilapidated living room that smelled of mold, earning a comment from Lovecraft about seeing if they could find some Penicillin to sell. Abram chuckled before Lovecraft went up to the front door, which was still closed due to them climbing in through the window, and kicked it open. However, instead of swinging on its hinges, it just simply fell over and crashed into the hallway.

Lovecraft walked onto the door and looked down the left side of the hallway with his gun, as Abram took the right; the only thing they saw were the dust bunnies flying into the deep crevices that occupied the rotted floorboards. They lowered their guns when nothing happened, and Lovecraft turned toward Abram. He slipped past his comrade and walked down the hallway that featured a large suite with big windows. However, as he took the first of his steps, another tremor rocked the building and threw him onto a nearby wall, while Abram was forced to the floor; his large form crashing into it with a loud bang.

"Motherfucker!" Lovecraft cursed, as the quake stopped, "Are you okay?"

"Fine, I just fell on my fat ass," Abram replied, taking up a crouched position. Lovecraft wobbled over to the doorframe of the suite and surmised that the recent storm had weakened the earth beneath the buildings; this whole place was becoming one big sinkhole.

Jumping across the safer rooftops to the east, Aaron and Ying surveyed the surrounding area, while also noticing that the sunlight was fading behind a cluster of grey clouds.

Ying shook her head, "If it rains, we'll be in the shit. Say goodbye to jumping across rooftops; it'll be surfing on mud."

"All the more reason to not be here if it starts," Aaron said, packing up his map. He told her to follow him and the two started hopping across the buildings once again, before they were met with a tall, 30-story, high-rise, that they could not cross over to, because its bridge had been blown away. Aaron allowed his gun to be caught by his sling and put his hands on his hips. He let out a frustrated sigh and pulled out his map. Ying walked over to one of the ledges and looked down at the deep canyons that used to be streets. She cleared her throat and, in an unladylike manner, spit her throat's contents into the trenches. Her eyes widened when she lost sight of it.

"Ruler Actual, this is Ruler Zero Two, message over," Aaron said into his radio, causing Ying to come back over.

"Send it."

"Ruler Zero Two has been cut off from its original route, we'll need to improvise a work around, how copy?"

"Solid copy. Be advised, the weather seems to be changing. In the event of inclement weather, you are to immediately call for evac," Lovecraft radioed.

"Roger that. Ruler Zero Two out," Aaron said. He turned to Ying and told her that there was a path if they went south, but they might have to fabricate parts of it in order for it to work. Ying turned to the direction he spoke of and found that they could manage, and agreed with his decision.

They followed this route and improved where they could, but they eventually hit another snag that took the form of a half-collapsed building that only a crazy person would think of using as a bridge. Unfortunately, Aaron and Ying could not afford to be sane, and as much as the fear crept into their heels, Aaron grabbed a loose piece of metal and set it across the gap. He waited for a second and when he saw that the building didn't go, he took that as it being stable enough.

Aaron started across the metal bridge and the moment his boot touched the roof, he felt it creak and shake violently, but it didn't not give way. Aaron could feel the sweat pool in his covered hair, as he started to walk as lightly as he could; pieces of wood fell into room just below the roof with every step Aaron took. However, to his surprise, Aaron made it across the roof, set up another makeshift bridge, and crossed it to safety.

He turned back to Ying and shouted across, "We're good, just try and step lightly, it'll be fine." Ying took in a breath and with a determined nod, started across the roof. She felt the same pressure as Aaron, the same creaks, the same violence, but the roof held and when she was about halfway, she really thought she could do this. That was until a large gust of wind tore through the surrounding buildings and were drawn up the thirty-story high-rise that Aaron and she were at previously. They looked up toward the building and saw an image that chilled the bone. Flying toward the ground was large chunk of a telecom tower that had been hidden by the thick cloud cover.

"Ying, run!" Aaron yelled, holding out his hand in order to pull her over the bridge. The woman started to run as fast as she could, but just as she reached the bridge, the tower crashed into the chasm next to the building and started taking it down with it. Ying screamed as she jumped toward Aaron's hand and somehow caught its gloved form, before she suddenly heard him scream, and in that moment, she realized that she was not being pulled up; no, *she had pulled him down.*

For the third time, Lovecraft tried to get a hold of Aaron and even resorted to contacting Ying, but for some reason, neither of them were answering. He pulled his hand away from his headset and in a frustrated motion, looked to the ceiling. Abram suggested that could have something to do with the weather, or that the signal was having trouble getting through the trenches. Lovecraft knew that all these were possible, but given their recent discovery, he knew that the problem could be all too sinister.

The problem they found was located inside of an old boarded-up gas station. All around the two men stood enough munitions for a small army and they all bore the marks of Lugers and Leggings, although somebody tried to scratch them off in vain. They had found Kara's guns and it meant that either the Chinese were here or that they gave them to somebody else. Lovecraft knew that Kara would want to hear about this once they got back, but for now, he decided to scuttle the place using the explosives that were also stockpiled here. However, as Abram started to set the C4 in place, an urgent distress call coming from a team of Contractors calling themselves 'Dokk,' passed through their comms.

"We are engaged by several, heavily armed hostiles at the junctions of South Yates Boulevard and East 79th Street. I have one K.I.A. and three wounded. We are held up in the old McDonald's. If anyone can hear me, we need help now!" the signal died off and on a day that already seemed be going so poorly, Lovecraft and Abram were left with a terrible choice.

Abram sat down with a heavy thud, "It'll take me at least five more minutes to get all this shit set. If we had known there'd be stuff to blow up, it wouldn't be a problem, but I guess that's the life of a Contractor. One day, you're killing I.S.I.S., and the next, you're getting wiped out by a bunch of hooligans. Too bad, the girl on that call sounded nice too."

Lovecraft couldn't accept that, "Maybe not." He motioned toward an open space in the window. Abram got up and looked out toward the gas pumps. Lovecraft explained that he had heard stories from some of the older police officers that during the cleanup, most of the Restricted Zones couldn't actually be sanitized. Needless to say, the sewers were still clogged, the streets were cluttered with rubble, and there was a high probability that the gas station's underground tank was still full.

"If we can't blow this place up, then we'll just bury it," Lovecraft stated, pulling a grenade from his belt. He ordered Abram to get to a rooftop and to run faster than hell, should the building start collapsing. Abram followed orders and ran across the parking lot, as Lovecraft walked over to the porthole. Using a crowbar he acquired from inside the station, he pried the cover off. Lovecraft hooked the tool onto some spare M.O.L.L.E. webbing, thinking that it might come in handy later, and grabbed his grenade. He stood there and held it for a moment, trying to prepare himself for the run that would have to be even faster than the one he told Abram to do. He pulled the pin and held the latch that traveled the length of its circular shape; it wasn't armed yet, but when he let go of this latch, the clock would start ticking. A typical fragmentation grenade had a five to six-second fuse before it would explode. That gave him five seconds to run across the lot and into a building, but that didn't mean he was safe. Lovecraft shook his head; he knew there was no way he could make it to safety in such little time.

The latch clanged as it hit the dusty asphalt, and as he threw it into the tube, he said, "Fuck it." Lovecraft turned and ran as fast as he could, but for the life of him, it felt like the lot had grown to the size of Siberia. A large explosion erupted underground and brought Lovecraft to a knee, as the earth started to collapse at its epicenter. He looked and saw the pavement disappearing. His body willed itself to action and he started running yet again, this time, trying to outrun the cracks that pursued him like snakes.

His foot got caught in a depression and this slowed him down enough that he was forced to jump toward the building. He reached out with a gloved, sweaty hand, in an effort to grasp the ledge of anything. However, all that was left for him was the air.

In the building above, Abram watched, with stunned eyes and pale skin. He had just watched Lovecraft fall into the hellish pit of fire and explosions, and part of him couldn't believe it. His legs clumsily started to move and although he almost fell down the stairs, he made it outside and called out to Lovecraft in a panicked tone. He threw his weapon to the ground and crawled over to the hellish ledge and found nothing but fire.

"Lovecraft!" he yelled, before ripping his radio from his vest. He started to scream into it, trying, just like Lovecraft had, to get a hold of Aaron. He got static every time that he yelled into it and in a brief stroke of insanity, he tried to look for some type of device to go looking for his leader with.

Yet, Lovecraft was much too lucky and experienced to let something so stupid kill him, and while Abram was distracted, the hooked end of Lovecraft's crowbar dug into the ledge. The Operator pulled himself over the ledge, with his helmet clasped in his other hand. He got up to his feet and walked over to Abram; his face covered in soot just like the rest of him. Abram saw him and thought he was looking at a ghost. The large Russian was stunned like a middle schooler who just got confessed to.

He looked over his ally's shoulder and shook his head at the fire, before holding up the crowbar, "Better than a knife. Let's go."

Ying's eyes were shut like tight clamps, as the feeling of falling dissipated; yet, she still felt weightless. She was scared to open her eyes, since she wasn't exactly sure what would meet her on the other side. Would it be Heaven where the streets were allegedly paved in gold, or would it be the dark pit? Ying couldn't help but feel that it would be the latter, which was why she held her eyes shut all the longer. However, when she heard Aaron's voice, she reflexively opened them. When grey clouds and semi-blue sky filled her vision, it struck her that she may not have actually died. She looked down at her body and found that she was suspended in a mess of hanging wire, a manmade spider web. She attempted to angle herself in such a way that she could see just how high she was, but that only earned her a metallic snap and in a breath, she was falling again, only this time she crashed into desk which skewered her left calf with a roofing nail, while also beating the hell out of her right knee.

Ying rolled off the now-broken furniture and was met with a bed of broken glass that cut up her forearms as she gasped for air. She pushed herself from the shards and found her rifle lying next to a section of wall. Ying crawled over to it and set her back against the wall; she felt the air slowly returning to her lungs and this gave her a moment to focus on some self-care.

"Ying!" her name was suddenly called, and the woman turned around and started looking for its source.

"Aaron!" she called out, trying to stand up, "Where are you?!" She groaned and swore loudly before she grabbed the nail in her leg and just ripped it out. Tears joined the sweat on her brow and as her blood stained a small section of the dirtied rug, she pushed the throbbing pain out of her mind and climbed to her feet. She used her gun as a makeshift cane and called out to Aaron again. She got a response this time, and it led her to a certain room that was vaguely similar to the one she found herself in. The only problem was, she had to do a makeshift jump across a hole and then had to climb over a few desks before she got there. She pushed the door open and once she entered, Aaron instructed her to look up. She did so and was stunned when she saw Aaron hanging above her; he was wrapped up in the same wire, even worse than that she had been.

"I saw you fall, I take it you're okay?" he asked.

Ying looked at her bleeding arms, busted-up knee, and punctured leg, and replied, "I'll survive."

He chuckled, "So it appears. Cut me down and I'll tend to those arms; they look pretty bad." Ying followed the many wires and found that a large clump of them ended at a hole in the floor. She hobbled over to this source and pulled out her knife. She silently prayed that this would be the only one and sawed her way through the cords. Aaron suddenly fell into a mess of computer monitors and Ying gave a sigh of relief.

Aaron took some time to get up and then set to work, helping Ying dress her wounds. She hissed when Aaron dabbed her with hydrogen peroxide; he apologized immediately, but never stopped. He then used a pair of tweezers to start pulling the bits of glass from her arms.

"Use your radio to get a hold of Lovecraft; he'll probably be wondering what happened to us... And sit still," he commanded, pulling a piece of glass out of Ying's elbow. Ying grit her teeth as he continued, and pulled her radio free from her carrier. Using the proper language, Ying contacted Lovecraft and informed him that they were actually alive and in one piece. She paused and listened to Lovecraft's instructions about the distress call and how that was where they needed to go.

Ying acknowledged these new orders and ended the conversation with Lovecraft just in time to cry out, "Son of a bitch!"

Aaron pulled the last piece of glass out rather roughly, which caused her exclamation, and happily announced, "That was the last one. Here, let me wrap it up and then I can start work on the other one." Ying had half a mind to punch him with the 'other one,' but allowed him to do it anyway, just because she was neither an idiot nor a two-year-old.

"Lovecraft and Abram are responding to a distress call at the junctions of South Yates Boulevard and East 79th Street. He wants us to meet—" she cut herself off to suck in some air, as a particularly deep piece was pulled free, "He wants us to meet up there and assist them." Aaron nodded his head and pulled out more gauze for this arm.

"Okay, how are your legs?" Aaron asked, resting his hands on his hips.

Ying smirked, "I can get those with my first aid. Give me a minute and I'll be good as new." Aaron nodded and packed up the Medkit. Ying pulled out her first aid and as she started treating herself, Aaron lit a cigarette and took a seat on a desk.

"I can't wait to not tell my wife about this adventure," he muttered, looking off into the distance.

"What do you tell her?" Ying asked.

"To stay safe and kiss the girls for me. She asks about Lovecraft and if I'm coming home soon, and then she informs me how my eldest is doing in school. She continues down the line until I know who I have to talk to and who I have to congratulate. We don't really like talking about my job, unless we're together and alone, so it just doesn't get discussed."

"How often are you able to get back there?"

"Every three months, if possible, but recently, I haven't been able to get home in over six," he admitted, puffing his cigarette.

"It must be hard; I've never really had something like that in my life. How does your wife manage?"

"Sometimes, I don't know. I guess we just got lucky, with our eldest being as mature and helpful as she is." Aaron flicked his cigarette off the building and stood up, as Ying finished wrapping her puncture wound. Both of them

190

picked up their guns and Aaron said that he would go slowly, but that she would still have to go reasonably fast. Ying nodded and thanked the fact that she had shot herself up with a few painkillers. The two of them set off; their first problem trying to find a reasonable path to their destination.

Automatic weapons' fire racked the walls of the old restaurant, as standing leader, Sue Park, covered the previous leader's body with a thin, white sheet. It had been over ten minutes since she had called for help, and in that time, the three wounded had joined their radio operator, and now, there were only three of them left, including herself. She picked up her K1A carbine and started to stand up, just as one of her remaining men shouted, "R.P.G.!" An explosion knocked Sue off her feet and showered her in gravel. Her ears rung and the room was spinning, as she pushed herself up; a warm liquid flowed from her hairline and dripped from her left cheek. She reached up to her chin and fumbled with her helmet strap. She pulled it off her head and looked at it; there was a smoky piece of copper shrapnel embedded deep inside of it. Had she not been wearing it, the shrapnel would have cut through the top of her skull, like a hot knife through butter. The blood was from the cut that formed when the helmet dented in.

Her dazed look traveled across the room and saw the white bone of a severed arm laying atop of the counter. It didn't belong to one of the already-dead bodies. Her eyes moved off from the gore and looked out the main door, where she saw five men with red-and-white armbands attached to their left arms. One of these was carrying the RPG-7V2 that just reduced one of her remaining teammates to crushed raspberries. Her hearing came back just in time for her remaining teammate's shots to ring out and riddle the man with bullets. His friends returned fire and even though her ally took two of them with her, she was riddled by a machine gun and coughed, as a lucky round ripped open her Adam's apple. Her submachine gun fell from her hands, as she collapsed to her knees. It appeared as though she would be allowed to choke to death in that position, but her head suddenly exploded, spraying Sue's face, and the thunderous crack of a high-caliber rifle echoed outside. Her body folding backward, like a perverse version of origami. She shook, as she looked toward the door again and saw that the enemy was now pushing toward her.

Frantically, she reached down and grabbed her weapon. She started shooting at them and caught two of them in the head, before they started shooting back. Sue ducked behind the counter again, as the enemy bullets split and bore into her cover. She started to cry as she dropped the empty magazine from her weapon and grabbed one of her two remaining full ones. She pushed it inside and switched her gun to semi-automatic, before peaking around the left side of the counter. She saw two more men walking through the front door and shot them three times each; the suppressive fire resumed, only this time, Sue was trying her best to fight back.

She continued to shoot until she was forced back behind cover, and only then did some faint static start to fill her headset.

"Dokk, come in, this is Lovecraft, leader of team Ruler. Do you copy? I repeat, this is Lovecraft, leader of team Ruler, do you copy?" it asked, with a static background.

Sue opened her comms and spoke into the mic, "Yes, oh thank God, yes! I'm trapped inside of the old McDonalds and will be overrun soon!" She hoped that she wasn't screaming too loud, but in the moment, she really didn't care.

Lovecraft's response came back almost immediately, "Roger. We're bringing the rain, keep away from the door." Sue looked as though an old lover had just asked for her hand in marriage; the hope gleamed like the tracers that burned above her head.

Lovecraft and Abram were atop a roof, overlooking the combat zone. Abram was laying down with the bipod deployed on his machine gun; his iron sights slowly drawing patterns across the men below. Lovecraft reached down and patted his back; that was the signal that he was clear to fire. The Russian immediately opened up and racked the assaulting men with automatic weapon's fire. He cut them down like a trained lumberjack and as he did, Lovecraft stood up and ran to a nearby skylight. He jumped down it and landed in front of a bewildered youth wearing another red-and-white armband.

He blew his head off with his rifle and continued down the hallway. Two shotgun-carrying men appeared at the end of the hallway and were soon dispatched by Lovecraft with his hardened aim. The Operator then heard running coming from his right and backed up a step, just as he did, a door was flung open and another shotgun blasted the wall where he once stood. Lovecraft took the opportunity to push the man's gun down with his own, sliding the side of his MK.18 across the top of the shotgun, he shot the confused man in the shoulder and then popped his head wide open as he recoiled. Machinegun fire rang out from inside the room and mutilated the man Lovecraft just killed, as the former ducked in the hallway. He pulled a frag grenade and tossed it into the room; its explosion shaking the building. Luckily, the ground around here wasn't as soft.

Lovecraft cleared the room and once he found that everyone inside was dispatched, he let Abram know that the enemy machinegun had been taken out, and that he was going to try and make his way to Dokk's position. Abram acknowledged all of these things and rolled away from his position; bullets were starting to impact the lip of the roof. He ran, full sprint across the top of the dilapidated building and jumped down the skylight, just as a highly accurate shot panged the air conditioner behind him. The enemy sniper had taken notice of them. He landed in the same place where Lovecraft did and saw his team leader rounding the corner that led to the stairs. Abram ran a little way down the hallway and pulled a Claymore mine from his pack. He hid it behind a cardboard box and stuck one of its tripwires into the loose plaster on the other side of the hall. After this, he set up in the former machinegun room and got ready to cover Lovecraft, who ran out into the street, just as he got set up.

Lovecraft took advantage of the confusion and killed all who stood between him and the restaurant. The people who were shooting at him couldn't get a clean shot and complained that he was just too fast. Sue saw him coming and peaked around the corner again. She shot the two men closest to the door, just as Lovecraft entered. She had heard stories of Lovecraft and the rest of Ruler; no Contractor who worked in Chicago didn't know who Lovecraft and Ruler was, but she had never actually seen him in person. He was much taller than she had ever heard, even those Contractors who had allegedly seen him and worked with him didn't say he was as tall as he was, maybe it was because Sue was rather short, but for her, his aged face and large frame was as intimidating as a mountain trail or a razor-wire fence.

Lovecraft's first impression of the carnage inside was that they had been just a little too late. He then pointed his gun toward the ceiling and motioned for Sue to come over to him. However, just as she started to move, a bullet hit the receiver of Lovecraft's gun and bore a hole in its side.

Lovecraft swore and jumped behind a booth. Sue ducked behind her cover again, as he dropped the magazine that was currently in his gun and tried in vain to pull the charging handle back. The whole operation was seized up and thus, made his gun completely inoperable. He called out to Abram and informed him of this, but he was also informed that a different sniper had suppressed Abram's position as well.

Lovecraft slung his rifle and as he pulled out his pistol, he muttered, "Great, this shit can never be easy, can it?"

"Unfortunately, it never is, Bro," Aaron's voice replied on Lovecraft's comms.

"Aaron, where are you guys at?" Lovecraft asked, slightly annoyed that his friend was listening in.

"We're arriving now. Tell Abram that he won't be stuck for much longer."

"Roger that." Aaron and Ying were pushed up into a building just two structures down from Abram. They slowly and carefully placed their steps, as their eyes were fixated on a lone gunman who had his eyes and rifle pointed at Lovecraft's position. Aaron averted his gaze to a nearby room and saw that there was a shovel laying on the floor. Stopping to pick it up, Aaron shifted his gun around and grasped its handle with two hands. They continued moving down the corridor and once they were close enough, Aaron took off at full sprint.

The sniper turned around and saw Aaron lift the shovel above his head, saying, "Good afternoon, bitch!" He swiped the man across the face with it and finished him off once he was on the floor. Ying got into a crouched position and watched the hallway, as Aaron radioed Abram, telling him that he should be safe for the time being. He inspected the room and his interest was immediately piqued when he saw that the sniper's rifle was a Knight's Armament SR-25, a rifle much too expensive for wannabe criminals.

He picked it up and muttered, "What the hell?" Just as he did though, the glass in the window cracked, as highly accurate fire ripped through the room. Ying swore as she hit the deck, and Aaron did as well, as he spun around a cabinet.

"Ying!" he called out to her, "This is more of your expertise!" He tossed her the SR and once she caught it, Ying checked its ammo and got back into a low position. She slinked her way into the hallway like a snake and for the first time, Aaron noticed that her eyes were as focused as a cat's. It was almost like she was hunting, but the only worthy prey were members of her own kind: Snipers. Thinking about it in hindsight made Aaron believe that she was trained to be a cannibalistic, apex predator; a devourer of men that could only be satisfied by the blood of her own species.

She slinked through the hallway like a wraith, and at a certain point, she stopped. She lifted the rifle up and held it against the doorframe with her left hand. From here, she could see out the apartment window and into the opposite building with her scope. Her trained eyes caught onto the delicate workings of the environment and quickly learned what was supposed to be there and what wasn't supposed to be there. A thin black line slightly hanging from a windowsill gave some small, but precise, movements; *that* was not natural. She steadied her breathing and hoped that this rifle was as accurate as she needed it to be. Ying squeezed the trigger and when the rifle went off, she saw the thin black line fall to the ground.

"Did you get him?!" Aaron yelled in.

Ying shook her head, "No, but I did get his gun." For the first time in his life, Aaron found himself speechless during a mission. The fact that Ying had just taken out a sniper by shooting his rifle was not just baffling; it was insane.

Ying could see that he was having trouble believing her and spoke for him, "It wasn't my greatest shot ever, but I think it worked for now. We should go and help the others before that sniper decides that he wants to come for our asses." Aaron could not believe that she was being so humble after making a shot that most people couldn't dream of making in their lifetime. However, her words did resurrect him, and he agreed with her. The two of them moved to the stairs and started to descend down the building.

Lovecraft and Sue were still held up inside the restaurant, but the enemy had dissipated enough that the two of them were more or less just taking pot shots at fleeing enemies. Aaron and Ying soon appeared in the street and joined them in shooting the stragglers. They cut down all that they saw, and Ying noticed that one of these runners had a bloodied face and similar hand. She knew this was the sniper and aimed carefully. Just as his head was about to meet the center of the crosshair, she fired and watched the red mist explode from him. The area fell quiet as his body rolled; Ying inhaled as she stood up and tossed the rifle to the asphalt. She grabbed her M4 from her back and followed Aaron to where Lovecraft and Sue now stood. Yet, they failed to see that one man was still half-alive and that he was currently pointing a pistol in their direction. It shook in his hand, but a shot did ring out, however, it did not come from his pistol. It came from Abram's machinegun, finishing him off at point blank. He shrugged his shoulders after and slung his gun.

Aaron walked up to Lovecraft and noticed that he was covered in black dust, "What the hell happened to you?"

Lovecraft looked at Ying's bandaged arms and asked her, "What the hell happened to you?"

Abram walked up, looked at Sue, and asked, "What the hell happened to her?" The four of them looked at each other and Sue couldn't believe that this exchange had just taken place. They stood there like statues for a second, and just awkwardly looked at each other.

Lovecraft decided that he would be the one to break the monotony, "Spelunking." Aaron looked at him like he was crazy, but left it at that, he had a feeling that whatever Lovecraft meant probably wasn't worth the time.

Ying went next and explained that she was the victim of 'Shitty American architecture.' Everybody, except for Aaron, looked at one another and tried to figure out exactly what that meant, but they soon gave up and then, they turned to Sue.

The woman felt terrible when she was suddenly put on the spot, since she was still trying to take them all in. She had heard of Aaron and the skull decal on his balaclava; he apparently was a master with tranquilizers and poisons, which he used to make traps. When she looked at Abram, Sue had heard that Ruler had, allegedly, brought a giant into their team, but she didn't think it was true until she saw him. Then there was this strange Asian woman that could have passed off as an Asian-American for just how curvy she was. Sue was predominately Korean, even though she was born in the States, and she could tell that Ying was neither Korean nor Japanese, thus, she surmised that she had to be Chinese. The one thing that Sue knew, for certain, was that this woman was scary. The way her eyes darted around at the slightest movement, the way that they seem to focus her like a carnivore, and how they softened once they recognized that it was her, made a chill run up her back; there was something off about her.

"Um, clever ambush." Sue looked to the asphalt for a second, "I should go and get the bodies ready." She started to turn around, but stopped once Lovecraft spoke up.

"We're not taking the bodies," he said.

She turned around and looked at him incredulously, "What?"

"You have no idea where you are, do you?" Lovecraft asked, and then answered it, "You are inside of a Restricted Zone without a permit. Nobody's coming to get them and we are the only ones who can save you."

"W-What are you talking about?! I...we...I can't just leave them here!" she protested. Lovecraft put his arms behind his back and instructed her to take as much time as she needed. The rest of Ruler started to have various conversations amongst themselves; some trying to figure out just what happened to Aaron and Ying, while the latter seemed extremely curious as to what would be for dinner that evening.

Sue watched them like the one kid in school who didn't have any friends, "You guys aren't serious, are you?" Everyone ignored her and those who smoked started reaching for their packs. Sue started to cry again as she turned around, dragging the buttstock of her gun along the ground; she walked back into the restaurant. She tried to cover the dead as best she could and even attempted to put the man who had been blown apart back together, but that only made her throw her bloodied gloves away in frustration. She sat in there for but a moment more, holding her head in her hands, as she tried to erase the memories, the sounds, and the smells. However, she soon realized, just as Lovecraft intended her to, that they were irreversible and would be with her forever.

"Hey, Gook!" a voice yelled in front of her. She looked up and saw Ying standing in front of her with rifle on her back and a small bag in her right hand.

"If you're going to complain about us not caring, then how about you pull their tags off before you start crying over them," she said, throwing her the bag. The fabric container hit the floor in front of her and spit out the dog tag of her commanding officer; her eyes immediately going wide. With shaky hands, she stooped down and pushed it back into the bag. She picked it up and held it close to her bosom; her eyes still leaking.

"We need to go," Ying said, after the woman finally picked up the bag, "You can cry some more later." Sue reluctantly followed her out of the building and rejoined the rest of Ruler. She noticed that Lovecraft had called it quits on fixing his gun and had picked up an AKM; he was busily going over a map with Aaron, while Abram searched the dead bodies for ammo and bandages. The two of them walked up and Ying announced that they were ready.

"Great. Well, lucky for us, there is still light left, which means that we can continue the search. We'll stay a full team though, since splitting up seemed to be a terrible idea," he replied.

Ying nodded and then asked, "So where do we start?"

Aaron answered this question, "Simple, we look inside the trenches. A majority of them are reasonably deep in this area, and our hope is that it cuts deep enough for us to see anomalies with the naked eye." Aaron returned after he said this and apologized to Lovecraft for only being able to find three mags for his AKM; these guys were surprisingly devoid of Russian surplus weapons. Lovecraft told him it was okay and started unpacking his STANAG magazines and handed them to Sue, saying that, 'she would need them more than he would.' He then replaced them in his plate carrier with the AK mags. After he finished this, he instructed them to move, and led them deeper into the zone.

Beneath their feet, wires hung like jungle vines, and holographic displays informed anyone of very-specific details regarding the area. In the center of the room, sat the half-robotic woman that attacked Aaron and Lovecraft in the hospital. She stared at her metallic right hand and admired the sharp nails that were welded onto her fingertips. The woman had no feeling in her fingers because of this, and even though many had tried to fix this over the years, none were successful. She often wondered why she had feeling in her arms, torso, legs, and even the spines on her crown, but not her hands. Her purple eyes glowed in the shadow cast by her crown, until there was a knock at her door, and they turned bluish when she shifted her gaze. The door to her room slid open and a robot carrying an old machine gun entered the room.

"Lady Valravn," he began, "the Master has need of you in his chamber." She acknowledged this and pulled two wires out of her head, before pulling two others out of each arm. She stood to her full height and started to walk. She ducked underneath the doorframe and walked out into the cramped, dark hallway that looked like it was out of an 80s sci-fi movie. Valravn could hear blow torches cutting metal in an adjacent hallway, and when she looked down a different one, she saw a man with dark goggles for eyes, eating a soup ration. She turned her gaze back to the front and her heavy, metal feet carried her to a set of large doors.

Outside this door was a small object; a doll that sat in a wheelchair. Now this was not a typically sized doll, no, it was about as big as 13 or 14-year-old girl, with an elaborate black bonnet covering her snowy hair. The bonnet, just like her dress, was covered in elaborate white lace. Her eyes were as blue as a newborn's, and her face was marred with deep lines that indicated that her face, and most of her body, was no more than a plastic counterfeit.

Her blue eyes suddenly moved to gaze at the tall, steel lady that stood with long hair just as white as her own, "Hello, Lady Valravn. Master is waiting for you inside, should I play my part as your translator?"

Valravn nodded at the small Lolita, "Yes, Coffin." The doll, whose name was just revealed as Coffin, smirked, as she assumed her other role in these tunnels. With no movement of her own, Coffin started to wheel around toward the door. There was a small battery pack and an antenna attached to the back of her chair and this allowed her to control her movement with her mind. Valravn often wondered what it was like for her to be able to wheel herself around. Was it like walking around, just noisier? Or perhaps, was it like riding around in a miniature car? She could never know, and would never ask because it would be too rude, but if she had to guess, had to hypothesize, the latter would be more likely than the former.

A holographic screen appeared in front of the door and asked for a password, which Coffin entered, without typing or speaking. The door started opening and, for a moment, both women were blinded by the light in the room. In its center was a large chair that was similar to Valravn's, but it was a bit larger and was built under a large mainframe that connected to the city's A.I. The Master was sitting in this chair and was covered in a grey robe and had over 40 wires plugged into his being. He had no face, instead, he had a black-visored helmet that wrapped around his whole head. The light that highlighted him was produced from the metallic confines of the mainframe above; it was a being that allowed him to see the whole city all at once.

"Hello, Val. It is good to see that your repairs have been completed," he greeted, the visor covering his face, displaying an image of happiness.

Valravn's eyes turned pink as she knelt down and whispered into Coffin's ear. Hidden from the prying ears of her leader, her speech was broken, and she could barely pronounce words that were above two syllables. This is why Coffin's second job was to be her translator.

"Valravn gives her thanks and asks why she was summoned," Coffin relayed. The Master's visor was painted with the number four that quickly flashed to a red five, and then the words, 'False Prophet' appeared in red background, before disappearing into the black.

"My sensors have indicated that the team of Contractors that you engaged with at the hospital are now above us. They are looking for an entrance to this place," he revealed.

"She asks if you would like her to drive them away," Coffin said, immediately after he finished.

"Stay calm, Valravn, and listen. The reason they are digging around is most certainly because of our black sheep, Lancelot. He has been active yet again, and the Contractors are starting to get nervous, especially ones of the Chinese variety," he explained, raising a hand to silence her.

She whispered to Coffin again, "She says that they are still looking for him, but since the recent hit on the Chinese, there has been no trace."

"Yes, he is hiding from even my eye," he motioned to the mainframe, "but this cannot go on for much longer. The Chinese people he attacked, are nasty and ruthless people, just like our creators, and they have started arming some of the Fascist militants who occupy the space above us. I fear that our traitor will soon become a victor if nothing is done," as the Master admitted this, the words, 'time to attack' appeared on his face and then disappeared.

"Lady Valravn suggests that we redouble our efforts, or we allow the Contractor to find him and put him down."

The mathematical equation, '$1+1=2$,' appeared on his visor, before he said, "Both are good suggestions, but I have already made a plan. Valravn, after you engaged those Contractors, I did some research on them, and their leader's name is Lovecraft. He's the one that electrocuted you." Valravn's eyes turned red and she turned away from his gaze for a moment. "However, I have also just learned that they have come at odds with the Chinese Contractors whom our bastard blew up. Thus, I want you two to initiate a dialogue with them and negotiate a truce." Valravn's eyes turned cyan as she succumbed to confusion.

Coffin, however, was ready to give her thoughts, "Master, it's pretty obvious that we are not on friendly terms with these, or any Contractors. So what evidence is there that we won't just be blown up the minute we show our faces?"

"Simple, you don't show your faces right away. You contact them and agree to meet with them. Bring your guards and allow them to keep their weapons; just be fair. After extensive study of Lovecraft's background, there is a very good chance that he will agree to meet with you, so long as you don't endanger them. Additionally, we have two common goals in the need for Lancelot to be put down and these Communist maniacs to be removed from the picture."

Valravn now countered through Coffin, "She wants to know what we should do if they don't accept and they try and take us."

"Go with them, but only go if they guarantee that you will be held and not handed off. We must first give peace a try or we are no better than what Lancelot would have us be," he said, his visor turning a bright white that then faded to black, "Go, you have your orders. Any of the finer details, I leave up to you. Oh yes, Valravn," she turned back around curiously, "try not to get shot up this time. We're running out of scrap metal."

Chapter 11
Black Hate

Gravel fell from the high ledges and took residence in deep chasms, as the boots of Ruler trudged along. Sunlight bathed the ruined buildings and made the broken glass twinkle like stars, as Aaron's eyes looked into the trenches below. They had been searching for a few hours and had yet seen nothing. He looked behind them and saw that Sue was falling behind a bit. He then looked in front of him and was met with the nape of Lovecraft's neck. Aaron looked at the ground for a second and knew that he needed to say something. He needed to talk some sense into Lovecraft; he needed to make the reasonable man see reason again.

"Lovecraft," he said, getting his leader's attention, "I need to speak to you." The man in question stopped, turned, and gave the order for them to rest in a nearby building that was still in fairly good condition. Ying, Sue, and Abram sat down on a fallen beam that could have easily been mistaken for a railroad tie, and the Chinese woman pulled an electric lantern from her backpack. She set it in the center of the room and then the three of them stared into it, like the bonfire in a fantasy novel.

Lovecraft and Aaron walked into an adjacent room where the latter pulled his helmet off, then his balaclava. He ran a hand over his smooth face and then turned to his friend, who stood next to a window and looked out.

"Dude," Aaron began, "what are we doing out here? We've been walking around for over two hours and haven't found anything. We can't keep this up, especially when we have an exhausted refugee that may need better medical attention than what I can give her. I'm no medic, Lovecraft."

Lovecraft looked at him with unimpressed eyes, "We have to find something, or we will be no better than a week ago. This investigation is at a stalemate and I will not let it be so."

"We have found something, Lovecraft," Aaron retorted, "Although, it is not what you had intended. We have found one survivor of a team that we could have, *you* could have, just left to die. Nobody would fault you if you had, but that's not it. There is countless evidence that the Chinese are arming militant cells in the Zone. Yet, you would kill Sue in favor of finding the tiniest, most insignificant, shred of evidence of the Master."

"It's not like she's going to spontaneously combust."

"Don't talk to me like you do with Kara. She understands that you do not mean it, but for me, it is the most insulting thing that could be done." Aaron got closer to Lovecraft, who recoiled a bit, but still held himself up like a wall, "What are you scared of, Lovecraft? Hmm? I remember a time when somebody like Major Kei would make you vomit and then you would have eradicated him like shit on your boot. Now, I wonder if I had just dreamed it all up."

"I was younger back then, Aaron. I've gotten smarter in my age."

"You are 30 years old, Lovecraft. You're not fucking 60, like you seem to think you are. Also, you've not gotten smarter, you've gotten more politicized." This cut to Lovecraft's core and made him ask the same question. He looked toward the door and saw the light from Ying's lantern streaming through the bottom crack. He remembered the promise that he had made the young woman and remembered how he took pity on her. It was the whole reason that she wasn't sitting in a jail cell right now.

Lovecraft suddenly sighed and pulled over an old chair. He sat down in it and pulled out his cigarettes.

"I'm tired, Aaron, and disturbed. This whole predicament we've gotten ourselves in is disturbing. However, now that Ying is here, I realize just how much I suck at being around people."

"You seemed to be doing pretty well. I mean, you even get along with Kara, so how much worse is it to be around them?"

"It's not easy. Especially when they bring their own problems down on us." Aaron could understand his feelings. The Chinese problem was something that they neither predicted nor wanted. However, Aaron knew what was the more-pressing matter at hand, and while the Master could become a bigger problem, he wasn't at the moment.

"It isn't easy," Aaron affirmed, "But that's life. Now, the thing that you need to figure out is just how you want to lead these people. Do you want to lead them and make them believe that you are *the* Lovecraft, or do you want to keep them safe? They know the job they were assigned to do, do you?" To say that Lovecraft enjoyed being lectured by his subordinate was a blatant lie. He hated it; especially, since he was the one who trained Aaron, but he knew that his friend was right.

"Of course I do. We move out in ten minutes; radio for evac…we're leaving," Lovecraft ordered, standing up. Aaron nodded, with a satisfied look in his eyes, as Lovecraft stepped past him and opened the door.

He walked down the hallway and toward the light which the small lantern proudly produced. He saw that Abram was in the midst of a tale that he deemed to be scary, but when Lovecraft listened to it, he had to smirk. The story was not as scary as he claimed; although, Sue looked like she was about to cry, and Ying had her arms and legs crossed, defiantly staring at the lamp. She shivered a bit and played it off as the cold.

Lovecraft's heavy boots carried him into the room, and Abram stopped mid-sentence once he saw his leader. He grabbed a dirty stool and sat next to them.

"Riveting," he congratulated, "but not as terrifying as the women would have you believe."

"Really?" Abram asked in disbelief, "I would assume you have something to share?"

Lovecraft nodded and then smiled, as he began, "This was a few years ago, in a place called Rock, Kansas. I know, stupid name for a town; it's like some smartass naming his town, Dirt. It's a small, not-even town to the east of Wichita, and directly south of Douglass, and in our line of work, we usually find ourselves driving through small places such as these. Well, most of the time, you just pass right on through because it's very rare for Contractors to get involved in small towns, however, this time, it was a different story. It had just rained, and the road was a mess with leaves and branches. We were driving up to Minnesota, but had taken a detour due to a bunch of crap happening on the Interstate, and as we drove along, we noticed an M.R.A.P. pulled onto the side of the road. Naturally, we found this strange and pulled up behind it.

"Aaron and I got out of the vehicle and started looking around, you know. Then we opened it up and found nobody inside, even though it still had plenty of gas. So we do the one thing any team would do and started searching the radio for emergency signals, or just any signals in general. As you can probably guess, we didn't find anything, so that left us only one option. We set off into the wilderness and using our NODS, we tried to find this missing team. Eventually, we come up to this barn and it looks like the door had been busted open from the inside. We planted our steps carefully as we went inside, the straw was wet and smelled of repugnant mold. This was where we found the team, but I guess it would be more appropriate to say we found what was left of them." Lovecraft looked around the room to gage the reaction and he was very pleased. Sue was shaking a bit, Abram looked like he was engrossed in a book, and Ying just jerked every time there was a noise she did not anticipate.

"Did you find out what took them out?" Abram asked.

Lovecraft shook his head, "The general consensus was a pack of wild dogs, but that makes about as much sense as a polar bear committing a terrorist attack. The locals were spooked enough to more or less abandon the town; part of me still wants to go back there and figure out what exactly happened." Sue muttered that it sounded like a death wish just as Aaron came into the room. His eyes adjusted to the electric light and sniggered at the agitated expressions that the women held.

"Personally, I buy the wild dog story, but Lovecraft still thinks there is something supernatural going on." He turned to Lovecraft, "The helicopter's on its way."

He got up from his stool and told Aaron, "Great, give me the coordinates and everyone else, get yourselves ready for transport." With that, Aaron informed his leader as to where they were to be picked up and the rest started packing up their things. Abram conveyed his disappointment that his claymore didn't get anybody, and Ying comforted him by saying, "Maybe next time." He agreed with her and hefted his machinegun up to his chest. Ying picked up her stuff and when she turned toward Sue, she saw the woman struggling to find a place for the bag of dog tags. She stepped over to the struggling woman and kicked the bag; this knocked the smaller bag from her hand and the contents spilled onto the floor.

Sue looked at her in anger and spat, "What the fuck was that for?" Ying detected the venom in her voice; yet, was unimpressed.

"Pain is not so easily stowed away." She bent down and pushed the dog tags back into the bag. She then reached inside of her bag and found an M.R.E.

She threw it to the floor, "That is why you make more room it." Ying set the bag in the M.R.E.'s place and then closed Sue's pack. Flashes of her comrades ripped through her mind like thunder, as each tooth of the zipper locked in place. She felt her heart burn, as she remembered those who knew nothing of her torment; those who were forced to die in the wrong.

"You sure have a funny way of saying that I should leave something behind," Sue said, standing up and hitting Ying's shoulder, as she moved toward the others. The Chinese woman barely felt it and immediately forgave her for it; after all, every heart has the right to its own sorrow.

It was after this that Ruler set out and as they climbed to the rooftops, a Chinese agent watched from almost 600 yards away. He quickly stopped watching them and ran down to a long-range radio. He started giving his report and stated that he may have just seen Ying Li, but could not confirm.

At an abandoned hotel on the outskirts of I-55, the sound of smacking flesh could be heard from inside of a closed-off bedroom. It was the kind of noise only heard when two people joined in the act of lovemaking. The two participants in this were Kie and his subordinate, Captain Zhi Yan, who was once Ying's Commanding Officer. Now, she was Ying's replacement. Kie drug his hands down her lower back and then moved them up her sides, till his hands were firmly wrapped around her breasts. Zhi's blue-haired head jumped up in ecstasy, and revealed the nastiest burn scar that anyone could imagine. It covered the right corner of her mouth and almost the entirety of her chin. It was the reason that Kie always took her from behind; he didn't want to see such nastiness during these acts.

There was a knock at the door and Kie immediately withdrew himself. Zhi rolled over onto her back and tried to get him to come back with the shake of the head. He ignored her, of course, and walked over to the door. Annoyed, she got up and went to take a shower, as Kie threw on a robe. He opened the door and saw that another captain stood outside. The soldier informed his leader of the situation and said that he should come down to the Terminal Room. Kie thanked him and dismissed him, before closing the door to begin dressing.

Zhi dressed as well, and both of them stood in the elevator, as they descended into the building's bowels. However, while Zhi had her insignia to differentiate from Kie, there was also another piece of her uniform that no one else had. It was a ballistic mask that covered her entire face; she used this to cover up that embarrassing mark. The other thing that set her apart from other officers, besides her blue hair, was a fur-lined, leather jacket that she usually wore over her uniform. It was an old jacket that had the Chinese military insignia on its shoulder boards and due to obvious circumstances, she did not have it.

The elevator door opened, and they walked into a stuffy, concrete room that had a large blue screen on the left-hand wall. Three men stood in the room, two with headsets and one without, who was the sergeant in charge. He turned toward the elevator and stood at attention once he saw the two officers. He told him to be at ease and after that, the sergeant began explaining the circumstances behind the scout's findings. There was apparently a firefight between one of their sponsored factions and an unknown Contracting group. Unfortunately, the sponsored faction was eliminated and most of its stragglers were being picked off by Scavers from the Bazaar. The sergeant then informed him that they dispatched a scout to get a gage on the situation, but, due to the poor logistics in this Zone, he arrived late. He then instructed one of his subordinates to bring up the scout's video.

"He captured this right before being ordered to pull out. Now, the video is not of the best quality due to the range that the binoculars had to capture, but it is good enough to at least make a speculation," the sergeant explained. He let the video play and through the shattered pixels of green and black, they saw four figures walking across the rooftops. The one they immediately picked out was the tallest one who wore Russian-styled gear. The next one in front of him was dressed in all black and stuck out like a strange apparition. Looking behind the tallest, they saw a strange woman who didn't appear all that impressive and behind of her, stood a woman who was unmistakably their missing sniper.

Zhi was the first one to speak and when she did, her voice was laced with displeasure, "Impressive, the little nymph managed to survive, but why is she with them?" Nobody answered her question, and as the video continued to play, a thin, black line suddenly cut vertically across the screen in front of Aaron; in that same moment, the video returned to normal.

"What was that?" Kei asked, causing the sergeant to turn to his subordinates. They shared a few words and then the sergeant explained to Kei that it could be a number of things such as: faulty equipment, radio waves, or there was just too much light and the night vision was having trouble correcting it.

Kei trusted his word and asked, "Do we know who this team is?"

"Unfortunately, we don't know and can't find out, unless we have a team leader or call sign. However, we believe that this one right here," he pointed to the woman in the far back, "was at the center of the firefight and due to this, she will probably go to the hospital."

"She will be a sitting duck for us to extract information from, Zhi," Kie called. Zhi stood at attention and he instructed her to head to Chicago and pull this information from its source. She accepted and walked out of the room in order to prepare for her mission.

Back in the Flood Zone, Ruler boarded another Blackhawk, where there was a medic waiting for Sue. She sat next to him, while the others took their own places. As Lovecraft sat down, his broken rifle placed between his feet, his phone forced itself off silent and alerted him with a single, high-pitched beep. He pulled it free from the confines of his pocket and tapped on the alert, which read, "WARNING: UNKNOWN SIGNAL BLOCKED." The screen switched to a display that gave him the time it first appeared, how far its source was, and a speculation as to who it belonged to. His nose crinkled and deep lines formed in his brow, as the Chinese characters filled his eyes.

"Problem?" Abram asked, noticing his leader's expression.

Lovecraft looked at him and said, "Yes. Ying!" The woman turned toward him and suddenly found his phone in her lap, "What do you know of this?" She looked at the writing and her face immediately fell.

"I should have worn a mask," she muttered grimly. She handed the item back to Lovecraft and took her seat once again. Everyone looked at him, as he turned the phone off; they all had the same question, but none were brave enough to ask it. Lovecraft also had no desire and no patience for such questions; he was tired and as soon as they were relieved of Sue, the better. It was not because he held any personal resentment toward her, but one could not deny that she was in the way and given her current emotional state, Lovecraft really did not want to risk getting shot in the ass because she was spacing off.

The pilot notifying them that they would be landing shortly broke Lovecraft from his thoughts, and when they did land, there was a medical team waiting for Sue. They handed her off and, after he informed Ying that she was being taken to the hospital for the time being, they departed. They ate at a cheap restaurant on the way home and returned to their compound a little after one in the morning. It was here that Lovecraft informed them of his plans for the next day.

"Tomorrow, Aaron will be in charge for most of the day," he began, "I will be running various errands in response to the growing Chinese threat. If I'm not back by five, call either Barons or Kara; I'll be speaking to both of them tomorrow." He looked around to each of them and they all nodded, except for Ying, who stayed behind as the others walked away.

"Can I ask you to do something for me? You know, if you have time tomorrow."

"No, Ying, I will not buy you tampons," Lovecraft smirked, trying to shake her gloomy expression.

It worked to some degree and caused her to smile, as she said, "No, it's nothing like that. I just wanted to know if you would pick up some flowers and give them to Sue for me?"

Lovecraft found this immensely surprising and asked, "You really do care for her then?"

"I never said I didn't, but I will also admit she's not my favorite person in the world. However, I do feel sorry for her and would at least like to convey that, even if she doesn't accept it. I just wish she didn't act like a child so much." Lovecraft could see the seriousness in her face and chose his words carefully.

"If I have time. Ying, don't make fun of her grief, because I could very easily make fun of yours." He started to walk away from her.

"I'm not making fun of her grief. I just wanted her to focus on the fact that she still was alive and needed to stay that way. It would have been a waste if she caught up and died for no reason."

"I agree, however, I have a sneaking suspicion that you're hiding something deep inside of you and it's tearing you apart. Yet, that's none of my business, so if there are no further questions, I will be going to bed," Lovecraft finished, by walking past her and retired to his room by shutting the door. Ying suddenly found herself mulling over his words, while also working through the situation she was in. She shook her head and muttered that her hair would turn white at this rate. Ying ran a hand through her hair and then retired to her room for the night, where her dreams were a mixture of scattered memories and familiar faces.

Lovecraft drove down the crowded Chicago streets around noon the next day. He was on his way to Lugers and Leggings, after he called ahead and made sure that Kara was free. He already knew that Thursdays were typically slow days for her, but he was never one for assumptions. He rounded the corner and immediately noticed that there was a military jeep pulled in front of Kara's shop. He pulled up behind it and grimaced in annoyance once he saw the German flag painted on the side.

"Not these fuckin' boy scouts," Lovecraft muttered, opening his door. He walked around the town car and pulled open its other door. From here, he pulled a case containing his broken rifle and carried it to the front door.

Upon entering, he was greeted by the sight of Michael Dumont talking to Kara, while his team stood behind him. He looked past them and saw that Monica was standing on the stairs, most likely with her M4 hidden behind the wall. Sammy stood next to Kara's office with his arms folded behind his back, his eyes watching their every move.

"I've told you a thousand times now, I do not know any Menagerie Alexandre. I have never known any Menagerie Alexandre," she turned to Lovecraft, "and if you can't see, I have a customer, so I'm going to have to ask you get off my property."

Michael turned toward the door and was shocked to see him, "Lovecraft? It's been a while; I didn't expect to see you here."

"The feeling is mutual. Now, might I ask why you're harassing her?" Lovecraft asked, motioning toward Kara with his hand.

Michael glanced back at her and then explained, "This is just standard procedure for when searching for a specific person, and—"

"Standard procedure does not piss off the owner and her Contractors. You are a dumbass if you think that you can fool me with such blatant crap. Leave, before I report this to the Union and get you deported," Lovecraft threatened. Michael looked at his men and then carried themselves out the door. Lovecraft watched them get in their vehicle and only turned away once they were gone.

"I can't believe they actually bought that," Kara said, smirking at him. He turned to her and noticed, for the first time, that she was wearing a long, black dress that hugged her curves beautifully. There was a section of red lace that formed an Asian-style dragon running all the way from the bottom of the skirt to the beginning of her waist. The top was solid in the front, with the back being completely open, and when coupled with her dark green hair, red lips, and the gold earrings hanging down from her hidden ears, she looked lovely.

"You look nice," Lovecraft said, setting the case on the counter. Kara blushed, realizing that it was just a straightforward compliment, and there was no other cynical follow up. Monica watched the way that Kara, the girl that she had raised since she was 16, reacted to this, and shook her head at just how obvious she was. It was almost cringe worthy how flustered she got.

Kara soon recovered and thanked Lovecraft shortly before asking him what brought him here besides the obvious; she was not told of any case over of the phone.

Lovecraft popped the locks on the case open and replied, "Ran into a snag on my last mission, and now, my MK.18 is FUBAR. Lookin' for a replacement and I need this one disposed of."

Kara's flustered demeanor had now totally disappeared thanks to them being in her element and snickered a bit, "Come on, L.C., it can't be that bad. All you'd have to do is hand it over and I can probably fix on the counter right now." Lovecraft had the brief thought of trying to argue her point, but he decided to just show her what he meant instead. After all, a gun with a bullet hole in the side was quite the sight. Lovecraft opened the case up and spun it around so Kara could take a look at it.

Her eyes immediately focused on the wreckage of the rifle, and it appeared as though the shock of the situation had frozen her in place with a smile affixed to her lips. She just sat there and stared at it for a moment and at its end, she grabbed the rifle.

She looked at it for a second, and after Lovecraft thought her face had permanently frozen in place, she said, "It's fucked. In fact, it's so fucked up, I think I may have to file a police report. Where in the… How in the…" Kara folded her hands in front of her mouth, "Okay, L.C., do I even want to know how this happened?"

Lovecraft mulled over the story in his head before deciding it wasn't a good idea, "Pretend it just happened randomly and I'll tell you the story of how I banged a flight attendant in the back of a strip club. Deal?"

The shop owner's pupils expanded and almost filled the entirety of their green borders, just like a cat's, "Deal!" She grabbed the broken gun and turned to Sammy, "Sammy! Pull the salvageable parts from this and then destroy it." He took it and disappeared behind a black door right next to the stairs. Kara then motioned for Lovecraft to follow her, although he stated that he knew how this worked. The two of them walked into Kara's office and as Lovecraft admired her gold AK-74, its owner punched a few numbers into a keypad on the inside of a cabinet.

The wall suddenly groaned before the back of it opened to reveal a black staircase that was lit with blue lights. This was where Lugers and Leggings kept its stock of military-grade weaponry that were only available to Contractors.

Kara turned to see that Lovecraft was still looking at her Kalashnikov and asked, "Something wrong?"

"No, just a feeling," Lovecraft said, turning toward her.

"What? You suddenly afraid I'm going to eat you down here. My nickname is superficial." She smirked at him.

Lovecraft scoffed, "No, my superstition is reserved for Movie Night, dark tunnels, and for whenever Jesus decides to grace us with his presence again. I just had a feeling that I might see an old friend very soon."

Kara didn't know what he meant by this and opted to change the subject, as they walked down the stairs, "Speaking of Movie Night, after this is all through with... Fridays, like usual?"

"Sure, but I'm picking the movie next time. You watch *Hot Rod* way too much." She started arguing with him about how she did not, and that it was one of the best movies ever. He proceeded to argue this point as well, and before either of them knew it, they were standing at the Arsenal Chamber door. With an annoyed twitch of the eye, Kara turned away from Lovecraft and swiped her hand down in front of the door. Its red lights immediately turned blue and then it slipped away automatically. The two of them walked into a massive rectangular room that was roughly half the size of a gymnasium. It was rather dark, but there was just enough light to make out the walls, where countless firearms hung from the walls. Kara walked into the middle of the room and said something in French that Lovecraft could not understand.

Upon the word being said, which he later found out meant crow, a panel lifted from the floor and presented them with an electric blue, holographic keyboard.

"You finally got it working?" Lovecraft asked.

Kara chuckled, "After two years of headaches, construction, and bloody knuckles, it's finally complete. This is also the first time I've used it, so I'd be lying if I said I wasn't a little bit excited." She took a moment to run her hand through the keyboard, which caused a shimmering effect, before asking, "Are you ready?"

Lovecraft nodded and waited for her to ask him the questions whose answers would then be typed into the computer. Kara clicked a few holographic keys and then smiled once it gave her the green light.

"So what country are we shopping from?"

210

"U.S.A." Kara typed his answer into the machine and a rather large back panel was highlighted. The rack holding up the guns was draped in an American flag.

"Platform?"

"AR15/M4."

"Brand?"

"No preference."

"Specialty Rifles?"

"No."

When Kara typed this in, four robotic arms appeared from the ceiling and removed several different rifles; most of them were HK416 variants, but there were also a few Bushmaster ACRs, a MK. 16, and even an AR-15 shotgun that was pulled from the pool.

"Barrel length?"

"14 inches." More rifles were pulled away.

"Specific specs?"

"Monolithic rail, 45-degree throw, nitride barrel, and an iron-bonded bolt carrier." These requests narrowed down the pool considerably.

"Do you want it to give you head too?" Kara asked, sarcastically.

Lovecraft rolled his eyes, "Only you would actually have something like that, Kara. Continue."

"Why would I have that, Lovecraft? I don't know if you noticed, but you're the only one with a dick in here. Cerakote?"

"F.D.E. and I beg to differ, because while one is permanently attached to my body, your whole being is one."

"Maybe that's why women love me? I had this 60-year-old woman hit on me the other day and I was so confused as to whether or not I was supposed to be flattered or not."

"Wow, Kara, making Granny's panties wet is a new feat. Yet, you still can't seem to find a guy to make you that excited." Lovecraft shrugged his shoulders, "Maybe you should just give up and go gay before you become the crazy cat lady who doesn't own a cat."

The robotic arm grabbed one of the racks and began to bring it over to Lovecraft and Kara, "I applaud you for finding such a creative way to call me crazy, but the thing is, most people in my age bracket have kids and everyone knows what children are." The rack stopped in front of them and the rifles swung due to the suddenly lack of momentum.

Lovecraft looked at her without a single clue as to what she meant, so she enlightened him, "Children are the spawn of Satan." He rolled his eyes at her just before she instructed him to see if any of these rifles were to his liking and he suddenly felt as though he were at a high-end suit fitting. The tall man walked amongst the rifles, which there were 16 in total, and ran his hand across some and lifted others. Kara clicked her heel on the floor and a cylindrical chair rose from the floor. She sat down and crossed her legs before resting her head in her palm; she loved to watch his mind work. There was something fascinating about watching him figure out what he liked and what he didn't like; it was like he was putting together a complex puzzle that only he could figure out. The sight brought her back to a time that took place almost a year-and-a-half ago; the memory tickled her spine, but before she could explore it further, she heard him pull a gun off the wall. She looked up and saw him pull a Daniel Defense M4 from the rack.

The assault rifle met each one of his specifications and even added a few more features. The first was that it already came with an Eotech, so now Lovecraft would have a spare if he bought this one. Another was that the Eotech sight had a riser underneath it, which Kara informed him, was to allow the shooter to fire the rifle from a chin wield, thus minimizing that stress on one's neck. Besides that, it came with canted iron sights, and an infrared laser.

Lovecraft was impressed with this rifle and couldn't help but notice that it was just what he needed right now.

"I might die from this, but how much is this going to cost?" he asked, suddenly feeling his wallet get heavier. Kara smirked at him and held up three fingers.

"Three? Really?" Lovecraft asked, in minor disbelief.

Kara shrugged her shoulders, "With all the shit going down on the southern border, we're saturating the market with M4 variants. Soon, an M4 and an AK-47 will be the same price at this rate."

Lovecraft looked down at the rifle and found that almost impossible to believe. He ultimately decided to buy this rifle and once they returned to the front, they started filling out the paperwork which took them about 30 minutes. After it was done, Lovecraft was hungry, and he still needed to discuss the Chinese matter with Kara. So there was only one logical course of action.

As Kara handed him the box for it, he asked, "Wanna go to lunch?" She was baffled, and stuttered a bit when asking him to repeat himself.

"I'm hungry and I know that you don't eat lunch on regular basis, so treat it as me looking out for your health," he played it off as if it were a normal request. Kara was so stunned that she really didn't hear herself excuse herself to get her coat and purse.

She only returned to the land of the living once she saw Monica sitting on her couch, shoving a cheese stick in her mouth.

"What's up?" she asked with her mouth full.

"Lovecraft asked me to go to lunch with him," she said, in a voice full of disbelief.

Monica stared at her and simply asked, "Are you on drugs?"

"I wish, it would make this a lot more normal. I'm going to get my things." Monica watched her step inside her bedroom and then emerge with her repaired Nano weave coat and handbag on her right shoulder.

"Take an umbrella," Monica called after her, "weather said we might get some rain this afternoon." Kara nodded and grabbed her umbrella. As she started down the stairs, she could feel butterflies in her stomach. When she emerged into the store once again, she tried to push them down into her feet and then tried to replace them with confidence. It worked to a degree.

"Ready?" Lovecraft asked. She nodded and while he grabbed his box, Kara held the door open for him. Outside, he stowed the rifle in the trunk, while Kara helped herself to the passenger seat. Once he got in, they drove to a small, Japanese restaurant, and in a few minutes, they were in a booth, sitting across from each other.

"This is nice, thanks," Kara said, putting down her menu to speak.

Lovecraft kept his up, "Well, I still needed to talk to you about the Chinese, and I knew that you'd be as hungry as I, so why not kill two birds with one stone?"

Kara smiled and then used one of her airbrushed nails to catch the top of his menu. His attention was immediately garnered and internally sighed, this was going to be…interesting.

She pulled it down to the table and said, "Well, if you're going to talk to me, my eyes are up here."

Lovecraft chuckled, "Weird, I never knew you needed your eyes to hear."

"Smartass. Why are you trying to be so inconspicuous anyway?"

Lovecraft looked around and said, "I'm being hunted by sasquatch. I hear that he won't come after you if he can't see you."

"Yes, and T-Rexes can't see you if you don't move. Seriously, if you're going to be paranoid about the Chinese seeing you in public, you could at least act like a normal person," Kara chastised him.

"Coming from the person who dyes her hair green and based her business off a strip club. Forgive me for being the sore thumb."

"You know you love my green hair, but I should probably stop distracting you from the topic at hand."

Lovecraft squinted at her, as he realized just how off track she had gotten him, "We were operating in one of the Southern Restricted Zones and as we were leaving, the jammer on my phone blocked a foreign transmission. You can probably guess what language the I.D. was in."

Kara sighed, "I also take it that they noticed Ying's lady bits as well."

"Most likely, and now, we need to figure out what's our next course of action. Obviously, we have to deal with this little Commie prick, but just how we go about that is influenced by Barons and yourself," Lovecraft explained.

Kara already knew her position in this and was more annoyed that they hadn't gotten somebody to wait on them yet, "I'm fine with whatever you guys feel like doing, but I'd still like to do it my way…even though I know you'll hate it."

"Humor me."

"After the ambush in California, we recovered a cellphone and the Legion can use that to pinpoint where the Chinese are holding up in. I'd like to contact the Chinese and get myself captured; I'll turn myself into a sleeping bomb."

Lovecraft shook his head, "I assume you mean that figuratively."

"No, I'm going to blow myself up like some goat fucker. Come on, L.C., I wouldn't give up my life that easily. Continuing, what I mean by 'bomb,' is I'll have the Legion sneak my gear inside and once a set point passes, I'll break out and render flesh. Simple."

"No, Kara. I can't let you do something so reckless. Yes, I know that you are on par with an Operating Contractor, but what you're asking is suicide."

"If you could do it, why can't I?"

Lovecraft squinted at her, "What do you mean?"

"Come on, Lovecraft. My instincts are too sharp to simply look over the fact that you are not just another Contractor. Your past is just as bloody as mine," Kara shrugged her shoulders, "Maybe that's why we get along so well."

"If we get along so well, then why do I dislike you so?"

"Because you hate it when I'm right. Now, what do you say about continuing this conversation over Udon and beer?" With that, Kara called over a waiter and then a few minutes later, they were able to eat. Contrary to what Kara suggested, they barely talked while they ate; yet, they started right back up again once they finished. Kara paid for the bill, albeit after Lovecraft objected, and as the two of them stepped outside, they heard rain hitting the awning. Her male counterpart sighed, as Kara smirked and opened her umbrella. She handed it to Lovecraft, but noticed that his hand shook as he accepted it. He seemed to not notice as he held the object above them.

"Are you all right?"

"Why wouldn't I be?"

"Because your hand is shaking." Lovecraft looked at his hand front and back. It was clearly shaking on its own and Lovecraft could not feel it.

"Well, isn't that interesting? Come on, I gotta get you back before dark." A worried expression was painted across Kara's face, as he ushered her back into the car. The drive back was a quiet one, although Kara never left Lovecraft without at least one sideways' glance every once in a while. He pulled up to Lugers and Leggings and handed back her umbrella. She asked him again if he was okay and he insisted that he was. Kara reluctantly nodded and left the car.

Lovecraft shook his head and pulled away. He had known his hands were shaking the minute he woke up that morning, but it wasn't the first time and it certainly wouldn't be the last. He worked his way to the Police Headquarters and just sat in his car. He reached up and grabbed his wrist; his right hand stopped shaking immediately, even though he couldn't actually feel the pressure on his wrist. Images of flames, blood, teeth, and compound fractures filled his head, as he ran a hand over his face. He could still hear the faint ringing in his ears that he thought, at one point, would render him deaf.

"You're a monster," a sudden voice said in his ear, causing him to jump. He looked to the back seat, the origin point of the sound, and found nothing but air. He knew who's the voice was and his hand started shaking, not out of fear. For most who knew anything about Lovecraft, they would know that he was not a particularly angry person. Sure, there were times that he was frustrated and raised his voice, but when it came to anger, Lovecraft didn't partake in it. He wasn't impressed with anger and when it was used against him, all he did was mock them. If there was one thing that Lovecraft knew was beneath him and could not hurt him; it was anger.

So what was it then that made him shake? What emotion could possibly make this machine of a man shake with enough power to bend steel? Simple, *hate*. Lovecraft was not an angry person, but he was a hateful one. At one point, a person surmised that hate breeds anger, but what happens if hate smothers the anger it creates? This is yet another simple question; it creates a person like Lovecraft. A cold, piece of rod iron, that does not kill quickly, but maims, tortures, rips, tears, and butchers; this definition is also shared by monsters. Kara was right; he was no ordinary Contractor and she was no ordinary arms dealer, but while she had been known for her ferocity and hot-blooded rage, Lovecraft was known for being a cold-blooded tactician – a man who could and would win at everything, even if it killed him. As stated before, Lovecraft is the only one who could have tamed Kara, the green wolf, and just like that, hate smothered wrath yet again.

Lovecraft grasped his wrist yet again, only this time, he locked it in a death grip. He willed away these feelings and once he did that, the feeling in his arms returned and the shaking stopped. He let out a sigh and then wetted his lips, as they had become very dry; he opened the door to his car and walked down the street toward the main door of the Police Headquarters. He glanced down a nearby alleyway and saw the same prune-haired girl sitting with her back against the building opposite the police's. She was reading a copy of *Little Red Riding Hood* that was obviously stolen, but honestly, who gave a damn? He glanced at the girl and then took it as a blessing, since she didn't seem to notice him; he didn't need any more distractions.

His boots carried him through the doors and all the way up to Barons' office. There, he relayed the events that happened yesterday, as well as Kara's opinion on the matter. He obviously had his objections and most of them were the same ones that Lovecraft had. Yet, Barons did have to admit that it was a better plan than nothing. The two men continued to discuss their options, but they both knew that without the support of a government official or the Contractor's Union, there was very little they could do legally.

"If we had that support, what could we do?" Lovecraft asked.

"The Chinese would immediately be banned from the U.S. and there would also be a warrant out for Kei and the rest of the Snow Leopard S.D.U. As to what I could do specifically, name the place and you'll have all the police and S.W.A.T. support you could handle," Barons replied, lighting a cigar.

Lovecraft nodded. "Then sit tight; I may just have the official support we need," he got up after saying this, and made his way out of the building. When he walked outside, he was glad to see that the rain had stopped and that nobody had parked by him. Things were looking up. He glanced down the alleyway again and was surprised to see that the prune-haired girl was gone. However, the stolen copy of *Little Red Riding Hood* was set on the wet ground. It was left open on a grotesque picture of the wolf and it appeared to stare right into his soul. Lovecraft disregarded this and returned to his vehicle. He pulled his phone free from his pocket and noticed that Aaron had texted him while he was talking to Barons. Opening the message, it reported that Abram, Ying, and he had left and went to a bookstore, due to the woman complaining about not having anything to read. It also requested that he call everybody, including the Coast Guard, should they not be home by the time he returned. He sighed and pinched his brow, but couldn't dwell on it as he had something more important to do. He dialed an unnamed contact in his phone and listened to it ring.

Once he heard the line click, he said, "Hello, is the Ryan's residence?"

Meanwhile, Ying, Abram, and Aaron were milling around a bookstore called 'The Den.' There weren't many people inside, which was interesting because it was nestled in the heart of downtown Chicago. Ying's grey sneakers squeaked on the hardwood floors, as she searched through each of the store's genres. There were books from all around the globe represented here, and Ying was quite surprised with some of the things that caught her eye. From Alexandre Dumas to Philip K. Dick, Ying was able to find almost everything

216

under the spectrum. She even found a few sections of erotica and blushed when she did.

The young Chinese woman felt very overwhelmed by her findings and accidentally bumped into someone, since her mind was so fogged. She quickly spun on her heel to apologize, but the words died in her mouth, as she saw Kara staring back at her. Ying stood there with her mouth open for a bit, and couldn't find the words to express her shock.

"Ying?" Kara asked, just as surprised as her.

"Kara? What are you doing here? I thought you were supposed to be with Lovecraft."

Kara pulled out her phone and checked the time, "Yeah, I was with him and that was about an hour ago, and as to what I'm doing here…" she thrust a small basket toward her, "…shopping." Ying looked at the basket and saw that she had already collected a few books written by different authors such as, Stieg Larsson, Dmitry Glukhovsky, Sen Takatsuki, and Miyamoto Musashi. However, the one that really caught her eye was a book titled, *How to Get a Guy to Like You in 48 Hours*. Ying found this funny and immediately pointed it out.

Kara blushed and said, "H-Hey, I don't make fun of you for your problems. I just am having some trouble with um…" she rubbed the back of her neck and then moved one of her other books on top of it.

Ying smirked and finished her sentence for her, "Finding guys that aren't just interested in your vagina?"

Kara sighed, "You've been hanging around Lovecraft too much. By the way, what are you doing here? Shouldn't you be on lockdown considering it's easier to defend you at the compound?"

Ying frowned, "Yeah, that's where I'm safest, but I'm bored, and if I'm going to stay locked inside somewhere, I might as well have something to read. So, I'm shopping as well." Kara shrugged her shoulders, she couldn't really argue against a person's own boredom, but she did have to ask whether or not Ying really understood the position she was in right now. If you were being hunted down by an elite Special Forces unit, Kara really didn't think it was worth the risk to go and get a piece of literature.

"Um, Ying, you do know that your people are not idiots, right? I'm not trying to burst your bubble here, but if it were me, I'd start singing if I knew you did something so reckless," she said, trying to make Ying see her point.

The Chinese Operator did see her point and even though she loved the way Kara said, 'bubble,' Ying couldn't help but feel the word's sting, "I know, but I'm…restless. I can't sit still, otherwise I feel like I'll never get to the end of this."

Kara understood what she meant and was somewhat sympathetic toward her plight, "I appreciate the fact that you're so zealous when it comes to this fight, but you also have to be patient, Ying. If you're not patient, we can't help you, and trust me, we want to help."

Ying smiled at her words, "Thanks, Kara."

The woman chuckled, "Don't thank me, thank Lovecraft. I don't really have any personal investment toward you, but I'd say that I've met worse people." Kara pulled her phone from her pocket again and checked the time, "Well, I've enjoyed this little meet and greet, but I've gotta go. I have a shop to run and all that." Ying nodded and said her goodbyes, although Kara had a little bit of revenge in store for her.

She walked past her and then said, "Oh yeah, if you're looking for porn, try the internet. I saw you looking at the erotic stuff and all I could do was shake my head. Maybe you'll think about that next time you make fun of my books, Tomato Head." Ying's eyes widened at the name that perfectly described the current color of her face. She watched the sultry woman waltz away and wished that she hadn't said anything. Ying started to walk away and folded her hands in front of herself, as she walked past the pornography again; her eyes locked forward.

When Lovecraft got home that evening, everyone wanted to see his new gun, so he withdrew it from its box and let them hold it. They all sang their praises for it and couldn't believe that he had gotten it for the price Kara offered. He stated that he was, 'just happy that he wouldn't have to do that much to it.' Everyone agreed with him, since they all had experience in dealing with barebones firearms. He packed it away and took it to his room, before returning and sitting in his chair at the table. Aaron had started dinner and Lovecraft took the moment to relax; it felt like he had run a day-long marathon.

"So how did it go today?" Abram asked, opening a can of pop.

"We have everything we need. All there is now, is to figure out a course of action that minimizes our risk," Lovecraft admitted.

Ying heard this and knew that now was the time to divulge the secrets of her unit; the same secrets that she had sworn an oath to protect for the glory of the state. Then, again, was there really any glory in her state? Was the People's Republic of China actually the people's? Was China even *her* state? All these questions, she had asked herself many times, and although she already knew the answer, it still felt strange.

She rolled up the sleeves of her flannel, revealing the beginning of her tattoos, and asked Lovecraft, "Are we ready to discuss my unit and what you need to expect?" Lovecraft turned to Abram and then called Aaron in; they settled back and allowed Ying to continue.

She asked for a piece of paper and once Aaron handed it to her, she started to write on it with the pen he also provided her.

"So, at the top of Snow Leopards, is Major Kei," she circled his name for everybody to see, "but that's old news. The thing we haven't discussed is the other officers he has under his command." She drew two lines that branched away from Kei, "The first is Captain Zhi Yan, she was my commanding officer and she's what you English speakers call a cunt."

"Seriously or figuratively?" Aaron asked as a half-joke.

Ying looked up at the ceiling and gave it some thought, "Actually, she's an ugly cunt. Zhi Yan wears a ballistic to hide a nasty mouth wound she received in the Alti. Stupid bitch thought she was invincible and almost got her head taken off by a Russian sniper."

"I guess Alex actually did hit her; I owe him a drink if I ever see him," Abram said, piquing Ying's interest.

"So that was his name, tell him he's lucky that I wasn't running my rifle that day. Anyway, getting back on topic, I need to tell you something else before we continue." Ying took a moment and walked into the kitchen and grabbed the biggest bottle of liquor she could find, it just so happened to be a bottle of tequila, and carried it into the kitchen. She stated that she would need to be drunk for this and immediately downed a glass.

"The west's main goal for the future was the invention and mass production of Bionics. They were going to bring the dream of Cybernetic Individuals, Cyborgs, to life, but China also had a version of this goal. The government decided that investing in genetic research would be more profitable than bionics, and they were much more successful than the west. Lucky for us though, it ended up much like the west's Bionics; a failure," Ying explained, her cheeks very red from the alcohol.

"And let me guess, you guys are the lucky few that it actually worked on," Aaron surmised.

Ying nodded, "My bones are so hard that they can't break. The closest they've ever been to actually doing it was the attack that led me to you guys."

"I don't believe you," Abram said immediately. Everybody else looked at him and silently agreed; what she said was just too crazy to believe.

Ying chuckled, "I thought you might say that. That's the reason I wanted to be drunk. Follow me to the garage and I'll show you."

She shakily got to her feet and led them out into the dark garage. She immediately grabbed a sledgehammer and held it so each man could see.

"Okay, I'll bet you all 20 dollars that the bones in my hand won't break," Ying said with a playful smirk.

"That's not really something you should be joking about, Ying," Lovecraft said.

She deadpanned, "Are you going to bet or not?" Lovecraft gave an annoyed groan before conceding. Abram and Aaron also took her bet and after smiling, said that she needed help with this and volunteered Abram. He had apprehensions about smashing Ying's hand with a hammer, naturally, but she assured him that it would be okay. She walked over to a metal workbench and laid her left hand, palm-down, on top of it. Abram hefted the tool up to his waist and then moved its heavy, metal head over her appendage.

Ying pulled her belt free from her pants and before biting down on it, she said, "Abram, don't miss." He nodded to her, as she bit down on the belt. He raised the hammer up and then crusted her hand with a loud, metallic thud. Ying screamed and wiped her eyes as her whole hand and portions of her forearm went numb. Her stomach started to hurt; she was in so much pain, and her legs started shaking, but she forced herself to stay standing. Abram looked down at his handiwork in shock.

"Hey guys, Ying was right," he announced, dropping the hammer. Lovecraft and Aaron ran over to her and they saw that her hand was not horribly mangled as it should have been, but only bright purple. Ying watched them look at it and through heaving breaths, she flexed the muscles in her hand and showed that she was fully dexterous. Aaron was baffled, but grabbed her by the shoulders and tried to help her move. This was not a good idea, since once she tried, the room started spinning and she almost pushed Aaron to the ground, trying to run outside.

She just barely made it and heaved what little there actually was in her stomach; the world started returning to normal after she stayed on all fours for a bit. Lovecraft knelt next to her and rubbed her back, as he told Aaron to get the Medkit. He complied and with Abram's help, Lovecraft guided Ying back inside.

"I'll take my 60 dollars now," she said, as Aaron gently bandaged her hand.

The three men looked at each other and soon dug their wallets from their pants, with Aaron saying, "Ying, you might be the craziest bitch I have ever seen in my life."

The Chinese woman smirked at this, "I'll take that as a compliment." They handed her earnings over and Aaron gave her something a little more special in the form of several ibuprofen. She gratefully accepted this and downed them with a glass of water. They then returned to her filling out the hierarchy of the Snow Leopards and filled them in on what their specific weaknesses were.

"As for our equipment, there's nothing special, except each Chinese soldier is equipped with a ZW-5 Exo Rig that greatly increases our physical prowess, but it's nothing to worry about, so long as we have Abram here. His E.M.P. grenades can render them useless and can even trap soldiers inside of their suits," Ying explained.

Lovecraft's mouth formed a line as he thought about all this, "Ying, I can't help but notice that you've failed to tell us the strength of your former commanding officer, Zhi Yun."

She was somewhat surprised at this, "Right, the bitch's healing properties were enhanced, but that doesn't mean she's invincible. Just shoot her in the vitals and she'll die before her body can heal itself. Whatever you do though, do not try and capture her. Kill her and be done with it; hell, cut her head off just to be safe."

"Why do you hate her so much? She's not a zombie, is she?" Abram asked.

"No, but she did watch while Kei… I'll let you finish that sentence for yourselves. The basic thing is, if you end up capturing Kei, you kill Zhi Yun. None of the room clear bullshit; I want you to hunt her down like a dog and then bury her in a soggy grave. Seem fair?"

The three men looked at each other and then nodded to her; although, none of them actually believed that they would do something so graphic. Ying smiled at them and suggested that they eat soon, because, as always, she was hungry. They decided that this was a good idea and Aaron went back to the kitchen. They eventually ate their fill and returned to bed, however, Lovecraft stayed up longer than any other.

He retreated to the outside and sat at the same bus stop that he first met Abram at. He was clad in only a red T-shirt and a pair of jeans, but the cool night air was still warm enough to not be unpleasant. Lovecraft sat there and thought about Ying's words. He then compared it to the conversation he had with Aaron so many years ago. He shut his eyes and he suddenly felt himself stuck to the bench like melted candy.

"Uncle get out of my head," he demanded. Once he did, an old man, who sat in a wheelchair, disappeared into a puddle of blood-red liquid behind him. Lovecraft opened his eyes and jumped up upon seeing Coffin sitting in front of him, with her lively eyes staring at him.

"Actually, my name's Coffin, but I'll assume you were sleeping," she said innocently. Lovecraft immediately pulled his gun and pointed it at her.

"Unfortunately, Contractor, we are not here for a fight, nor am I able to fight you. However, we bring a message—"

"We?" Coffin's eyes moved to a side alley and then moved her wheelchair in that direction, causing Lovecraft to look over. Valravn's white hair was the first thing to catch the light and Lovecraft immediately trained his sights on her. She wore a dark purple dress and her eyes were colored in fluorescent blue.

"This is Valravn, I think you already know her," Coffin introduced.

"Just a bit," Lovecraft said, "How do I know that you're not here to fight?" He turned to Coffin and added, "I'm asking her, not you. If you try anything, I can just kick you over." It was times like these that Coffin wished her face wasn't plastic, so she could give people dirty looks.

Valravn responded to his question by raising her hands and trying her best to convey that she meant no harm. However, she was struggling to pronounce the proper words and then Lovecraft put two and two together.

He turned to Coffin and asked, "Are you her translator, and what is wrong with her?"

"I am, and her vocal cords are damaged. The Master's message was given to her and I've come to form the words that she lacks." Lovecraft looked at Valravn and lowered his pistol, until it was at his hip.

"Step into the light and stay there. I'm going to call my team and if I am in one piece by the time they get here, I'll believe you," he ordered, pulling out his phone. Valravn stepped into the light, as Lovecraft called Aaron and told him to get everybody up and to make sure they were armed. He then ended the call and put his phone away.

A few minutes later, Abram, Aaron, and Ying marched outside, their guns pointed toward the street.

"Shit," Abram swore, as he recognized the white-haired woman.

"Lovecraft!" Aaron called out, as they started moving down the stairs, weapons forward. Upon hearing his name, Lovecraft threw his hand back and sent it in a downward motion and used two fingers to flick toward himself. Aaron didn't know what had gotten into him, but he told the others to lower their weapons and they continued their journey.

Ying flinched once they made it to Lovecraft; these people were just like the man who attacked her. She held her assault rifle into her shoulder, but with the barrel pointed down. She did not like being out here or around them. Valravn looked at her and her eyes turned light pink, but when she saw Abram, her eyes turned red and she reflexively turned her side defensively. Abram raised his machine gun at this action, but was stopped when Lovecraft put his hand on top of it. He looked at him and then turned to Coffin for an explanation.

"Forgive her, she does not like this man, since he was the one who hit her with the magnetic pulse. She couldn't function correctly for a few days and was in a lot of pain," she explained. The three men could only think of the injuries they suffered and how long it took them to fully recover.

"Yeah, we know the feeling. So what is the message your master sent us; could it be another threat?"

"No, he has recognized the fact that you are hunting the Chinese military and wishes to help you in some way. You see, the Chinese have been arming the local denizens around our home, and it is looking a bit grim for us."

"So you're saying that the enemy of your enemy is your friend?"

"Yes…if you'll have us. In exchange, the Master is willing to provide you with the identity of your assassin."

Lovecraft scrutinized her words with his eyes, "The Master is our assassin. We just have no idea where to look for him."

Coffin looked to the ground for a moment, "It is a lot more complicated than you think, Lovecraft." After she got down saying this, Lovecraft's phone rang. Her eyes fell, as Valravn knew what it would be for.

"I'm terribly sorry, Contractor," Valravn struggled, "But, I thought we had more time."

"What do you mean?" Lovecraft asked.

Coffin replied by motioning toward him, "Answer your phone; although, your Korean friend is most likely dead. I'm sorry."

Chapter 12
Vintermorgen

"Welcome to Chicago, Illinois! We are extremely happy to have you and hope that your trip here went as smooth as possible," A cheery, female voice said over the intercom of O'Hare's Terminal. In this place, holographic advertisements hung and even walked on air, while robots handed out coupons for nearby restaurants. People nearly ran into each other as they tried to get to their boarding gates and also sought to get out of the building as quickly as possible. Amongst these people were heavily armed Contractors who carried everything from common nine-millimeter pistols to rare, South African Galils.

"Foreign Contractors!" a police officer called, as people started to stream in from a gate, "Please form a line parallel to the civilian passengers and have your temporary licenses ready for inspection!" The Contractors, who stuck out like a sore thumb due to their fatigues, formed a line, and a beauty with curly blonde hair stood fifth from the front. She had a pair of ear buds shoved into her ears, and was semi-singing a song by Disturbed. Her torso was draped in a flecktarn jacket, but other than that, she was dressed like a civilian. This fact greatly pleased the tall man behind her, who was taking small glances at her rear end whenever possible. The blonde woman knew he was doing this and wore a playful smirk on her face, her perfect rear seemed to move back and forth to the rhythm of her music.

The song ended and she pulled one of her ear buds free and turned to look at him. He smiled when she did, but he felt the fear of God suddenly strike him when he saw the insignia pinned on her jacket collar; she was a Major. He immediately froze in place and his eyes shot ahead of him; he dared not look again. The female Major was amused by his reaction and smiled to herself; although, there was the slight feeling of disappointment, as some part of her wished he hadn't backed down. It was the way everybody acted when they found out she was in charge and was one of the main reasons she had been celibate for over three years. It seemed nobody wanted a hardened military officer who was well into her 30s, even though she looked as though she were in her late 20s.

"Next!" the police officer called, and the woman was suddenly pulled from her depressing thoughts. She shook her head free and walked forward, whilst fetching her temporary license from her pocket. She handed it to the officer, and he looked at it, he then looked at her with a suspicious glare. He looked at her long enough to make her feel uneasy, and then he stamped the piece of paper.

"Welcome to the United States, Major Vintermorgen," he said, before yelling for the next person. She took her temporary license back and saw that there was a green 'A' stamped right above her name; Major Olivia Vintermorgen. She pulled out her wallet and slipped it next to her driver's license, and then returned her loose ear bud back to its rightful place, as she went to find her bags.

Olivia then found herself sitting inside a large waiting room at the Contractor's Union; her hair was pulled back into a ponytail that hung from the back of her flecktarn patrol cap. Her hair was still wet from the shower she took at the small flat she had been provided, and the front of her cap had a medic's cross attached to it. She had changed from her civilian clothes and was now clad in her fatigues that matched the German camo her hat was in.

She looked to the left and the right awkwardly, as the room could seat over 40 people; yet, she was the only one there. This made her wonder if the lady at the front desk had given her the right information. When one went to the Contractor's Union to get their temporary licenses turned into permanent ones, a Contractor is filed into a room and given a number much like a D.M.V. There were only four rooms for her to go inside and they were labeled: Civilian, Former Military, Active Military/Operator, and Foreign Military/Operator. Olivia sat in the last one.

Her attention was garnered when she heard a door open behind the protective kiosk. Her green eyes followed the tired form of a caramel-skinned man; his eyes here framed by a thick pair of blue glasses. He didn't look out into the room; instead, he focused his gaze on a piece of paper in front of him.

"Number one," he called to nobody. Olivia looked around the room on reflex and then looked at her number; she was number nine.

You've got to be kidding me, she thought, slamming the back of her head into the wall. She listened to him as he got to five and she wondered what god was playing the cruelest joke on her. However, Olivia could only venture a few guesses, before her mind was rocked by an indescribably sharp pain that ran the length of her entire left leg. She gasped aloud and fumbled with her breast pocket, before pulling a white pill bottle out of it. She threw four pills into her hand and downed them without water. Her forehead had begun to sweat from the pain and now, all she could do was pray that the painkillers worked faster than the last time; it never did. Olivia shut her eyes and slowed her breathing to a normal level.

"Number nine!" the man at the desk finally called. Ironic, since Olivia now no longer wished he had called her. She reluctantly stood up and limped her way over to the kiosk. He slipped a piece of paper underneath the glass and told her to sign it. Her permanent license was attached to the form.

She looked at it in bewilderment and asked, "What?" The man didn't look at her as he asked her if she could read English. She stated that she could and then he stated that he didn't know what the problem was.

"Huh? I didn't even say anything, and you just slid me my license. Aren't I supposed to have an interview or a test or something?"

He finally looked up at her and said, "Look, I really don't want to be here, and you already took the test back in your own country. Now, there was one flag that was brought up and it was about how you've been on a regiment of particularly strong painkillers since you turned 30 years old. Care to explain why?"

"I was injured by an I.E.D. on the French border and I didn't heal properly," she explained, subconsciously rubbing her sore leg.

"Good enough. Sign the forum and take your license," he ordered, turning away from her once again. Olivia was rather appalled by the way he acted and had a notion to give him a piece of her mind, but she was stopped by the sound of her superior's voice running through her head. She grabbed the pen and signed the piece of paper before pulling the license free. She replaced her temporary one with the permanent and left the building.

She walked outside and immediately felt the humidity wrap around her neck, as the sun blazed above. Olivia put her hand up to the bill of her hat and tried to pull it further down, in hopes to keep her face from burning. She then pulled her phone from her pocket and unwove her ear buds. Olivia pushed them into her ears and tuned it to her first playlist, and as Metallica's *One* filled her ears, she walked down to the bus stop. She walked down there alone, got on the empty bus alone, and was dropped off at her first stop alone. Olivia had one more stop to make before she could go home and relax for the day, but in order to make it to the next bus stop, she needed to walk around the block – which was practically baking. In response, she rolled up her sleeves and revealed her large and swollen arm muscles that denoted her athleticism. Olivia started to make her way around the block and had her gaze glued to the sweating concrete.

It was because of this that she ran into a woman carrying several large boxes once she rounded the next corner.

"Oh, I'm terribly sorry!" Olivia apologized, as she lifted a heavy metal box off the concrete. She really hoped that whatever was inside of it wasn't expensive or breakable; however, she immediately lost focus on these thoughts, when she noticed that the box she had picked up was a box of warheads. She had seen pictures of these Russian boxes many times and knew that the writing on it said they were for R.P.G.-type launchers.

"Heh, don't worry about it too much. That's what I get for not letting one of the interns help me," came a voice that was slightly diluted by a French accent. Olivia looked up in half panic when she heard the accent, her days on the French border suddenly coming back in full force, but when she looked and saw green eyes framed by extremely dark-green hair, her mind was defused for a moment.

"Honestly, you'd think that the truck drivers could deliver it closer to my shop. Thanks for picking it up, though, if you'd like to help me, it would be much appreciated," she offered with hopeful eyes. Olivia was still at a loss for words though, as she tried to figure out how somebody got that much hair to look that good while being put in a messy bun. Whoever this was, she was the kind of person that Olivia had read of in books that were so beautiful, they charmed even people of the same sex.

"Um, are you okay? Did the heat get to you?" the woman suddenly asked, pulling Olivia free from her own mind. Embarrassed, Olivia apologized again and asked her to repeat what she asked. She laughed and repeated herself, whilst also bringing the woman's thick German accent to attention.

Olivia agreed to help her and found that the woman's ditzy nature was rather contagious, maybe even infectious, but it was good.

"Follow me, my name's Kara, by the way," she instructed, leading Olivia in the opposite direction of her original destination.

"Major Olivia Vintermorgen."

"Major?! Well, aren't you something. I bet the men are just hanging off those boots of yours."

Olivia had to chuckle at this, "No…not really."

"Bullshit. Really? I find that very hard to believe."

"Well, it is true. Why is it so hard to believe?"

"Because, you're very pretty, but I guess we don't have to have somebody at this very moment. My shop is at the end of the corner." Olivia appreciated her words and garnered a small amount of hope from her. However, she was not allowed to dwell on this forever, as a news drone flew over their street right at that moment.

"This weather forecast is brought to you by Lugers and Leggings." Olivia heard the name and found it slightly humorous, while also being slightly

intrigued by it. She wondered how an old pistol from her home country was synonymous with leggings and she made a mental note that she would have to find out one day.

"Ooh, I want to listen to this," Kara said excitedly.

"Lugers & Leggings, the beauty of annihilation." Kara bounced up and down excitedly, while saying that it sounded perfect.

"Perfect?" Olivia muttered, wondering why Kara was so excited over an advertisement. She didn't get a chance to ask her because as soon as she stopped bouncing, Kara was already making her way back down the sidewalk, and forced Olivia to run after her, much like a cartoon character. She soon wound up behind Kara, and thanks to the heat, was somewhat winded; Mother Nature was giving her no breaks today.

"We're here!" Kara announced, much to Olivia's gratitude. She looked up to the store's sign and her face immediately dropped when she read 'Lugers and Leggings.' Her mind started to sputter like an old car and allowed her to finally connect the dots between the munitions she carried and the advertisement that Kara seemed so thrilled about: Olivia could feel the word, 'moron' being drawn on her forehead, and it was at these moments that she wondered how she made the rank of Major.

As Olivia's head fried like an egg, Kara walked up to the door and kicked the bottom of it twice. She waited a few moments and door was opened by Monica, who wore the expression Kara knew that meant she was concerned. She chided Kara for not letting her help and took the two remaining boxes from the taller, yet younger, woman.

Kara held the door open for Olivia and said to Monica, "Oh my God, I am so sorry, Monica," her tone was mocking and sarcastic, "I should really think of my health. I mean, how would I go play bingo with the girls or go to bed at four-thirty if I wrenched my back? I guess I need to double my supplements for sure."

Monica set the boxes on the counter, as Olivia entered the building, "Babe, you've been hanging around Lovecraft too much; you're started to sound like a sarcastic twat."

Kara chuckled, "And he'd call you a crabby old bitch right now. Stop calling me babe as well, I don't want people to think that we're lovers or in an incestuous relationship like some English tramp."

Monica scoffed and then laughed herself, "Stop being so melodramatic, Kara. People know that I'm not your actual mother and I've called you babe since you were but a babe. You can't expect me to stop now." Kara sighed and then turned to see that Olivia was standing next to the counter, with her arms behind her back; she had been listening to them bicker the whole time.

"Who is this, Kara?" Monica asked.

"This is Major Olivia Vintermorgen, a brand-new Contractor." Olivia looked bewildered, immediately once Kara said this; she had never said such a thing.

"How did you know?" she asked.

"The look on your face gave it away. There's only one thing that can make a person look like a fish out of water, and that's when you first get your Contractor's license," Kara explained, stepping away from Monica and walking behind the counter. Olivia touched her face, when Kara pointed out that she looked a little lost.

"So have you found a contract yet, and what tier are you?" Kara asked, taking one of the boxes and setting it on the floor and out of view.

"I'm a, uh, Operator, and I don't have any."

Kara smiled at this, "Well, I'll be damned. You are something special, aren't you?"

"Well, no, I don't particularly think so. I'm just a Combat Surgeon."

Kara almost fell over and even Monica's attention was garnered when she said this. Olivia asked if it was something she said and after Kara recovered, she asked the woman a very blunt question.

"Okay, I thought your stupidity just came from your naivety, but now I must ask for your sake. Are you an idiot?"

Olivia looked at her in shock, "No, I'm not."

"Then how do you not have any contracts already lined up? Like, is your agent a retard or something?"

"Agent?" Kara could not believe her ears. This woman was an Operating Contractor, practically a Civilian Navy Seal, and she didn't have a clue as to how most Contractors did business in this country. However, it was as she thought of this, that a thought, a small thread-like notion, wafted through her mind and caused her to ask her next question.

"What did the Contractor's Union say to you?"

Olivia suddenly started putting the pieces together and stated grimly, "Sign here, take your license, and get out."

Kara nodded, "They fucked you and from my guess, it wasn't enjoyable." She used her eyes to search underneath the cash register and when she found a stack of yellow papers, she grabbed one, "Come here, Sauerkraut." Olivia shook her head at the nickname and walked over; she was slightly amused by it. Kara withdrew a pen and started to point to various aspects and blanks on the paper. She explained to her that this was the sheet that they used when hiring new Contractors and that she could represent herself like some Operators, but having an agent would make it easier on herself. She also reaffirmed that she could do it herself and there would be no repercussions, and that pay would be set by the Contractor, but she recommended that she didn't put herself too high otherwise she'll just get laughed at.

Kara let Olivia digest this information before she continued speaking, "Now, as for the fact you are a Combat Surgeon and at the very least, a medic, I would highly recommend that you let that be known to as many potential contacts as possible. In fact, it would be one of the first things I would put forth. As for me and Lugers and Leggings, you won't have to look much further for any ordinance that you may need. We also sell medical supplies, but given the current situation on our Southern Border, you might have a better chance trying to swindle them off a nurse at the local hospital."

"Would they really go for that?" Olivia asked, uncertain.

"Everybody's poor nowadays, and Contractors are actually some of the most trustworthy people one can sell to. Plus, Contracting pays well, so they know you have the money to pay," Kara explained.

While her boss helped Olivia understand how being a Contractor worked, Monica got a message from Lawrence on her phone. She had wondered where he had been since she hadn't seen him since yesterday, and when she inquired as to where he was, the only thing the rest of the Legion said was that Kara had an assignment for him – and when she went to Kara, the only thing she said was that Lovecraft requested him. It was frustrating.

Yet, when she opened it up, there was no explanation, no emotion, not even a damn greeting. All it said was, *"Tell Kara that she needs to turn on the news."* Monica was beside herself, but she carried the message to Kara, who immediately pulled out her phone. Her eyes scanned the latest news headlines and once she saw that there had been an incident at the hospital, Kara knew that this was the reason Lovecraft called her. She saw that there were a lot injured and she knew that Olivia would be able to help enormously.

She looked up at her and asked, "Hey, kind of a weird question, but how soon can you get your gear ready?"

Olivia looked at her in confusion, "Um, I was put up in a small flat not too far from here, why?"

"Because, shit just hit the fan." She turned to Monica and instructed her to drive Olivia to this place and then to get her down to the hospital. She acknowledged her orders and soon led Olivia to an old U.A.Z. four-by-four, located just behind L&L.

Once they were driving, Olivia asked, "How bad do you think it is?"

"If Kara threw you in with how green you are, then I'd expect mass casualties. You ready for something like that?" Monica asked, going ten over the speed limit. Olivia's face darkened when the thoughts of what she had seen back home filled her mind. She stared at her bare hands that would soon be covered by white latex and took in a breath.

"I always am," she replied.

It didn't take them long to get to where Olivia was staying, and it took the blonde-haired woman even less to run the stairs, because the elevator was too slow. Once inside, she quickly pulled off her shirt and black bra and threw on a blue sports bra. She then covered that with a red tank top, thinking of the heat. Bags and boxes were thrown around the room, as she laced her belt through her pants' loops and snapped her holster onto her upper thigh. She wanted to save the heavier and more cumbersome gear for last and decided to kick off her boots, which she soon replaced with a pair of blacked-out skate shoes. After she got done tying them, Olivia threw her bag onto the bed and began packing tourniquets, bandages, antibiotics, steroids, painkillers, epi pens, and really anything that she could carry comfortably. She dusted off her goggles and then pulled off her hat; she steeled herself for this would be the hardest part. Olivia went over to a particularly heavy case and opened it to reveal a Paraclete plate carrier that was fitted out with level-five body armor. She really hated how cumbersome this thing was, but when it came to the possibility of getting shot, she could overlook it.

She slipped it over her head and Velcro-ed it around her body. She then fastened its shoulder pads securely around her lower arm; one of which featured a blue cross. She pulled a pair of white, latex gloves over her hands and all the way up on her forearms, before returning her hat to its rightful place. She put her backpack on and now, there was just two more things she needed to grab.

Olivia went over to a medium-sized, hard case that she opened with four loud clicks. From inside, she pulled an FNX-45 pistol that was colored in dark earth and pulled its magazine free to check its ammunition; no, she was not supposed to have it loaded on the plane, but who was going to check a Contractor's stuff in the first place? Olivia had owned this pistol for a long time and had modified it with a red-dot sight, muzzle break, and a laser; however, the paint was starting to come off and in some places, it didn't even look like it had a finish. The other weapon she pulled out, which was also her primary weapon, was an HK433 assault rifle, that was almost as old as her pistol, but it certainly looked a lot better than her pistol. She checked its magazine and then threw three more spares in her carrier and then grabbed three pistol magazines and slipped them into the carriers on her belt.

Olivia quickly shut the box and quickly moved to her door. She ran back down the stairs and when she got back in the vehicle with Monica, the woman complimented her on how fast she was. Olivia felt that she was slower than usual, but still accepted the compliment. The two women drove through downtown Chicago and decorative trees started to sprout around them. Monica pulled her license and told Olivia to get hers out. As they got closer to their destination, the wind started blowing, and while it felt better than the boiling humidity, the darkened sky told of its true nature. The first raindrop fell onto the bill of Olivia's hat and her bangs blew around her green eyes. Monica pushed her sunglasses up on her head, as the sun fully disappeared, and the blowing wind pushed aside the trees to reveal the flashing lights in front of them.

The German medic stared in awe as there had to be at least five, heavily armored, police cruisers forming a roadblock. Amongst these cars were equally heavily armored S.W.A.T. members that carried their UMP-45V3s, and .50 Beowulf's extremely close to the chest. One of them stepped in front of Monica's vehicle and held his hand up, indicating for her to stop. She did so and he came around to her window, while two more officers stepped in front of and beside the Soviet four by four.

"Afternoon, ladies, can I see your stuff?" he asked. Monica grabbed Olivia's license and gave both of them to the officer, who looked at them both front and back before returning them, "Have a better day."

"Good choice of words," Monica commented, before rolling up her window and proceeding through. The rain started to come down harder as they continued on, and Olivia was left to collect her thoughts, as she stared at her license.

"What happened here?" she asked, having finally looked up. There were various emergency vehicles parked along the road, as well as armored vehicles that were other Contractors. Some of them were even lounging in raincoats nearby.

Monica shrugged her shoulders even though Olivia wasn't directly looking at her, "All I know is that there was some mass shooting here last night; other than that, one of my comrades was sent here upon the request of Lovecraft, another Operator, and after that, I don't have a clue."

"You mentioned him before when we were with Kara. Who is he?"

"Probably the smartest and scariest motherfucker I've ever met. He's a cruel bastard who expects results no matter the problem, and rarely takes prisoners, but I guess that's just a side effect of the missions he gets put on."

"What kind of missions are those?"

"He's directly employed by the Chicago Police Department, as most of the highest-ranking Contracting Groups are, and he, as well as the rest of his team, are Barons' resident cockroach stompers. Basically, if you have terrorist activity, a mass shooter, or any other kind of nasty bitch, Lovecraft, and the rest of his team, are immediately called in if they're available."

Olivia had to chuckle a bit and told Monica, "You sound like an ex-lover of his, from the way you speak about him."

Monica blushed as she pulled over, "Um, no, unfortunately, that's a scenario that exists only in my dreams. I'm much too old and dry to keep up with a man like Lovecraft."

"I could give you some medicine for that, if it's that bad," Olivia offered with a little too much sincerity for Monica's liking.

"I wasn't serious…" Monica trailed off, her pride currently bleeding out, "Anyway, get out of the truck. It's time for work." With that, she opened her door and grabbed her M4 from the back seat. Olivia also jumped out of the truck, with a heavy thud coming from her feet due to the weight of her body armor. She slung her gun over her shoulder, but suddenly, she saw that there were over 30 blue, body bags that were strategically hidden behind a couple of ambulances. Olivia pulled her right foot back and off one of them. They had unknowingly parked next to.

"Jesus, what a mess," Monica muttered, when she pushed a bloody arm back inside of a burst body bag with her foot. The air stunk and it was this stench that was starting to attract flies, which made Olivia's skin crawl.

"This is really bad. They need to get these bodies out of here otherwise people are going to get worse than gunshot wounds," Olivia said, stepping over a few more of them.

"It looks like they're trying to move as fast as they can," Monica said, whilst pointing to a series of ambulances loading up bodies. Olivia nodded and then looked up to the building and saw that all of its windows were blown out and some even featured a halo around them that was made of soot. There was metallic click from underneath her shoe and when she looked down to investigate, Olivia found a thin piece of surprisingly sturdy metal that was machined into the form of a dart.

"What's that?" Monica asked.

Olivia rolled it between her latex fingers and replied, "I don't know, but it seems familiar…" she trailed off before taking the dart and shoving it inside her pocket for later. She stood up and followed Monica into the building where the tale of last night's terror began.

Blood hung from fresh flowers placed on the bedside of the room that Sue formerly occupied. Glass and metallic darts covered the floor, as blood dripped from the wall next to the door and almost flooded the whole bathroom. A white strand of hair fell and disappeared in the L.E.D. light, before revealing itself again by landing in a drop of blood. There was a deathly silence in the room and it scared Ying, as she stood there in the middle of this room, her boot mere millimeters from the stained line of hair. Her black hair struggled in vain to shield her eyes from this carnival, this parade of absolute tragedy. Her eyes betrayed herself and imprinted this fully in her mind, like it was the greatest thing she had ever seen.

Her hands were still, her body was still, and her eyes refused to blink. She had turned into a statue and maybe, just maybe, staying as such an object would be worth it. The bathroom was where they found her; just hanging there, with all her clothes torn away – just like her dignity. They had left her to bleed out, and judging from the semen they found inside of her, the Chinese even used her as Ying's replacement for a while. Sue was dead, Magnolia was dead, Magnolia's staff were dead, the hospital was in ruins, and it was all committed by a special strike team lead by Ying's former C.O.: Captain Zhi Yun. Ying's index and middle fingers started to rub together rapidly, like they were anxious to find something.

"Excuse me?" Ying's eyes and being stirred into motion upon hearing a familiar voice. She turned around so quickly that when her right foot hit the floor, her boot heel produced a loud cracking sound on the tile. Her eyes dilated for a second, before she saw Monica's red hair, and then she refocused on the glasses-clad face of the middle-aged French woman. There was a shorter woman with long blonde hair pulled back in a ponytail behind her, but Ying disregarded her as not important for the moment. She did have to admit that she was rather armored for a medic, but that was about as much time as she gave to look at her.

"Monica? What are you doing here?" she asked, rather surprised. Olivia looked the Asian woman over and she wondered why she was using such old gear; even the green jacket she wore looked rather dirty. The other thing she noticed was that this 'Ying' was almost as busty and developed as Kara; a trait that was almost never seen in her ethnic region. She was rather impressed and a little cautious about it.

"I got a text from Lawrence. Do you know where he is?" Monica inquired, looking around the damaged room.

"Probably with Lovecraft. I'll show you the way." Ying started to move out of the room and as she passed Monica, the older woman told her to stay still. She did so and Monica reached up to Ying's hair and pulled out a strand of hair.

The younger woman gave her complaints and Monica apologized by saying, "Sorry, you had a grey." Ying nodded and they started to walk further down the darkened hallway. The power was still out and even though the electricians were working tirelessly to get it back on, there was only so much damage they could repair. The women's weapons clattered against their backs, as they walked up a flight of stairs that were covered in more of the strange darts.

"What are these things, Ying?" Monica asked, kicking them out of her way.

"Flechettes. The Chinese raided the place using shotguns loaded with it; and started slaughtering everybody. It wasn't exactly effective, but any ammunition is effective when all you need to do is shoot."

Olivia now knew why the dart in her pocket seemed so familiar. The French had used flechette artillery shells on them during one of the many border confrontations, "They didn't want them to die quickly. They wanted them to bleed to death."

"Your skills of observation are impeccable, Snow White. Who are you anyway?" Ying asked.

Olivia replied, "*Oberstabsarzt* Olivia Vintermorgen, I just arrived today."

"Ober-what? I don't speak German."

Olivia nodded, "*Oberstabsarzt* is essentially a medic that is the rank of a Major. I'm also a Combat Surgeon."

"So what, you just like sightseeing? What are you doing here if you're a Combat Surgeon, shouldn't you be further south?"

Olivia shrugged her shoulders, "I don't have any contracts, and Kara said that I could be of some use here, so here I am."

"Hate to burst your bubble, but most of the people here died last night. You may be able to save one of the dying, but there may not be time." Ying ran a hand through her hair, "Come, Lovecraft will probably have some use for you." She turned around and started walking up the stairs again. Monica and Olivia followed her and as she passed one of the few good windows, Olivia could have sworn the reflected image of Ying's hair was bright white, but that was impossible.

The three of them went to the top floor and what Olivia saw almost sent her into shock. The floor was littered with dead bodies, most of whom wore Chinese flags on their arms. Olivia covered her mouth with her hand as the stench hit her hard; Monica did the same, but Ying didn't seem to notice it at all.

"I see Ruler's been busy," Monica commented, trying to step around the bodies.

"These were the security force left here in order to capture me. Sorry, but we've only been able to move the bodies from the first few floors." Ying reached into her pocket and pulled out a wad of surgical masks. She handed one to each of them and then put one on herself. The three of them started walking once again and as they did, Olivia had time to look at the dead Chinese soldiers. Each one of them had been shot in the head and some of them, although a small majority of them, had been shot in the chest as well. She was not a coroner, but if she had to guess, then she would assume that the ones who had been shot in the chest were the ones they thought were still alive. It was cruel, but from the way Ying spoke with her hollow voice that almost held no accent, it almost seemed as though they had it coming.

This, however, did not prepare her for the sheer brutality that Ying was about display. The three women trudged their way through the gore, but as they reached the end of the hallway, Ying noticed that there was a blood trailing leading away from them into one of the other rooms.

Her face fell and she walked around the corner and saw a Chinese soldier trying to hide in a corner, "Hey, look, one of them is still alive." Olivia and Monica appeared behind her, just as he flipped himself onto his back. He started to mutter something, but in the space of a single breath, Ying pulled her pistol and finished him off with three rounds of nine-millimeter. She did it so fast that it felt like she had stolen the air out of Olivia's lungs, but in reality, Ying didn't do it that fast, and the only reason it felt so fast was because the German Operator didn't expect her to perform such a ruthless act.

Ying put away her smoking gun just as they heard a set of rhythmic thuds approaching them. The three of them turned around and saw Abram appear from around the corner, with his flashlight on and his face covered just like theirs. Seeing him for the first time, Olivia couldn't believe how tall he was; the story of David and Goliath immediately being pulled from her memories, as she gazed at this individual.

"Ying, I heard shots," he said, with an Eastern accent that piqued Olivia's interest.

Ying pointed into the room with her pistol, "Making sure the dead stay dead."

Abram grunted as she put her pistol away, "Keep it to a minimum; we can't have the cleaners shitting themselves over loose gunshots." He turned to Monica and the strange German he didn't know, and said, "I'll assume you're here looking for Lawrence. He's on the roof with L.C." Monica turned to him, nodded, and then motioned for Olivia to follow with her head. The German soldier looked at her and then turned back to the dead Chinese soldier. She continued to look at him even as she walked away, but she couldn't look at him forever.

She continued to follow the Eastern man with the others and noticed, for the first time, that he was Russian, due to the faded flags on his Altyn helmet. Their feet echoed through the dark, bloody, and damaged halls, as they came to the door that lead to the roof.

"They're up there, you're free to go up," Abram said, crossing his arms whilst leaning next to the door. The three women went up the metal stairs and opened the top door with hollow creak, as the rain, once again, started pelting their faces. Olivia gazed across the roof and found it to be extremely flat, with its ends being lined with a black half-wall which was probably to prevent people from committing suicide. The far, top, right-hand corner stood a makeshift, tarp tent that looked like it belonged in a ghetto.

Underneath its protection, there were four men; three standing and one sitting. The one who was sitting was dressed in black, Crye Precision, combat gear, and wore a balaclava imprinted with a skull underneath his ballistic helmet. The first of the three men was a police officer, which was obvious, given the word, 'POLICE' was scribbled across his body armor. The second one wore a tan plate carrier similar to Monica's; thus, Olivia presumed this was Lawrence. The third and final one stood a head taller than both men, and was covered by a black trench coat that went down to the knees of his Multicam pants. His head was shaved on the sides, while the top was left to grow just like the unkempt stubble that decorated his face. He pointed to a piece of paper with his gloved hand and made sure that each man understood his orders, whilst the women walked up to him.

"Lovecraft," Ying got his attention, "visitors for you."

Lovecraft stopped talking and turned toward them; Olivia's heart jumped when she saw his vacant, grey eyes look over at her. They were just like the eyes she had seen when the night terrors oppressed her earlier years.

"Ying, you have blood on your face," was the first thing that Lovecraft said, in a voice that made the back of Olivia's neck harden like ice. The Chinese woman reached up to her face and with a swipe, found that he was correct. She went to go clean her face off, as Lawrence turned and noticed his comrade.

"Good to see you," he greeted.

"The feeling is mutual. I heard, and saw a little bit, from Ying, that this was China's doing; care to explain?" Lawrence nodded, but differed to Lovecraft who would know the story better. Monica turned to him and Lovecraft began weaving a tale of black and bloody darkness that ended with the slaughter of Sue and began the total annihilation of the Chinese military in the U.S.

Monica understood everything he said, but Olivia couldn't really believe what was happening. The Chinese were declaring war on America via proxy and black operations. She sure picked a hell of a time to get sent here.

"Sounds like you lit the world on fire last night. Why haven't you called Kara, and about this tip you got – who gave it to you?"

"I left my phones, both of them, at the compound, and as for the tip, it will be a part of a discussion, all of us, including Barons, will be having sometime in the next few hours," he explained, not trying to give up Coffin and Valravn just yet.

Monica nodded, "Okay, who's that?" She pointed past Lovecraft and to a small figure sitting in the opposite corner, silently watching them. Olivia had to take a step back, as she had apparently glossed over this person who was covered in some sort of black, hooded dress. Her hands were covered by red, leather gloves and her feet, as well as her legs, were wrapped in deep, crimson ribbon. She sat with her back against the low wall and her knees were tucked into her chest; the black dress, with its pleather hexagonal pattern, covering the majority of her body, had fooled Olivia into thinking that she was nothing more than a trash bag.

Her face was more like a mask. Her eyes were completely hollowed out into horizontal ovals, and the only other feature that existed was a convex addition to simulate a nose. Everything else was just smooth, hardened, white plastic that was half hidden by her hood.

Lovecraft looked at her and then turned to Monica, saying, "She's…a deadly acquaintance."

Monica slowly nodded her head, "I'll bet. What does she hunt, mice?" Lovecraft took a moment and then indicated with his eyes that the redhead should look behind her. Monica looked at him like he was crazy, before turning around and taking a step back, as this strange little girl was now immediately behind her. Olivia gasped when she saw whoever this was standing next to her; she didn't even make a sound as she crossed the length of the roof in about a second.

"I don't hunt," she said in a voice that was befitting of a third grader, "I hurt people." Monica's face grew to one of duress, as the girl's creepy face seemed to bore into her soul. Olivia felt the chill return to her skin and it wasn't from the rain, it was from this girl's voice. It was absolutely eerie hearing an innocent voice talking about such a topic.

"Kay, sit down," Lovecraft commanded, rolling his eyes. The strange girl bent her arms behind her back and folded her hands together. She bent forward and moved her head like she was giving Monica an over-exaggerated wink. She then walked between Monica and Olivia, before climbing up on the half wall. She sat down the ledge and dangled her legs over the edge; she kicked them back and forth just like a kid. Olivia watched her for a few more seconds, but could not shake the feeling that there was something off about her.

"Seriously, who is she, Lovecraft?" Monica asked again, a little more on edge. Lovecraft sighed and from his body language, he really didn't want to explain just who Kay was or to which person she was subjected to. However, as he was about to speak, he heard a buzz off to his left and Monica cried, as she tumbled to the roof, blood running from her shoulder, staining her white shirt. Olivia saw her fall and reflexively pulled her assault rifle from her back. She started firing single rounds across the park and into the buildings on the other side. To her surprise, there were additional tracers joining hers and when she looked over, she saw that Lovecraft had grabbed his weapon and was sending rounds toward the buildings. Olivia stopped shooting and went to care for Monica, as Aaron took cover behind the wall. Lovecraft ducked behind the wall, as Ying began crawling over to them; Lawrence was by Monica's side, as Olivia pulled her backpack off and grabbed some antiseptic, as well as an Israeli bandage. The bullet itself had been caught by Monica's plate carrier after it had exited her arm, but it still fucked up her arm pretty good.

Another round impacted the wall, as Lovecraft kicked the table and made his helmet fall from it. He used his gun to retrieve it and once he had it on his head, he started talking to Abram in order to find just where the shots were coming from. The police officer was hiding underneath the table with his hand on his headset, as Ying crawled next Olivia and watched her put a clotting solution on Monica's wound.

She recognized the wound and said, "It's a Chinese sniper and he's using an FY-JS sniper rifle."

"Any idea who or where it could be?" Lovecraft asked, as another shot rang out and several civilians started running from the front of the building.

Ying heard their screams and had an idea, "Permission to do something you won't like?"

"Granted." Ying nodded and stood up for everybody, including the sniper, to see. She wasn't a gambling person, but she had gotten a hint of this sniper's skill from his first shot and knew that the odds were reasonably stacked in her favor. The sound of a bee whizzed right past her left cheek, but didn't come close to her skin. She saw the muzzle flash and got back behind the wall and pulled a compass from one of her pockets.

"Bearing two-forty-three, 13-story building, fifth floor," Ying said, clicking the compass shut and pulling her rifle back up.

"I've said it once and I'll say it again, you are a crazy bitch, Ying!" Aaron yelled down.

"Sometimes crazy is just what you need to get yourself out of this shit," the police officer muttered. Olivia was watching the events unfold and couldn't believe her eyes. This Asian chick had balls, or ovaries she guessed, of steel. Furthermore, she noticed that Kay had seemingly disappeared from where she once sat. It didn't really matter where she had gone at that point and time, but it was still concerning that she had vanished without a trace. Olivia felt something nudge her arm and when she looked down, Monica was sat up and busily pulled her M4 into her hands.

"Abram, did you copy Ying's directions?" Lovecraft asked over his comms.

"Solid copy, but I can't get a shot from this floor. I'd have to be up there with you guys to see the building." Lovecraft cursed under his breath before he turned to Lawrence and asked him if any of his men had any range. He confirmed that he did and then listened as Lovecraft told him to have this person come up the stairs and throw his rifle to Ying. He was very explicit on the fact that he should follow these instructions to the letter; lest he end up getting shot.

"It would be easier if I just called in a V.T.O.L. and had them take it out," the police officer suggested to Lovecraft, who immediately shot it down, saying that, "It was better to get hit by a stray bullet than it was to get crushed by a collapsing building." He was, of course, referring to the possible civilian activity in the area; an act that surprised, but was also highly admired by Olivia.

The door to the roof suddenly flung open and from its dark confines, a Romanian PSL flew through the air and landed near Ying. She slightly grimaced at the sight of Eastern Bloc D.M.R., as she highly doubted it would be accurate enough to confirm the kill, but they no choice. If this was the extent of their ranged capability, then she would have to make it work, otherwise they were all well, and truly, screwed. She wrapped the sling around her left arm and then nodded to Lovecraft, signaling she was ready.

He nodded to her and he told everybody to get ready, and when their weapons were to their shoulders, he yelled, "Suppressive fire!"

Aaron, the police officer, Lovecraft, Olivia, Monica, and Lawrence, all flung their barrels over the low wall, six barrels in total, and they started shooting at the building Ying indicated. The female sniper waited about a second, before throwing her barrel over the wall, and from there, she waited with the chevron of the Soviet era scope roughly where she believed the sniper would appear. The six of them stopped firing and when they did, Ying saw the darkness shift in front of her reticle.

She fired and watched the vapor trail zoom downrange before it started to tumble, just what she was afraid it would do, and cracked the cinder block frame of the window. Yet, her eyes clearly saw a dark liquid spurt out of the opening and as she aimed again, Ying shot for its source. She held her breath for longer than usual and only exhaled when she saw a bolt-action rifle hit the windowsill. Relaxing her shoulders, Ying flicked her tongue into the air like a snake, before turning toward Olivia and Monica.

The German medic watched her do this action and the only thing offered as an explanation was a wink. Lovecraft was the first to stand up and, after he didn't get shot, he gave the all clear. He called the officer over and instructed him to send somebody and have them clear the building. As Olivia watched him, the rain finally let up and as the sun began to return, it cast its light over the roof, but seemed to avoid Lovecraft entirely. Instead, it appeared to cower from him, which created a dark circle around those near him, including her. She shook her head as the cold chill of fear formed its crystals amongst her bones, and when she looked back, the light had returned to its normal rules, and this made her wonder if the events back in her homeland were driving her crazy.

"Hey, did you forget to put your ear pro in? I'm talking to you!" Lovecraft yelled, finally getting Olivia's attention.

"W-What?" she asked in bewilderment.

"I asked you for your name. Unless you're one of those 'next-generation' kids who only have one letter; if that's the case, then I'm just going to call you stupid."

Olivia looked at him and choked on her words, "I'm...Olivia...*Major* Olivia Vintermorgen."

"Hmm," was all the acknowledgement he gave her rank, "You're quick, almost as fast as me, but three seconds too slow. How much did you sucker Kara into paying for that level of skill?"

"I didn't, she asked me to come because my skills may have been necessary."

Lovecraft looked at her like she was retarded, "I guess there is some truth to all those 'Dumb Blonde' jokes."

"Excuse me?!" she asked, not believing her ears.

"What skills do you possess anyway?" he asked, completely ignoring her outrage, "We have plenty of medics here, both Contractor and City." Everybody watched their exchange and all of Ruler, as well as their acquaintances, knew that Olivia was being tested right now. There were only two outcomes to this test: the first was proving that she was tougher than nails, and second, was proving that she deserved no place beside Lovecraft or the other Operators he commanded.

Olivia clenched her fist and forced herself to swallow her pride, "I am a combat surgeon, with more experience than any of your damn civilian medics."

Lovecraft huffed in amusement, "So you do have some attitude other than a fish outta water. You need to be sharpened, but you'll fit right in, Olivia." The German woman suddenly felt exhausted and when it finally hit her that

Lovecraft had just been testing her the whole time – she not only realized that he was the biggest douchebag she had ever met, but that she also wasn't that mad.

Abram appeared in the doorway and joined the rest of them, as Olivia took off her hat and wiped her brow.

"So what's the plan now?" the Russian asked, bracing his machine gun against his shoulder.

Lovecraft slung his rifle and said, "Well, seeing as I don't have any of my damn phones here, let's go visit Kara. I'm sure she'll want to hear about this." They all agreed and as they walked off, Kay watched them from behind her mask. She stood on a lonely, steel I-beam that was suspended at least a hundred feet above the ground by a crane. Below her, on the actual construction site, was the eviscerated body of a Chinese soldier, one of his hands still held the spotting scope he was issued.

Kay sat down on the beam, as the wind blew her hood back and turned her pink hair into a wild mess. She reached up and took her mask off, as the sun broke through the clouds and sent sporadic beams of light over the park and the rest of Chicago.

"Good luck, Lovecraft. Our Black Knight," she muttered.

Chapter 13
An Equal and Opposite Reaction

The tip of Kara's nose touched the top corner of her glass counter; her eyes locked onto the surface of the smooth container. Strands of loose hair blew gently in around her head, as an overhead fan helped circulate the air-conditioned room. However, while there was nothing remarkably unique about her hair, besides its color, there was something rather peculiar about the soft, yellow feathers that adored the area around her face. She breathed slowly and ever so often, there would be a soft patter, like someone tapping their fingernail across the glass, before an orange beak would touch her nose.

Suddenly, her companion and she, were startled by the sound of Ruler's Humvee and Monica's Russian jeep. They entered the building in this order: Lovecraft, Monica, Abram, Aaron, Olivia, and finally, Ying. However, they all had the same reaction when they saw what Kara now held to her chest.

Lovecraft, naturally, was the first to rouse himself from his dumbfounded state, "Kara…why do you have a…duckling?" Everybody stared at the baby fowl held gently in her hands; it looked like it enjoyed the warmth that's Kara's breasts had to offer. Although, it still looked at them cautiously, like it might try and eat them, which was an amusing thought.

"Well, it's a long story that we really don't have—"

"We have time, Kara," Monica said, crossing her arms, "Please explain how you came into the possession of a bird that is commonly found with a…parent."

Kara started to giggle nervously, "Well, you see, I didn't steal it or anything. It was given to me."

"Bullshit," Lovecraft, Aaron, and Abram said in unison; the three of them looking at one another afterward.

"It's not bullshit!" Kara exclaimed, before describing an elaborately detailed story of how a customer and his son came in into the shop. The boy sang praises for how his father just bought him a 'lucky egg' and how something magical would happen if he held onto it for a while. Well, once they left, Kara noticed that he had forgotten his egg on the counter and, to her horror, it started to hatch.

"And let me guess…" Lovecraft pinched his brow, "…the first thing it saw was *you*."

Kara took a breath, "His name is Daffy and he's precisely four hours old."

"You named it?!" Aaron asked, slapping his helmet with his hand. Lovecraft calmed everybody down and insisted that they didn't have time for this. He garnered Kara's full attention and explained to her the events that had taken place in the last 12 hours. Kara glanced at Ying a few times during the explanation and wished that Lovecraft would allow her to go ahead with her plan.

"So what do we do?" she asked.

"This is the first time the Chinese have openly attacked us, but it does not mean they have the advantage." He pulled a slip of paper from his carrier and handed it to her. The French woman read it and was confused for a second.

"This is an old construction site."

"We need somewhere that we can be safe and the only way that's going to happen is if our new allies can watch our backs." Kara looked skeptical at the address before pushing it inside her shirt.

"I'll have the Legion join us there. Is there anything else?"

He nodded, "Don't shoot at anything unless I say so." Kara was about to ask what he meant by that, but she stopped halfway and decided that it was better to not ask. She looked at each of them and intended on finishing there, but Ying's hair caught her eye before she started to say her goodbyes.

"Ying, I think the sun caught your hair a bit. Its…lighter than it was."

The Chinese woman reached up and swept her hair in front of her face, but couldn't see anything, "I think it's just the lighting in here, Kara." The shopkeeper nodded in agreement. Although, she had a sneaking suspicion that it wasn't just her imagination. She shook it from her mind and thanked Lovecraft for the heads up. After this, she said her goodbyes and Monica went upstairs to lick her wounds. Olivia joined Ruler inside their Humvee, since they had agreed to drop her off at her flat.

"So who are the Legion anyway?" Ying asked Aaron, who was in the driver's seat.

"Lovecraft will have to answer that. It's too complicated to tell when you're preoccupied," he replied, turning down a vacant street. Ying turned her attention to Lovecraft, who started to speak.

"In 2044, when the world was lit on fire by the failure of technology, the European Union collapsed under the weight of its own greed. France, Kara's home country, was hit the hardest, and this allowed for a young, charismatic man from Luxembourg, to take control of the country. The only problem was that he had a copy of *Mein Kampf* in his back pocket." Olivia listened to him alongside Ying, and remembered those days when their currency might as well have been dirt. She remembered writing to her stepmother on almost a weekly basis to see if they were managing without her help.

"All foreigners were ordered out of the country lest they face a firing squad. The newly formed secret police, who are former members of the Gendarmerie, rounded up all those who could afford to get on a plane. Now, if you know anything about the French military, then you'd have heard of the Foreign Legion. Well, they're not around anymore, and the reason for that is they were all kicked out of the country. The same country they fought and died for. Well, where there is anger, there is an ambitious entrepreneur who holds just as much resentment for her country as they. She also just so happens to have connections with the exiled commanders of the Foreign Legion. They swore their allegiance to Kara and became her bodyguards, her own personal army."

"That's a scary thought," Ying surmised.

Lovecraft nodded, "The French government thought the same thing and immediately declared the Foreign Legion international terrorists who worked for Menagerie Alexandre. The secret was out and now, the Foreign Legion could no longer call itself its own name. So they became the Legion of Grey Men; Contractors who posed as regular civilians. Yet, they have about five-times more experience than most other P.M.C.s."

Aaron pulled over onto the side of the road and asked Olivia, "This it?" She confirmed that it was and thanked them for taking her there.

However, before she climbed out, Lovecraft called to her, "Hey, Blitz!" She stopped moving and looked at him, with question in her eyes.

He pulled another note from his carrier and scribbled down the address of where they were meeting, "If you can't make it, go with Kara. You're skills maybe necessary." She nodded and took the note from him. She stepped onto the sidewalk and watched them drive away. Her blonde hair blew and swirled around her hat like a furious storm, as her green eyes watched them disappear around the corner. A drop of water impacted the bill of her hat and that was her cue to go inside.

She hurried her way into an elevator and then made her way inside of her residence. Inside, she stripped out of her heavy armor and then pulled herself free of her sweaty underclothes and undergarments. She sat on her bed naked for a moment and just enjoyed the feeling of her body being able to breathe. She pulled her hair free from its ponytail and shook it out, as she noticed that there was a mirror right in front of her. Olivia gazed at her bare chest and scrutinized the fact that it still looked like when she was 17; barely good enough to call attention to her. She was thankful that, in her words, her ass was better than her boobs, otherwise people might have mistaken her for a very beautiful boy.

Olivia uncrossed her legs and bore the full brunt of her womanhood to the mirror, but was disappointed yet again. There was nothing wrong with her. She looked just like every other woman and she just couldn't understand why men didn't see that. Suddenly, though, she shook these thoughts from her mind and snapped her legs shut. She rubbed her face with her hand and then stood up. The sound of her footsteps carried her into the bathroom, where she took a shower and then dressed herself. She curled up on her bed and looked at the note Lovecraft had given her. Her eyes danced across it and then, only then, did she realize that she didn't know when she was supposed to be at this place.

She rolled onto her back, "Fuck…" She then grabbed her phone and looked up the number for Luger and Leggings. Olivia called them up and once the phone was handed to Kara, she explained her problem. Kara understood and told her that Lovecraft hadn't told her the time either, which meant that he hadn't set a time yet, and was probably waiting to talk to Barons, Chicago's police chief. Olivia felt her heart lighten a bit, as she thought she had missed some vital information. She gave her thanks to Kara, who then asked if she needed a ride. Olivia accepted this and said that they gave her everything but transportation.

Kara laughed and said, "Welcome to America, Hun. They'll give you everything *but* the thing you need to succeed." Olivia shared in her amusement, before Kara told her that as soon as she heard something, she would be over to pick her up. Olivia thanked her again and both of the women hung up.

Time progressed and Olivia decided to take a nap after talking with Kara. However, it went longer than she intended, since the next thing she knew, it was dark outside, and her phone was ringing. She barely got dressed and tapped her foot, as the elevator brought her down. She ran outside where she saw Kara sitting inside of an orange four-door that looked like it should have been owned by some douchey 19-year-old.

She waved to the German from inside and Olivia waved back, before running to the other side of the vehicle. After waiting for a car to pass, Olivia opened the door and found a Taco Johns bag in her seat.

Kara's hand immediately flung toward it and moved it to the backseat, "Sorry, I got hungry on the way here." Olivia told her it was fine and took her seat. Kara offered her something from the bag, and even though she was hungry, she respectfully declined. However, she didn't know Kara, and had no way of knowing that the offer was a loaded question.

She shoved a wrapped taco into her hands and pointed a finger at her face, "Nonsense, I can see that you haven't eaten all over your face. You must eat, if not, how are you going to maintain enough energy to vanquish the enemy?" It was at this point that Olivia figured out just how eccentric Kara was, but still ate what was given to her. Seeing this made Kara feel good, and with this, she began to pull her car onto the street.

"Be sure and hang on, okay?"

"Why?"

Kara gave Olivia a smile that bared her teeth and started to rev her engine, "Because this baby's *super*." Before Olivia even put two and two together, Kara hit the gas and made Olivia sink into her seat. She had been right about the car the whole time, only instead of an immature preteen, it was owned by a crazy French lady. Olivia started laughing as her adrenaline started flowing and it just vaguely reminded her of the battles she had partaken in; just without the blood.

Eventually though, they had to slow down and when they did, Kara turned down a dark street that was freed from the lights of Chicago's holograms. The car's headlights reflected off a tower of steel I-beams, tarps, and scaffolding. The protective fence around the construction site perimeter featured a small hole that was impossible to see without the aid of a light. Kara stopped the car in the middle of the street and threw it into reverse. She backed into a nearby alley and turned the car off.

"We're a bit early," she stated, before stretching her arms. Olivia did the same and made herself comfortable. However, her attention was suddenly brought back to Kara, when she heard her pull something from her person. Her eyes widened when she saw her black-and-gold pistol for the first time. Her mind clouded when she tried to figure just how much the gold sights, hammer, barrel, compensator, trigger, and magazine must have cost. Not to mention that she had never seen such a pistol before; it must have been fairly old.

"Holy crap, Kara!" Olivia exclaimed.

Kara looked at her quizzically, "What?" Olivia motioned toward the pistol. "Oh, I'm kinda surprised you noticed this; I got it from a friend in the Russian government."

"You're not a Russian spy, are you?" Olivia asked, like a wide-eyed kid.

"I might be." Olivia stared at her, trying to see if she was being serious. She certainly sounded serious, but she knew it was false when Kara's stoic expression broke and transformed into a contained laugh. She bragged about how she had her going for a bit, until they saw a blacked-out car pull past them and then back into the alleyway across from them. Kara opened her car's center console and pulled a flashlight from it. She flashed it toward the car twice and, after a second or two, the other car replied with a single flash.

Kara sighed as Olivia looked at her quizzically, "Well, Barons is here." Kara reached into her coat and pulled her Marlboros out.

She put one in her mouth and lit it, just as Olivia asked, "You know those are bad for you, right?"

Kara looked at her like she was a pathetic high schooler, "So are bullets, pop, radiation, and drinking from the faucet." Olivia sealed her lips after this and only opened them every so often to cough from the smoke. Kara chuckled every time she did it and after a bit, the cigarette finally burned out. She threw it from the car and informed Olivia that she sounded like a mouse when she coughed. The medic didn't know how to respond to this; luckily, she didn't have to, as Ruler's Humvee drove past them and was followed by a half-ton that belonged to the Legion. Kara pulled the slide back on her pistol and announced that it was time. The two women stepped out of the car and Kara walked to her trunk.

She opened it and grabbed her golden Kalashnikov from its floor. She brushed a hand across its finish before slinging it on her back.

Olivia's eyes widened when she saw the rifle, "Who the hell are you?"

"The Queen of Black Gold, sweetie," Kara replied, slipping a pair of black leather gloves onto her hands. Olivia frowned at the woman, as her high-heeled boots carried her past the older woman; she had heard the name somewhere before, but for the life of her, she could not recall where or why. It felt like she had heard something similar to it as well. She watched the woman, clade in her distinctive trench coat, walk down the sidewalk, as the men in the other car started to get out. Olivia followed her and soon found herself sitting at a table illuminated by construction lights.

She sat roughly in the middle of the table, with Monica on her right and Lawrence on her left. Across from her sat Aaron, Abram, and Ying, while Sammy, and the other members of the Legion, stood behind them. At the head of their table was another table set horizontally, so that those who sat there could look at those at the first table. Lovecraft sat in the center of this table, and on his right was Kara and on his left was Barons, who Olivia found, was rather unhealthy. In all of this, however, Olivia couldn't help but notice that there was a chair at the end of their table that was currently empty.

Barons bent over to Lovecraft and asked him if everybody was there, but he insisted that they were missing two others.

"Relax, we're waiting for our trump card."

"How do you know they'll show?" Barons asked in his gravelly voice.

"Because, if they don't, then they'll be our enemies, and I can assure you, they don't want that." Barons relaxed in his seat at his words. "Just tell your men to be cool and don't shoot at them. It'll reflect poorly on the department." Barons huffed at his words and adjusted the fedora on his head. Seeing that Lovecraft was done talking, Aaron leaned in and asked for permission to grab the awning from the back of the Humvee. His concern was that it may rain here at any moment, and with the dark clouds polluting the night sky, Lovecraft couldn't help but agree with him.

Upon getting permission, Aaron took Abram, and the two of them went to go fetch the cover. Lovecraft took to the opportunity to light a cigarette while they waited. This seemed to cause a chain reaction amongst the members at the table, as Olivia suddenly found herself assaulted by smoke on both sides. Aaron and Abram soon returned and began setting up the awning. Olivia assisted them just to get some fresh air. However, as they did this, their hidden allies appeared.

Lovecraft sat in his chair, but his eyes studied the darkened construction site around him. He noticed how the shadows would shift and somewhat come toward the light, but would always back away.

Lovecraft watched it for a bit before calling out to it, "Valravn. Come sit." Everyone, except for those in Ruler, looked at Lovecraft and then turned to the darkened area in question. Those who had never seen Valravn flinched, when a skeletonized metal hand grasped a pillar and dug its titanium tips into the concrete. A single, bright amber eye appeared from behind the pillar in an effort to properly gauge her situation. Those who were not prepared for such a thing flinched once again and rested their hands on their side arms. Lovecraft commanded them to relax and when they eased themselves, Valravn moved from behind the pillar and started to walk toward them; her eyes returning to their normal shade of blue.

The sound of a wheelchair suddenly echoed around the concrete structure and Coffin appeared from a pillar just behind Valravn. Those at the table noticed that they were, in a simple term, not human, and those that were working the Master Case knew that this was what they were dealing with. Kara knew that this…woman, was what Lovecraft had seen in the hospital basement that day; she couldn't help but admit that she had been skeptical until now. Olivia shook her head and then shut her eyes for a few moments, before coming to the conclusion that she was not seeing things. She wondered if the American's had accomplished their cyborg program and just not told anybody. Barons couldn't be sure if he had taken too much Advil before coming here, but Lovecraft was, apparently, seeing them too, so that was at least comforting.

However, he didn't like that these two women were agents of the Master; a fugitive.

Valravn tested the chair with her hand and found that it could not possibly hold her weight. She moved it to the side and then struck a sitting pose where the chair once was; her knees locked into that position and it appeared as though she was sitting on air. Everyone stared at her with half-open mouths, as she did something that was normal to her, but physically impossible to anybody else. Coffin suggested that she at least put the chair underneath her in order to make everybody more comfortable. Valravn looked at the chair and slipped it underneath herself so it looked like she was sitting normally. This made those at the table relax a bit, but there was still some tension in the air.

"This is Valravn and Coffin. Valravn is representing the Master and Coffin is her translator," Lovecraft introduced. He then went around the table and introduced each member by name so that everyone knew each other.

"Might I ask why there are members of a wanted fugitive's group sitting at the table with us?" Barons asked, glancing at the cyborgs.

"Because I'm getting results," Lovecraft replied, dismissing him. He grabbed a few papers in his hands and started to recount the events that took place in the last 24 hours. He then switched to another paper and described the genetic modifications the Snow Leopards had gone through. Ying offered to show them just like she had showed the rest of Ruler, but Lovecraft stopped her.

"Unfortunately, Ying, injuring you now would prove to be more bad than good," he said, before turning back to his notes. He read off the names of each of Kei's officers, including Ying's former captain. He listed off their abilities that they had been given and that they had all been raised from adolescence to be soldiers. Thus, they would be just as smart as they were.

Olivia raised her hand, "You mentioned the advantages that they had been given by their modified genetics. Well, are there any direct counters to it?"

"Almost all of our vascular systems were messed up in some way. It made us highly susceptible to infection, disease, and poison," Ying replied, "I was once laid up for a month with the flu; it was excruciating."

"That does prove a significant weakness, but how do you keep healthy if you're so prone to illness?"

"Well, I think that my words may have been poor there. We rarely do get sick in actuality, it's just when we do, our immune system isn't fast enough to catch up to it."

Olivia nodded, "Still, poisons could be the unfair advantage that we need. If we have poisons that paralyze or others that impair sense, it may prove vital to our mission."

Aaron pointed toward himself with his thumb, "I'm the hazardous materials guy. I'll see if I can conjure up something for us to use offensively. In the meantime, I would suggest dipping our knives and some rounds in Hydrocyanic Acid."

"Cyanide," Olivia clarified for everybody.

Aaron nodded, "It'll be a useful, last-resort option, should we not have ways to defend ourselves traditionally." All were in agreement with this and seeing this allowed Lovecraft to move onto their next topic: planning.

"Very well. Blitz, get with Aaron and get us something to subdue these guys without lethality." Olivia gave him a nod. "Next matter is planning, and I'm hoping that our friends here know where the Chinese are stationed, because without that, we're fucked."

Valravn leaned over to Coffin and whispered something that she soon repeated, "The Chinese are holding up in an abandoned planetarium off I-55. We believe it's called—"

"The Gardens of Babylon," Lovecraft interrupted.

"You know of it."

"Just a little. I was one of the key hands in arresting the guy who owned it. Although, I didn't really pay that much attention to the details. However, with this knowledge in hand, it is with great reluctance that I approve Kara's unorthodox plan, only with a few changes." Everyone, even Kara herself, looked at him like he had gone crazy. He looked at all of them and continued speaking, "Kara will use the phone she collected in California to contact the Chinese and will then meet them to give away our location. If the ruse works, she will guide Kei into our trap and then will eradicate the rest of the Chinese forces there."

Monica looked at him and asked, "Like…alone?" Lovecraft nodded and Monica suddenly turned even whiter than she already was. Olivia leaned over and asked if she was okay. She muttered something in French that Olivia didn't understand, but Kara did.

Kara interpreted for her, "She said she's going to be sick."

"Oh, I have some anti-nausea pills," Olivia said, pulling her pack off. Valravn and Coffin looked at one another and then started to awkwardly look around the room. Aaron watched, as Lawrence took Monica and helped her out of the area; he shook his head and then glanced at Lovecraft. His face was hard as stone. Ying bore worried expression on her face as she watched them; she couldn't believe the effect that those words had just had on Monica and it filled her with doubt. Abram lowered his head and smoothed back his greased hair. Barons just puffed his cigar and rolled his eyes; if Kara didn't come back, it would be better for him in the long run.

Kara suddenly heard Lovecraft's chair push out and when she turned, she saw him walking away. His gloved hands were packed into tight fists as the first sprinkles started to fall.

"If that is the only objection," he said, throwing his coat over himself, "then the judgment is final. Kara, I give you free reign to carry out your plan; I'll send the location to your phone." Ruler started to pack up and those from the Master's tent walked back into the darkness. Kara chased after Lovecraft and eventually caught up to him when they were surrounded by black pillars.

"Lovecraft wait, I—" she was cut off when Lovecraft spun around and flung his fist at her. She parried it with her own hand and guided it away from herself. Lovecraft then threw his other hand toward her ribs and she blocked that one with her knee. Reflexively, she jumped away from Lovecraft and dodged another jab, and sought to go for his waist. She knew what this was, and her memories brought her back to those first few weeks in her second year. The cold snow on her bruised skin and the half-frozen blood that dripped from her nose and stained her grey sweatshirt. Yes, this was just like the test he gave her long ago.

Lovecraft moved out of the way and was now behind Kara. She knew this and rolled away from his arms that tried to grab her. She started to go on the offensive by throwing several well-placed, but ineffective, punches that Lovecraft blocked with his arms. Kara recoiled back and then tried to kick him in the leg. However, it was not a good idea, since he was ready for this and grabbed her leg. Due to the fact that she was wearing heels, it was not that hard for him to pull her off balance. Lovecraft pulled her forward and jabbed at her face, but stopped before he made contact with her. Kara stared at the carbon fiber knuckles that hovered mere centimeters from the tip of her nose; it was rather comforting – like being close enough to see death, but not actually die. The look he gave her was one of pain because even she knew that she still wasn't on par with him.

He let her go and unwound his fist, "Don't make me regret the decision I made."

She looked at him and then looked at the floor for a second, "Monica will hate you for this."

"Shocking, somebody hates me. I guess the crabby old bitch will have to get in the spitting line." Had it been under a better setting, Kara would have laughed, but she just gave a meek smile. He turned around again and started to walk off.

Kara called out to him again, "Lovecraft, I don't hate you." He stopped for a second, but didn't say a thing. He started to walk again, only just a bit slower than at first.

Chapter 14
Poison Dart Round

The wind whipped through Lovecraft's hair as he stood atop the compound; his mind mulling over the events that had taken place three days earlier. He had given Aaron and Olivia some time to try and build something that they could use against the Chinese, while he and Barons worked to keep the peace. Several other Contractors, and their men, had been informed of the situation, and two of these were Marlene and David, who were doing active raids inside the Flood Zone, as Lovecraft stood there. Suddenly, he heard the door behind him open, and he saw Aaron standing in its wake.

"You should really come back down. There could be marksmen," he warned.

Lovecraft looked around for a moment, "If there were, I'd already be engaged. I'd also recommend not telling everybody that; turning this place into a prison would hurt morale. How is it coming?"

Aaron shrugged his shoulders, "It'll work, but we're having trouble with consistent detonation. Although, if the question is if it will work, then it will."

"So what you're saying is bullets are still better."

He shrugged his shoulders again, "I'd personally use it, but I'd be a moron if I choose to trust my life to it." Lovecraft carefully inspected his stance, as Aaron shoved his hand into his pocket. He knew something was up.

"I know you have something to say, so what is it?" Aaron looked at him and smirked; he couldn't hide anything from his leader, teacher, and best friend.

However, this was a fleeting expression, as was evident by it fading into a more serious one, "Is this really what we're doing nowadays, L.C.? Sending people to do our dirty work." He chuckled a bit, "You know, I remember a time when you were the one to go and kill the whole army, while I sat back and dealt with the paperwork."

"You speak of simpler times, my friend. Back when we were both young and a time before I promised myself I would not act in such arrogance again."

"So sending Kara on a suicide mission is better than breaking the promise we both made? You do remember we both made that promise, right? The promise to be better than what we had been, so we don't fail ever again. Do you even love her at all, or are you just a selfish cock like Barons?"

"What are you talking about?" Lovecraft asked, the emotion in his voice hollowing out even more.

"Dude, sometimes you're denser than lead, but you do realize that the chances of Kara coming back are almost next to nothing, right?"

Lovecraft took a few steps and turned back around to where he was looking off the building again, "She can do it."

"Sure, she can do it…but you could do it too, and you have a much higher chance of making it out."

Lovecraft's right hand started shaking and caused him to begin cracking its fingers with its thumb, "My judgment is final. Kara will do this; I have full confidence in her." Aaron knew that he would get no further beyond this point and started to leave, yet he had one more thing to say to Lovecraft and it would cut him to the bone.

"Lovecraft, my sister's *dead*. You should ask yourself whether a promise to a dead person is more important than the life of a living one." Lovecraft's eyes fell, as his left hand started shaking, and even though Lovecraft was the only one who could see him, the old man, was back again.

"Maybe you should kill him as well," he suggested, even though Lovecraft ignored him. The leader of Ruler reached into his holster and pulled his pistol out, the firearm Kara had got him for his birthday last year, and stared at it.

"I'm not as dense as you believe," Lovecraft muttered to himself. His hands stopped shaking as he held onto the tool and before he knew it, the world had calmed down and he remembered something. Kara's birthday was next week. He swore under his breath and tore off to find his phone which could get him a map to the nearest jewelry store.

While Lovecraft dealt with his own problems, Olivia put the pin in the final Paralysis Grenade. She wore a respirator and wiped the sweat from her brow, as she placed it next to its brothers inside a pressurized box. She cracked her latex knuckles and then pulled the gloves from her hands. She threw them into a waste bin labeled, 'Biohazard,' and then went to reach for another pair, since she was about to work with cyanide. Was it safe to do this in a regular room? No. Was it stupid? Yes. Could Aaron and she possibly kill everybody in the building? Yep. Did it need to be done? Absolutely.

The door suddenly opened, and Aaron came back in, wearing a respirator much like hers. He grabbed his own pair of gloves and asked, "How goes it?"

"Grenades are done. I was getting ready to start working with the cyanide, what did Lovecraft say?"

"Eh, he's still stubborn as a mule. Kara's still going to do her part, but I don't—" he stopped when they heard a heavy set of footsteps heading toward them. There was a knock at the door and Olivia stepped out, considering that Aaron was already suited up. She met Lovecraft in the hallway and immediately noticed that he was more involved with his phone than anything else.

"Hey, Blitz, how's it going in there?"

"Good, we got our grenades done."

Lovecraft nodded, "Cool, tell Aaron that I'm stepping out for a bit."

"What? Where are you going?" Olivia asked.

"Need to run some errands. Unfortunately, life doesn't stop for the Chinese military." Olivia looked down the hallway and when she saw Abram and Ying sitting at the table, she got an idea.

"Well...if you're going to be gone, why not take them with you?" She pointed to the two soldiers, "I think you aren't the only one in need of a distraction."

Lovecraft looked up from his phone and deadpanned, "You're not going to have sex with Aaron; many have tried, and the only one who has succeeded is his wife. Seriously, you'd have a better shot at fucking the president."

Olivia blushed and tripped over her words, "Th-That is not my intention. I was just trying to get you out of here so you don't die if there's an accident."

Lovecraft gave her a slow and exaggerated nod, "Uh huh, and Hitler just wanted to baptize the Jews in chambers of Holy Water."

"Did you just call me a Nazi?" she asked, a strand of hair breaking free from her ponytail and landing in the middle of her face. Lovecraft laughed at her expression, "Don't flatter yourself. You'll never by that crafty." He smiled and laughed again, "But people might just be stupid enough to let you do it anyway."

It was Olivia's turn to deadpan, as she fixed her hair, "You are literally the smuggest, and most offensive bastard I have ever met."

"I try my best," he retorted with an even smugger look. Olivia shook her head and rolled her eyes, before telling him to leave and to take the others with him. He waved her off while still chuckling to himself. He really needed the laugh and to his surprise, the German woman was rather entertaining in her own right. Much more than Lovecraft ever thought she would be. He approached Abram and Ying, and told them that he had errands to run and they were coming with him. In truth, he was only going to get one thing, but it did offer his teammates an opportunity to feel normal for a bit. He looked at Ying and noticed that she was wearing one of the three outfits she had, and decided that today would be the day that changed.

He told them to load up the Humvee while he grabbed something from his room. He opened the door and immediately pulled an extra debit card that was hidden inside a book. He stuffed it inside his coat pocket and grabbed his assault rifle before leaving. Lovecraft met them inside the Humvee and all three of them sped off into the cityscape.

The weather was better than yesterday; the air was cool, winds light, and only the faintest idea that March was about to transition into April. The three of them drove past various streets that were littered with trash and graffiti that graphically painted the picture of people's opinions with things such as, "WE WANT JOBS!" "Fuck Rahm Emanuel and his children," and "The only good politician is a disemboweled one." It was annoying for Lovecraft, who wished that he didn't have to deal in politics, to see these, but that was an unfortunate part of the job that might just force him into retirement one day.

They pulled onto an empty street and then turned onto another one where Abram pulled onto the side of the road. There were a few more cars than the first street, but it was nothing out of the ordinary for a weekday. The three of them entered into a large glass structure that had police officers and Contractors standing outside of it. The three of them showed their licenses and once inside, Lovecraft told the other two to gather around him.

He handed Ying the debit card he fetched from his room and said, "Ying, you can buy all the essential items you need, but please try and be reasonable with *my* money." Ying looked at him incredulously, while Abram nodded his head in approval. She took the card and wondered what he had to gain from giving her this kind of freedom.

"Abram, keep her safe…and try and keep her from wasting all my money," Lovecraft ordered, earning a chuckle from the Russian.

"Don't worry, I'll keep her from buying any diamond-encrusted underwear," he laughed, as Ying looked at him in stunned embarrassment. This nearly brought both men to tears; they laughed so hard.

"O-Okay, then. Where are you going? Shouldn't we stick together given our circumstances?" Ying asked, trying to save some face.

"There's no need," Lovecraft said, patting his M4, "I can take care of myself." With that being said, Lovecraft left and disappeared behind a crowd of people.

Ying watched this and asked Abram, "Hey, why does he always seem to just disappear?"

Abram stroked his beard for a second and replied, "Because, Lovecraft is a man who knows better than to involve other people in his business. Put simply, he values his privacy."

Ying cocked an eyebrow, "Why do you think that is?"

"There were men stationed with me and they acted just like Lovecraft. The reason for this was because their loved ones were hurt in some irredeemable way because they simply knew too much."

"What is that supposed to mean?"

"My country is a very corrupt place and it is not always safe for everybody. Anyway, the thing I find fascinating is how Lovecraft manages to stay so calm; it's like he's a piece of iron. We should really get to going; it'll be dark before we get done discussing the philosophy of Lovecraft." Ying nodded and together, they hit every shop that the young woman would need. She acquired a few new outfits, a few books, and even some movies that she could play out in the kitchen. Now, carrying her anti-boredom arsenal, Ying passed by a pet store and took a moment to look inside of its windows.

"Wanna go inside?" Abram asked, taking Ying's bags from her. She nodded and he turned to see that they were rather close to the main entrance. He told her that he was going to run these to the Humvee and to not leave the pet store until he got back. Ying nodded once again and entered the store as he ran off.

The woman at the counter welcomed her and asked if there was anything she was looking for. Ying shook her head and stated that she was just looking around; although, there was one section that she was very interested in seeing.

"Um, do you have a reptile section?" Ying asked, taking a moment to smile at a small yorkie in a cage.

"Yes," the lady nodded enthusiastically, "it's back and to the left. If you need or would like to look at anything, I'll be right here." Ying smirked at her and gave her thanks. She trodden on the hardwood floors and eventually came to a section of four shelves lined with bright, green tanks. Ying walked between them and saw a collection of reptiles, ranging from a bearded dragon to a green tree frog that seemed to be very weary of people. However, while these were still very cool, Ying was more interested in the legless reptiles that inhabited the middle and bottom cages. She ran her hand along each of the names and studied them carefully, yet none, for lack of a better term, jumped out at her. They had your standard ball python, a rat snake, and even a water snake, but nothing that piqued her interest, until her fingernail accidentally tapped the glass of the middlemost tank. From a small hole in the corner, a snake with a hook-shaped nose appeared and smelled the glass with its tongue.

Ying instinctively froze, but when she saw that it had placed its unique nose right in line with her finger, she moved it down. He followed her finger down. She smirked and moved her finger to the side and then to the other; he followed her with his head the whole way.

She chuckled like a kid did when something made them happy; Abram knew this laugh well and it brought a smile to his face as it reminded him of his girls – who were very far away.

He stepped around the corner and asked, "Having fun?"

Startled, Ying jerked her head up and her friend in the tank started to curl his body up defensively. She took a breath when she recognized that it was Abram, and she began playing with the snake again.

A mirthful smile spread on her face as she watched him, "I like snakes. They're so simple, yet some carry the power to crush boulders, and others can kill whole armies."

Abram nodded, "That is rather impressive, but how did you come to like them? I'm sure you are aware that not many women have such a fondness for snakes as you apparently do."

"I was shipped to Borneo as one of my first assignments, and my mission was to eliminate a local oil tycoon so that China could move into the market. Well, the night before I found my target, I decided to get some sleep next to a tree. The next thing I knew, there was something tickling my ankle and it caused me to wake up. I woke up and saw a King Cobra sliding across my boot. I froze. I waited until it finally crossed my boot, which took forever, since the thing was so fucking long, and pulled my pistol out. Moving to the snake's side of the tree, I sought to shoot it, but there was something I failed to notice."

"The snake was female and she had eggs," Abram finished for her.

Ying smirked and nodded, "She had comeback to check on her clutch and really only noticed that I was actually there, when I started to climb the tree. She reared up on me, but stopped for some reason; her hood didn't even come out. She just stared at me and I stared at her before I finished climbing the tree. I watched them from above for a while and then fell back asleep. When I awoke the next morning, she was still there, but didn't notice me when I looked down again. I climbed down and never saw her again."

"Weird shit happens on an op, Ying. Maybe it was just like your friend there," Abram said, gesturing to the snake. Ying smiled at it, but had to stop when Lovecraft texted Abram. The two of them left the shop and met Lovecraft inside the Humvee. There was white box on the dash that had not been there previously, yet Lovecraft barely seemed to notice, as he looked at his phone.

He put it away once they entered the vehicle and said, "When we get back to the compound, get your stuff ready. The plan starts at three."

The sound of bare feet slapping across tile filled Kara's bathroom, as she stepped out in a red bathrobe. She grabbed a remote next to her bed and drew the curtains, as Monica stepped in; she was dressed like a businesswoman, but also wore her body armor. Kara undid the belt on her robe and let it fall to the floor; her eyes glancing at her clock as her nakedness came into view. It read two-forty.

Monica stepped forward and took Kara's hair into her hands and started to braid it. Her young leader knew that she was going to say something and she reached for her cigarettes.

She lit it as Monica asked, "You know you don't have to do this, right? W-We can find another way that doesn't involve—"

"Maman, enough," Kara commanded, pulling her tobacco from her lips.

Monica stopped talking for a bit and then, as she tied the ponytail around the braid, she said, "I know you love him," Kara's eyes lowered a bit, as she was confronted with the fact, "He's the one who you've been keeping a secret about, the one who you've been trying to hide your feelings over. Yet, I know, and I also know that this will not impress him."

"I don't seek to impress him," Kara said, turning around and confronting her, "I seek to prove it to myself that I am not some useless bystander."

"Then you will kill yourself to prove some useless pride?! Menagerie, your mother wanted me to protect you. I can't do that if you go and get yourself killed."

"You're not wrong, Monica," Kara said, getting closer to her, "but…what you are wrong about is my name. I'm not Menagerie anymore. I stopped being Menagerie when we came to the States, remember? I have no family, I have no history, I don't even have a last name. I will do this as Kara, I will leave as Kara, and whether or not you want to be a part of my life is up to you."

"What are you meaning, Kara?" Monica asked, setting a hand on her hip.

Kara felt her heart break when she realized that she would have to set Monica straight, "Have you forgotten? Tickets back to the U.A.E. are a dime in a dozen for me."

Monica dropped her authoritative stance, "Kara, you can't mean…"

"But I do mean it! I cannot fucking tell you how annoying and petty it is to be challenged on every goddamn decision I make. I think you have forgotten that *I*, not my mother, is the holder of your paycheck, and *you* are paid to follow my orders, as well as protect me. So let me put it in layman's terms for you; do your job or you are fired," Kara hated her words, but they needed to be said. Monica, for lack of a better term, was demoralizing for the young woman, and it just couldn't stay that way. The older French woman took her glasses off and wiped her eyes, as Kara turned around.

"Help me get dressed. I'm getting cold." Kara walked to the closet, opened it, and then shoved all her clothes to the side. Monica walked up behind her and watched her punch a code into a keypad. The wall slid away and was replaced by a blinding L.E.D. light.

"Ma'am, what do I tell the men when they find out that you're wearing this again?" Monica asked, folding her hands in front of herself.

Kara walked forward and took one of the garments, "Tell them the truth. I chose to wear it, because I'm still just as good as they remember." Monica nodded and helped Kara get dressed. The sound of zippers being pulled up, buttons being clicked, belts tightening, and chains being spooled filled the room, before Kara threw her coat over her shoulders. She threaded the gold buttons through its holes and popped its collar to where it stood behind her head, and her braid hung a bit. She looked at the clock and grimaced, as she saw that it was ten minutes to three. She quickly went over to her make-up station and looked at the bottle of cyanide Olivia had given her. She unscrewed its top and mixed it into a bottle of black fingernail polish.

Kara threw the rest of the cyanide away, painted her nails with the tainted polish, and then gave herself just the bare minimum amount of makeup she would need to look normal. She figured that if she was going to pull this off, looking like everything was okay would be a necessity. She stood up and grabbed a pair of black gloves that featured gold fingertips.

"Our man on the inside has hidden your weapons in the place you specified, and has also left your transportation in the surrounding area. You can find it using the G.P.S. on your phone," Monica informed her.

"Thank you. Now, go join Lovecraft and the others, they'll need you more than I will," Kara commanded, pulling out the enemy phone.

Monica nodded and turned around with a melancholic look in her eyes. "Monica."

She turned back around when she heard Kara call her, "I'll see you for dinner tonight." Monica smiled and walked away, her heart focusing on the hope that she would. Kara watched her walk down the stairs and then she turned to the phone again. She thumbed through the contacts until she found the one, she was looking for and called it. Her red lips smiled as she heard the line pick up.

Kara was soon placed in a hard, steel chair; her head covered by a black bag. The Chinese had taken her and now, Major Kei stood next to Zhi behind a blacked-out mirror. He watched her as she sat there, with her hands splayed out on the table; the metal tips clicked on its metal surface like claws.

"Why is she here, Captain?" he asked.

"She's claimed to have information relevant to my mission."

"Are you saying that she has information on Ying?" Zhi cringed at his anxious tone and grabbed a small file that she had put together on Kara.

"You should talk to her, but be careful. She's…talkative." Kei cocked an eyebrow, before Zhi kissed him on the cheek and sent him along. It was her way of reminding him just who she was now.

Kara heard the buzzer and smirked when she smelled Kei walk into the room. He smelled of cinnamon.

"Hello, Major, you smell nice," Kara complimented, surprising Kei who was moving to sit down.

She heard the seat pull back and smirked underneath the bag when he sat down, "You've kept a lady waiting. I'm mildly insulted."

"I do not care about your feelings, Miss…Kara."

"Hmm, you're a feisty one. Maybe you should take this bag off and get to know me a little. After all, that other woman who smelled of blueberries seemed to know you *very* well." Zhi was stunned, as she realized that Kara was able to identify her just from the smell of her soap.

"You may not talk about my subordinates or my relationship with them while we are in this room. My focus is the information you promised."

Kara chuckled, "I also see that you're a fun Nazi, or should I say, fun Commie. I really can't tell the difference anymore."

"I would encourage you to be quiet."

"Oh yeah?" Kara pulled the bag off her head and flashed her green eyes from between her green bangs, "And how would that help me give you information?" Kei sighed and rolled up his sleeves, before lunging across the table, throwing his chair behind him in the process, to grab Kara's coat collar.

She giggled, as she was pulled across the table, and her face was brought right up to Kei's, "I knew this was gonna be fun! You should be a rollercoaster!"

"I have little patience for people like you."

Kara laughed at him, "Well, that's too bad, because you're going to have to entertain me if you want to learn anything about your fallen sniper."

"Where is she?"

"Don't worry, she's far better than your men in California." This comment made Kei pick Kara up and then slammed her head into the black mirror, cracking it somewhat. Most of the soldiers on the other side flinched, but Zhi watched in an enamored expression. The light in the room turned harsh for Kara, as her whole body went numb; her brain trying to frantically recover from the shock she just received.

"You should never start with the person's head; they can't feel the—" Kara was silenced by Kei punching her in the face, which she couldn't feel at all.

She looked at him with a frown that was only enhanced by her smudged red, lipstick, "I told you so."

He grabbed her by the collar again and lifted her off the floor, however, her toes still touched it, thanks to her abnormal height.

"I told you to stop talking. Now, where is she?"

"Well, make up your mind, tiny—" He punched her in the face again.

"Seriously, how am I supposed to answer your questions—" He punched her again. Kara was laughing internally, since he was only hitting so hard that it messed up her makeup and withdrew some tears.

"Where in the fuck is she?!" he demanded.

"Oh don't worry, Major Kei," she laughed mockingly, "I'm going to tell you where they are, *both* of them."

Kei was about to hit her again, but stopped when he heard the emphasized word, "Them?"

Kara chuckled, "Yes, Major. You see, Ying does not belong to you anymore and now, you have a choice. Go after Ying, who is on her way to testify against you in Washington, or go after the man who is on the warpath to kill all of you, Lovecraft. You know, it's kind of funny, Major. You spent all that time turning her into a slave and now, she's spending all her time to break her master; it's very poetic. She's on her way to O'Hare, but you might just catch her—" Kei dropped her to the floor and immediately left the room, as Kara watched him with a coy smirk. A Chinese soldier stepped inside the room and stood in front of the door with his back to the door.

Kei walked out of the room and was immediately asked which person he was going after, and he told Zhi that he would be going after Ying. She nodded and then got her men together and they joined their Major outside. They mounted up in a convoy of eight vehicles that were bound for Chicago, while Kara sat on the floor, rocking her feet to and fro. She turned to the guard whilst slipping one of her gloves off and complimented him on his eyes.

Meanwhile, on a secluded road named 95th Street, which was situated deep in the Spears Woods, Ruler was coordinating police and Legion forces in the building of an ambush. The road was completely covered in men moving earth, shrubs, branches, and trees around, while those that had demolitions experience planted IEDs along the road. They all wore Multicam or some other type of camouflage, as they got themselves situated in their respective spots.

The plan was simple, teams One and Two would take up concealed positions in the forest, on either side of the road, and would detonate the IEDs. Once that was finished, they would engage the Chinese with their assault rifles. These teams would be led by Aaron. Teams Three and Four would be further back in the forest, and would provide heavier suppressing fire using their machine guns. This was helped by the raised positions they were building out of the materials available to them. These teams would be led by Abram, who would also be acting as a bodyguard to Ying. Team Five would be led by Monica and would be the hard wall of A.T. rockets that would ultimately stop the convoy if needed. However, Lovecraft always believed in having a plan B, so Lawrence would lead Team Six, should the need arise. They possessed four technicals, one featuring a heavy KPV Anti-Aircraft gun, and a heavily armored police truck that would then engage the convoy with extreme prejudice. If this came to pass, then Kei would no longer be worth capturing. Through all this though, Lovecraft still felt that it could fail and kept something up his sleeve that even his team didn't know about.

With all these things set in place, Lovecraft stared at the men below, with his binoculars trained on the men setting the IEDs. He set them down slowly when he saw them moving away from them and then turned to see an older gentleman wearing police S.W.A.T. gear.

"All the roads have been closed. This is the only way to get into the city," he reported. Lovecraft dismissed him back to his computer and got on his radio. He contacted Abram and asked if the machine gunners were ready, and once he got the affirmative, he let him go and thought himself, *It's all up to you now, Kara.*

Blood dripped from Kara's fingernails, as she wiped them off with the dead soldier's balaclava. She smiled, her eye shadow casting deep, black lines down her face. Kara pulled the soldier's knife from his belt and used it to pop a vent open in the room. She reached inside and pulled a green duffle bag from inside and opened it to reveal her Grizzly, AK-74, a bunch of ammo, and a 14-inch survival knife that had serration running the length of its spine. She put her pistol in its holster, the knife in its sheath, and the ammo on her coat's belt. Kara loaded her Kalashnikov and pointed it at the black mirror.

"Time to start the party," she muttered, before covering her face with her arm. She unloaded into the mirror with a single burst of fully automatic fire and praised the Lord for hearing protection, as the sound echoed around the whole room. The small, 5.45 white phosphorous rounds tore into the mirror and then brought the whole thing down, as the chemical burned through it. Kara walked through the former mirror and found a Chinese soldier standing behind a consul; he wasn't even dressed in his combat gear. Whipping out her pistol, Kara shot him in the head, before another Chinese soldier stormed the room; this one was dressed in his combat gear. Kara ducked behind the console, shielding herself from the bullets ripping apart the cement wall behind her, and ducked out once he ran out of ammo. She stood up and shot him right in the eye, the W.P. round causing his head to swell like a pumpkin before exploding. The green-eyed woman smirked at her handiwork before walking past it and into the hallway with her rifle raised. She looked to her right and saw that a squad of soldiers had taken a position at the end of it. Ducking back into the room as they fired, Kara counted to three and then peeked out. She sprayed the deadly rounds down the hallway and the sight of severed limbs filled her vision, shortly before the end of the hallway erupted into flames.

Her eyes watched the flames flicker for a bit, as an alarm sounded; now everybody knew what was happening. She checked her Kalashnikov and then grabbed a fresh magazine from her belt. She used the new one to kick out the old one and then cocked it with her thumb. She started to walk down the other end of the hallway and killed any who stood in her way; doing this stained her boots a dark red. The lights had dimmed into a bright red and left her as just a black image on a red background.

She continued on and when she came to a particular corner, stuck her weapon's muzzle brake around it. However, she quickly brought it back to her and put the weapon to wear its side touched her chest; the reason for this presented itself in the form of a Chinese soldier trying to hit the weapon out of her hands from around the corner. Using her pistol grip for control, she thrust the rifle's buttstock forward and clocked him in the nose. Her barrel was now over his foot and that was where she shot him, just before another appeared from a room behind her.

Kara felt the bullets hit her in the back; the nanoweave saving her from everything but pain, and she turned around to rush soldier with the extended knife she carried. She plunged the blade deep into his belly, right where his plate carrier stopped protecting, and disemboweled him, before executing him with her pistol. She turned back to the man whose foot had all but melted away, and with an angry yell, jabbed the knife through the bottom of his jaw and lifted him to the ceiling. She ripped the blade from his head and sent his body crashing to the floor. She fell to her knees and held herself up with her arm, as the broken lead fell from her back. Kara grit her teeth as she pushed herself back up to a standing position, before she ran a hand across her face. Her glove came back with a mixture of blood and make-up on it; Kara figured that she must already look like a mess, but she pushed this from her mind and continued on her mission.

At the outskirts of Chicago, the Snow Leopards were speeding down various back roads, as they made their way toward 95th Street. Little did they know, the forest held a deadly secret. Four teams of Legion snipers, dressed in Ghillie suits and lead by Sammy, were watching their every move and giving minute-by-minute information on their location. The trees had eyes and the Chinese could not escape their sight.

Sammy spoke into his radio, "Sniper Team to Team Five, message, over." Monica's voice responded and gave him the go ahead, "Be advised, eight times Chinese vehicles head toward the A.O. E.T.A. five minutes."

"Solid Copy." Monica switched the channel over to Aaron's, "Aaron, five minutes." The contractor nodded when he heard this and then instructed his men to put their gas masks on. Gloved fingers scratched the detonators' triggers anxiously. Lovecraft stood on top of the roof of his building and watched the entire area with his binoculars. To his right, Kay sat; her black robe flowing in the wind.

"This is quite the exciting set up," she said, kicking her feet off the edge of the building.

Lovecraft turned and was surprised to see her sitting there, but he didn't show it, "Is Valravn on her way?"

"Yes."

"Good," he said, lifted the binoculars up again.

Kara walked down the darkened corridors and left a trail of blood in her wake. The fire alarms echoed through the building, as the white phosphorous ignited chemicals in the medical area. Kara stepped into an area that appeared to be a makeshift command center; it also appeared to be abandoned. However, Kara was not so easily perturbed, and walked around the computers with her pistol pointed toward the floor. She walked around the desks and almost called it quits, until she heard a loud thud from inside a door that she didn't see at first. She turned the barrel of her pistol to the door and fired three rounds through it. The response she got was an audible slump. Kara moved to the door and when she opened it, a woman choking on her own blood, fell out of the small closet. She finished the woman off quickly and just watched her for moment.

She was dressed in civilian clothes and didn't even carry a weapon; yet, the thing that struck her the most was this woman was *not* Chinese. Kara kicked the body over, thinking she must have been mistaken and got a better look at her face. No, she was not Chinese at all. It was during this time that she heard something behind her and when she turned, she saw the choke of a shotgun.

Having no time to react, Kara was thrown to the floor, as the close-range blast painted her coat white. Dazed, she couldn't move, as the Chinese soldier slung his shotgun and yelled at her in Chinese. He pulled out a knife, bent down, whilst still yelling at her, and drove it into her chest, but it bounced off and even came back bent. He asked her why she wouldn't die, but she couldn't understand it and let it be known.

"I can't speak Chinese, you Commie fuck!" she yelled, before biting his hand. He yelped in pain, before he heard the sound of fabric tearing. Looking down, he saw that Kara had stabbed him through a weak spot in his armor and shock caused him to stand up. The French woman pulled the knife free and watched as he collapsed against the wall. She stood up and ran a hand through her hair whilst muttering something about them hiding in the woodwork. Her eyes moved back down to the strange foreigner and then looked to the now-dead Chinese soldier and found that he had a blue card hanging from his plate carrier. She retrieved it from him and read that it was for an area designated: The Box. Kara looked to the many monitors in this room and found a map on one of them. She didn't know what buttons did what, but she figured out how to pan the display around and when she did, 'The Box,' was actually very close to her current location. Kara decided that this was her next destination, but as she went to leave, her eyes caught something on another monitor. She turned toward it and saw that it was security camera footage of the next hallway; there were five soldiers pointing guns at the door. Kara smirked and grabbed her AK off her back.

At 95th Street, police and Contracting forces waited with bated breath, as they heard the convoy coming toward them. Aaron's men were clad in gas masks and were waiting anxiously for the convoy to be spotted by local units. They were completely hidden from view and relied on the eyes of another to call when they were good. One looked to the other when the ground started to vibrate, and then the one readied his grip on the detonator. The sound got progressively louder, as two sets of eyes flicked back and forth. The first vehicle passed; everybody in the trench readied themselves. They got the call shortly before the second vehicle passed, and a second after the second IED exploded, the first one did.

The Chinese watched as the first two vehicles in their convoy exploded and the third crashed into the back of the second. A yellow gas permeated the air as the fourth vehicle, Zhi's vehicle, hit the brakes hard. Abram immediately gave the order for Teams Three and Four to start firing. The Chinese captain started to frantically call for help, as their armored trucks ate the bullets that sought them. However, when she got no response, she realized that they were on their own. The first Chinese survivors fell in the street due to the gas and couldn't move; Zhi ordered that the Seventh and Eighth vehicles to collapse on the Fifth vehicle, Kei's Vehicle, while the Sixth was to ram the wreckage out of the way. The vehicle's followed her orders, and just as the truck moved the wreckage away: a rocket flew through the air and planted its explosive warhead into the driver's side of the windshield.

Kara stood in front of the large door that lead to The Box, and was half-concealed due to her clothing. She stood in a single, hazy light and while her eyes were shadowed by her bangs, the rest of her was not – it showed that she had taken some damage on the way there. A hole, lined with gel-like blood, resided on her right arm and was patched with an equally bloody bandage. Her right cheek was bleeding slightly, as well as her left eyebrow; her left hand throbbed with the pain and was almost totally equal with the pain in her knee. She looked up to the door and took a moment to admire the fact that the Chinese had done a lot of renovations. She only admired this for but a moment though, and walked to the door and swiped the card in front of it.

The doors creaked open and she saw two Chinese soldiers standing in the middle of the room, and immediately blew their heads off with her weapon. The muzzle break of her AK-74 smoked like a chimney, as she lowered the weapon; she had been running it hard and to say that the W.P. ammo wasn't tearing it up was wrong. It was widely known that this ammunition was only meant to be used in small quantities or in machine guns because of its potency; however, she couldn't dwell on that when she noticed the cages around her.

The iron smell of blood polluted the air and Kara realized just what the two Chinese men were doing in there. They were killing civilian prisoners. She covered her mouth and nose with her sleeve, as she walked down the row, bodies on all sides. Kara shut her eyes and when she opened them again, they were fixed on the door ahead of her. It was a technique that she had seen Aaron and Lovecraft use many times and it was a method to keep yourself calm when others may have descended into panic. She got to the other side and swiped the card again. The door opened and showered her in white light as she stepped into a large, cylindrical room that was lined with a catwalk about nine feet above the floor. She immediately saw that there were four entrances, including the one she just came through, and having no prior knowledge as to where she was, Kara decided to go through the next door on her right. Yet, as she moved toward it, she was stopped when a knife embedded itself in the door controls.

The forest battle intensified, as the remaining Chinese troops disembarked and started to return fire. While this was an improvement for them, it didn't mean much, considering that half their forces were already dead or incapacitated. Two men stood next to Zhi behind one of the trucks, and were helping her attempt at suppressing the right side of the road. However, the attempt didn't last long, as the heads of the two men suddenly exploded, and when it was Zhi's turn, the heavy 7.62 NATO ricocheted off her ballistic mask and imbedded itself in her shoulder. It was an incredible stroke of luck, but one that still threw her to the ground. Aaron saw her collapse through the red dot and circle emblem of his Eotech, and immediately got on the radio with Abram. He told him to tell his men to cease fire, as Kei jumped out of his vehicle and attempted to run away. He took his opportunity to run into the woods, but Zhi caught his foot and tried to get him to stop, since she saw the enemy rushing them. He kicked her hand away as she pleaded with him and continued his course. However, as he got to the end of the first truck, one of his soldiers was shot in the neck and the heavy round over-penetrated him. The round grazed the side of Kei's head and caused him to duck. Aaron stepped up as the Chinese soldier fell and his eyes graced Kei's face.

"Major Kei, it's so good to finally meet you," he said. Kei pulled his sidearm free, but cried out in pain, as Aaron shot it out of his hand. This severed three of his fingers and as he writhed on the ground in pain, Aaron kicked the severed digits away from him.

"Please try and resist more. I have to bring you in alive, but not in one piece," Aaron said, as Olivia appeared from the other side of the truck.

She pointed her gun at the downed man, "That him?"

"Affirmative." Olivia called her men over as Aaron kicked Kei over and tied his hands back with a wire tie. He started struggling and tried to turn over, until Olivia pulled her pistol out and shot it next to his ear.

She grabbed his collar as he squirmed, and ghosted the barrel next to his other ear, "Move again and I will fully deafen you." He stopped moving and Aaron was now able to tighten the wire.

"What do we do with the remaining Chinese, Commander?" one of Legion asked.

Aaron turned to him as he pulled Kei to his feet, "Let the police have them. If you find hiding ones, execute them. No mercy."

Olivia looked at him as the soldier left, "That's a little barbaric, isn't it?"

"Nah, don't like the treatment, don't do the crime." He made Kei sit next to the truck and took a moment to pull his gas mask off. He commented how it felt better to breathe fresh air before he called Lovecraft down. It took him a few minutes, but he soon arrived on sight, with Monica and her men, as well as Kay, who danced around the prisoner. She cupped her masked face with her hands as she got a good look at him.

"Good job," Lovecraft congratulated before looking around, "Where's Abram?"

Kara whipped around and swapped the catwalk with her incendiary rounds, exploding the concrete walls and setting a pair of flags ablaze. A man appeared from the smoke and threw another knife at Kara, who was forced to block it with her gun. He then pulled out a long sword and slashed her across the shoulder with it, before she pushed him away.

Panting, she looked at him and noticed that he had a red tuft of fabric on the top of his helmet, and he wore a type of mask that looked ancient in design.

She remembered him from the list that Ying had made and called him by his name.

"Spartan, I must admit you are the first of these Chinese *Heavies* that I've seen. I'm quite disappointed that I will have to exterminate something so rare." She laughed, buttoning her collar so that it went up to the bridge of her nose.

"You fancy yourself as something special, don't you?" he said in English, "Yes, you have skill, but that rifle, those bullets, are your crutch. The crutch that I will kick out from under you." Kara smirked underneath the buttoned collar before she started firing; she loved it when they talked back. Spartan dodged her rounds and threw another knife at her, as the embers wafted through the air. Kara dodged it, but found that a smoke grenade had also been tossed and now, she could barely see. A blade suddenly came from nowhere and hit the top of her rifle, knocking it to the floor. As it clattered to the floor, the sword was then brought back and then thrown into Kara's arm. However, it slid off, thanks to whatever was under her coat.

She pulled her pistol out and shot into the smoke before jumping out of it. She looked at the cut in her sleeve and was annoyed by the fact that Nanoweave was bulletproof, but not cut proof. It was more designed like a spider web and acted like a net to catch bullets. However, knives just tore right through it. The reason why this happened was the sharp blade would grab hold of the fibers and pulled them apart; much like breaking a wishbone.

The Spartan jumped from the smoke, but missed Kara with his slash; the French woman then aimed her pistol and shattered the blade of his sword with three, well-placed bullets. Her pistol's slide locked to the rear and when Spartan saw that Kara was out of ammo, he pulled his second, emergency sword and continued his attack.

Kara blocked the sword by catching its blade between her elbow and knee, and then blocked it with her arm, but this still didn't stop him. She took note of how he seemed to have an inhuman amount of stamina and, while this high level of prey excited her, it did not mean well when it came to her survival.

She blocked his blade once more with the side of her hand and then used this same hand to hit him in the throat. He recoiled and Kara then kicked his left knee, turning him to that side, she jumped behind him and wrapped her braid around his neck. She put her foot on his back and pushed him forward, while her arms and head pulled back. Spartan struggled as he was choked by Kara's hair; he dropped his sword and grabbed the braid with both hands. Kara grunted and groaned from the physical exertion that was required of her. However, she was forced to stop, when a knife was shoved into her back and then another cut her braid off at the base. Kara gasped in pain as the knife stopped at the very bone of her shoulder blade. Her unknown assailant pulled the knife free and then tossed her off of Spartan. Kara hit the floor and coughed, as she realized that she had just been thrown some 15 feet in the air. She rolled over and saw that a woman with teal hair was helping Spartan up; she undid her collar and smiled with bloody teeth.

"Helloooo, Madame Plague. I thought I would just have to exterminate one of you." Kara rolled over onto her hands and knees. From here, she saw that Plague was wearing one of the Chinese exo suits that she had seen. This had to have been the reason that Kara was thrown away so effortlessly. The Chinese soldiers turned around and both of them raised their weapons; Plague's being a pistol and a gauntlet of syringes filled with an unknown substance.

Kara smirked at them with her newly shortened hair crowding her eyes, "Two on one, really?" Neither of the soldiers flinched at her words. "Fine, then I have a confession to make." She started unbuttoning her coat, "I've been holding back on your boy there. Now, I can fight you just like the British SAS in '33."

Plague and Spartan looked at each other, but couldn't figure out what she was talking about, until Spartan noticed something about her. He brought an image up from his memories and imagined he was looking at Kara. The image in his mind and Kara were one in the same, and it was only then that he realized that he was not fighting some mystery woman named Kara; he was fighting the Emerald Wolf, Menagerie Alexandre. He felt the sweat collect underneath his mask, as Kara shrugged her coat off her shoulders.

Underneath, she wore a padded, black body suit of leather and Kevlar. Her hands were still covered by her gloves and her arms were covered in black fabric sleeves that stopped at her shoulders. The piece of armor that bent and broke blades was a shiny piece of AR500 steel that was cut into an upside-down pentagon. This was held onto her body by a series of belts that wove into another piece of metal on her back that was smaller. She wore a black tactical belt around her waist and her drop-leg holster attached to this, as well as another holster that was very peculiar – almost as peculiar as the silver chains that snaked their way into it. Finally, a pair of shin guards sprouted from the top of her boots and even covered her knees.

Kara reached into the unique holster and pulled out a long metal rod that had its end sharpened into that of a needle, "Shall we do this one at a time?"

Both Chinese soldiers leapt into action, as Kara threw the weapon. Plague pointed her pistol at Kara, but it was knocked out of her hand when the French woman pulled on the sword's chain. The unique piece of metal on Kara's back turned out to be a motor that automatically retracted the chain when pulled back, this allowed her the ability to disarm Plague while she blocked Spartan's sword with her arms; the fabric coating them had steel wire woven into it and this made her arms impervious to the sword's damage.

She guided his sword away from herself and then smacked him in the head. Kicking him away from her, Kara turned to see that Plague was reaching for the pistol with a bloody hand. Immediately, she threw her sword out again in an effort to stop her. However, she noticed that such a hasty throw would cause her to miss. Thinking quickly, she grabbed the chain and guided it back toward the Chinese soldier. This caused the chain to wrap itself around Plague's neck, before Spartan punched Kara and knocked her to the floor. Him doing this caused the chain to pull a now-choking Plague to the floor. She grasped at the chain desperately, as it squeezed the tears from her eyes and suffocated her voice; her head was turning into the color of an eggplant, as Kara head-butted Spartan. She then got up, wrapped the extra length of the chain around his neck, and then used his height to aid her jump to the rafters. Spartan fought against the chain as he followed Kara with his head. Yet, he stopped fighting, when he saw Kara attached to a metal rafter by her feet. Her boots were magnetized and each had a small, orange light on the side of them.

Kara then swung herself over the rafter and threaded the chain over the beam. Spartan and Plague were suddenly carried into the air; Plague was barely conscious at this point, but ceased to be when the chain jerked her head and broke her neck. The sound was very much like that of a bag of air popping. She hung limply from the chain, as Kara watched them from below, yet Spartan was still alive, and that was when she realized that he didn't need air to live.

Kara chuckled in the husky and sensual way she always did and said, "I see now. The Chinese engineered you to be able to survive without air; you truly are an abomination. I wonder if Ying knew about this?" Spartan fought his way out of the bind and dropped to the floor.

He picked up his sword and Kara continued to taunt him, "Well, come on, Mister Super Weapon. You've earned your right to fight me, now come show your glorious state what a loyal bitch you are." Spartan, consumed by emotion, got up and charged Kara whilst yelling. She rolled her eyes at how stupid he was being and waited till she heard the splitting of metal. Looking down, she saw his newly broken blade touching her breast plate. She reached onto the back of her belt and pulled an old percussion cap-revolver off of it. Its barrel was inscribed with the words, 'Black Belladonna.'

"In most stories, the dog dies. This story is no different. However, nobody's going to cry over fucking trash like you." She pulled the hammer back and sent a round right into the eyehole of his mask. She didn't stop there though; five more shots rang out, as she emptied the pistol into his face and neck; she made sure that he would not be getting up.

Kara sighed when she was done, her heart felt like it was about to explode and her hair was matted with sweat and dried blood. She huffed and puffed as she pulled her chain sword back. The friction from the motor kicking in severed Plague's head, and her decapitated body fell to the floor, as Kara returned the sword to its place. She spied a canteen on Spartan's belt and helped herself to it. After drinking all of its contents, Kara tossed it away and then went around retrieving her weapons and coat; she put a new magazine in her Grizzly, as well as a new cylinder in the percussion, before grabbing her Kalashnikov to replace its magazine.

A door suddenly slipped open and she whipped around with her pistol ready to fire. Although, she withdrew it once she saw Valravn appear from it.

"What are you doing here?" she asked, confused.

"Lovecraft asked that I make sure you got out alive. I see that you have everything under control." Kara nodded and then pulled a memory card from her belt. She retraced her steps and slipped the memory card into the control room's main computer and, after a few seconds, it stored the entire hard drive on itself. Kara and Valravn then exited the base and while Valravn disappeared into the woods, the French woman walked down the roadways and found an old U.A.Z. hidden behind a clump of bushes. She got in and reached behind her in order to undo her braid, but it was then that she remembered her hair was now much shorter.

Lovecraft, Aaron, Olivia, Monica, and Lawrence pushed their way through the bush and found Abram sitting up against a tree, holding his bleeding chest. Lovecraft, Aaron, Monica, and Lawrence spread out, as Olivia ran to him and began treatment.

"I thought you guys would never show up," he coughed.

"Sorry, man, we were dealing with the Chinese. What happened to Ying?" Lovecraft asked.

"They took her."

"Who took her?"

"The fucking bitch who she used to call, 'Officer.'" He jerked before being pulled back by a mixture of pain and Olivia. The German doctor applied some new clotting agent and a bandage, as Lovecraft turned to him.

"Did you get her with one of her poison rounds?" he asked.

"I tried, but God, she was so quiet that even Ying didn't hear her."

"Lovecraft, what do we do?" Aaron asked, still looking around. Lovecraft looked to Olivia to give him an idea of how Abram was and she told him that Abram needed to get to a hospital right away. He nodded and ordered a stretcher to be brought to their location.

He then moved next to Aaron and slung his rifle, "The Chinese aren't stupid. They have a plan; a fallback point should their leader get captured. I think we have just the person to ask."

Aaron nodded once when he understood what Lovecraft meant, "What would you have us do to him?"

"Make him tell. Tear him limb from limb if you have to; just make sure he's still alive so that he can tell you."

"Excuse me," Olivia's voice cut between them and forced them to look at her, "I may be able to help in that area."

Lovecraft and Aaron looked at one another, "How?"

Chapter 15
Reign of the Machine

The next day, March 31st, was a cold and rainy day. It was a day that perfectly matched the moods of those in Ruler and the team's allies. Abram lay in his hospital bed, looking through the window, while Aaron stood next to the doorframe. The water sliding down the glass reminded Abram of when Ying confessed her love for snakes.

Lovecraft sat in a nearby chair and stared at the floor; his back hunched forward with his hands folded. His head was filled with thoughts of how they were going to get Ying back, but he kept running into the same dilemma – they were too preoccupied with Abram. They couldn't leave him alone for fear of a repeat in the incident that took place with Sue, and they couldn't take him with them due to his injuries. This meant that somebody would have to stay with him, and while the Legion and the police had agreed to guard him, Lovecraft didn't like the idea of not having at least one of them there to fend off the Chinese Heavies. He only came to one, terrible conclusion: he would have to do it.

Lovecraft suddenly stood up and announced, "I'm going to check on Blitz." Both men nodded and returned to their quiet mullings. He stepped out the door, passed Monica, who was on the phone with Kara, and ducked through a doorway that led to a concrete stairwell. He looked up at it, like it was some magical instrument, but his actual thoughts were that of melancholic nostalgia. He imagined them being wooden as he ascended, and near one of the doors, the old man appeared.

"You were always a—" He was cut off as Lovecraft walked through him. The man continued ascending the stairs in his black trench coat, until he got to the seventh floor, but just as he started to push the door open, he jerked his head around and saw the girl with the yellow raincoat staring back at him. He stared at her for a second and then Aaron's words about his sister echoed in his mind; he opened the door and didn't look back as she disappeared. He walked through the crowded hall, a byproduct of having one floor completely locked down, and came to a door that had two police officers standing next to it.

They stepped aside and allowed him to open the door. Once entering, he was treated with the almost artistic sight of Olivia, dressed in a black tank top and black combat pants, punching Kei in the jaw, which threw a spray of blood to the floor that splashed with a wet plop. She wrung the pain out of her gloved hand, before turning around when she heard the door close.

"I thought you said you weren't going to beat it out of him," Lovecraft said, as he looked to the tray of empty syringes in the room.

Olivia chuckled before pulling her bloody gloves off, "I didn't," she threw the latex gloves into a trash can labeled 'Biohazard,' "I shot him up with the drugs and he sang like a bird; the beating was for what he did to Ying."

Lovecraft nodded, "I take it you found something?"

"There's an old power plant near a place called Des Plaines, do you know it?"

"Of course, it's right next to O'Hare."

Olivia nodded, "Seegers Road, next to Weller Creek. That's where the power plant is, along with the Chinese." Lovecraft congratulated her on a job well done and suggested that she take a shower to cool herself down. She didn't argue this and called for the police officers outside to come and get the unconscious Kei, as Lovecraft stepped out.

He made his way back down the stairs, past a few doctors and nurses, and when he made it back to Abram's room, he called Aaron out into the hallway.

His older friend shut the door behind him and asked, "What is it?"

"You'll be staying with Abram tonight."

Aaron looked at him incredulously, "Okay, and what about you?"

"I'm going to get Ying back."

Aaron snorted, "By yourself? Wait, you're not seriously going to grab your old gear, are you?" Lovecraft nodded and Aaron could barely comprehend this, or rather, he couldn't believe it. Never in a million years did he think that Lovecraft would ever consider donning his old gear again.

"And why am I staying here in this scenario?"

"Because, we are one team member down, and if you and I both leave, then there will be nobody here for Abram. I also can't lose you to some stupid bullshit when you're my second in command. If anything happens to me, then you need to take control of Ruler."

"You sound like you expect to die."

"No, I'm just being realistic. If two of us die on the battlefield and then one dies in a hospital bed because the guards were outmatched, then that's it, no more Ruler."

Aaron wiped his brow with his sleeve as Lovecraft's logic weighed on him, "Are you sure you're going to be okay digging all that up?"

"I'll be fine. I just need to go on a walk first." He turned around and left Aaron standing in the hallway. Ruler's second in command stumbled back into Abram's room, and the Russian's ears had caught the entire exchange.

"Lovecraft's returning, isn't he?" he asked.

Aaron looked at him, "Yeah, he'll be back."

Abram shook his head, "No, I meant he's returning to his real form. The thing that tamed the Wolf herself. Tell me, how did you meet him?"

Aaron paused for a moment, stunned from his question, but this gave ample time for Olivia to walk in. She opened her mouth to say something, but stopped when she felt the heaviness in the room.

"Um, am I interrupting something?" she asked.

Aaron pinched his brow and said, "No, you can stay. It's not like this stuff is a secret." Olivia didn't know what he was talking about, but shut the door anyway. She walked to the other side of the room while Aaron sat in one of the chairs.

"When I went to high school, I didn't have many friends. I was a loner and a loser, but that didn't mean I liked it. One day, we got a new student in our class. Even back in that day, he was called Lovecraft, and he was just as alone as I; only he wanted it that way. I just started to hang around him, even though he found it really annoying, and soon, we were friends. Then, I found out about his dirty little secret. You see, Lovecraft lived out his nights, killing the local city trash, and that was where he earned a majority of his money. I had noticed that he always seemed more tired than others in the morning and I, being the genius that I was, sneaked to where he lived and followed him. Long story short, he saved my ass from getting roasted and after that, he started to train me. Of course, there's always more to this story, but I'm not as good a storyteller as Kara or the man himself," Aaron finished. The story drew a nod from Abram, and Olivia's eyes were glued to him.

"Lovecraft is a good man. He's the best leader I could've asked for, but, Aaron, is Lovecraft actually as merciful as he claims to be?" Abram asked.

Aaron looked at them and said, "It's a matter of perspective really. The best way to describe Lovecraft is the alias that his enemies used to call him, 'The Machine.'"

"What does 'used to' mean?" Olivia asked, looking like it was her first reaction to a great myth.

"We killed them all, he and I, and I know how he fights. The Chinese will stand no chance, they will beg for mercy and won't find it. Lovecraft's main weapon is hate, and this begs the question: how does the one who wields hate as a weapon show mercy? The answer is: by not using the weapon."

Abram immediately had an epiphany, "That's why he's not been going after the Chinese as earnestly as he should have."

"Because, he knew that they were poking a bear trap that's even worse than Afghanistan. It's brutal," Olivia added, crossing her arms.

Aaron nodded, "When he comes back, and he will, don't act differently. He swore to me, many years ago, that he would never fight so earnestly again, and now, he has to. I believe that the real victim here is, in fact, Lovecraft."

The light faded, but the rain and the clouds did not. These were Lovecraft's companions, as he walked down the wet sidewalk toward Lugers and Leggings. Water dripped from his hair, as he tried to keep the memories at bay, and he was anticipating when he got to the door because it presented a distraction. However, somebody stood outside the door and when he looked at her, Lovecraft realized that she was a protester. A scowl formed on his face as he walked up to the door.

"Excuse me, sir. Have you ever stopped and realized that there have been over 20 school shootings in the last 20 years?" Lovecraft ignored her and fished the spare key out of his pocket.

As he put it in the keyhole, she said, "Um, if you sign this petition, we could reinstate the old Chicago gun laws and save our children from this terrible fate."

Lovecraft looked at her, then behind her, and then behind himself, "We? No, you mean you."

"Well, with your help—"

"There were 25."

"Excuse me."

"There were 25 school shootings, because I was a first responder to 15 of them."

The girl looked at him incredulously and this caused him to explain, "I'm a Contractor, and the gun I used to kill those 15 school shooters is the same one you're trying to ban." She started to stammer, but Lovecraft shook his head, "Face it, you have no idea what you're talking about. Also, the laws you're trying to reinstate were in place during the murder crisis in the 2010s. You may as well take your 300-dollar scarf, 210-dollar shoes, 100-dollar pants, and 80-dollar tee shirt to your mom and complain to her. Maybe she'll tell you that I'm just an asshole and then she'll rub your back as you drink warm milk."

The girl looked down, "My mom was shot and killed last year."

Lovecraft stopped unlocking the door and turned to her, "Welcome to reality, kid. The world sucks, it's a black place, and while I will fight till I die to protect you, you will find no pity in me."

She looked up to him, as a red neon sign turned on across the street, "Who are you?"

Lovecraft's face was half covered in red, while the other was completely black, "A person who has realized that the ugly truth is a more faithful woman than your beautiful lie." He disappeared inside the shop and left the protester to mull over his answer. She soon threw her sign into an alleyway and walked home; a home that had once been for two, but now held only one.

Walking through the door, Lovecraft looked around the darkened store. He looked at the holographic open sign and saw that Kara had remembered to turn it off this time, it gave him some comfort to know that Kara had made it back in one piece.

He locked the front door and called out, "Hey, Kara, you here?" There was no response, as was expected, so Lovecraft looked around a bit, before he started to climb the black stairs to her apartment door.

As he climbed, he realized that there was an old feeling of comfort when he was inside here. He looked behind himself and then looked forward, but there was no memory present that wanted to haunt him. Just like the ghosts of the battlefield, they followed him wherever he went, but not here for some reason. He shook his head and continued on until he got to her door, a door that she insisted on painting red even though he told her not to; it looked really tacky.

He knocked on the door and asked, "Kara, you there?" It took almost a minute before the door unlocked and its occupant looked at Lovecraft like she was seeing a ghost when she first saw him.

"L.C.?!? I didn't know you were coming; y-you usually call." Kara was positioned in such a way that Lovecraft could see that she was in a blue bathrobe, but the entire left side of herself was hidden from view.

"Is this a bad time?" he asked, really hoping that it wasn't because he was already in a bad mood.

Kara looked back at the apartment, stroked her bottom lip, and then said, "No, it's fine, but the place isn't clean, and I need some time to get dressed."

"Kara, if you're getting dressed, or if there is somebody else here, I can wait downstairs till you're done." It took Kara a moment to realize what Lovecraft was insinuating, due to the throbbing pain in her back, but when she did, the door was fully opened, and she showed Lovecraft her left arm, which was happily residing in a sling. She explained to Lovecraft, how putting your clothes on and having sex is, and would be, very hard and awkward with only one arm.

"That sucks, Kara, your two national past times got taken out in one go," he said, in his perfect monotone.

Her eye started to twitch as she stepped out of the doorway, "I will seriously fucking slap you." He stepped inside, as Kara started to walk back into her bedroom. He looked around and found that Kara had her weapons all taken apart and ready for cleaning, but, Lovecraft surmised, she was having some trouble, just like with everything. There were muddy footprints on her carpet and, after checking his own feet, he realized that Kara had tracked them. The coffee table was cluttered with a sewing kit and large Medkit; there were some dirty bandages left on there too. He looked at all of this and slowly walked over to the table. He set about cleaning it up, throwing the bandages away, packing up the sewing kit, and also closing the Medkit. He looked at the carpet and then looked to a nearby cabinet which was where Kara kept her cleaning supplies. He opened it and knew that the proper tools for cleaning such a mess were not present. Although, he knew that he could at least try. After that, Kara could just work on the stains later.

His newfound purpose consumed him, but as he did this task, Lovecraft couldn't forget the responsibility he needed to carry out tonight. It brought bags under his eyes and produced a buzzing in the back of his mind that, unless ignored, would make his mind wander to the more pressing subject. It was driving him crazy.

"Hey, Lovecraft," Kara voice came from the other side of the bedroom door, "Can you...give me a hand?" She had startled the man and he took a moment to recollect himself before he opened the door. He already knew where this was going, but didn't mind it. Kara had done more than he thought she was capable, and he was glad that she made it back in one piece. He walked into Kara's bedroom and saw her standing there in a pair of jeans and her arms held over her chest. She was holding a black bra to herself, but it was unclasped, just like Lovecraft anticipated.

Kara looked over her shoulder, "Hey, could you help me here?" Lovecraft nodded and took his gloves off for more dexterity. He reached for the garment, but stopped halfway when he saw that her hair was shorter. However, it was not this simple fact that stopped him so easily. No, it was what her hair had been covering this whole time that stunned him; her scars. He had never seen them before, surprising as this fact was, and reached his hand forward toward the one on her neck. He stopped halfway when Kara asked what the holdup was. Lovecraft told her it was nothing and hooked the two ends together for her.

However, before he let go, he looked at the knife wound on her back and it caused him to ask, "You do your stitches yourself or did Monica?"

"Monica, why?"

"Because, it looks like she did it without her glasses on. Sit on the couch, I'll redo it for you," he said, grabbing his gloves and walking out into the other room. Kara followed him and sat on the couch, as Lovecraft fetched the sewing kit again. He told her to sit with her legs up on the couch while he got behind her.

"Jesus, what the hell did she do, use a fuckin' nail to sew this shit up?" Lovecraft cussed, dabbing an alcohol pad on it.

"Is it really that bad?"

"No, but it still looks like hell. I'm gonna start pulling this out, okay?" Kara nodded, and he began his work. He grimaced as he watched the wound open, and blood started to dribble out of it. He wiped it off, eliciting a hiss from Kara, and then he pulled it fully open again. It was as he started to sew it back together again, that he noticed that Kara would squirm every time his hand would touch her skin.

"I'm not hurting you, am I?" he asked, looking at the back of her head. Kara was embarrassed to admit that he was tickling her, which was surprising to him.

"I didn't know you were ticklish," he said, getting back to work.

"Well, you've never touched me before," she chuckled, "I know you came here for something, so what is it?"

"Maybe I just wanted to check up on you, make sure you actually did make it back in one piece," he retorted, grabbing the scissors.

"You mean you actually worried about me? I'm shocked, but I saw that gloomy look on your face. Something happened while I was gone, and you need something from me. So what is it?"

Lovecraft finished with her stitches and snipped the ends of the threads off, "Ying got captured and now, I'm going to bring her back."

Surprise spread over Kara's face when he said this, "By yourself? What about Aaron and the rest?"

"Aaron is guarding Abram, who was injured trying to protect Ying. I can't lose more men, so I'm just going to do it myself. As for what I need, do you have any 12-gauge dragon's breath?" Kara stood up and Lovecraft stood with her. She looked him in the eyes and saw that they were the eyes of a man dealing with his past; she had seen this many times. Kara responded positively to his question and started to pull the sling over her head.

When Lovecraft inquired as to what she was doing, Kara replied, "I can see it, Lovecraft. You're struggling with this, and while I don't know what you've done, I will tell you that the past means nothing when lives are on the line. I'm not going to be the bird with a broken wing while I explain this to you." Kara threw the sling on her bed and then grabbed a tee shirt, "Gold is worthless to the dying. Water is worthless to the starving. Food is worthless to the thirsty." She stood in front of him and folded her hands in front of herself, "Medicine is worthless to the dead. Peace is worthless in times of war. Justice is worthless in a place where there is no law, and your past doesn't matter when it comes to your present. I want you to remember this while I grab what you need." She guided him down the stairs, into the shop, and back into her office.

She unlocked a cabinet and pulled out two blue boxes and handed them to Lovecraft, "Everything has its own value, Lovecraft. Take it from someone who's had to give up her past, present, and future for someone else's; people are more valuable than anybody's past."

"Is it really that simple for you, Menagerie?"

"Yes, it is. Why? Because, that's what you've taught me. Dwelling on things forever will only degrade who you are, that's why I've accepted Kara as who I am now. I am no longer Menagerie and it was you who gave me this second chance." She took a moment to put a hand up to his face, "Take it from somebody who everybody hates; you can always choose to be different. Now, you need to go back, and be the person whom everybody feared."

He looked at her and cocked an eyebrow, "I can't. I don't want to."

"You are going to become that person again. Why? Because, you're the only hope that Ying and everybody else has; killing to save one life will earn you others." Kara took a moment to collect her thoughts, "My door will be unlocked when you come back. I hope you pick a better movie than last time."

"Kara, you do know that I may not come—"

"Fuck the facts, Lovecraft. I'm tired of losing those around me." She grabbed his coat and pulled him toward her, green eyes bore into slate grey ones, "You are not some simple soldier who's going to take out the enemy, you're a force of nature just like me. You will come back because you're Lovecraft, the one we all believe in, the one who wields hate as his sword."

"Who told you that?"

"I've known for quite some time, since your record speaks for itself, but it doesn't concern me. I just want you to make it out." She let him go and slowly retracted her hurt arm. She sucked in some air for a moment and looked at the carpet for a moment.

"When you get out, my door will be unlocked," she said, folding her arms over her stomach. Lovecraft nodded and shoved the boxes into his pockets. He then retreated to the door and left Kara's; he now headed toward the Compound where he thought he had buried his past for good.

It was dark by the time he got there, and when he opened the door, it was as quiet as a tomb. Lovecraft looked around the bright kitchen, it was the only light they left on when they left, and knew that there would be no distractions unlike earlier. He balled his hands into fists and walked down the hallway which was pitch black in comparison to the kitchen. He started walking, but stopped when he felt a cold wind hit his unshaven face. The darkness took on an unusually blue high and he immediately knew what it was.

"Amanda..." he called in his deep, rough voice, "out of my head, now!" The raincoat-ed figure who stood behind him immediately disappeared. Lovecraft continued walking and came to his room. He turned the knob and pushed it open with a creak; the light from his window drawing raindrop lines on Lovecraft's face. Eyes glued to the bed, he walked over to it and ran his gloved fingers over the mattress; the scratchy material sliding across the leather mesh. He then grunted as he grabbed its frame and folded it against the wall. This revealed a corrugated metal hatch that had been painted black. Opening it, he hesitated a moment to look at his shaking hands.

Crunching them up into fists again, he reached into the dark pit and withdrew the one weapon that his assault rifles could never dream of reaching its kill count; Lovecraft's Vepr twelve-gauge shotgun. It was based on the Russian RPK machine gun, a super-sized Kalashnikov, only it was now chambered for shotgun shells. Lovecraft's was Cerakote jet black and engraved to the point that there were very few clean places left. He set it aside and pulled out all his old gear, which he started to change into. His plate carrier was worn underneath his coat, while a chest rig was draped over that. He belted a strange device onto his back that had four, short antenna erected toward the ceiling, and then he put his helmet on his head. He tested the night vision before trading out his Oakley gloves for a different set of gloves that were covered in metal plating that had been sharpened to that of a razor.

As he secured their Velcro beneath his coat's sleeves, a voice came from the hallway, "You cannot hide from us, Contractor," the voice said in snarky, authoritative tone, "Your past will not so easily be cheated."

Lovecraft glanced over to the door and he saw the old man sitting in the doorway; his wheelchair glowing like a fire. The Contractor turned back to his work, as he continued to speak his insults.

"Did you think that you could dig up the past without the past noticing? You were always that stupid." Lovecraft flexed his hands in the gloves, "You were the reason she died; you know that, right? Your stupidity got her killed, and then you killed me. You're a traitorous bastard, Lovecraft. An actual monster, but even that term is too human for you. Maybe you are just a machine, more machine than the dolls you've allied yourself with. You cannot and never will be able to change, boy!"

Lovecraft stood up and turned to him, almost invisible due to his dark clothing, "I know." He grabbed his shotgun and attached it to the device on his back, thanks to an internal magnet, "but, Uncle, I. AM. NOT. YOUR. MACHINE." He turned to the orange specter and started walking toward him, "You are also, no relative of mine." Having said this, Lovecraft walked right through him and transformed him into a pillar of sparks, just like he did so many years ago. Lovecraft stepped into the light, and, when using the direct light, one could just barely make out the date '11/21/40' scratched into his helmet. Lovecraft screwed a suppressor onto his pistol and returned it to his holster, before he left in the town car.

A stray draft blew through Ying's grey-and-black hair, as blood dripped from her nose. Scales rubbed against the chains which bound her; the head of a cobra nuzzling itself next to her cheek. Pain, the burning of her blood, the wetness of her tears, and the snake were all that Ying had come to know since coming here. There was a hole in her left thigh where a needle had been shoved, and its contents now ran through her body, it made her burn all over, yet she still felt cold. She kept wishing that somebody would come and let her out, or at the very least, give her some water, but every time, she was reminded that guards had said she would be dead in seven minutes or less. Yet, she couldn't remember if she had counted eight or nine minutes since then.

Ying looked to the floor and shut her eyes. She remembered her days back with her family and those other days with Ruler; her *other* family. Fleeing into these memories, she sought to hide from the pain and the snake, which she surmised was to be her former comrade's final solution to her existence. Ying wanted to leave, she wanted to go home, and she wanted to be with her friends again. This need brought on the memory of her getting captured and she remembered what Zhi did to Abram.

"That bitch!" Ying said, lifting her head. She struggled against the chains and threw the snake from her in the process. It curled around her knees when she stopped moving, and Ying uttered the words, "I refuse to die."

The world around the Chinese base was made of cast iron; it was locked down so tight. Their wounded numbered in the double digits and a majority of their supplies had been burned up by Kara's attack. The number of wounded was so bad, in fact, that two injured women had been asked to leave the infirmary so they could cater to those with more severe wounds. Thus, the two women, one with a completely wrapped head and the other with a broken arm, made their way to the makeshift, women's barracks. The one with the broken arm led the blind one to the door, where they found another female soldier standing guard. She allowed them access and once inside, the less-damaged woman set her blind friend down.

She told her that she was just running to the bathroom for a second and that she should wait for her. The wounded woman couldn't see through the bandage, but nodded anyway. She heard the bathroom door open and then close, but didn't know if she was actually alone or not.

Inside the bathroom, the woman could barely see, as she walked over one of the mirrors. For being a power station, the lights weren't that bright, but she was given some help, thanks to the fact that there were lights above each mirror. She flicked it on and saw her damaged face for the first time; it pained her to see just how many stitches there were. She opened the mirrored cabinet in an attempt to find some band aids, but right as she grabbed the box, there was a noise behind her.

The woman jumped and turned around as fast as she could, but there was only a thick wall of black behind her. Her breathing quickened as her eyes danced across the faint outlines of the stalls; she called out in her own tongue to ask if anybody was there. When no answer came back, she let out a breath before turning back to the cabinet; she chalked it up to her nerves being on edge. She pulled a bandage out of the cardboard box and started to move the mirror back into place. However, she dropped the package when she saw Lovecraft standing behind her. She gasped, as he grabbed the back of her head and slammed it into the mirror, crushing it into little pieces, just like her skull.

Lovecraft let her go and she flopped to the floor like a dead fish. He pulled his suppressed pistol from its holster, as the dead woman's head started to leak all over the floor, staining the underside of his boots, as he turned out the lights. He opened the door and the blind woman called to her friend, but questioned it when she did not get an answer back. She was about to call out to her again, but her breath caught in her throat once she felt Lovecraft's pistol put against her chin.

"You people took something from me, and it really pissed me off. Now where did you take her?"

"Take who?" she replied in broken shaky English.

Lovecraft rolled his eyes, "Ying Li, you dumb bitch. Tell me so I don't have to splatter your brains all over the wall like your friend."

She squeaked at his words, "I don't know, but if she's anywhere, it'll be on the fourth floor. That's where we keep the makeshift holding cells." Lovecraft praised her cooperation and moved away from her, but he still wasn't done.

"Tell me, Chinglish, are you scared of the dark?" he asked. The Chinese woman didn't understand what he meant and when she started to ask, she got her head blown off. Lovecraft was almost invisible against the black background and he retracted the smoking suppressor into the depths of his coat.

The door suddenly flew open in front of Lovecraft, as the guard outside was drawn in by the sound of his pistol. Her eyes were drawn to the woman on the bloody mattress, but this was the last thing she saw, as metal gloves wrapped around her head. She was lifted into the air, her gun falling to the floor as she kicked back and forth, and with a snap of the fingers, her neck was broken. Lovecraft threw her lifeless body to the floor and pulled his pistol out again. He collected a keycard off her body and stepped out into the hallway. It smelled of mold, and as he checked on his surroundings, he noticed that the security cameras were functioning. Pulling out his phone, Lovecraft tapped a few icons and a set of cameras faded into static.

This let him move around freely, but also alerted the officer watching the cams. He noticed that a series of five cams had gone down in the women's section, and grabbed his radio.

"Team One, can you investigate the women's dorms. Seems some type of power outage, over." He got the acknowledgment back almost immediately and when he set the radio down, Zhi came over to him.

"Is there a problem?" she asked, adjusting her ballistic mask.

"No, ma'am. Probably just some faulty wiring due to this building's age. I'll have Team One stand guard after they confirm what the problem is," he replied, grabbing his cigarettes.

Team One moved into Lovecraft's area; their flashlights painting the rusted walls as their comms were filled with static. Two of them split off into two separate hallways, while three other ones guarded the main entrance. Lovecraft walked into a room that was filled with rolls of copper wire and as one of the roamers passed his room, he jumped through the doorway, knocking the door out of the way, and threw a line of copper wire around his neck. He dragged the struggling, gasping man back into the room where his sounds were never heard again.

His friends called out his name because they heard the loud bang of the door, but when they didn't get an answer, two of them picked up their Bullpup rifles and moved toward the hallway. They found his gun laying on the floor, with its flashlight pointed toward the center of the dark hallway. They called his name again, but there was still no answer. The sweat beaded on their brows, as they started to look around them; their flashlights melting the shadows from the cracked open door. One of the men saw this and moved to the door, causing the other man to get on the other side of it. Little did they know that when their attention was pointed toward the door, Lovecraft stepped out of the darkened hallway and walked right past them.

They hesitated for a moment, but when they did open the door, they both stormed it, and their lights danced across it. However, this room was so dark that the cheap iridescent lights could barely make a dent into the black wall. They called out their comrade's name, but once again, there was no response. They sighed in disappointment and turned around, however, what they didn't know was that on the floor, mere inches from one of their feet, lay the gloved hand of their dead friend.

They exited the room and tried to get their radios to work. Unfortunately, they had no luck and when they returned to their original post, they realized that the third man, whom they'd left there, was gone. One gave a frustrated sigh and called out to the missing man. There was no response, and he swore under his breath, but the other soldier quickly grabbed his attention and showed him a Chinese flag that he had found on the floor. They both looked around and stayed still for a moment to listen. They couldn't hear anything of note, but that was the eerie part, there was a low hanging ambience around them that stuck like mud. It was too quiet for a manmade structure, especially one of this age.

"Okay," one of them whispered for no apparent reason, "we find Yu and then get backup from Team Two. There's something not right about this place."

"Should we be searching for survivors?" the other asked.

"Later, if we don't make it back, then they'll never be found. Grab onto my carrier and don't let go for anything, understand?" The other Chinese soldier listened to him and grabbed hold of his drag handle. They started down the other hallway and started to call out to their other companion. They kept their barrels pointed to each other's blind spots, but in this darkness, it was all a blind spot. They passed room after room, and checked each one, but they could not find the man; he was just gone like all the others. They rounded another corner and saw that there was a light on inside of the next room. They wondered if this could be one of the women's dorms or if their comrade was inside. They went up to the door and tried the knob, but found it locked. They looked at each other for a moment, before they forced it open, and found the room to be completely empty, except for a few beds and another gun laying on the floor. They went inside, but they failed to notice that there was someone in the dark hallway behind them; a long suppressor hanging off his pistol.

The two men looked at the gun, but the one who had come up with their course of action also noticed that this room had a bathroom just like some of the larger dorms. He announced that he was going to check the bathroom and moved away from his friend. When he got to the door, the one inspecting the rifle got something thick and syrupy on his gloves. He shined the light to it and his eyes went wide, when he realized that it was blood. Yet, he couldn't speak a word about it, since Lovecraft slit his throat at the same time. Lovecraft grabbed the soldier and slowly dragged him back into the hallway, as his friend, who was now the last one left alive, kicked the bathroom door open.

"Is there anybody in there?!" he cried, looking around the dimly lit room. He turned on the lights and took note of how only one of the three overhead lights came on, and it was buzzing to boot. He called out again and received no answer again. Shaking his head, he went to leave, but his gut started telling him to check the stalls. He trusted it and crouched to look underneath the doors. He laughed when he saw a pair of Chinese boots. Going over to the stall laughing, he pressed his hand against it and said the game was over, but when he started to push on it, he realized that it was unlocked. What lay inside, horrified him. His friend had been shot in the head and two naked women had been piled on top of him; they must have been this dorm's occupants.

He backed up as fast as he could and called to his friend. He realized then that he was gone too. Panicked, he ran into the hallway where he saw his comrade standing in a corner.

"Hey, this is no time to taking a piss! We need to get the fuck—" He touched his shoulder and jumped back, as he fell backward, which revealed his throat that had been completely ripped open. He exclaimed and ran back down the hallway at full speed. He needed to get to safety, he needed to get to a place where whatever, or whoever this was, would have a considerably harder time getting to him.

He rounded the corner and saw the main entrance to the area. He was home free, he could make it and tell everybody what was going on, but that was a fleeting dream, as Lovecraft appeared from around the corner and grabbed him by the collar.

The taller man slammed him against the wall and said to him, "Greetings, Comrade." He then grabbed the soldier's belt, while his other hand still held his collar, lifted him up, and threw him head first into a stack of barrels. The soldier groaned, as he rolled onto his back where Lovecraft's boot found its place on his chest.

He pointed his pistol at the soldier's face, "Fourth floor, that's where you keep your prisoners, right?" The soldier groaned and acted like he couldn't understand Lovecraft. His interrogator's expression grew impatient when he saw this, and the result of this was him moving his foot off of him. However, he wasn't done. He reached down and grabbed the Chinese by the neck, the sharpened metal on his gloves cutting into his skin.

"Let's not sit here on ceremony, you Communist fuck. You're Special Forces and a Contractor. You can understand me. Did you hear me? You. Can. Understand. Me." Lovecraft watched his reaction and his eyes flicked to a back corner where he saw a FLIR camera. He turned back to the soldier and shook his head.

"It appears that you know much more than you claim. Should we give them a good show?" he asked, tightening his grip. The man monitoring the camera watched in horror as the taller, white image repeatedly hit the Chinese soldier, until he was dropped to the floor. Without missing a beat, he hit the alarm and all the lights came up in the building. Chinese soldiers scrambled to their positions, as Lovecraft watched all the lights come up around him.

He huffed as he pulled out his phone, "Your lights will not help you," Red lights appeared on a device that hung off his back, "because even they belong to me." The lights, the cameras, the alarms, even the flashlights on the guns, turned off.

Lovecraft pulled his night vision over his eyes and then grabbed his shotgun off his back, "Be a little more patient, Ying, I'm going hunting."

Zhi stormed into the camera operator's room and demanded that he explain why he hit the alarm. He told her that an intruder in the women's section wiped out all of Team One. Zhi couldn't believe what she just heard and personally ordered Team Two to cut whoever this is off from the rest of the building.

"There's only one way to the rest of the building and he's not making it any further. Tell Rock to meet me in front of the infirmary, we will not let such bullshit stop us," Zhi said, grabbing her rifle. She left the room and once the coast was clear, the camera operator looked back to the monitors and noticed that almost a dozen cameras were offline.

Lovecraft walked through the hallways with the darkness clinging to his attire. He stuck to the shadows and had already killed half a squad since leaving the Women's Section. He believed them to be Squad Three and, if his hunch was correct, Squad Two would be up ahead. They would be attempting to cut him off from the rest of the building, and since he already knew this, Lovecraft just walked right in. The room was pitch black thanks to his device, but Lovecraft had no problem seeing, thanks to his night vision. He looked around and watched the men of this Second Squad looking around; they were probably trying to figure out why the lights suddenly went out. Lovecraft noticed that their leader was holding an angle on the door itself while the rest of his team were spread out amongst the machines in the room. Ducking behind a machine, Lovecraft eventually found himself standing right behind the enemy leader. He pointed his shotgun behind his head and then blew the appendage clean off, his allies turning around in time to see their leader slump over. The last thing the four of them saw, however, was the blinding flash of Lovecraft's Vepr.

A light suddenly turned on behind Lovecraft and when he looked, there was a man standing in front of him with a bulletproof shield that covered his entire body. He blocked Lovecraft's way with the shield and, thanks to the path forward, being an old catwalk, it was more effective than it should have been.

This annoyed Lovecraft, but he had an answer for every problem. He kicked the mag out of his shotgun, taking note of how stupid it was that the shield guy was letting him do this, and replaced it with one that was filled with green shotgun shells. He cocked the gun and then fired it directly at the shield; the shot that was loaded was a fragmentation type and upon contact, it detonated. The round blew a large hole in the shield and damn near ripped its user in half; his blood coating the side walls. He fell backward and the shield fell with him, covering his body, before Lovecraft calmly walked past.

"Shooting me would have been more effective," he muttered, going into the next room. Zhi swore as she got the report that both Teams Two and Three were out of action, and Team Four had been forced to withdraw due to the number of injured. She couldn't comprehend that one man was doing this to them. It was insane, yet some of China's most elite warriors were being mowed down like they were in the Korean War.

Zhi suddenly broke out of her musings when Rock, the other genetically modified soldier, arrived.

"Where have you been?" she asked.

"Trying to get in contact with Team Four, you?"

"Holding down the Infirmary, and don't worry about Team Four, they just got bitch slapped and are retreating here."

"How many are there?"

"One."

"One? You're joking."

"Do you really think I'm joking about this shit?!" Rock looked at his superior and then asked what he could do. Zhi told him to go and buy time, but don't get killed. She'd need him later on. He nodded and then she told him that whoever was killing all of them was nearing the Power Generators and after that, he'd have complete access to any floor he wanted.

"I'll stop him there," Rock said, before taking his leave and running to his new destination. Zhi watched him and made sure her weapon was ready to go; she had a bad feeling about this.

When Rock made it to his destination, he crossed his arms and waited for Lovecraft to appear. The man didn't disappoint and announced his arrival by throwing a Chinese soldier through the door. He landed in front of Rock and revealed that his entire body had been shredded by buckshot. The Chinese soldier was shocked by the brutality and looked up, once he heard the broken-down door move. His eyes widened when he saw a man, who was almost a foot taller than he was, step out from the darkness. He was dressed in a black trench coat that would have rendered him almost invisible in this dark building.

Lovecraft pushed his night vision back on his helmet and asked, "Who the hell are you supposed to be?"

"I am Bik Ming, also known as 'Rock.' You have killed many of our men and even captured our beloved leader; your massacre and your life ends here," he introduced himself.

Lovecraft chuckled, "So you're Rock. Sorry, I imagined more of a boulder than a pebble." He got no reaction out of him, even though that Rock couldn't believe he was so nonchalant about his situation.

Lovecraft raised his shotgun up and said, "Well, are you just going to stand there or are you gonna let me pass?" Rock responded by throwing his weapons to the floor; he put his fists up. Lovecraft's back slumped and disappointment filled his mind. *Everyone wants a fist fight*, he thought, as he shot Rock right in the chest; the blast sending him backward. Tiny little balls of lead rolled from his body and scattered on the floor.

"Sorry, kid, but I don't have time for your bullshit…" Lovecraft trailed off, as he noticed one of the balls hitting his boot. He looked down and when he looked back up, he saw that Rock was standing up again.

He laughed and clapped his hands, "So Ying wasn't lying! Your skin really is harder than metal! Isn't that a bitch." Lovecraft put his shotgun on his back and spread his arms wide, "Well, come on then, you fucking cockroach, hit me." Rock charged him and swung, only Lovecraft walked around and said he was too slow. He swung again and this time, Lovecraft ducked out of the way. He came up behind Rock and put his arm around his neck; he used Rock's own body weight to throw him across the floor.

"Your skin may be harder than stone, but you hit like a bitch." He threw another punch at Lovecraft, who caught it with his hand, "I told you so." Lovecraft pushed Rock's own fist into his face several times, before he pushed him away all together. Having gained more than enough breathing room, Lovecraft drew his pistol and shot Rock three times. Naturally, the Chinese man stood to block them with his arms, but he suddenly felt blood trickle down his arms and down one of his legs.

He looked to Lovecraft who was brandishing his pistol toward him, "Depleted Uranium, it'll go through anything." Lovecraft then went on the offense; hitting Rock with so many strikes that he could only try and block him. Seeing that he had the upper hand, Lovecraft went for his legs and shot him in the back of his left knee and in his right ankle. Rock cried in pain, before collapsing to the floor. Lovecraft shot him in both arms and then popped two rounds into his stomach; Rock collapsed onto the floor and Lovecraft rolled him over.

The leader of Ruler pulled a frag grenade from his belt and pulled its pin, "Here, Cockroach, hold onto this for me." He dropped it next to Rock and ran through the other door. The last line of organized defense went up in a blinding flash of light. Now, even Zhi couldn't keep him from destroying everything.

Lovecraft walked through the darkened hallways and eventually came to the infirmary which was right next to the stairs. He looked into the cordoned-off area and left it alone, as most of the injured were hooked up to tubes or were unconscious. They certainly weren't going anywhere, anytime soon. However, there was something that concerned Lovecraft immensely; it seems that nobody was guarding these injured. He brought his night vision back down and tightened his grip on his shotgun. He proceeded up the stairs and was welcomed by a dark hallway that was lined with four-paned windows.

White light streamed through the windows as black raindrops ghosted their way down the glass. It smelled of dust, as Lovecraft slowly started walking down its length. The doors to his right were all locked with devices that accepted key cards and he hoped that his worked on them. However, before he finished that thought, the hallway started to explode. Bullets stripped two of the lenses from his panoramic night vision, cut his left cheek, ricocheted off his helmet, and blew a hole in his left shoulder. Lovecraft dove into an alcove that was cut into the wall, and waited as his wounds screamed.

Zhi got up from her kneeling position and walked down the hallway, her barrel smoking, as she drew it toward the alcove. Lovecraft threw his gun on top of hers and punched her in the face; the sharp metal cutting grooves into her mask. Zhi retaliated by trying to bring her assault rifle on him, but he knocked it out of her hands. He smacked her across the face, knocking the mask off, and got a good look at Zhi's mutilated face.

She knocked his shotgun from his hands and then kneed him in the plate carrier. She was wearing one of the Chinese's exoskeletons and its added strength crushed the protective plate against Lovecraft's ribs. He shrugged this pain from his mind and pulled his pistol free. He planted three shots into Zhi's kidneys, before spinning her around. Lovecraft put her into a choke hold, but it was soon interrupted by Zhi pulling her knife and jamming it into Lovecraft's leg. He groaned in pain and this was enough for her to get out of the hold. She turned around and started to reach for her own sidearm, but was stopped when Lovecraft shot her in the arm and then overpowered her. He picked her up by her plate carrier and threw her out one of the windows with a crash; her body made a wrenching noise as it collided with the earth.

Lovecraft put his broken night vision on his helmet, retrieved his shotgun, and took a moment to rest. With painful breathes, Lovecraft continued on, hobbling his way down. He counted 13 different doors as he reached the end of the hallway. He groaned and started to swipe his stolen key card in front of them, at least it was opening the doors. He continued to open every single one until he came to the tenth and when he opened it, he saw Ying wrapped up in chains. The hair at the top of her head was bright white while its ends were her natural black. She had obviously been beaten, if not tortured, due to the blood that dripped from her body.

"Ying!" he called, only to stop when the cobra slithered out from under her. Lovecraft killed it with his pistol and stood in front of Ying.

"Lovecraft? You're bleeding," she said, lifting her head.

"Later." He pulled out an item that looked like a piece of fabric, but, when he threaded it underneath the chain, it cut Ying free once he tugged on it. Ying gasped as she fell and was caught by Lovecraft, who braced her against himself. He returned the item to his pocket and began working on Ying's wounds, before treating himself with what was left.

"Is it just you?" Lovecraft nodded and pulled the knife from his leg, "Is Abram…?"

"He's fine, what about you, Miss Salt and Pepper?" Ying was confused by what he meant, so he pulled out his phone and showed her using its camera. Ying took it and covered her mouth with her hand.

"They did this to me?"

"No, you did it to yourself. Your body's own defense mechanism against the stress you were under. Do you feel any different?"

Ying shook her head, "No, I hurt, that's all."

"What about when you see what your countrymen have done?"

"It is disgusting! They're like a bunch of animals, no, little, shitty vermin is what they are. I want to kill them all, to destroy their very existence to the point that everybody forgets who they were. Their sins are unforgivable, and I will never forget what they have done to all of you," Ying replied, leaning up against one of the walls.

Impressed, Lovecraft stood up and put her arm over his shoulders, "Very well, let's get out of here."

She nodded and he carried her out into the hallway. He kept his shotgun pointed to the end of the hallway as they walked, but Ying kept looking around.

"What happened to Zhi?"

"I threw the ugly bitch out of a window, why?"

"She's not dead; you need to get me to an armory so I can walk on my own."

"How do you know?"

"Because, she's different now. She's a lot more…irate."

"Irate? What does that mean?" Lovecraft asked, helping her down a set of stairs.

"Means that she's going crazy. I don't really know how to describe it, but she's not calm anymore. She's tail-spinning and I think it's due to Kei being captured."

"Great. So you're telling me that I just pissed off a Chinese super weapon. I'm going to assume there's more bad news?"

Ying shook her head, "I don't know. She locked me in that box and I haven't been able to hear much, but I did notice that her skin looked softer than it did and the scar on her face is disappearing."

"Meaning?"

"I think she, or her cells, have mutated and gotten stronger." Lovecraft expressed his annoyance at this as they came to the end of the stairs. Both of them hobbled through the dark halls until they came to a red door and Ying made him stop. She told him that this was the armory, but before she could attempt to open the door, she fell on her hands and knees to throw up.

She vomited up a bunch of bile and alarmed Lovecraft, "Ying, are you okay?!" She nodded while she was still down and wiped her mouth with her shirt sleeve; she couldn't tell him that the snake had bitten her or that she could feel a fever inside her cheeks. Actually, it was more than a fever; it was like she could feel her individual blood cells moving throughout her body. Ying tried to block these feelings from her mind and stood up despite her weakened state.

Bracing herself against the wall, she put in her code and was happy to see that they hadn't gotten around to purging her access. The door slid open and the room was illuminated with blue neon. Guns and ammunition lined the walls, but Ying's goal were the exoskeletons that lined the back wall.

"Get me to the last one on the right, it's a female model." Lovecraft helped her over to it and listened to Ying's instructions when she told him how to secure the rig to her body. He locked it to her joints and as she was about to release its safety locks, Ying made the comment of how the last time she wore one of these, her convoy got blown up. Lovecraft told her not to worry and that if the worst should happen, this time, only she would be blowing up. It wasn't the most comforting thing ever, but she should at least expect as much in their situation. Ying disengaged the locks and stepped out of the terminal; the technique required to operate one of these machines slowing coming back to her.

"Should I call you Arnold now?" Lovecraft asked, as she grabbed a QBU-88-2 off the wall.

She looked at him with a confused expression, as she grabbed the rifle's ammunition, "I don't get that reference." Disappointment filled Lovecraft's face, as he hefted his shotgun in his arms. Ying stepped past him; the new metal pads on the bottoms of her shoes thudding across the floor.

"Zhi will be waiting for us, and she'll probably be pissed when we meet her. Are you ready to kill the strongest of us?" she asked, cocking her gun. Lovecraft nodded and followed her into the hallway.

The two of them made it to the outside of the building just as dawn started to break. Ying had commented on how Lovecraft had apparently killed everyone, although he said that it was impossible. He had only just gotten to the second part of the building and when he did, it was deserted. Ying found this concerning, but stowed it in the back of her mind as there were more pressing matters at hand.

The outside of the derelict power plant had been dug up in preparation for new construction, however, that construction never came to pass. Now, all that was left was a muddy mess that clung to their boots. Lovecraft kept looking over his shoulder; he had thrown Zhi out here and it was here she should have been. However, he couldn't see anything but piles of mud, and with the unnatural hair color that she possessed, it would be easy to see her. Yet, he suddenly saw a muzzle flash in the distance and a bullet ricocheted off his helmet, as the mud around him started to explode. Ying called out his name as he fell backwards; Zhi crawling out of the mud that she buried herself in.

She wore an exoskeleton, just like Ying did, and used its enhanced speed to get right up on Lovecraft. He tried to defend himself, but she had so much room now, that she evaded him and threw him well away from Ying, who started to unload onto Zhi. The bullets passed right through her and were almost immediately healed when she grabbed Ying's rifle.

Zhi broke it before running the back of her hand over Ying's face; the force throwing her into a mud puddle.

Zhi held her face in the water and said, "Oh dear, Ying, I'd thought you'd be dead by now. But, you're so weak right now that you may as well be dead." Zhi pulled her up from the water using Ying's hair and then smashed her fist into Ying's stomach.

She allowed the girl to collapse to the ground and the pointed at her, "You wait right there while I deal with the true threat." She left her in a mixture of mud and water, while she walked over to where she threw Lovecraft. This involved her climbing over another mound of dirt, and when she reached the summit, she didn't see him anyway.

She frowned and used her eyes to look all over the area, "Now where the fuck did you run off to, bastard?" Zhi suddenly heard something behind her and threw her arm back to hit it, however, it was stopped by Ying's hand.

"I'm the threat here, bitch," she said, before punching her in the face. Zhi recoiled from her newly broken nose and couldn't react to her former subordinate grabbing her hair. She whipped Zhi around and threw her down the dirt mound; Ying watched as she rolled onto more level ground before jumping into the air.

Zhi rolled away as Ying sunk her fist into the mud that she used to occupy; her hand wouldn't budge as the sticky clay solidified around it. Seeing this, Zhi seized her opportunity and wrapped her arms around Ying's midsection. She lifted Ying up, pulling her arm free in the process, and then threw her onto the ground as hard as she could.

"You were always so smug about him fucking you! You'd always rub my nose in it and make me feel like I was dirt," she said, straddling Ying, "But then I saw the bruises and it was just what a whore like you deserved." She started to hit Ying, but couldn't get through her guard. Ying had heard her words and was already tired of hearing her bullshit; now, she was done hearing it. She folded her hands together and thrust them vertically between the captain's arms, knocking them away, and then threw them forward. They crashed into Zhi's chest, not doing as much as they should, thanks to her armor, and knocked her off balance. This allowed Ying to get her hands underneath the captain's knees and used her aided strength to flip Zhi onto her back. Ying stood up, and pulled Zhi up soon after. She punched her in the face again, breaking her nose again and ripping open her scar, and as she recoiled, Ying pulled her back and then punched her on the other side, cutting her cheek open. She then forced Zhi to her knees and full force kicked her in the face; this action broke Zhi's jaw and sent her tumbling into a bloody puddle.

"Yes, Zhi, I totally bragged about getting raped. It was so fucking fun. It must have been fun for you too, getting to take my place after I disappeared. I'm sure you loved it. After all, your butchered mouth had always been made for sucking cock." Ying grabbed the spine of Zhi's exoskeleton and ripped it off, "However, none of your fun could ever match how much fun I've had fucking you up."

Zhi picked herself up and pushed Ying away to where she was, only about two steps from her.

Ying watched Zhi pull another knife out, "Oh? Lost your technological superpowers and now you have to use an instrument to fight me. Even for gutter trash like you that's low." Ying shook her head, "You were the strongest among us, Zhi. The golden bulwark that shined brighter than the sun. Yet, even you were corrupted by Kei."

Zhi took this opportunity to fix her jaw and, once she did, she said, "I *am* the strongest among you! I am like Gawain and I will never lose to a Lancelot like yourself! I am invincible! Look! Look, at the wounds you have given me. Are they not already gone?! You can't hurt me; a stupid bitch like you could never put a scratch on me."

Ying turned away, "You always did like comparing us to those of the Round Table... But you forget, Zhi, that Gawain was Lancelot's best friend and you are no friend of mine."

Zhi raised her knife into a combative stance as Ying moved to the side, "You were never a member of our Round Table."

The dirt shifted from behind Zhi and when she glanced toward it, she saw the dark silhouette of Lovecraft standing behind her. Ying lowered her guard and backed even further away than she had been pushed. Lovecraft threw another dead Chinese soldier down in front of him; his wounds smoldering from whatever ammunition was inside his gun.

He had a hand in his coat pocket and his shotgun was pointed to the sky, "Knights of the Round Table? What a fuckin' joke; you do realize, Zhi Yun, that Arthur's kingdom was a failure, and so were his knights?"

"What did you say?!"

"Arthur Pendragon was a failure. Like David, when his men went off to war, he left his knights home and they destroyed everything he built. Why? Because Mordred was filth no better than shit, and Lancelot was still human. You are no knight, you are no Gawain, and you are, most definitely, not invincible. You're just a monster and I'm going to prove it to you." He brought his shotgun down and shot Zhi in the leg; the shot that was loaded was a Dragon's Breath round and it quickly went to work, setting her pants on fire. Zhi felt down and screamed, as her skin started to boil. She frantically took off what was left of her exoskeleton and then unzipped her jacket, throwing the infamous garment toward Ying's feet.

"Hurts, doesn't it, bitch?" Lovecraft asked, walking closer to her, "The fire will burn faster than your regeneration can repair. Thus, you won't be able to cheat death like you used to." He pointed his shotgun at her arm and shot that with the fire shot. She screamed obscenities at him before he pointed the shotgun at her head. Ying reached down and grabbed the jacket that Zhi had thrown away. She dusted it off and started to take the top of her exoskeleton off.

"Do you have anything else to say, Ying?" Lovecraft asked. Ying shook her head, as she pulled her arms through the arms through the jacket's sleeves.

Lovecraft shrugged his shoulders and shot her in the head. He covered her entire body with fire and then left her to burn; her cries having stopped once his first shot rang out. He turned to Ying, who was zipping the jacket up, and motioned with his head.

She followed him and the two of them sat down on a nearby dirt mound; the fur that lined Ying's collar blew in the wind and tickled her nose. Lovecraft unclasped his helmet and pulled it from his sweat-caked head; the air felt good.

"Where were you while I fought her?" Ying asked, bring her knees up to her chest.

"I was killing off the missing Chinese soldiers. When she threw me, I noticed that there were people moving around in the woods. So I went after them and prayed that you could handle her. You didn't disappoint," he explained. He let the silence take hold again, but didn't let it last.

"Why was there a snake in there with you?"

"That was their final solution, should I not die, but I guess I'm the one of us that's actually immune to poison." Lovecraft nodded and then started to pat his pockets in search of his cigarettes.

"You don't seem so surprised."

Lovecraft found what he was looking for and put a cigarette in his mouth, "You said that Zhi mutated and became stronger. With this knowledge, I can only deduce that you are capable of the same thing. Thus, I should not be surprised if you're magically immune to snake venom or what you have."

Ying understood Lovecraft's logic and held her hand out, "Can I get one of those?"

Lovecraft looked at his cigarettes, "I thought you didn't smoke?"

"I don't," Ying clarified, but still held her hand out. Lovecraft handed her one and lit hers before he lit his own. The two of them sat there for a few moments and allowed themselves a break. However, once Lovecraft was ready, he asked Ying if she was. She agreed and they both stood up; they started to walk to where Lovecraft had parked the car. Yet, Ying stopped next to Zhi's charred corpse. Turning to Lovecraft, she asked him for his pistol and emptied a magazine into her head just to be sure. She returned it to him and they continued on; she would later fall asleep on the way back to the hospital.

Sneakers, caked in clay, strolled down the whitewashed halls of the hospital. Zebra-like hair flew in loose strands, as their owner rounded a corner and came to a door that had guards on either side. Dirty, red Chinese stars flexed on top of Ying's shoulders, as she pushed the doors open; her leather clad arms swung back to her sides. The fur that stuck out from her collar, tickling her chin, as she stepped past Monica, the French woman looking at her with stunned, yet happy, expressions.

She slowed herself down once she neared Abram's room, the place where the rest of Ruler was. She still wore the lower part of the exoskeleton, but she had forgotten about it due to her excitement. Ying stopped at the door and took a breath so she didn't look so winded. She had wiped the mud and blood from her face in the car and now, she calmly walked through the door.

Everyone stopped talking when the sound of her feet echoed throughout the room. They all turned to her with equally shocked expressions, like if she had been a ghost.

Ying smiled and gave a chuckle, "Well, you certainly look better than I do, Abram." She then turned to Olivia and Aaron, "I'm not a ghost." The three people all started talking at the same time and all of them, at one point or another, asked her if she was okay. Ying laughed and took a seat, as Lovecraft stepped inside the room; everybody stopped talking again.

He stopped and looked at everybody like they were crazy, "What? I had to use the bathroom," he continued, till he was leant up against the wall, "Nobody gonna ask me if I'm okay?"

"Well, are you?" Aaron asked.

"Sure, just got stabbed in the leg, cracked a few ribs, and got shot in the arms a bit. You know, nothing I can't handle," he replied. Olivia smirked and then asked if everything was over now. Ying nodded and folded her hands in her lap; she had never felt more relieved after a mission, or event, than right now. Lovecraft added that it was over for now, and told Olivia to take Ying to a different room so they could treat her properly. The German woman nodded and let Ying say goodbye to Abram, whom she thanked, for trying his hardest to save her, and Aaron, before escorting her out.

Lovecraft took her seat and let out an exhausted sigh. He cracked his fingers as Abram and Aaron looked at him

"I know it's not a proper thing to ask, but how was it? To be back?" Aaron asked, a little unsure.

Lovecraft lifted his head and replied, "It felt just like old times, Bro, but I was also made aware that I am getting way too old to be doing shit like that. My joints have been popping and grinding ever since I took a moment to rest." He chuckled at this a bit, and so did Abram, who could sympathize with him. Aaron joined in this amusement, but also suggested that Lovecraft get checked out like Ying. He declined, like Aaron knew he would, and said that he couldn't because he had a promise to keep. He would, however, let Aaron change his bandages and stitch up whatever needed to be stitched, since it was a pain in the ass to do it himself. Neither men asked what this promise was that Lovecraft held, since they knew how much he hated it when people pried into his business, but their imaginations had already given them an answer.

Olivia helped Ying out of the metal skeleton and lifted her onto the hospital bed; this earned her some praise for her surprising strength. She took Ying's shoes off and set them next to the door.

"Could I trouble you to change into a gown?" Olivia asked, although she already knew the answer.

Ying shook her head, "The only changing I want to do is when I change into my pajamas tonight. Until then, you're going to have to buy me dinner if you wanna take my pants off."

Both of them laughed and Olivia comment, "You're feeling rather chipper."

Ying shook her head, "No, I feel alive…for the first time in years."

Another night descended on Chicago, and as the holographic advertisements lit up the night sky, robots and abnormally dressed people took advantage of the city's nightlife, while the Contractors and the police watched on; it was going to be a busy night. However, one person in the city was alone in her apartment; yet, her heart was beating with as much energy as the outside world. Kara lay on her couch with a white yarn blanket draped over her lower half. She massaged her bare feet together anxiously, as she glanced back and forth between her television and the clock. Her mind raced as she constantly reminded herself that Lovecraft was over two hours late and he hadn't called. She kept trying to convince herself that he had forgotten with all that was going on, but she couldn't shake the notion that something could be wrong. She checked the clock again and saw that it was well past 12 o'clock and even though she wanted to wait a little longer, she had work tomorrow.

Reluctantly, Kara turned the T.V. off and got up from the couch. She knew that there was no sleep to be had this night, but she would try, just like everybody else would. However, as she started to walk, there was a sudden knock at her door that caused her to spin on her heel. Kara darted to the door and took a breath as she opened it; outside, Lovecraft stood, with his arms at his sides.

"Sorry, I couldn't decide on what movie—" He was cut off as Kara threw herself at him and hugged him tightly. He stood there awkwardly, not entirely prepared for this, but eventually put an arm around her.

She pulled away and said, "What's wrong? You always call if you're going to be late."

Lovecraft looked as if something dawned on him suddenly, "Right, I thought I had forgotten something. It's been a long few hours for me, you see, and I'm not…put together like normal." Kara smirked and invited him in where they had drinks and watched a few episodes of an animated show. Lovecraft told her how it went and how Ying and Abram would be staying at the hospital for a few days before the aftermath began. He stated that he would try his hardest to keep her free, but also expressed doubts about the situation. Kara understood this and listened as intently as she could.

"I have a favor to ask you. I've noticed some flaws in the way my team operates and I'd like to put in an order for something better," Lovecraft said, changing the subject.

Kara frowned, "Are you sure you want to talk about work right now? From the sounds of it, the best thing for all of you would be a vacation."

"You wouldn't be wrong, but I'd like to tell you now so I don't get on a waiting list for it or, God forbid, I forget."

Kara nodded and smiled at him, "Write it down for me before you go and I'll get right to it first thing in the morning." She watched him for a bit and noticed that after this exchange, he had dozed off. She looked at the clock and saw that it had just rolled over to one and wondered if she should wake him up. Another thought graced her mind as well; this one made her blush, but not to the point to where she didn't consider it and, eventually, decided to take it.

Kara sat her tea down on the coffee table and scooted closer to Lovecraft. She put her head on his shoulder and thought to herself that if everything should go downhill from here, at least she could remember this. Being this close to him was what she wanted, and if the world would end right now, she didn't mind; peace was what this was. It was an escape from reality and for her, it was so much more. She ended up falling asleep as well; the steam from her tea disappearing, as the apartment lights shut off due to their automatic timer. Neon blue filled the room, along with one blinking red light, and shrouded both of them. It was April first, happy birthday, Kara.

Chapter 16
Beginning's Curtain Call

The sun beamed in the blue sky a week later, and Kara was busily stacking gun cases onto a table at the gun range. She had just arrived and was there for a specific purpose; to see if all her hard labor had paid off. A week ago, Lovecraft had assigned her the task of gathering weaponry for Abram and Ying – should it prove that she needed it. It had taken her a week, and while it has been a busy week for her, it was even busier for Ruler. Two trips to D.C., a trip to Taiwan, and almost two days of paperwork to fill out; this was the aftermath of their actions against the Chinese, or so she heard.

Kara placed two long and heavy gun cases up on the table and decided to start with the one she placed on her left side. Tying her hair back, she opened the case with a series of clicks. She pulled out an Accuracy International, AX338 sniper rifle. This had been the rifle that Ying chose and Kara made sure that it was brought up to her job specifications. This process involved attaching a rangefinder to the scope that could be seen from inside its lens, upgrading its muzzle break into something that wouldn't break people's windows, and, hardest of all, lightening the damn thing so that it, not only would be comfortable for the reasonably small woman, but also so that it could be manipulated in close spaces, should Ying not be able to switch to her other weapon.

She accomplished this upgrade by replacing a majority of its parts with carbon fiber variants. She would have liked to replace the barrel, but there were too many risks in this. Kara deployed the bipod and set it up so that she could shoot. She loaded five rounds into the magazine and got behind the rifle. She shot all five rounds and was pleased to see that even a person with her lack of skill was able to shoot a quarter-sized group with it.

Satisfied, Kara moved it to the side and the next gun she grabbed was Ying's other firearm. This one was for her to use when a long-range rifle wouldn't be appropriate. Kara picked up an AAC Honey Badger that had gotten the same treatment as the AX338. She pushed a magazine into its receiver and flipped it to fully automatic. Kara emptied the entire mag in one go and was happy to see that there were no problems. She then grabbed the last of Ying's guns, a Glock 19, and emptied a mag with that one as well. She was satisfied with all the weapons she had procured for the sniper and now, she moved onto Abram's weapons.

His were much more complicated to enhance, due to the Russian government setting restrictions on what they allowed their Contractors to use. Yet, Kara was able to upgrade his PKM to a PKP 'Pecheneg' thanks to her contacts inside the other country. It didn't solve the problem that he would be using different ammo compared to all the others on his team, but at the very least, he wouldn't be stuck in the 80s anymore. Plus, she may have figured out a way to 'work' the Russian's system.

Kara pulled down the sleeves of her black shirt and loaded the machine gun with a belt that only held ten bullets. It cycled these rounds beautifully and that's all she cared about when it came to machine guns; if it jammed after the first ten rounds, then it probably wasn't anything that the operator couldn't clear on his own. Kara moved it away, swearing over how heavy and annoying it was, and then grabbed his replacement gun.

It was held in an unmarked case that honestly could have been mistaken for an old suitcase; the kind that children found in their great-great-grandmother's closet. However, the rifle it contained almost made Kara shove her fist through a wall; it was such a pain in the ass to get. Honestly, working with other companies was ridiculous sometimes.

She opened the case and pulled out a very rare assault rifle, a Krebs custom AK-type rifle. It had been reworked to fire the 5.56x45 cartridge and even accepted STANAG magazines, thanks to its modified receiver. This was how Kara intended work around the Russian restrictions; after all, it was technically Russian. She loaded its 30-round magazine and, if all went correctly and they didn't screw her, the plastic box should be empty in about four seconds. She cocked it and pulled the trigger; it sang just like it was supposed to, and Kara couldn't have been happier. She started packing them up one by one and then loaded them into her car as fast as she could. Kara had already grabbed the necessary paperwork earlier and once she had buckled her seatbelt, she sped off and headed to Ruler's compound.

She soon pulled up to the building about 40 minutes later, and got out of the car excitedly. Her heeled boots clicked up the stairs that led her to the front door; her right arm tightly holding onto the paperwork. She knocked on the door and was greeted by Abram who had just recently returned from Russia. He invited her in and Kara thanked him as he stepped aside and allowed her to see Aaron and Lovecraft sitting at the kitchen table. Aaron was dressed in a red tee shirt and grey jeans, while his opposite, Lovecraft, wore a long-sleeved, black shirt and a pair of khaki combat pants. He was telling some story of his trip to D.C., but he stopped when he saw Kara walk in.

He got up and walked to her, saying, "Are they done?" Kara smirked at him and said that they were. He told Aaron and Abram to go get the stuff out of Kara's car while he filled this out. Kara smiled at them as they walked past her; she then turned to Lovecraft and walked toward him.

"How is she?" Kara asked, handing him the paperwork.

Lovecraft took the papers and pulled a pen out of his pocket, "She's fine. She's in her room getting dressed right now; the trip to Taiwan was kind of a shock for her. Turns out, her aunt is Japanese."

"Really?"

Lovecraft nodded, "I took some lessons a long time ago in the Japanese language; never thought I'd have to use it though. Luckily, her husband is Chinese and after that, Ying took over the conversation."

"Did you get her signature then?"

"Yes." Lovecraft handed the paperwork back to Kara, "The U.S. Government also let her go. They renewed her Contractor's license and her Contractor's Immigration pass, but under a different name. As far as they are concerned, Ying Li died in the ambush to capture Kei. The name they gave her is Ying Nam."

"Heh, the government is getting generous. I wish they would have let me keep my name," Kara responded, crossing her arms.

Lovecraft scoffed, "Names only mean so much to those who aren't happy with their own. Anyway, if you must, just call her Ying Li, it will just make things easier for everybody."

Kara smirked and waved it off, "I'll just call her Ying. It's not that big of a deal." Kara took a moment to fold the paperwork and slipped it into her pocket, "Now where is it?"

Lovecraft cocked an eyebrow, as Aaron and Abram walked back in, "Where's what?"

Kara rolled her eyes that they began setting the crates on the table, "Your Vepr, stupid. I've never seen one in the wild and I've heard yours is…ornate."

Lovecraft deadpanned, but motioned for her to follow him, "I want to punch you in the throat sometimes." Kara snickered and said that he liked her too much to do something so brutal. Naturally, he reminded her that he almost did that first night they met, but she shot back and said that it didn't count because they didn't truly know one another.

He opened the door to his room and Kara took a moment to admire his small library, while he opened up the armory underneath his bed. Lovecraft pulled the weapon out and handed it to her; she immediately started admiring the engravings in its black finish. She commented on how it felt like a Saiga, another AK-style shotgun, on steroids, and that the engravings were rather beautiful. Lovecraft wasn't one to dwell on such compliments and took it back from her before she could make an offer on it.

"It's not that spectacular, you know?"

"Maybe to you, it's not, but it *did* just kill a lot of Chinese soldiers with it. I think there's still some blood on the end of the choke too." Lovecraft looked at the end of the shotgun and told her to 'Fuck off,' when he realized that she had tricked him. She cackled like a witch and let him lead her out of the room. The two of them then returned to the kitchen and as Lovecraft sat down, Ying stepped out of the bathroom in her new gear.

She stepped into the room and while she was surprised to see Kara, she was more anxious about what they thought of her choices. She wore a black tank top that was tucked into a pair of Crye combat pants; they were held up with a khaki-colored belt. The pants were colored in Multicam and were essentially just like Lovecraft's, only cut for women. Her boots were a pair of dark, almost-chocolate-brown hiking boots that Abram had suggested. The second layer she wore, her plate carrier and the like, was a mixture of gear that was meant to keep her load the lightest it could be. Thus, the Multicam J.P.C. she wore had plastic attachments that connected to her belt; this was so that it held the carrier in balance and limited the fatigue on her shoulders. Her carrier was set up very much like everyone else's, and this was so there would be no confusion if worse came to worst, and they needed to get to her Medkit. Her holster was the only abnormality on her person, because it was stuck to the front of her carrier, just above her magazine pouches. The reason for this was so she could use the bionic legs they had captured from the Chinese; she had invaluable training when it came to using such an apparatus, and Lovecraft had already insisted that they use it.

Ying had no qualms with this, as she knew just how much of an advantage the enhanced strength gave her. The only problem was, she didn't know how she was going to maintain it without the proper tools or the replacement parts. Yet, Lovecraft assured her that they could find such things should the need arise, and she stopped protesting after that. The final pieces of clothing and gear that Ying wore were a pair of black Oakleys on her hands, a G.P.S. strapped to her left bicep, and a communications headset that she wore around her neck so that she could hear. Her tattoos were on full display, which Kara and a few others absolutely loved.

Ying looked to each one of them and asked, "How do I look?"

Kara immediately jumped at the question and said, "You look awesome! Your tattoos make you look like a badass!" Ying blushed at her exuberance, but thanked her anyway. The others shared the same sentiment, while Aaron bragged to Lovecraft, saying, "See? I told you her boobs wouldn't be a problem. Just gotta, 'Squish 'em into place,' as my wife says." Lovecraft shook his head, as Aaron and Abram started laughing. Ying turned a shade of red that had yet to be discovered, as Kara put a hand on her shoulder whilst laughing.

"So how are you, Miss Salt and Pepper?" Kara asked, referencing her new hair color. Lovecraft protested this nickname and said that he had already thought of it.

Kara stuck her tongue out at him, as Ying answered, "I'm better. It's exhausting being the first person to have a confirmed case of Marie Ant-Antio- How do you say it?"

"Antoinette," Lovecraft helped her.

"Yeah, that syndrome. I'm also apparently half-reptile now too," Ying confessed, causing Kara to just stare at her.

"You're what?"

Lovecraft decided to help her out, "Olivia ran some blood work after we got to the hospital and, after she told us that the Chinese had used snake venom on her and that she had also been bitten by the snake I killed, we found out that her cells had mutated and…let's just say that she really, really likes sunlight." Kara looked at Ying and she immediately pulled out her lighter. She flicked on the flame and hovered it around Ying; there was no reaction.

Lovecraft looked at her and said, "Kara, stop." She didn't respond and closed her lighter.

She mumbled that at least she thought it was funny before seriously asking, "You mention that the poison turned you this way. Does that mean you're poisonous in some way?" Ying explained to her that the poison had apparently neutralized when it changed her dynamics. Yet, she still had to be cautious for the time being, and be very careful if she bled on anything, sneezed, had sex, or did anything that involved bodily fluids. This really didn't make Kara feel any safer, but she feigned it by smiling and agreeing that it was good. She then changed the subject to the items that she brought and suddenly, she turned into Santa Claus.

Kara watched, as Ying and Abram opened their boxes and they both showed their delight at the times they received. Abram could not believe that Kara was able to get such an exotic weapon, and Ying was just in awe at the amount of work the French lady had put into making her weapons like that of the gods. She especially loved the small leveling device on the side of her rifle; it was extremely satisfying to see the bubble to move back and forth as she turned the weapon. Kara appreciated all the words of praise they gave her and was kind of beside herself. There was a difference when it came to being praised by total strangers and being praised by people one considered to be family. She took it in stride, however, and thanked them in return for trusting her with such delicacies that could save their lives one day.

This exchange of gratitude soon devolved into hearty conversations that honestly felt like a breath of air after the suffocation they suffered under the Chinese. However, this merriment was momentarily interrupted, when there was a knock at their door and Olivia stuck her head through the door.

"Hello?" she asked in her shallow accent, "The door was unlocked." Lovecraft beckoned her inside and she accepted the invitation. She set her purse by the table and looked over the miniature arsenal that was spread across the table.

"Holy crap! I thought the Chinese were done for?" she asked, incredulously. Kara and the rest laughed, before telling her that they were upgrades for Abram and replacements for Ying. Olivia nodded and congratulated the both of them before asking Ying how she was. The young woman gave her the same answers she gave Kara, and Olivia was glad to hear that she was, at the very least, okay.

Lovecraft waited till she was finished and then pointed toward the hallway. She nodded and he excused himself, saying, "Duty calls." He entered his room with her and took a seat at his desk while she sat in chair next to him.

"I'm sure you're here about the contract I gave you. Otherwise, you could have just not respond to it and went elsewhere," he said, being his usual, overly logical self.

Olivia rolled her eyes and tried to get the idea that it was kind of charming out of her head as she pulled the contract out. She put the yellow paper on his desk and pushed it forward; her signature decorating the bottom of it.

Lovecraft looked at it, grabbed it, and said, "Excellent." He set it off to the side and opened a new window on his computer and started typing in her information. He asked if she had any questions and she said that there weren't many, but she had one and it concerned how her paychecks would work.

Lovecraft nodded and explained, "You will be paid in a check every three weeks, and it will start out at 50-dollars an hour, and the hours are dictated by the time that we wake up. For instance, if we get woken up at five in the morning, then that's when our day starts, and it will end at 12:00 A.M. every day; no exceptions. Your pay will increase every six months that you stay on, until you've been here for two years. At that point in time, you will be earning around…" he took a moment to do the math in his head, "…90-dollars an hour, so that means, if we were to just say that you work six hours consistently after two years, you'll be earning over three grand a week." Olivia's heart nearly stopped when she heard this and could have sworn that the only thing that made it start pumping again was her swallowing it.

"A-Are you serious?" she asked, dumbfounded. Lovecraft looked at her and asked if she was expecting more and she quickly backtracked, explaining that she had not expected such a high wage.

"Well, you are an Operator, so you do get paid the best, but our missions are harder than everybody else's. Besides, don't count your chickens before they hatch, Olivia, you won't actually be rich," Lovecraft explained.

"How so?"

Lovecraft turned his computer screen to her and showed her Ruler's bank account; her eyebrows went to the ceiling when she saw the seven-figure number.

Lovecraft pointed to this number and said, "This number is our generalized budget where costs for ammunition, food, rent, utilities, medical supplies, and the like come from." He then pointed down to a significantly smaller number, "This is the account that our payouts go into. Right now, Barons pays out a set bounty for each task we complete. However, I keep a majority of the payout in order to pay for things like food, utilities, and ammunition. This means that you will never be getting paid the proper amount for the work you've done. But I do provide 'free' lodging and food for everyone on my team. Now if you have any problem with this, I can just tear up this piece of paper and we can forget this ever happened."

Olivia's eyebrow furrowed and then she asked, "Can I use the money in my paycheck for anything I want?"

"You can use that money for anything you want. Buy some new bed sheets, buy some special food that you want, hell buy some porn if you're so inclined; I really don't give a damn. Besides, it's not like you won't get a decent amount every now and again, everybody, even Ying, will get a sizable bonus for their birthday and every year that they, for lack of a better term, survive. You'd also be in charge of our medical logistics and would have a say in what medicines we spent our money on."

Olivia considered this and deduced that part of Ruler's extraordinary combat record was due to this strict economic discipline. After all, very few would dispute, that when your men were as highly trained as those in Ruler, high-tiered gear and lots of money would only help such a combat record.

Olivia sighed and decided it was okay, saying, "Fine, just so long as you're fair and don't start taking more than what you've already said." Lovecraft nodded and finished typing her information again, before handing her an additional forum.

"Just sign that and I can send it off to Barons. After that, we're all set. I'll let you know when you can start moving in." He paused for a moment, till she was about halfway through her name, and then added, "Make sure your weird Nazi propaganda is put in unmarked bags before moving in as well."

Olivia stopped writing and a smile formed across her lips as she looked up, "Tell me, are all of your jokes going to be aimed at me and how I'm, allegedly, a Nazi?"

"Oh no, Blitz, I'll probably make fun of your social life, your love life, your physical attributes too. Why? Because, I think that you are a stick in the mud and need to laugh more often." Olivia's eyebrow twitched beneath her blonde locks, and she couldn't help but notice that Lovecraft had completely disregarded the first half of her question. She began signing her name again and wondered if there was any possible way for her to strangle him in his sleep. It was a fun thought, but prison wasn't *that* desirable. She took a breath and handed it back to him, and he congratulated and welcomed her as Ruler 05. Olivia appreciated this and with it having been said, the two of them went out to the others.

The announcement was made and congratulations were sent to Olivia in the best ways they could. The German woman accepted each of them, although she really didn't know if this was the best choice for her; only time would tell. Kara suggested that they all go out for dinner this evening to celebrate and the agreement was unanimous. They decided that they would reconvene around seven o'clock. It was at this point that Kara said her goodbyes and left the team to their own devices.

Lovecraft told Abram to give Olivia a quick tour of their compound; he also told Aaron to help Ying get her new stuff set up in her room. The two men did as they were told, and as they were leaving, Lovecraft got a message on his phone that was from an unknown number. However, he knew who this was from the nature of the text. He immediately got up and put Aaron in charge, since he was stepping out. His friend gladly took the position like he always did, and it seemed like Lovecraft found himself driving down the road in a matter of seconds.

He eventually found himself standing on the third floor of a construction site just outside the Flood Zone. Plastic sheets were hung on the outside of the wall-less structure and they blew in the wind like helpless ghosts. His boots echoed on the white concrete, as he stepped through an unfinished wall. Lovecraft looked to the other end of the floor and saw Valravn, Coffin, and Kay sitting around a cast iron table. The latter of which was sitting on a steel I-beam that hung precariously off the building; she kicked her legs back and forth like it was something normal.

Lovecraft walked over to them and asked, "Does the Master only keep women in his stead, or is it just coincidence?"

Coffin answered this question while also asking one of her own, "Coincidence to be sure, but it is not that surprising. Valravn and Kay are some of the best people when it comes to working on the surface and were also the only ones available at the time. Would you like some tea?"

She brandished the kettle at Lovecraft, who declined, saying, "No thanks. I have business after this and can't stay." Kay commented that it probably had something to do with that hot arms dealer that he loves to be around; she was silence by Valravn. This shifted the point of attention to her and the folder that sat on the table next to her.

She grabbed it and said, "The Prime Minister's killer, his name is Solomon, and he used to be one of us."

Lovecraft deciphered her broken words and asked, "Used to be?"

Kay answered this question, "He was troubled and in constant pain due to his synthetics. Essentially, he was far too radical for us and wished to take revenge on our creators. He was so cute back then too; it's too bad he devolved into a megalomaniac…and a terrorist." Kay's answer left Lovecraft with more questions than he was comfortable with, but he was pressed for time and needed what they promised.

"Sounds bad, where is he?"

Valravn's blue eyes turned to purple and she replied, "Apparently, he knows that you're after him, and has taken to hiding in your own backyard, effectively under your nose." Lovecraft didn't know what she was referring to, so she opened the folder and showed him a map of Nebraska.

"He fled to Nebraska?"

Valravn nodded, "Specifically to your hometown." She then stood up and gave the folder to him, "If we never see each other again, I'm gonna say thank you for removing him in advance."

"Are you guys going somewhere?" he asked.

Coffin nodded in her chair, "We are fleeing this city. Our hand in the Chinese incident, although very minimal, has attracted attention to us again. Thus, we are leaving for the one place our enemies would never dream of going."

She was being intentionally cryptic and Lovecraft knew this, "Your enemies?"

"One problem at a time, Lovecraft. Your only concern should be finding and killing Solomon," Valravn said. He left it at that, while he wanted to push for more answers, the feeling in the back of his neck told him that he would not be getting any. Lovecraft tucked the folder underneath his arm and thanked them for their help. He turned around and began to walk toward the unfinished stairs he used to ascend the structure.

Lovecraft took the next few hours to study this folder, and he made sure that he remembered as many of its details as he could. The manifest itself was extensive. There were at least 20 pages of observed habits, physical characteristics, and people this cyborg associated himself with. On top of that, there was a map, obviously stolen satellite imagery, and pictures of Solomon, although they were quite blurry. Lovecraft stroked his chin, lined with stubble, as he read; his other hand was busy taking and making notes to the documents. He continued to scrutinize every page, but found nothing out of the ordinary, beyond a few dead ends that seemed irrelevant for the time being. He would investigate these further when he had more time, but left it on his to-do list and left it there. However, he soon came to the last page in the folder, and it was as interesting as it was alarming.

The paper itself was old, *very* old. Its color had yellowed, and its edges were beginning to turn brown. He saw Solomon's name on the top of it, but couldn't decipher much more, since most of its text was covered in black ink. He flipped it back and forth before taking a moment to think about the words that he could still see. Lovecraft eventually realized that he was looking at some sort of report that had been written by whoever built Solomon. He sighed in frustration and returned the piece of paper back to the folder, and just as he was closing it, his computer beeped, and its printer started churning out a document. He immediately knew that this was Olivia's approval papers and got a marker ready.

He grabbed the papers once they finished, which was strange that there was more than one, and started to read through them before covering the more sensitive information with the marker. He came to the second sheet and saw that it was a letter from the German military. He began reading it and what it spoke of, concerned him, but it was nothing to duck and cover over. He covered what he deemed too sensitive for anybody but himself, and bragged a manila folder. He labeled it 'Olivia V,' and carried it over to his filing cabinet. He slipped it right next to Ying's folder and then turned back to the table. Lovecraft knew that he needed to hide this folder and knew just the place to do it.

Lovecraft took the folder and opened up his armory. He placed it underneath two ammo boxes and made sure that it was completely invisible. Satisfied, Lovecraft returned everything to where it should be and looked at the clock. It was six o'clock. Almost as soon as he looked away, there was a knock on his door and once he gave his consent, Aaron opened the door. He came to tell Lovecraft that it was getting close to when they were supposed to leave, and that he should start getting ready.

"Who are you, my mom?" Lovecraft asked, before smirking. Aaron rolled his eyes and shut the door. Lovecraft proceeded to go shower and once he was done, he met the others in the kitchen.

"Have we decided where to go?" Lovecraft asked, sitting down at the table.

"We're going to one of the local pizza places, because most of us have never had this famous 'Chicago Pizza,'" Ying explained, her mouth close to watering. Lovecraft nodded and started tying his boots, as Aaron came out of his room and joined them. With him now here, they left and met Kara at the restaurant which was named after its owner, 'Saroni.' They got a table and Kara sat next to Lovecraft, Aaron sat next to Abram, and Ying sat next to Olivia. They all held casual conversations before they ordered, and when their food finally came, they each ate at their own pace. Ying's was about as fast as an SR-71 and one had to ask if she was even tasting what she was eating. Olivia did notice that every time Ying started eating, however, she would slowly pick off her pepperoni and eat it at that same speed. It was when she had one pepperoni left that Olivia made her move and pulled it off of Ying's pizza and popped it into her mouth.

The action was so fast that Ying barely saw it, but she suddenly realized that there was no more pepperoni left and she had seen Olivia's hand move. She just stared at the pizza, as Olivia waited for her reaction.

"Ying?" Olivia asked, and this break in the monotony brought water from Ying's eyes. Olivia immediately started to panic and offered Ying her pizza, while the Asian woman called her a 'meanie.' Everyone laughed at them, before they went back to their food. Kara knew that this exchange was going make the two women fast friends. Kara reached for her another slice of pizza and on her way back, her arm nudged Lovecraft, and he immediately turned to her. She turned to him, nibbling on the point of her pizza slice, and just looked at him. He cocked an eyebrow and she just shrugged her shoulders; they turned away after this and carried on. The dinner continued with merriment and was the kind of fun that everybody was sad when it had to end.

That night, Ying fell asleep in her window, with the moon illuminating the white in her hair. Her rifle was braced up against the sill next to her, and her former captain's jacket hung in her closet. A computer had been moved into the room for her, and the last touch that signified the room as hers was the gold plaque on the door that read, 'Ying Nam.' In between the two words, another word had been carved into it using a knife. It read, 'Li.'

The next morning, Lovecraft sat on the roof, watching the sun come up. It felt like it had been an eternity since he had an opportunity like this. The folder that he had been presented was resting in his lap; he had been paying half-attention to it.

He was suddenly ripped from his thoughts as he heard the familiar squeak of the door behind him. Lovecraft got up and turned to see not one, but all of his Contractors standing behind him, dressed in full gear.

Aaron crossed his arms and asked, "So what's next?" His smirk, just like Lovecraft's from the other day.

Lovecraft walked up to them and said, "First, we get Olivia moved in." Everybody looked at the corresponding woman, "Then, we go on a little cross-country trip." He opened the folder and presented the map to them.

"For some of you," he began, "this will be your first time in this part of the country, but for Aaron and me, *this*," he pointed to the map, "is our home." They all looked at the city more closely, and Aaron just held his smirk.

"Omaha, I haven't seen it in years." He turned to look in the distance for a moment, "So that's it then? Go to Omaha, get some payback for the Japanese, and then go home?"

Lovecraft's expression fell to one that was almost unreadable, as he turned to look at the sun again, "Actually, I think we're just getting started."

Interlude 2

I am no politician, I am no military officer, I've never gone to college, and didn't finish high school. I'm just a woman who, as a girl, avenged my grandfather and paid dearly for it. My captors have become my friends and my friends have also become my family.

"You have to understand that, when the events involving the Chinese combined with those of the Master, there was a considerable threat and weight. It was like two terribly strong armies combined to take out the smaller, weaker one, and I think that's what Lovecraft was fearing the most," Kara explained, to me.

It was lucky then? That the Master wanted to assist in their suppression.

Kara chuckled at my question, "It was extremely lucky, but not totally unpredictable. If there's two opposing douchebags in the same area, then they're bound to hate each other. All you have to do is look at Hitler and Stalin to see that law at work." Kara took a moment to collect her thoughts, as I wrote down more notes, "If I am to be honest about one thing, it would be that, to this day, I don't see how Ying survived it. She was, and still is, tougher than nails, but I've never met somebody who could take that much punishment." Kara scoffed at the thought, "A Basilisk indeed."

Pardon?

"Basilisk. It's the name we called Ying; it's similar to how Lovecraft was called Machine and I was called Green Wolf."

I see. I made sure to jot this down. *So now that the team is more or less together what happened—* I was suddenly interrupted by the alarm on my phone, and grimaced as I realized that I was out of time. I looked to the French woman and extended my hand to her. She shook it and thanked me, and affirmed that we would be meeting next week. The woman gathered her coat and said her goodbyes before disappearing into the cold, winter air.

I sat there for a bit after she left, and started flipping my pen around my fingers. Looking at my notes, I tried to see if there was anything that I would need to ask her about the next time that I saw her. This resulted in a few underlined points, but nothing of major concern. However, I did wonder why the Chinese seemed so weak in her account. Did their war with the Russians really weaken their forces that bad? Could their logistics not keep up with their advance in America? Or were the Heavies just flawed from the start? I have a feeling that these soldiers were blinded by easy victories, but the real thing to consider is whether or not Lovecraft was really that good, or if he's been embellished.

Unfortunately, a lot of historical fact backs up Kara's claims and even elaborates on them. Still, I'm skeptical. I might just have to ask him...

Epilogue
The One Who Feeds

Cold, that was how the darkened sky felt above the semi-forested fields of Tennessee. Puddles rumbled across barren asphalt, as they were suddenly disturbed by heavy, rubber wheels. These wheels belonged to a heavily armed F.B.I. convoy that had elements of a C.B.R.N. unit with them. They were guarding an ambulance that contained Zhi Yun's body.

She was being taken to a remote research facility in north-western Tennessee. Switchboard had expressed interest in her body when they learned of its remarkable, regenerative abilities, but the F.B.I. would only hand it over once the military had studied her first and when they got approval from the attorney general. Thus, this facility was under direct military control and, once the F.B.I. handed her over, it would be the military's problem.

Two F.B.I. S.W.A.T. soldiers sat in the lead vehicle and complained that it was a waste of resources to guard a dead body.

"Should've had the local police do this; they got lights and sirens just like we do," the driver complained; his name was John.

"But they don't have the guns we do, or the training," his friend, Ben, pointed out.

"You don't need our training to run a convoy cross-country. Hell, you probably wouldn't even need an M16; nobody, in their right mind, is gonna steal a dead body."

"What about the people who aren't in their right mind?" Ben asked, his white teeth showing between his black lips.

"Then you put them down. In my experience, retards can't shoot straight." The line of vehicles continued, until the area started to get more mountainous and the brush became thicker. It started to rain again as they pulled up to a dark building that was rather wide, but not tall enough go above the treetops.

The road ended in a circle, similar to a cul-de-sac, but there was a slab of decorative plants in the center of it. It was more like a roundabout without the let-ins. The edge of the street went right up to the building and this was where drop offs were made, however, there was nobody waiting for them outside.

John stopped the convoy and looked at the empty area, "What? Nobody to welcome us?"

"Yeah, with somebody this high-profile, there should at least be somebody." The two men looked at one another before they got out of their M.R.A.P. Their assault rifles hung loosely from their chests as they walked around. Their commanding officer, Enrico Alvarez, stepped out of his vehicle and started to get people set up.

"Hey, Commander," Ben yelled, before they both walked up to him, "there anybody here? Looks deserted."

Enrico turned to look at the building before putting a cigar in his mouth, "Looks like somebody in the army isn't doing their fuckin' job. John. Ben. Get in there and figure out why there's nobody to greet us; got enough time wasted without having to wait on the army."

The two S.W.A.T. members acknowledged their orders and started their walk across the loading area. They made it to the glass doors, which automatically slid away, and saw that even the front desk was deserted.

"The hell?" Ben asked, as they walked into the vacant lobby. The two men started to look into the various nooks and crannies in the room, but couldn't find a single person. They reported this to their superior, who then instructed them to hold position. He soon arrived with the rest of the men in the convoy; these men included the C.B.R.N. units – as well as their cargo. They all looked around, before the area was suddenly filled with light speculations of what was going on.

Enrico silenced everybody and then instructed two teams were to go and search the building. The C.B.R.N. and the rest of the main force were to stay there and guard Zhi Yun. Naturally, John and Ben got volunteered for one of the teams. They were a part of team two, which consisted of five men, and they were tasked with going through a door that went into the left side of the building.

"Still regretting the fact you got this job?" Ben asked, glancing to John.

He nodded, "This job just went from boring to downright eerie. My hair's standing on end just thinking about this place."

"I'll buy you a beer when we get back, might suppress the nightmares," Ben mocked, as the team started to move through the door. John muttered something under his breath before following them.

The hallway they entered was dark. It was so dark that it felt like their flashlights were just candles. To their right was a set of grey lockers that had a fire extinguisher mounted beside them, to their left were two metal doors. The first one was open and it was just a small storage room; it was a bit messy, but nothing out of the ordinary. The second was locked down hard, and when it was quite clear that it wouldn't budge, they brought up one of their members who had a special device for doors.

He popped the control panel's housing off with the butt of his rifle and connected the device to it. It took a second for it to work, and when it did, it only moved about an inch away from the doorframe. It was jammed, and when they looked through the small slit, they couldn't see anything. They called out to anybody inside, but left when they got no answer. Little did they know, the other side of the door was covered in blood, as the mutilated body of a man was furiously stabbed. The stabbing instrument was a long, scorpion-like tail that was made out of titanium. It retracted itself back into the ceiling once the F.B.I. yelled into the room.

Ben and John continued on with their team and passed through several hallways. They stopped for a moment when they heard a strange, grinding sound inside the air ducts. It seemed fairly consistent, so they chalked it up to a busted fan. However, on the other side of the wall from them, a woman's body was being pulled into the duct. The small entrance folding her body in on itself before she disappeared.

"Hey, do you think that noise was really a busted fan?" Ben asked, clearly on edge. John didn't answer and kept his eyes focused on the darkness in front of them. He could've sworn that, when they were sitting there, there was set of red eyes looking at him from a half-open door.

They continued on, until one of their members called out, 'damage' and they all turned toward what looked like a cafeteria door. The door itself was lying across the floor and once they were inside, there was the faint sound of music across the room. They looked to the music and saw a man, the first they'd seen, shivering next to the green light of a vending machine. Calling out to him, they ran across the room as he woke up.

"Get back! Stay away from me!" he yelled, trying to bury himself in the corner. They made their way to him and started to ask him questions, but he was erratic and seemed to not be able to understand them. He just kept repeating, "You have to leave!" and "She's in there!" Every time he said the latter, he would point to the source of the music. John picked up its source, an old radio, and inspected it; there was nothing wrong it.

"Come on, man, who's here?" Ben asked twice.

The man went wheezy and said, "The Devil! He's come here to eat us all! We're all already in his *belly*!" Ben backed away from the deranged man just before, to his horror, the man pulled a revolver from his pocket and shot himself. His body fell backward and the entire team looked at him with horrified faces. His blood dripped from the ceiling, as their leader shook himself to life and tried to get in contact with Enrico. He was having trouble and while this went on, the radio in John's hand started to play a series of songs that made the device sound like it was laughing. He pointed this out to his commander and they immediately spread out around the room. Something had been drawn by the gunshot and now, it came for them.

But nothing happened. There was no sound, and even the radio went silent. Sweat ran down John's face as he looked toward the door they came from; did whatever this was just wanting to scare them? No, it couldn't, there was nothing to gain by alerting the enemy to where you were. But that laugh on the radio, surely it meant something, it had to. John was joined by another man, but he suddenly slumped on top of him. John pushed him off and asked what he thought he was doing, but this question slowly fell into a scream when he noticed that the man's head was cut in half. Ben turned to the direction of the commotion, but fell to the floor, when his legs were cut out from under him.

Two, bladed, titanium appendages slithered out of the darkness like snakes, and began dicing up the team like they were cabbage. Pieces fell around John before he got up and grabbed Ben from the floor. However, as he tried to pick him up, he was stopped when his friend got caught on something. He turned and saw that one of the bladed serpents had split itself down the middle and had almost chopped his arm off, like a wire in wire-cutters.

John immediately shot the appendage off of his friend and began running back to the main entrance. However, when he got back, he fell on his knees; they were all dead. All of them. The C.B.R.N., the main force, even Enrico, were dead, and their bodies were used as demented decorations. Ben flopped from John's shoulders as the ceiling mounted speakers started to play an abrasive violin. John's friend had died on the way back and now the only thing he cared about was the figure standing before him.

Kay watched the exhausted man in front of her and wondered if he was as squishy as he looked. She moved her hand toward him and one of the metal tails burst through the back of her robe. It flew through the air and wrapped itself around John, bringing him back to its owner. She giggled as she shoved her hand into his body and felt around.

"Hey? Do you think that humans can die from pain alone? I *know* they can, that's why I better go slow." She pushed into a new cavity, "Feel that? That's your ribcage—" he started coughing and the blood landed on Kay's mask, "Sorry, that was your lung." She wrapped her hand around a vibrating muscle and pulled, "Just like picking an apple." She let him fall to the floor and held his heart in her hand; she crushed it before sprouting two more appendages that she used to cut his legs off and to cut through half his arm.

Kay threw him over to where Ben lay and said, "The same." She let out a sigh after and walked over to the pod that they kept Zhi inside of. She ripped it open with her serpents, and watched as it started to breathe.

"Oh dear, oh my, oh deary me! So resilient, aren't you, my little egg!" One of the tendrils flew forward and stabbed Zhi's body; this stopped its breathing. It then manipulated itself it such a way that it lifted her out of the tank and toward Kay. She ran her gloved hand across Zhi's half-burned body; her red eyes glowing through the dark holes of her mask.

"We're going to be so great together, my little egg. You're going to help me hatch." Kay pulled her mask off and the face of the prune-haired girl that Lovecraft had met at the police department appeared. The red of her eyes glowed through her brown irises, as she wrapped Zhi with her metal tentacles. The two of them disappeared into the misty air.